Menfreya

Harriet Delvaney, young daughter of an M.P., becomes obsessed with the Menfrey family and their ancient house with its turrets and towers standing on a cliff above the sea.

Harriet runs to Menfreya when life in her father's house becomes intolerable; and from then she is irrevocably involved with the family. Her father's sudden marriage and the mysterious death of his young wife, send her into a marriage which links her for ever with the Magic Menfreys. Menfreya is her home at last.

But the skies are dark over Menfreya as yet. Harriet's husband Bevil is one of the 'Wild Menfreys'. Can she expect a sudden reformation? Loving him as she does, she is tortured by suspicions when the beautiful Jessica Trelarken comes to Menfreya. The suspicions deepen into something sinister; and as one mysterious warning follows another, Harriet fears that it is not only her husband she may lose, but her life.

VICTORIA HOLT

Menfreya

Collins
FONTANA BOOKS

First published 1966
First issued in Fontana Books 1968
Ninth Impression January 1973

© Victoria Holt 1966

Printed in Great Britain
Collins Clear-Type Press
London and Glasgow

ONE

To see Menfreya at its best was to see it in the morning. I discovered this for the first time at dawn in the house on No Man's Island, when away to the east the scarlet-stained clouds were throwing a pinkish sheen on the sea, and the water which lapped about the island was like pearl-grey rippled silk.

The morning seemed more peaceful because of the night of fear through which I had passed, the scene more delightful because of my nightmares. As I stood at the open window, the sea and the mainland before me, with Menfreya standing on the cliff top, I felt as elated by all that beauty as by the fact that I had come safely through the night.

The house was like a castle with its turrets, buttresses and machicolated towers—a landmark to sailors who would know where they were when they saw that pile of ancient stones. They could be silver grey at noon when the sun picked out sharp flints in the walls and made them glitter like diamonds: but never did Menfreya look so splendid as when touched with the rosy glow of sunrise.

Menfreya had been the home of the Menfreys for centuries. I had secretly christened them the Magic Menfreys because that was how they seemed to me—different from ordinary people, striking in appearance, strong, vital people. I had heard them called the Wild Menfreys, and according to A'Lee—the butler at Chough Towers—they were not only wild but wicked. He had tales to tell of the present Sir Endelion. The Menfreys had names which seemed strange to me but not, apparently, to Cornishmen, for these names were part of the ancient history of the Duchy. Sir Endelion had abducted Lady Menfrey when she was a young girl of not more than fifteen, had brought her to Menfreya and kept her there until her reputation was ruined and her family only too glad to agree to the marriage. "Not for love," said A'Lee. "Don't make no mistake about that, Miss Harriet. It were the money that he were after. One of the biggest heiresses in the country, they say; and the Menfreys needed the money."

When I saw Sir Endelion riding about Menfreystow I thought of him as a young man, looking exactly like his son Bevil, abducting the heiress and riding with her to Menfreya

5

—poor terrified girl, little more than a child, yet completely fascinated by the wild Sir Endelion.

His hair was tawny and reminded me of a lion's mane. He still had an eye for the women, so said A'Lee ; it was a failing among the Menfreys ; many of them had come to grief—men and women—through their love affairs.

Lady Menfrey, the heiress, was quite unlike the rest of the family ; she was fair and frail, a gentle lady who concerned herself with the poor of the district. She had meekly accepted her fate when she passed her fortune into her husband's hands. And with that, said A'Lee, he soon began to play ducks and drakes.

She proved to be a disappointment—apart from the money —for the Menfreys had always been heavy breeders and she had only one son, Bevil, and then there had been a gap of five years before she produced Gwennan. Not that she had not made efforts in between. The poor lady had had a miscarriage almost every year and continued to do so for some years after Gwennan's birth.

As soon as I saw Bevil and heard that he was the image of what his father had been in his youth, I knew why Lady Menfrey had allowed herself to be abducted. Bevil had the same colouring as his father, and the most attractive eyes I had ever seen. They were of the same reddish-brown tint as his hair ; but it wasn't the colour which made one aware of them. I suppose it was an expression. They looked on the world and everyone in it with assurance, amusement and an indifference as though nothing was worth caring about. For me, Bevil was the most fascinating member of a fascinating household.

Gwennan, his sister, I knew best of them all, for she was my age and we had become friends. She had that immense vitality and the arrogance which appeared to be inherent. We used to lie on the cliffs among the sea pinks and gorse bushes and talk—or rather she talked and I listened.

" In St. Neot's church there's a glass window," she once told me. " It's been there for hundreds of years and on it there's a picture of St. Brychan and his twenty-four children. There's St. Ive and Menfre and Endelient . . . Menfre, that's obviously us, and Papa's name came from Endelient. And Gwennan was Brychan's daughter ; so now you know . . ."

" And what about Bevil ?"

" Bevil !" She spoke his name with reverence. " He's named

after Sir Bevil Granville, who was the greatest soldier in Cornwall. He fought against Oliver Cromwell."

"Well, then," I said, knowing a little more history than she did, "he didn't win."

"Of course he won," she retorted scornfully.

"But Miss James says the King lost his head and Cromwell ruled."

She was typically Menfrey; imperiously she waved aside Miss James and the history books. "Bevil always won," she declared; and that settled it.

Now the walls of the house were changing colour again; the rosy tint was fading and they were silvery in the bright dawn. I gazed at the outline of the coast, at the wicked rocks, sharp as knives and treacherous because they were so often covered by the sea. There was a range of rocks close to the island which were called the Lurkers. Gwennan said this was because they were so often completely hidden from sight and were lurking in wait to destroy any craft that came near them. No Man's Island, a part of this chain of rocks, was about half a mile from the mainland and nothing more than a hump in the sea, being about half a mile in circumference; but although there was only one house on it there was a spring of fresh water, which, again said Gwennan, was the reason the house had been built there. There was some mystery about the house and a reason why no one wanted to live in it—which, I assured myself now, was a good thing, for if there had been a tenant, where should I have spent last night?

It was not a place I should have chosen had there been a choice. Now the house in which no one wanted to live was filling with comforting light, but even so it was eerie, as though the past had been trapped here and resentfully wanted to catch you and trap you so that you belonged to it.

If I told that to Gwennan she would laugh at me. I could imagine the scorn in her high-pitched imperious voice. "*You!* You're too fanciful. It's all because of your affliction."

Gwennan had no compunction about openly discussing subjects which others pretended did not exist. Perhaps that was why I found her company irresistible, although at times it was hurtful.

I was hungry, so I ate a piece of the chocolate which Gwennan had brought for me, and looked about the room. At night the dust sheets had made ghosts of the furniture and

I had wondered whether I would prefer to sleep outside; but the ground was hard and the air chilly and the noise of the sea, like murmuring voices, was louder and more insistent outside than in. So I had climbed the staircase to one of the bedrooms and lain fully dressed on the covered bed.

I went down to the big stone-floored kitchen; the flags were damp; everything was damp on the island. I washed in the water I had drawn from the spring the day before; there was a mirror on the wall and as I combed my hair I gazed at my reflection thinking that it looked different from what it did in my room at home. My eyes looked bigger; that was fear. My hair was sticking out in all directions; that was because of a disturbed night. It was thick straight hair that liked to be untidy—the despair of the numerous nannies whose rewarding fate it had been to direct my childhood. I was plain and there was no pleasure in looking at my image.

I decided to pass the time in exploring the house to assure myself that I really was alone. The strange noises which had tortured the night were the creaks of boards; the rhythmic advance and retreat of the waves, which could sound like breathing or whispering; or the scamper of rats—for there were rats on the island, Gwennan had said, which came from the ships wrecked on the Lurkers.

The house had been built by the Menfreys a hundred and fifty years ago—for like so much of the district the island belonged to them. There were eight rooms besides the kitchen and outhouses; and the place had recently been furnished, waiting for the tenant who could not be found.

I came into the drawing-room with its casement window which looked out to sea. There was no garden, although it appeared that at some time someone had tried to make one. Now the grass grew in patches and there were gorse bushes and brambles everywhere. The Menfreys had not bothered with it and it was useless to, for at high tide the sea covered it.

Having no idea of the time, I came out of the house and ran down to the sandy cove, where I lay gazing at Menfreya and waiting for Gwennan.

The sun was climbing high before she came. I saw her in the cove which belonged to the Menfreys and which as a special concession they allowed the public to use so that it would not be necessary to close part of the shore and force people to make a detour. Three or four boats were kept tied up there and I watched her get into one and row over. In a short time it was scraping on the sand, and as she scrambled out I ran to meet her.

"Gwennan," I screamed.

"Ssh!" she shouted. "Someone might hear you—or see you. Go into the house at once."

She was soon with me, more excited than I had ever seen her; I noticed that she was wearing a cape, inside which were enormous pockets, and these bulged with what I guessed to be the food she had promised me.

She was waving a newspaper in her hands. "Look at this," she cried. "The morning paper. You're in it! *You* . . . on the front page."

She went to the table and spread out the paper on the dust sheet which covered it.

I stared at it. "M.P.'s daughter missing. Foul Play cannot be ruled out, say police." Beneath the headlines I read: "Henrietta (Harriet), thirteen-year-old daughter of Sir Edward Delvaney, M.P. for the Lansella district of Cornwall, disappeared from her London home two days ago. It is feared that she may have been kidnapped and will be held to ransom."

Gwennan drew herself on to the table and hugged her knees; her eyes were almost hidden as they were when her face was creased with amusement.

She pointed to me. "Well, Miss Henrietta (Harriet) Delvaney, you *have* become important, haven't you? They're searching for you. All over London they're searching. And nobody knows where you are except you and me!"

It was what I had wanted, I supposed; so I had, in a way, achieved my purpose.

I laughed with Gwennan. People were talking about me; the police were searching for me. It was a wonderful moment. But experience had taught me that wonderful moments did not last. They would find me, and then what would happen? It wouldn't always be a sunny day. Gwennan would not stay with me. Dusk would come and I should be alone on the island.

I had decided to run away on the night of the ball my father was giving in his town house, which was in a quiet Westminster square about five minutes' walk from the Houses of Parliament. He had always said that it was part of his parliamentary duties to entertain lavishly and constantly, and whether we were in Westminster or Cornwall there were always guests: dinner parties and balls in London, shooting parties and house-parties in Cornwall. Being only thirteen I was excluded from these affairs. My place was in my own room, from which I would emerge to peer over the banisters down into the hall and gaze on the splendour, or stand at my window and watch the occupants of the carriages as they stepped forth and passed under the red and white awning which was set up for the occasion.

Throughout the day the preparations had been going on; thick red carpet had been laid on the steps which led to the front door and along the stretch of pavement on which guests would step when alighting from their carriages; two young women from the florists had been busy all the afternoon putting flowers in vases, and plants in every alcove, cleverly arranging some of them to look as if they were growing out of the walls; leaves and flowers had been entwined in the banisters of the curved and gracious staircase up to the first floor, which was as far as the guests would go.

"It smells like a funeral," I said to my governess, Miss James.

"Harriet," she answered, "you are being ghoulish." And she looked at me with that pained expression which I knew so well.

"But it *does* smell like a funeral," I insisted.

"You are a morbid child!" she muttered and turned away.

Poor Miss James. She was thirty and a lady without means of support; and in order to live she must either marry or be governess to people like me.

The library was to be the supper-room and the flower decorations there were magnificent. A marble pond had been erected in the centre of the room and in it gold and silver fishes swam and on the surface water lilies floated. There were draperies of rich purple, the Tory colour. In the front drawing-room, which was furnished in white, gold and purple, there was a grand piano, for there would be music to-night played by a famous pianist.

I should be able to gaze down at the guests as they mounted the stairs, hoping that none of them would look up and see their host's daughter who would be no credit to him. I should be hoping for a glimpse of my father, for it was at such times that I saw a different man from the one I knew. Past fifty, for he had married late in life, he was tall and his dark hair was white at the temples; he had blue eyes which were rather startling in his dark face and when they looked at me they reminded me of ice. When he was being host or talking to his constituents or entertaining his guests, those eyes sparkled. He was noted for his wit and the brilliance of his speeches in the House; his remarks were constantly being quoted in the papers. He was rich; and this was why he could afford to be a Member of Parliament. Politics was his life. He had a private income from investments but his great fortune came from steel somewhere in the Midlands. We never mentioned it; he had little to do with it; but it was the great provider.

He was member for a division of Cornwall and that was why we had a house near Lansella; we went from London to Cornwall, for when Parliament was not sitting there was the constituency to be 'nursed'; and for some strange reason where my father was, there was I, too, though we saw little of each other.

Our town house had a large entrance hall, and on the ground floor the library, dining-room and servants' quarters; on the first floor were two large drawing-rooms and the studies; above that were three guest rooms, one of them occupied by William Lister, my father's secretary, besides my own and my father's bedroom. On the top floor there were about six servants' bedrooms.

It was a beautiful Georgian house and its finest feature, as far as I was concerned, was the staircase which curled like a serpent from bottom to top of the house and enabled one to look down from the top floor to the hall. But to me it was a cold house. Our house in Cornwall was the same. Any house where he lived would be like that . . . cold and dead. How different was Menfreya Manor; vital and warm, that was a house where anything could happen, a house that you would always dream of when you were away and never want to leave—a real home.

The London house was elegantly furnished to suit the architecture; so the furniture was eighteenth-century and there were few concessions to our Victorian age. I was always astonished when I went into other houses and saw their ornate furniture and crowded rooms and compared them with our Chippendale and Hepplewhite.

I have forgotten the names of the servants; there were so

many of them. I remember Miss James, of course, because she was my governess, and Mrs. Trant the housekeeper and Polden the butler. Those are all the names I can think of—except, of course, Fanny.

But Fanny was different. I didn't think of her as a servant. Fanny was security in a frightening world; when I was bewildered by my father's coldness I turned to Fanny for explanations; she could not give them but she could offer comfort; she it was who made me drink my milk and eat my rice puddings; she scolded me and fretted over me so that I did not miss a mother as much as I otherwise would have. She had a sharp face with deep-set dreaming eyes, hair that was a shade of greyish brown, and scraped up to a knot on the top of her head so tightly that it looked as though it hurt, a sallow skin and a thin figure; she was about thirty-five and barely five feet high, and she had always looked the same to me since I was a baby and first aware of her. She spoke with the tongue of the London streets and when I grew older and she surreptitiously introduced me to those streets, I grew to love them as I loved her.

She had come to the house soon after I was born to act as wet nurse. I don't think they had intended to keep her but I was apparently a difficult child from the first weeks and I took a fancy to Fanny. So she stayed on as my nurse and although she was resented by Mrs. Trant, Polden and the nanny-in-chief, Fanny did not care about that—and nor did I.

Fanny was a woman of contrasts. Her sharp cockney tongue did not fit the dreamy eyes; the stories she told me of her past were a mixture of fantasy and all that was practical. She had been left at an orphanage by persons unknown. "Just by the statue of St. Francis feeding the birds. So they called me Frances—Fanny for short—Frances Stone. You see it was a stone statue." She was not Frances Stone now because she had married Billy Carter; we didn't talk much about Billy Carter. He was lying at the bottom of the ocean, she told me once; and she would never see him more in this life. "What's done's done," she would say briskly. "And best forgot." There were times when she gave herself up to make-believe and a favourite game of ours when I was six or seven had been telling stories about Fanny before she was left by the statue of St. Francis. She told the stories and I urged her on. She had been born in a house as grand as ours, but had been stolen by gipsies. She was an heiress and a wicked uncle left her at the orphanage after substituting a dead child in her father's house. There were several versions; and they usually ended with: "And we shall never know, Miss Harriet, so drink up your milk for it's time you was abed."

She talked to me about the orphanage too, of the bells which summoned the children to inadequate meals; I saw them clearly in their gingham pinafores, their hands mottled with cold and blotched with chilblains; I saw them bobbing curtsies to those in authority and learning how to be humble.

"But we learned how to read and write, too," said Fanny, "which is more than some will ever learn."

She scarcely ever talked of her baby, though; and when she did she would clutch me to her and hold my head down so that I shouldn't see her face. "It was a little girl; she lived only an hour. It was all I'd gone through over Billy."

Billy was dead; the baby was dead. "And then," said Fanny, "I come to you."

She used to take me to St. James's Park and there we would feed the ducks or sit on the grass while I persuaded her to tell more versions of her early life. She introduced me to a London I had never known existed. It was a secret, she said; for it would never do for any of Them—the people at home —to know where she took me on our outings. We went to the markets where the costers had their stalls; gripping me tightly by the hand she would pull me along, as excited as I was by these people who screamed the virtues of their wares in raucous voices which I could not understand. I remember the shops with old clothes hanging outside—the queer musty unforgettable smell; the old women sellings pins and buttons, whelks, gingerbread and cough drops. Once she bought me a baked potato which seemed the most delicious food I had ever had, until I tasted roasted chestnuts hot from the embers.

"Don't you tell anyone where you've been," she warned me; and the secrecy made it the more exciting.

There was ginger beer, sherbet and lemonade to be bought and once we tossed with a pieman. It was an old custom with piemen, Fanny told me; and we stood and watched a young coster and his girl toss the penny and lose so that they got no pie; Fanny, greatly daring, tossed her penny and we won. We carried the pie to St. James's Park and sat by the lake devouring every morsel.

"But you haven't seen the market of a Saturday night.

That's the time," said Fanny. "Perhaps when you're older . . ."

It was something to plan for.

I loved the market with its costermongers whose faces portrayed all the parts one would find in a morality play. There was lust and greed, sloth and cunning in those faces; and occasionally saintliness. Fanny was most excited by the tricksters; she would want to stand and watch the juggler and the conjurer, the sword- and flame-swallowers.

Fanny had shown me a new world, which was right on our doorstep although so many people seemed unaware of it. The only occasion when the two worlds met was on a Sunday afternoon when, sitting at my window, I would hear the bell of the muffin man and see him coming across the square with his tray on his head and the white-capped and aproned maids running out to buy from him.

That was my life up to the night of the ball.

On such occasions everyone in the house was pressed into helping and Fanny was called into the kitchens for the afternoon and evening; Miss James was helping the housekeeper and I was alone.

My Aunt Clarissa was staying with us because my father needed a hostess. I disliked my Aunt Clarissa—who was my father's sister—as much as she disliked me. She was constantly comparing me with her three daughters—Sylvia, Phyllis and Clarissa—who were all golden-haired, blue-eyed, and, according to her, beautiful. She was going to be very busy bringing them out and I was to join them in this fearsome necessity for all young ladies. I knew I was going to hate it as much as Aunt Clarissa dreaded it.

So the fact that Aunt Clarissa was in the house was an additional reason why I wanted to be out of it.

I had wandered about the house miserably all day, and on the stairs I met my Aunt Clarissa. "My goodness me, Harriet," she cried. "Look at your hair! You always look as if you've been pulled through a bush backwards. Your cousins don't have trouble with their hair. They would never go about looking as you do, I can assure you."

"Oh, they are the three graces."

"Don't be insolent, Harriet. I should have thought that *you* might have taken special pains with your hair seeing that . . ."

"Seeing that I'm deformed?"

She was shocked. "What nonsense. Of course you're not. But I should have thought you might . . ."

I went limping upstairs into my room. She mustn't know how deeply I cared. None of them must, for then it would be quite unbearable.

In my room I stood before the mirror; I lifted my long grey merino skirt and I looked at my legs and feet. There was nothing to show that one leg was shorter than the other; it was only when I walked that I appeared to drag one behind the other. It had always been like that, from the disappointing day I was born. Disappointing! That was a mild way of expressing it. It was a hateful day, a tragic day for everyone including myself. I knew nothing about it until later when I began to discover that I was not quite like other children. As if it was not bad enough to be the cause of your mother's death; you had to be made imperfectly as well. I remember hearing it said of some great beauty—Lady Hamilton, I think—that God was in a glorious mood when he made her. "Well," I retorted, "He must have been in a bad temper when He made me!"

Sometimes I wished that I had been born anyone but Harriet Delvaney. When Fanny took me into the park and I saw other children I always envied them. I envied almost everybody—even the dirty children of the man with the barrel-organ who used to stand beside him looking pitiful while the little brown monkey held out the red cap for pennies. Everybody, I thought in those days, was more fortunate than Harriet Delvaney.

I had been told by several nannies under whom Fanny had served that I was a bad, wicked girl. I had a good home, plenty to eat, a kind father, a good nanny, and I was not satisfied.

I did not walk until I was four years old. I was taken to doctors who meddled with my legs and had long discussions about what was to be done and shook their heads over me. I was given this treatment and that; my father used to come and look at me, and there was something in his eyes which told me he would rather look at anything than me, but he forced himself to pretend he liked doing it.

I remember one day when I was in the garden of my Aunt Clarissa's house near Regent's Park. It was strawberry time and we had been eating the fruit with sugar and cream near the summer-house. All the women had parasols and big shady hats to protect their complexions, and because it was Phyllis's birthday there were several children on the lawn and they were running about playing together. I was seated on my chair with my offending hateful legs stretched out before me. I had come in the carriage and been carried into the garden by one of the footmen and placed in the chair where I might watch the other children.

I heard Aunt Clarissa's voice: " *Not* a very pleasant child. I suppose one must make excuses . . ."

I did not understand what she meant although I stored up the remark to ponder on later; when I think of that day I remember the scent of strawberries; the delicious mingling of fruit, sugar and cream, and legs . . . the strong legs of other children.

I can still recall the great determination which came to me as I almost fell out of the chair and stood on my own legs and walked.

It was a miracle, said the kind ones. Others thought I could have done it before and had been pretending all the time. The doctors were astonished.

I could only totter at first ; but from that day I walked. I do not know whether I could have walked before or not ; all I can remember is that sudden sense of determination, and of gratifying power as I tottered towards those children.

I gradually learned my pathetic little story, mostly from the servants who had worked in the house before my birth.

" *She* was too old to have children. Could you wonder . . . Having Miss Harriet killed her. Operation . . . Them instruments . . . Well, it's dangerous. Lost her and saved the child. But there's her with that leg. As for him . . . he was never the same again. Idolised her . . . Of course they'd only been married a year or two. Whether it 'ud have lasted, him being what he is . . . No wonder he can't abide the child, though. Now if she'd been like Miss Phyllis or one of her cousins . . . Makes you think, don't it? Money ain't everything."

There was my story in those few words. Sometimes I imagined that I was a saint who went about the world doing good and everyone loved me. They said: " Well, she's no beauty but one must make excuses and she's very good."

But I wasn't good. I was jealous of my cousins with their pretty pink faces and their silky golden hair ; I was angry with my father who couldn't abide me because my coming into the world sent my mother out of it. I was difficult with the servants because I was sorry for myself.

The only people with whom I felt I could be humble and perhaps learn to be good were the Menfreys; it was not that they took much notice of me, but to me they were the Magic Menfreys, living in the most exciting house I had ever seen, perched on the cliffs opposite No Man's Island which belonged to them and about which there was a story I had yet to discover. Our house was the nearest to theirs—much more modern—a mansion in which my father could entertain and look after the constituency. The Menfreys were his great friends. "They must be cultivated," I heard him say to his secretary William Lister. "They carry great influence in the constituency." So the Menfreys were to be tended like flowers in the greenhouse.

And it was only necessary to look at them—all of them—to believe in their influence. My father's secretary, William Lister, had said that they were larger than life. It was the first time I had heard the phrase and it fitted well.

The family were very ready to be friendly with us; they worked for Father during the elections; they entertained him and he entertained them. They were the lords of the district and when Sir Endelion told his tenants to vote, they voted and for the candidate he favoured; if not, they need not expect to remain his tenants.

When we went to Cornwall some of the servants accompanied us while Mrs. Trant and Polden stayed in London with a skeleton staff; Miss James, Nanny and Fanny among others came with us; and in Cornwall we had a resident butler and housekeeper—husband and wife, the A'Lees—who went with the furnished house we rented, which was very convenient.

I was allowed to go to tea at Menfreya and Gwennan came to have tea with me at Chough Towers. She would ride over with one of the grooms from Menfreya and it was during one of these visits that I learned to ride and discovered that I was happier in the saddle than anywhere else because then my defect was unimportant; I felt normal on horseback. The nearest I had ever been to complete pleasure was riding along these Cornish lanes, uphill, downhill, and I never grew in the least blasé in my appreciation of the scenery. I always caught my breath in wonder when, reaching the top of a steep hill, I had a sudden glimpse of the sea.

I envied Gwennan for living permanently in such a place. She liked to hear about London and I enjoyed telling her. In return I made her talk about Menfreya and the Menfreys, but most of all about Bevil.

As I stood in front of my mirror after the encounter with Aunt Clarissa on the stairs I started to think of Menfreya with a longing which went so deep that it was like a pain.

I was leaning over the banisters. There was music in the front drawing-room but it was almost drowned by the hum of voices and the sudden bursts of laughter. It was as though the house had come to life; it was no longer cold; all these voices, all this laughter changed it.

I was in my flannelette nightgown with a red twill dressing-gown over it; my feet were bare, for slippers could betray with the padding sound they made. It was not that any of the servants would have scolded me for peeping over the banisters but that I liked to pretend I was not the least bit interested in my father's entertainments.

Sometimes I dreamed that he sent for me and that I went limping into the room. The Prime Minister was there and he talked to me; he and everyone was astonished by my wit and understanding. My father's eyes were warm and sparkling because he was so proud of me.

What a foolish dream!

That night as I leaned against the banisters sniffing the beeswax and turpentine with which they were polished, I overheard the conversation between Aunt Clarissa and a man who was a stranger to me. They were talking about my father.

" Quite brilliant . . ."

" The P.M. seemed to think so."

" Oh, yes. Sir Edward's heading for the Cabinet. Mark my words."

" Dear Edward." That was Aunt Clarissa. " He deserves a little luck."

" Luck! I should have thought he had had his share. He must be an extremely wealthy man."

" He has never been happy since his wife died."

" He has been a widower now for many years, has he not? A wife would have been useful to him. I wonder . . . he didn't marry again."

"Marriage was such a tragic experience, and in a way Edward's a born bachelor."

"I hear there's a child."

I felt my face grow hot with fury at the note in Aunt Clarissa's voice as she said: "Oh, yes, there's a child. Henrietta. We call her Harriet."

"There is some misfortune?"

Aunt Clarissa was whispering; then her voice was loud again. "I often think it was a pity she wasn't taken and Sylvia left. Having the child killed her, you know. They had only been married a few years, but she was in her late thirties. They wanted a son, of course. And this girl . . ."

"Still, she must be a compensation to him."

A cruel laugh. A whisper. Then: "It's going to be my task to bring her out when the time comes. My Phyllis and Sylvia—named for her aunt—are about the same age, but the difference! . . . How I shall find a husband for Harriet I do *not* know . . . in spite of the money."

"Is she so very unattractive?"

"She has nothing . . . simply nothing."

Fanny had told me that listeners never hear good of themselves. How right she was! I had heard that I was wicked; that I suffered from tantrums; that I should go to hell. This from my various nannies. But I had never heard anything that was quite so wounding as that conversation between Aunt Clarissa and the unknown man. For long afterwards I could not bear the smell of beeswax and turpentine because I associated it with abject misery.

I could no longer watch, so I left the banisters and sped to my room.

I had already learned that when one is very unhappy it is advisable to turn from one's sorrow and plan something . . . anything that will make one forget How stupid I was to dream as I did, for in those dreams I never saw myself as I actually was. I was always a heroine; even the colour of my hair changed. Instead of being dark brown it was golden; my eyes instead of being green were blue; my nose was neat and straight instead of tiptilted in a way which might have added piquancy to some faces and merely looked incongruous with my dour expression.

Plan something quickly, I said to myself; and the answer came promptly: they don't want me here, so I'll run away.

Where to? There was only one place I wanted to run to. That was Menfreya.

"I'll go to Menfreya," I said aloud.

I refused to think of what I should do when I arrived because if I did the plan would founder right at the start, and I must shut out the sound of cruel voices saying cruel words. I must do something quickly.

I could catch a train from Paddington. I had money in my money-box which would be enough to buy the ticket and that was all that mattered. All I had to think of now was getting to Menfreya; when I arrived I would make further plans. I could not stay in this house; every time I walked down the stairs I should hear those voices. Aunt Clarissa was worried about finding a husband for me. Well, I would save her that bother.

When should I go? How could I make sure of not being missed for long enough to be able to get on that train? It needed careful planning.

So while in the drawing-rooms below me they listened to the music Papa had provided for the occasion and enjoyed all the delicacies that were served in the supper-room, while they talked together of politics and my father's chances in the Cabinet, I lay in my bed and thought of how I should run away.

My chance came the next day when everyone was weary. There were bad tempers in the kitchen; Miss James was irritable. I always thought that since reading *Jane Eyre* she thought that my father was going to marry her; and after occasions like last night's party that possibility would seem more remote than usual. She retired to her room at six o'clock complaining of a headache and this gave me my opportunity, so, calmly putting on my cape with the hood, the money, which I had taken from my money-box, in my pocket, I slipped out of the house. I boarded an omnibus— the first time I had ever done this alone—and one or two people looked at me curiously but I pretended to take no notice of them. I knew it was the right omnibus because it said Paddington on the side, so I calmly asked for a ticket to the station. It was easier than I had imagined.

I knew the station because I had been there with Papa, although I had never before been there in the evening. I bought my ticket but when I was told I had an hour and three quarters to wait before the train came in, I was horrified. That was the longest hour and three quarters I had ever known. I sat down on one of the seats near the barrier and watched the people, terrified that at any moment someone would come running in, searching for me.

But no one came and in time the train was there. I boarded it, finding it very different from travelling first class with Papa. The seats were wooden and uncomfortable, but I was on the train, on my way to Menfreya, and that was all that mattered just at that time.

I sat in my corner seat and no one noticed me. I was thankful that it was night; I dozed and woke up to find we had come as far as Exeter; then I began to ask myself what I was going to do when I reached Menfreya. Was I going to walk into the hall to tell the butler I had arrived for a visit? I imagined being taken to Lady Menfrey, who would immediately inform my father that I had come. I should be taken back, punished, forbidden ever to do such a thing again. And what would have been gained more than the preliminary excitement of the adventure?

How characteristic of me to rush into something and then ask myself where I was going. I was impulsive and foolish. No wonder they said I was difficult.

I was hungry; I was tired and depressed. I wished that I was in my own room, even though Aunt Clarissa might come in at any moment and look at me in that way which told me she was comparing me with Phyllis or one of the others.

By the time we arrived at Liskeard I realised that I had done a very foolish thing. But I could not turn back now. When I travelled with Papa, A'Lee brought the carriage to the station and we drove the rest of the way. Now there was no carriage so I bought a ticket for the branch line. There was a train which met the London express. It was waiting so I hurried to it.

We waited in the station for almost half an hour which gave me time to plan what I would do. As we made the short journey it occurred to me that as so few people were on the train I might be recognised and stopped. Although we didn't travel on this line Papa was well known in the district and I might be pointed out as his daughter.

At Menfreystow I left the train. There was not more than a dozen people and I huddled close to them as we passed the

little barrier and lowered my head as I handed in my ticket.
I was free. But what now?

I had to make my way to the sea and then walk about a
mile along the cliff path. There would be few people out at
this hour of the morning.

The little town of Menfreystow was still sleeping. The
winding high street—which was almost all there was of it—
was quite deserted; the curtains were drawn in most of the
houses and the few shops were bolted and barred. I smelt the
sea and struck out towards the harbour where the fishing boats
were anchored; and as I passed the fish-shed where the catch
was sold I saw the nets spread out and the lobster pots and
in spite of my uncertainty I experienced a moment of happiness. I always felt as though I belonged here although I did
not, for my father had not rented the house until he became
M.P. for Lansella and its district and that could only have
been some six years before. I stepped carefully over the
iron rings to which the thick salty ropes were attached;
I told myself I was foolish to have come to the harbour.
The fishermen were often about in the early morning and
if I were seen my presence would be reported at once.

I took one of the side alleys and came back into the high
street; this time I darted up one of the steep cobbled turnings,
climbed for five minutes, and then I was up on the cliffs.

The beauty of the scene made me pause for a few seconds
to admire it; there was the coast in all its glory and below
me the beach with the blue-green water very gently caressing
the grey sands; a mile or so along this coast was Menfreya
Manor and facing it No Man's Island where no one lived.

I started to walk thinking about Menfreya Manor and the
Menfreys. Soon I should see the Manor. I knew the exact
spot in the twists and turns of the cliff path where it would
be visible. And there it was, grand, imposing, a kind of Mecca
in my pilgrimage; the home of the Menfreys, the family
which had owned it through the ages. There had been
Menfreys there when Bishop Trelawny had been sent to the
Tower; a Menfrey had supported the Bishop and had
gathered his retainers to join the twenty thousand Cornishmen who were going to know the reason why; I pictured
Menfreys in feathered hats and lace-edged sleeves and
breeches, with powdered hair and lace cravats; there were
pictures of them in the gallery. I could think of nothing

more exciting than being a Menfrey—though I knew I should be wiser to turn my thoughts to more practical matters.

I had reached the spot from where I could see the battlements. Gwennan had taken me up to the top of the tower on one of those occasions when Miss James had brought me over to tea. I could feel the thrill of looking down the steep grey wall to the cliff, down, down to the sea and I could hear Gwennan's voice: "If you want to die all you have to do is jump straight down." I had had a feeling that she might order me to do so in that imperious Menfrey way and that as they were so used to being obeyed, she might expect me to do it. They had been giving orders for many generations whereas the Delvaneys had been doing so for only one. The steel business which was so profitable had been built up by my grandfather, who had begun as one of its humblest employees. Now of course Sir Edward Delvaney had forgotten all about his beginnings; he was polished, an educated man with a brilliant future; but although he was much cleverer than the Menfreys, I knew the difference.

I must be clever too. I must plan the next move. Gwennan often took an early-morning ride and she came this way, for she had told me it was one of her favourite rides.

If I hid myself in a cave in the cliffs which we had discovered I might see her. If not I should have to make further plans. Perhaps it would be better to go to the stables and hide there. But I might meet some of the grooms; besides there were the dogs. No, I must take my chance and wait in the cave. If she was riding to-day she would most certainly come this way.

I waited for what seemed like hours, but I was lucky in the end. Gwennan came and she came alone.

I called to her. She pulled up sharp and stopped.

When I told her she was amused. It was she who thought of the island. It was an adventure which appealed to her. She had me at her mercy now and she was delighted.

"Come with me," she said. "I know where to hide you."

It was high tide so she rowed me over to the island, making me lie in the bottom of the boat for fear someone should see me.

"I shall see that you're fed," she told me. "And as no one else wants to live in the house, why shouldn't you?"

That had happened the day before, now here was Gwennan

with the newspaper. I had not thought that my running away could be so important.

Gwennan said: "They were all talking about it at breakfast. Papa says that someone is going to demand a ransom for you. Thousands of pounds. Fancy being worth that!"

"My Papa would never pay it. He would be glad really to be rid of me."

Gwennan nodded, conceding the possibility of this. "Still," she said wisely, "he mightn't want the papers to know it and so pay up."

"But nobody's asking. I'm not kidnapped."

Gwennan was regarding me speculatively. "We're in need of money, you know," she said.

I laughed. "What! The Menfreys holding me to ransom. It doesn't make sense."

"It would," sighed Gwennan, "if Sir Edward paid us the money. You know we're finding it hard to make ends meet. That's why this place has been furnished. Papa said he didn't see why it shouldn't be put to use. It's been standing idle for years. So they painted it up a little, and they brought this furniture over. That was a year ago. We've been waiting for the first tenant. And it's you!"

"I'm not a real tenant. I'm just hiding here."

"Besides you're not paying rent. Still, if there's a ransom . . ."

"There isn't."

"No. But I'm not surprised you ran away. That hateful old Clarissa creature. I should have gone down and boxed her ears, if I'd been in your place."

"You wouldn't have been. You're beautiful and no one could say those things about you."

Gwennan slipped off the table on which she had been sitting, and uncovering one of the mirrors, studied her face. I limped over and we stood side by side, looking. She couldn't help but be pleased with her reflection—round face, creamy skin, faintly freckled, tawny hair, tawny eyes and an enchanting little nose with wide nostrils which I said made her look like a tiger.

"You always look as though you think people aren't going to like you—that's your trouble," said Gwennan.

"Well, why should I look any other way when they don't?"

"It reminds them they don't. They might forget it if you looked as if you didn't know it. Well, you'll have to stay here.

I'll bring food every day so you won't starve. You'll have to see how long you can hold out. How did you like spending a night on No Man's?"

" Oh . . . it was all right."

" Liar. You were scared."

" Wouldn't you have been?"

" Perhaps. It's haunted, you know."

" It isn't," I said fiercely. It mustn't be, and yet if it was I didn't want to hear about it; but on the other hand I couldn't resist urging her to go on.

In any case Gwennan wasn't going to spare me. " Oh, yes it is. Papa says there might be a tenant but for the whispers. People come and look at the house and then get to hear."

She spent an hour with me, and, when she went, promised to come back in the afternoon. She would have to be very careful not to arouse suspicions, for someone might wonder why she was suddenly interested in the island.

I should have been excited in her place; she had all the fun of it; I had all the difficulties.

I felt uneasy as twilight began to fall. I did not want to enter the house until I had to, so I sat leaning against the wall staring across the sea to Menfreya Manor . . . a comforting sight. There were lights in several of the windows. Bevil was probably there; I had wanted to ask Gwennan about him but I had refrained from doing so for Gwennan had an uneasy habit of reading my thoughts and if she discovered that I was interested in her brother she would be amused and not only tease me but exaggerate my interest.

It would soon be high tide and I watched the water slowly creeping nearer to the house. It came to within a few yards on this side and on very high tides I had heard it reached the wall and flooded the kitchen. That was at certain times of the year, I believed, and it was not now. But the encroaching sea held less terror for me than the dark house. Gwennan had brought me candles in the afternoon and before it was quite dark I would go in and light a few. The more candles there were, the less uneasy I felt. Perhaps I would leave one burning in the bedroom all night; then when I awoke startled I would see where I was at once.

I had no watch so I did not know the time, but the sun had long disappeared and the first stars were beginning to show themselves. I watched them—one moment not there

and the next there they were. I discovered the Plough and
then looked for other constellations which, I had learned from
Miss James, I could expect to find in the night sky. Fear was
creeping closer, like the sea, like the darkness. Perhaps if I
went to bed and lay down I might sleep for I had slept little
for two nights.

I went into the house and hastily lighted the candles; then
I carried one upstairs to the bedroom. I fancied the furniture
leaped into its places as I entered; I hastily looked about me
and shut the door. Then, carrying my candle, I went cau-
tiously to each grotesque hump and lifted the sheet, just to
assure myself that it was only furniture beneath and that
there was nothing hidden there but the pieces which had
been brought over from Menfreya Manor to furnish the
place for the hoped-for tenant. I was foolish. The fear
was within myself. If I could only drive it out of my mind
this would merely be a lonely house to me; I should lie on the
bed and fall fast asleep.

I would try this; but I would leave the candle burning.

I lay on the bed as I had the previous night and closed my
eyes, immediately opening them quickly to see if I could
catch something before it had time to hide. How foolish!
Some people said you didn't actually see ghosts, because
seeing was a physical process and ghosts were not physical.
You sensed them. And I sensed something in this house when
darkness fell, I was sure.

I closed my eyes again, and suddenly thought I was
travelling on the train and because I was so tired, I slept.

I awoke terrified. The first thing I saw was the candle and
I knew that I had slept some time because of how much of it
was burned. I sat up and looked about the room; it seemed
as though the sheeted humps suddenly stood in the places
they had occupied when I closed my eyes. I glanced at the
window. It was still night. Something had awakened me.
A dream? A bad one, because I was trembling and my heart
was bumping madly.

"Only a dream," I said aloud. Then I was alert. Above
the gentle murmur of the waves I heard a sound below.
Voices . . . and then the creak of a door.

I leaped off the bed and stood staring at the door.

I was not alone on the island. I was not alone in the
house.

Voices! Whispering voices! One deep, one of a higher pitch. I heard a sound that could have been a footstep.

"You're imagining it," I whispered.

No. There was the creak of a stair, and the unmistakable sound of stealthy footsteps.

My heart was beating so loudly that it stopped my thinking. *I* was standing against the door listening. Those were undoubted footsteps on the stairs. Then I heard a voice, a female voice. "Let's go. I don't like it."

A low laugh— a man's laugh.

One thing was certain. Whoever these were they were no ghosts, and at any moment they would burst into the room. I ran to the dressing-table and scrambled under the dust sheet. I had only just succeeded in hiding myself when the door opened.

"Ah! Here we are!" said a voice I knew.

"A candle . . . *a light*, Mr. Bevil." That was the woman.

"Whoever is in the house is hiding here," said Bevil Menfrey.

He was pulling off the dust covers and I knew it was only a matter of seconds before he reached the dressing-table.

I looked up at him and even at such a moment I thought how magnificent he looked in candlelight. He had become older since I last saw him. He was indeed a man. He looked enormously tall and the candlelight threw a long shadow of him on the wall with the smaller figure of the woman cowering behind him.

"Good God!" he cried. "It's Harriet Delvaney. Come out, you little wretch. What are you doing here?"

Then stooping he gripped me by the arm and pulled me up.

"Can't say I admire your choice of a residence. How long have you been here?"

"This is the second night."

He turned to his companion and I saw that she was a young and pretty girl whom I did not know.

"Well. The mystery's solved, then."

"What are you going to do, Mr. Bevil?" asked the girl; and then I knew that she was one of the village girls who wouldn't be invited as a guest to Menfreya, so I wondered what she was doing here at this time of night with Bevil.

"There's only one thing to do. I'm going to row her straight back to the mainland; and we'll have to let her father know she's found."

"Oh . . . the wicked little thing!"

"And what about you?" I asked.

That made Bevil laugh again. "Yes," he said, "what about you and what about me? No recriminations on either side, eh, Harriet?"

"No," I said, not understanding, but suddenly almost happy, first because I was not going to have to spend the rest of the night alone on the island and secondly because he was amused by what I had done and because I understood that just as he had discovered me where I should not be, so had I discovered him.

He looked down at me. "You shouldn't have left the candle burning," he said. "Very careless. We saw the flickering light in the window almost as soon as we landed." His face was suddenly stern. "Do you know, Miss Harriet, that there's great consternation about you? They've all but decided to drag the Thames."

He was joking; but he was puzzled, and again I felt that glow of pleasure. Never before had I had his undivided attention; I could see that he had quite forgotten his companion.

We went down to the boat, and in a short time we had reached the mainland.

He said to the girl: "You go now."

Her mouth slackened and she looked at him in surprise but he said impatiently, "Yes, go."

She gave him a rather sullen look and lifting her skirts about her thighs, stepped over the side of the boat into the shallow water. Her feet were bare and she stood for a moment with the water lapping about her ankles to look back and see if Bevil was watching. He wasn't. He was looking at me, his hands resting on the oars.

"Why did you do it?" he said.

"I wanted to."

"You ran away to spend a night on that island?"

"Not to do that."

"How did you get there?"

I didn't answer. I was not going to involve Gwennan.

"You're an odd child, Harriet," he said. "I suspect that you worry too much about things that are not half as important as you imagine them to be."

"You can't know how important my being lame is to me." I was passionately angry suddenly. "You say it's not important. Nor is it, to you. But you don't have to limp about, do you? Of course you can imagine it is not important. It isn't to *you*."

He looked startled. "My dear Harriet, how vehement you are. People don't like you less for being lame. That's what I'm trying to tell you. But that's not the question at the moment, is it? You have run away. There's a great fuss about it. And now you are discovered. What are you going to do? You're not planning to run away from me, are you? Because I shall catch you and bring you back. I want to help you." He leaned towards me. His eyes were quizzical and not without tenderness, which warmed me and made me happy. "Was life impossible there?"

I nodded.

"Your father, I suppose." He sighed. "My poor little Harriet. I'm afraid I'll have to take you back. I'll have to say I found you. If I didn't I'd be an accessory after the fact or something like that. Who brought you over? Gwennan, I suppose. She's been glowing with importance all day. So it *was* Gwennan!"

I did not answer.

"Honour bright," he said. "Very creditable. Well, there's nothing to be done but face the music. But tell me this: What were your intentions?"

"I don't know."

"You mean you just ran away without deciding where you would run to?"

"I came down here."

"By train, I suppose. That was daring of you. But you should have had a plan of campaign, you know. And what did you hope to achieve?"

"I don't know."

He shook his head. Then his face was suddenly tender again. "Poor Harriet, it must have been bad."

"I heard Aunt Clarissa talking about the difficulty of finding a husband for me," I blurted out. "Because," I added, "I was . . ."

"Well, don't let that worry you. Who knows, I might marry you myself."

I laughed.

"I resent that," he said mockingly. "Here I am making a perfectly reasonable suggestion and you treat it with scorn."

"Well," I said, "it wasn't serious."

"People never treat me seriously. I'm too often flippant."
He shipped the oars and leaning towards me, kissed me on
the forehead. I was fully aware then of the charm of the
Menfreys.

When he helped me out of the boat he held me for a
moment, his face close to mine.

"Don't forget," he said, "there'll be a row. But it'll pass.
Come on. Now we go and face the music."

The dogs started to bark as we crossed the courtyard.

The hall was dimly lighted by two gas jets in what looked
like lanterns, and there was just enough light to show the
vaulted ceiling and the armoured figures at the foot of the
staircase.

Bevil shouted so that his voice echoed up to the rafters.
"Come and see what I have found. Harriet Delvaney! I've
got her here."

Then the household was alive. The sounds of voices started
up everywhere.

Sir Endelion and Lady Menfrey came first; then some of
the servants, and I saw Gwennan at the top of the staircase
looking at me with wide accusing eyes.

I felt relieved, because the time had not yet come when I
said to myself: What next? I felt excited because this
night's adventure had brought me closer to Bevil.

I sat in the library drinking hot milk.

Lady Menfrey kept murmuring: "Harriet, but how could
you? Your poor father . . . Frantic . . . quite frantic."

"We've had to telegraph him," Sir Endelion told me
apologetically, pulling at his moustache. I thought then how
much nicer sinners were. Sir Endelion wasn't half as shocked
as Lady Menfrey; nor had Bevil been.

Bevil sat on the table, smiling at me, as though he wanted
to keep my spirits up. I couldn't feel unhappy or frightened
while he was there.

Gwennan had come in quietly so that she wouldn't be seen
and sent back to bed; she was watching me intently.

"What he will say I can't imagine," sighed Lady Menfrey.
"At least we've done our best. . . ."

"You'll have to face the music, my dear." That was Sir
Endelion, and he sounded just like Bevil.

"Exactly my words," said Bevil. "Don't let us repeat ourselves. I think that Harriet should go to bed and sleep; then she will be in better form for the musical interlude."

"I've told Pengelly to have a bed prepared," Lady Menfrey said.

"The room next to mine," added Gwennan.

"Gwennan, my dear, what are you doing here? You should be in bed and asleep." Lady Menfrey looked worried. Her family, I guessed, were a source of continual anxiety to her.

"Awakened by the arrival of Harriet," said Bevil. "It must have been a great shock to her."

"It was," retorted Gwennan defiantly.

"Such a surprise?" asked Bevil.

Gwennan scowled at her brother.

"The last place *you* would have expected to find her."

"You too?" suggested Gwennan. "Otherwise you wouldn't have decided to go there to-night."

Sir Endelion burst into loud laughter; Lady Menfrey looked bewildered. I thought what an exciting household this was; and fervently wished that I belonged to it. I could see that all except Lady Menfrey were taking a lenient view of what I had done; and Lady Menfrey's opinion did not count for much.

"Had I known Harriet was there I should not have gone there last night, I do assure you," retorted Bevil.

I put my glass on the table.

"Gwennan," said Lady Menfrey, "since you are here, perhaps you will take our guest to her room."

I said good night to Bevil, Sir Endelion and Lady Menfrey, and Gwennan and I mounted the staircase together; and even at such a time I could not help feeling thrilled to be in Menfreya.

"Your room's next to mine," she said. "I told Pengelly I wanted you to be there. So you didn't tell . . ."

"They know. There was nothing to tell."

"About me, I mean."

I shook my head.

The room they had given me was large—all the rooms were, at Menfreya—with a window seat round a bay window which looked out to the island. On the double bed was a pink flannel nightdress.

"One of mine," pointed out Gwennan. "You've to get undressed right away."

I hesitated. "Go on," she said. "Don't be so prudish."

I wriggled out of my clothes while she watched me, and when I was in bed she sat at the end hugging her knees, her eyes still on me.

"I'm not sure that you won't go to prison," she said. "After all, the police were brought in and when that happens you never know." I could see that while she taunted me her mind was busy with plans for my rescue. "But I don't suppose that would happen. Your father would bribe them not to. I'm in for it, too. You see they'll want to know who took you over there and who robbed the pantry. Mrs. Pengelly missed that leg of chicken I brought you yesterday. And other things. Suspicion points to me . . . and I shall be in the dock with you. That should be a comfort. Mamma and Papa will go into deep conferences, and a decision is about to be made. And by the way, Bev will be furious with you."

"Furious with me, why?"

"Because you spoilt his little adventure. Since Papa furnished the house he uses it for his seductions. It's romantic and the ladies' fear of ghosts adds a piquancy to the occasion. He can be bold and protective and the purpose is achieved in half the time."

"You're making it up. How could you know?"

"My dear Harriet, all the Menfreys know about each other. It's a gift we have. All the men are devastatingly attractive to women and all the women to men. We can't help it. We have to accept it."

I looked at her and believed it was so; the thought saddened me.

"I'm tired," I said. I wanted to be alone, to go over those moments when Bevil and I were in the boat together, to remember every word he had said.

"Tired!" cried Gwennan. "How can you be tired when you think of to-morrow? What a good thing I didn't send that ransom letter."

"There was no question of a ransom letter."

"Wasn't there? I've been drafting it. You don't think I'd let an opportunity like that pass! The Menfreys never miss their opportunities."

"I don't believe it." I closed my eyes.

"All right," she said huffily and leaped off the bed. "Go to sleep and dream about to-morrow. I shouldn't like to be in your place, Harriet Delvaney. You wait till your father comes."

Gwennan and I were watching for his carriage so we saw it arrive. Very shortly afterwards I was summoned to the library.

Never have I seen his eyes so cold; never had he looked at me with such dislike; and never had I felt so ugly as I did when I limped into that room. Strangely enough when I was aware of my deformity I fancied it became more obvious; and in his presence I was always conscious of it.

"Come here," he said, and as usual the tone in his voice when he addressed me made me feel as though cold water was being poured down my back.

"I am shocked beyond belief. I could never contemplate such ingratitude, such selfishness, such wickedness. How could you . . . even you—and I have learned that you are capable of many undutiful acts—but how could you be capable of such conduct!"

I did not answer. The last thing I could do was try to explain my reasons to him. I wasn't entirely sure of them myself. The roots were too deeply embedded; and I knew even at this time that those few ill-chosen words of Aunt Clarissa's were not the entire reason why I had left home.

"Speak when I ask a question. Do not give me insolence as well as ingratitude."

He took a step towards me and I thought he was going to strike me. I almost wished he would. I believed I could have endured a hot hatred rather than a cold dislike.

"Papa, I . . . wanted to get away. I . . ."

"You wanted to run away? You wanted to cause trouble. Why did you come here?"

"I . . . I wanted to come to Menfreya."

"The whim of the moment. You should be whipped . . . insensible." His mouth twisted into an expression of distaste. Physical violence was repulsive to him, I knew. Any dog which disobeyed him was not corrected; it was destroyed. I thought then: He would like to destroy me. But he would never whip me.

He turned away from me as though he could not bear to look at me. "Everything you want is yours. You have every comfort. Yet you have no gratitude. You delight in giving us acute anxiety and causing trouble. When I think that it was to give you birth that your mother died . . ."

I wanted to scream at him to stop. I could not bear to hear him say this. I knew that he had thought it often, but to hear the words gave the horror deeper meaning. I could not bear it. I wanted to creep into a corner and cry.

Yet instead of the pain I felt, my face was forming itself into those ugly obstinate lines and I could not prevent it. He saw this and the loathing which was deep in him for this monster who had robbed him of a loved one that it might have life was temporarily unleashed. He took brief comfort in giving freedom to the bitter resentment which had been smouldering for years.

"When I saw you . . . when they told me your mother was dead I wanted to throw you out of the house."

The words were out. They hit me more cruelly than any whip could have done. He had crystallised the scene. I saw the ugly baby in the nurse's arms; I saw the dead woman on the bed; and his face. I could even hear his voice: "Throw it out of the house."

It was there for ever in my mind. Previously I had guessed at his dislike; I had been able to delude myself that I had imagined it; that he was a man who did not easily express his feelings; that deep down he loved me. But that was over.

Perhaps he was ashamed. His voice had softened a little. "I despair of ever imbuing you with a sense of decency," he said. "Not only do you make trouble for yourself but for others. The entire household has been disrupted. We have been invaded by reporters."

He was talking to hide his confusion; and I was only half listening because I was thinking of his anger when he looked at the baby in the nurse's arms.

"At least," he said, "you must not abuse the hospitality of Menfreya any longer than necessary. We will leave at once for Chough Towers."

Chough Towers was an early Victorian mansion about a mile from Menfreya. My father had rented it furnished from a family called Leveret who had made a fortune from china clay which they quarried near St. Austell. The house was almost as large as Menfreya but it lacked the character of the latter. It was an ugly house and, as I have said, always seemed cold and impersonal; but perhaps that was because my father had rented it and it was his personality which had pervaded it; inhabited by a happy family it might have been a happy house. The rooms were large and panelled, with big windows looking out on well-tended lawns; there was a large ballroom on the ground floor of fine proportions, at one end of which was a wide oak staircase; everything that could have been done to give an air of antiquity to the place had been done. There was even a minstrels' gallery, which I always thought looked incongruous in such a house; the conservatory was pleasant because it was full of colourful plants; but everything else was over-ornate and heavy; the baroque towers and battlements were false and it was absurd to have called it Chough Towers for I never saw a chough near the place. It was a showy imitation, pretending to be what it was not.

It was surrounded by a park but the trees in the drive had obviously not been planted more than thirty years before; there were none of those tottery old yews one found at Menfreya. I was in love with Menfreya, and perhaps I felt the difference more keenly than most. Chough Towers was I suppose a beautiful house in a beautiful setting, but it had no echoes of the past, no secrets; it was just the outward sign of a self-made man's desire to build himself a dwelling as grand as those enjoyed by people whom, a generation before, he would have been expected to bow to as the gentry. But a house is more than walls and windows—or even fine ballrooms and conservatories, a park and lawns.

It suited my father because he only spent a certain time of the year in the vicinity; and he was not sure that he wanted to buy a house there. If he lost his seat in the House he would certainly not wish to retain Chough Towers.

As we entered the house I was aware of the hushed atmosphere. I suspected that the servants were talking of me, perhaps some of them were peeping at me. I had become an object of interest because my name had been in the papers. It would be again—for the discovery of my whereabouts would have to be known since there had been such concern about my disappearance.

"You will go straight to your room and remain there until you are given permission to leave it," said my father.

And how glad I was to escape.

I was a prisoner. I was to have only bread and milk until

further notice. None of the servants was to speak to me. I was in disgrace.

I was defiant, and pretended I didn't care, but my feelings alternated between misery and elation.

I would sometimes be able to shut out all memory of anything but Bevil, sitting there in the boat. I could see his strange eyes alight with tenderness—no, mockery really. " I might marry you myself .   ." He was joking ; and yet perhaps not entirely. In any case in my present state it was pleasant to delude myself into believing that he might have meant it. It was a gay and happy dream.

Then there was that other—dark, gloomy ; the death chamber, the shrivelled-faced baby ; I had seen new-born babies and thought them ugly, and surely I would have been particularly so. I could picture the mad impulse of a normally restrained man. I could feel the revulsion, the longing to be rid of the unwanted creature whose coming had cost so dear.

On the second day of my captivity my father came to my room. My spirits rose because I saw that he was dressed for departure.

" You will remain in your room for a week," he said, " and I hope that you will be considerably chastened at the end of that time. Has it occurred to you that your life might be cut short at any moment? I should like you to consider during the next days that you are heading for eternal damnation. For your own sake—I know you are too selfish to do it for mine—reform your ways. You will remain here until it is time for you to go away to school."

I was too astonished to speak. I was suddenly torn from the contemplation of hell's torments to consider an entirely new life. School!

" Yes," he went on, " you are in desperate need of discipline. If at school you are disobedient, you will be severely punished. Miss James was too lenient with you, I fear. She will be leaving us now, of course."

I thought of Miss James packing her bag and crying discreetly because she was frightened of the future. Poor Miss James! She would haunt me for weeks to come in spite of the alarming prospect before me.

" So she is to be dismissed . . ."

" You see how your thoughtless actions affect others."

A frightening thought occurred to me. Fanny! What of Fanny?

I whispered her name under my breath, but he heard me.

"She remains. She will be employed in another capacity. And when you are on holiday you will need a maid."

Waves of thankfulness! Fanny was safe. Why had I not thought of what the consequences might have been to her before I ran away? My father was right. I must think before I acted.

He continued: "It is my earnest wish that you should learn a little selflessness. This wantonly thoughtless action of yours has caused me great trouble. Remember it; and should you ever feel tempted to be so wicked again, pray consider, for you will not find me as indulgent next time."

"You are going away, Papa," I said.

"I am going to get on with the work which you interrupted."

He looked at me and for a moment I thought he was going to take me in his arms and kiss me. To my amazement I realised that I wanted him to.

If he had, I should have cried; I should have told him how unhappy I was, how sorry that I had had to be born, how I would willingly go back into that limbo where unborn babies were and stay there, if by doing so I could bring my mother back to him.

That was one part of me; the other part hated him.

And the part that hated was uppermost; it showed itself in my sullen expression.

He turned and left me.

The atmosphere in the house was considerably lifted when he went.

Within an hour A'Lee was unlocking my door. He was carrying a tray which was covered by a cloth, and as he came in he said: "Well, Miss Harriet, the master be gone back to London and us be alone again."

He set down the tray, winked at me and whipped off the cloth to disclose a Cornish pasty, golden-brown, hot and savoury, fresh from the oven, and a glass of cider; and with it was a large slice of raisin cake.

"It was all Mrs. A'Lee could lay her hands on at a minute's notice."

" It looks delicious."

" And tastes so, if I know Mrs. A'Lee."

" But I'm supposed to be on bread and milk."

" Me and Mrs. A'Lee, we never did like the sound of that."

I sat down at the table and cut the pasty. The savoury steam made my mouth water and A'Lee looked on with satisfaction.

" Well, now, that be an end to that bread and milk nonsense."

" My father would be furious if he knew. You'd be dismissed . . . both you and Mrs. A'Lee."

" Not we two. We go with the house, don't 'ee forget. He never did like us. We ain't like his London butler, I reckon." A'Lee took the cloth which covered the tray, folded it over his arm and minced round the room. His attempts to mimic the over-refined accents of Polden, whom he had seen once or twice when Polden had come to Chough Towers to superintend some special occasion, were so wide of the mark that they made me laugh, as A'Lee had intended they should.

" No," he said, " we be good enough for Mr. Leveret and we be good enough for 'ee."

" Don't you wish that Mr. Leveret had continued to live here?"

" Oh, them was the days. Mr. Harry may come back. But he be so busy down in St. Austell and in other parts they do say. Reckon we belong to be working for the Leverets rather than fine fancy gentlemen from London like . . ."

" Like my father? You don't want to work for him, do you, A'Lee?"

" Well, he do have a nice little maid for a daughter."

" And she at least likes you better than that stupid Polden."

" Well, she be a real right lady, she be."

We laughed together.

" That be my own brew of cider. I'd make it for Mr. Leveret. Mr. Harry he got drunk on it one day. Not much more than eight he were. He come sniffing round the barrel and I didn't know that he'd been helping himself. That were a time, that were. Don't 'ee get too much of a taste for it, Miss Harriet. It be real heady stuff."

" Not much chance. I'm going away to school."

" Yes, so we be hearing. Well, you'll be back, I reckon. And her's to go with 'ee, so there'll be fireworks like as not."

" Who?"

"Miss Gwennan up at Menfreya."

"Oh . . . A'Lee! Is it true?"

"You be real proper pleased."

"It makes all the difference."

He shook his head. "I don't know. Them Menfreys . . ."

"You don't like them much, do you, A'Lee?"

"Oh, 'tain't rightly a matter of liking or not liking. They'm wild. And they'm made for trouble. 'Twas due to Menfrey trouble that you be here . . . sitting on that chair enjoying Mrs. A'Lee's pasty like it be a nectar of the gods—which it might be, for that there couldn't have tasted much better, I'll be bound."

"Due to Menfrey trouble? But why?"

"Well, why be you here? Because your father, Sir Edward Delvaney, he be the Member. For nigh on seven years he's been the Member. But before that it was always a Menfrey who went to Parliament in London for us. There was never no foreigner here till these last seven years."

"Sir Endelion was the Member for Lansella, then?"

"Of course he were. And his father before him. Ever since there was Members it's been the Menfreys for Lansella."

"And why did Sir Endelion give it up?"

"Why bless you, my dear, he didn't so much give it up as it gave him up. The Queen they do say be terrible strict and her wouldn't have any of her ministers with a bad name, you see. And Sir Endelion he were something big up there in London. Might have been one of the real heads but for this. Prime Minister, say . . . or some such thing."

"What was the scandal?"

"The usual. You never have to ask *what*, when it's Menfreys my dear; it's *who*."

"A woman?"

A'Lee nodded. "Regular scandal. Up in London, too. Down here we be used to 'em. The Menfreys was always good to the girls who got into trouble through them. Find them husbands most likely or homes for the babies. But this were in London. Some very high-born lady, and her husband divorced her all along of Sir Endelion."

"Poor Lady Menfrey!"

"Oh, she be a gentle lady, she be. She forgive him like; and for the first time any of us remember we didn't have a Menfrey up in Parliament for us. That's how your father came."

"They don't seem to mind."

"There's some that say he be nursing the seat for Mr. Bevil."

"So . . . he will go into politics."

"Well, Menfreys always has. Must have a say in the Government, says they. They're regular ones for having their say. Mr. Bevil he'll come back, I reckon. All in time. And then there'll be a Menfrey up in London for Lansella."

I finished the cider and swallowed the last of the raisin cake.

"That was good, A'Lee," I said; and I was thinking of poor Lady Menfrey and how angry she must have been—or sorry. Unhappy in any case. I could imagine Sir Endelion coming back to Menfreya, turned out of Parliament because of scandal.

No wonder they were called the wild Menfreys.

Later that day Gwennan came over to see me.

"As soon as I heard your father had gone I came over," she said. "We're to go to school . . . together. We're undisciplined, and they can't control us. What fun! They would never have thought of sending us if you hadn't run away. This is the end of all that."

"It's not the end," I contradicted. "How could going away and starting a new life be the end of anything?"

TWO

Three years had passed since I had run away, and they had been happier years than I had known up to that time, although I was not as popular at school as Gwennan was. I was more studious, and although not brilliantly clever, my desire to shine at something helped me considerably. My diligence pleased my teachers and because of this I was moderately happy.

Friendship between my family and the Menfreys had grown. My father was particularly interested in Bevil, for A'Lee had been right when he said that the Menfreys always went into politics. Bevil had decided to do just that; and I supposed that one day he hoped to bring back the family tradition of representing Lansella. In the meantime he had come down from the university, had travelled through Europe on a sort of Grand Tour, and was helping my father in his work with a prospect of gaining an opportunity of standing for Parliament when it arose.

When I had seen them together I was astonished, for my father was quite charming with Bevil, who, I was sure, had no idea how different he could be with his own daughter.

Summer holidays were spent at Chough Towers and that was as good as staying at Menfreya. My father had decided that London air was not good for me, so I was not an encumbrance there, but put into the care of the A'Lees—which suited me, particularly as I spent the greater part of my time at Menfreya, where I was regarded as one of the family.

I was growing more restrained; I was still resentful against the world, but able to control my feelings more easily. Sometimes I dreamed that my father was trying to throw me out of the house or was chasing me with a whip. I recall vividly the cold terror in which I always awoke from these nightmares.

I told no one of these dreams—certainly not Gwennan. But Fanny knew. Often I would wake up and find her at my bedside, because I had shouted in my sleep. Sometimes she would just get into my bed and hold me in her arms until I slipped into peaceful sleep; at others she would talk to me about the orphanage. I rarely had these dreams when I was away at school.

Because I had for a short time feared I might lose Fanny, I realised how important she was to me. She it was who sewed the name tabs on my school garments, who insisted that I changed my clothes if I were caught in the rain.

Gwennan envied me Fanny.

" You're lucky to have a maid of your own," she told me. " She'll be with you to the death."

I enjoyed being envied by Gwennan; so that was something else for which I had to be grateful to Fanny.

Gwennan was the most attractive girl in the school and the most outrageously outspoken. She charmed her way out of trouble and I believe that had she not been able to do so she might well have been expelled. She had been right when she said that the Menfreys were fatally attractive to the opposite sex. There were one of two affairs when we were at school which were undetected, but of which she liked to boast. How far they went I was not sure; I could not always believe what she told me. I was constantly afraid of what she would do next, but what I was most afraid of was being left out of her confidence.

It was she who told me that Bevil was going into Parliament and that my father was helping him. He was waiting until there was a constituency for him and then he would nurse it and hope for a seat at a by-election or the next General Election.

" Your father can do so much for him, so Papa and Mamma are anxious that we shall all be friends. That, my dear Harriet, is why we go to school together and you're so welcome at Menfreya."

" It seems a horrid reason."

" Reasons often are."

" So that's why you're my friend?"

" No. *I* could not be bribed."

" I don't see how *I* could bribe you."

" Not you. But all that money could. Mamma and Papa want us to be friends, you know, because of Bev. But I have my own reasons."

" What?"

" You're such a foil to my beauty." She laughed. " Ha! Now you look sick. Silly. As if I *need* a foil. I never did believe in them anyway. No, I like you because you're so angry about everything, and ran away and all that You stayed that night too on No Man's and didn't bring me in. I'm glad you're going to marry Bevil."

" Marry Bevil!"

" Well, you are in love with him, aren't you? My dear and precious life! as Mrs. Pengelly would say. You *are* blushing. You look better red than sallow. So it's not a bad idea. I should cultivate that, Harriet."

" I don't know what you mean about . . . marrying."

" Then you're blinder than a dozer bats. You know how they work things in families like ours. They choose our husbands for us . . . like royalty. Bevil is for you and Harry Leveret for me. Poor Harry has red hair and you can't see his eyelashes. I don't believe he's got many; but I'll tell you what he has a lot of, and that is pounds, shillings and pence ; and my family happen to think that is a great deal more important than eyelashes. And you have the same. That is why we are so happy to invite the Leverets and the Delvaneys to Menfreya Manor. It stands to reason, doesn't it?"

"They are very . . . mercenary."

"Have a heart, Harriet. They're poor. They have the grandest house in South Cornwall and it's an old monster that eats up the pounds, shillings and pence. You've no idea. We're feckless. We always have been. Monsters demand the blood of rich young virgins like you and Harry—for you are, I know, and I'm sure Harry is. So we need you."

"Does Bevil know this?"

"Of course he knows it."

"And he doesn't mind?"

"Mind? Why should he? He's delighted."

"You mean he likes me a little?"

"Don't be silly, Harriet. You're an heiress. Your father's got all that money and who else has he got to leave it to?"

"I don't think he'll leave anything to me."

"Of course he will. People always leave their money to their heirs . . . however much they hate them. It's pride, or something."

"But it's beastly . . . for you and Bevil, I mean."

"Bless you. We don't mind." She stood up and folded her hands together trying to look like a saint. "It's for the sake of Menfreya," she added.

It was soon after that when she showed me the table in the hall. "Once," she said, "it was set with precious stones. Rubies, I think. See, they've all been taken out. They were used up one by one by my ancestors . . . to save Menfreya. Well, now there are no rubies left, so it has to be wives and husbands."

"I shall be a wife more precious than rubies," I said.

We giggled together. That was how it was with Gwennan ; however much she hurt me, we would always laugh together; and however much she scorned me or criticised me, I was always her closest friend.

When my father decided to give a fancy-dress ball at Chough Towers, Gwennan determined to go. We were sixteen and neither of us officially "out," but Gwennan badgered Lady Menfrey until she agreed that we might watch from the gallery if my father gave his permission for us to do this ; and since Lady Menfrey asked it, it was graciously given.

"We need clothes," said Gwennan, but even Lady Menfrey, who could usually be persuaded by her family, did not take that seriously.

Gwennan glowered; she raged and stormed ; and for days

she talked of nothing but costumes and how we could get them. Then one day when I went to Menfreya I found her in a state of excitement.

She greeted me with the words: " I've something to show you. Come on. It's where you've never been before."

Menfreya always seemed mysterious to me because there was so much of it which I had never explored, and the thought of seeing a new part excited me, so I eagerly followed Gwennan, who led me through the house to the east wing which was never used and was the oldest part.

" This wing needs so many repairs that until they can be done we can't live in it. Who'd want to anyway? I came here yesterday but I didn't like to stay because it was getting dark." We had climbed a short staircase and reached a door which she pushed but could not open.

" It was hard to open yesterday, but I managed it. Before that it hadn't been opened for years, I expect—not since Bevil and I came here ages ago. Don't stand there. Give a hand.

I put my shoulder to the door and pushed with all my might. It moved slowly at first and then flew open to disclose a gloomy passage which smelt of age and damp. We walked down this.

" We must be near the east buttress," I whispered.

" There's no need to murmur," Gwennan shouted. " No one can hear us. We're shut right away. Buttress is right. That's where I'm taking you."

My teeth were chattering, with excitement not cold, although there was a chill in the air.

" Fancy having all this and never coming here," I said.

" Somebody went over it once and gave such an estimate for what had to be done that we forgot all about it. That was the time when I came here exploring with Bevil."

" When you were children?"

She didn't answer. " Mind these stairs. Hold the rope." We had come to a small spiral staircase ; each step was steep and worn in the middle; the rope acted as a banister and a means of pulling oneself up the stairs. Gwennan stood at the top and grinned at me. She held up her hands. " Look at the dust."

" What made you come here?"

" You'll see. Look at this door. It was put in a long time

after this place was built. Once there was just a panel which you could slide and let yourself into the room."

"What room?"

"This leads to a sort of passage and then . . . into the haunted room. This door's hard to open, too."

It was; it gave a whine of protest which sounded like a human voice warning us not to go in—at least that was what I suggested, and it made Gwennan shriek with laughter.

"Trust you to think up that! Now . . . through here. It leads to the buttress."

The air was really chill now; the passage was narrow, the wall of stone. We were almost in the dark and I reached for Gwennan and clutched her skirt.

The passage opened out into what was scarcely a room— more like a circular aperture. There was no window but a slit in the deep wall open to the air, and through this came a little daylight.

"What a strange place!" I cried.

"Of course it is. They used to keep prisoners here in the old days. Then of course *he* kept *her* here . . . and then it became haunted."

"You are incoherent, Gwennan."

She watched my amazement with gratification as I looked round the place. Strangely enough there was a mirror propped against the wall; its glass was mottled, its frame tarnished. And there was a trunk, green with mildew. I noticed another passage like that we had come through and pointed this out to Gwennan.

"Come on, then. I'll show you." She led the way into the passage, where, facing us, was another spiral staircase like the one we had just mounted. She began to climb it, counting the steep steps as she did so. There were forty, and at the top we were out in the open air on a narrow circular walk which took us round the buttress.

"This is where she used to come up for air," Gwennan announced.

"Who?"

"Her, of course. If she really does walk, I reckon she comes up here."

The sides of the buttress were battlemented. We knelt on a ledge and leaned over to look down from the very top of the house to the sea below. Gwennan pointed out the corbels on which she said they used to stand the pots of boiling oil they threw down on anyone who came attacking them. "Imagine them," she said, "climbing up the cliffs and getting out their battering rams. That was years and years ago . . . long before *she* was here."

I filled my lungs with the fresh air and clung to the hard stone of the battlement. I thought then: How I love this house where so many exciting things have happened; and so many people have lived and died. I wanted wholeheartedly to belong to it, to be one of them.

Gwennan had started to tell me the story. "She was employed here as a governess to the children and this Menfrey—my ancestor—fell in love with her. When Lady Menfrey found out she dismissed her and told her to get out of the house. She thought she had gone, but she hadn't. You see, *he* couldn't bear her to go away, so he brought her to this place because no one knew it was here then. He used to visit her in that room down there. Can't you picture him, Harriet, creeping into the disused wing and sliding the panel? I bet it was a panel then, and he'd have a candle or perhaps a lantern . . . and they'd be together. He had to go away for a while. To London, I expect . . . to Parliament . . . and the clock in the tower stopped. You know the tower clock which is supposed to stop when a Menfrey is going to die."

"I didn't . . ."

"You don't know anything. Well, the clock in the tower is supposed to stop when one of us is going to die an unnatural death. That's why Dawney has to be careful to keep it going. We don't believe these old stories—or we say we don't . . . but other people do. That's what Papa says, and we have to remember that. Goodness knows why."

"Well, what happened? Why did the clock stop?"

"Because she died. She died up here . . . in that room down there . . . and so did the baby."

"Whose baby?"

"Hers, of course. You see, it came before it should . . . and no one knew. They both died. That's why the clock stopped."

"She wasn't a Menfrey."

"No, but the baby was. It stopped for the baby. Then Sir Bevil came back."

"Who?"

"I expect he was Sir Bevil . . . or Endelion or something . . . he came back and found her dead. They sealed off the room and never thought about it for years and years . . .

until someone found it again and put the door in instead of the panel. But nobody would come here. The servants wouldn't. They say it's haunted. Do you think it is?"

"It feels cold and melancholy," I said.

She hung over the battlements with her feet off the ground so that I was terrified that she was going to fall. She did it purposely, I knew, to show how reckless she was.

"Let's go down," I said.

"Yes, rather. There's that trunk. I looked inside. That's why I brought you. But I wanted to show you this first."

We made our way back to the circular room and Gwennan lifted the lid of the trunk. The green growth came off on her hands, which made her grimace; but the contents of the trunk caused her to smile.

She was tugging at what looked like a piece of topaz-coloured velvet, but I wasn't interested; I was thinking of the woman who had been loved by a Menfrey. "I thought you could have this brown thing," she said. She dropped it on to the floor and brought out a roll of blue velvet which she began draping about her. I picked up the topaz-coloured velvet. It was a dress, with a tight square-cut bodice and wide sleeves that were slashed to show golden satin beneath. The skirt must have contained yards and yards of velvet. I held it up against me and when I looked at my reflection in that mottled mirror I could not believe I was looking at myself.

"It suits you," said Gwennan, her attention momentarily distracted from herself. "Put it on. Yes, put it on."

"Here?"

"Yes. Over your clothes."

"It's so cold I'm sure it's damp."

"It won't hurt you for a minute. It's just the thing for the ball."

I caught her excitement as I slipped the dress over my head. She was beside me, pulling it, fastening it, and in a few seconds there I was . . . transformed.

It was cut low and my grey merino showed at neck and sleeves, but that did not seem to matter. It became me in a way nothing else ever had. As I lifted the skirt, something fell from it, and picking it up I found it to be a snood, made of ribbon and lace and decorated with stones which might have been topaz.

"It goes on your hair," said Gwennan. "Go on. Put it on."

Now the change was complete. That was not poor lame Harriet Delvaney who looked back at me from the mottled mirror. Her eyes were greener and much larger, her face animated.

"It's a miracle," said Gwennan. She pointed at the reflection. "It's not like you at all. You've turned into someone else." She laughed. "Well, I'll tell you something, Harriet Delvaney. You've got yourself a dress for the ball."

She came and stood beside me wrapping the blue velvet about her, and I was glad she was with me. If she had not been I should have felt something very strange happening to me. But then, of course, I was the fanciful one.

She took my hand. "Come, be my partner in the dance, dear madam."

She skipped round the room, her hand in mine. I went with her and we had been round the room before I realised that I was dancing—I, who had told myself I would never dance.

She too had noticed it. "You're a fraud, Harriet Delvaney," she shouted and her voice echoed oddly in this strange place. "I don't believe there's anything wrong with that foot of yours after all."

I stopped and looked down at it; then I caught the reflection of the girl in the mirror. It was an extraordinary moment, like that in the garden when I was a child and had suddenly got up and walked.

I was exhilarated, I couldn't understand why; I felt it had something to do with the dress I was wearing.

"Well, that settles it," said Gwennan. "We're going to the ball. And now get that off and we'll take these things and we'll see what we can do with them."

We went back to Gwennan's room together; I felt then as though I had begun to live in a dream.

My father came down to Chough Towers the day before the ball and gloom descended on the house. Meals were always an ordeal when he was there. Fortunately for me—but not for him—William Lister joined us and we would sit at the long table in the dining-room—which overlooked one of the lawns—for what seemed like interminable periods of time. My father led the conversation, which was usually about politics, and William made discreet replies; if I spoke my father would listen with obvious patience, and usually ignore what I had said; if William tried to reply to me my father often changed the subject. So I decided that it was better to say nothing, and hope that the meal would soon be over. A'Lee would be at the sideboard directing the parlourmaids—there were two of them; and it always seemed incongruous that we three should need so many people to wait on us—particularly as I knew how much bustle would be going on in the kitchen. I would rise when they reached the port stage and leave them to talk. How glad I was when it was time for that!

Once my father said to me: "Have you no conversation?" and I merely flushed and said nothing, when I wanted to shout: When I do speak you ignore me.

At least my mind was so occupied with thoughts of the dress which now hung in my wardrobe side by side with the one Gwennan would wear and wondering if Bevil would see me in it and be charmed with what he saw, that I ceased to think very much about my father. Gwennan had said we must tell no one about our discovery because there might be attempts to stop us using the dresses. However, I could not keep Fanny out of the secret and she had helped to make up the blue for Gwennan and altered the the topaz velvet for me. She saw no harm in it, she said; and afterwards we could put them back where we found them. She hung them out on the balcony—to air them, she said, and get rid of the musty smell. So, after we had smuggled them over to Chough Towers, there had been long sessions in my bedroom which Fanny had seemed to enjoy as much as we did.

On the night of the ball, Fanny brushed my untidy hair until it lay flat about my shoulders; then she helped me into the dress and sat me down before the mirror so that I could watch while she finished my hair and put on the jewelled snood. My face looked back at me—my green eyes greener because they were so brilliant, a faint colour beneath my skin; I could almost believe I was attractive in that dress.

"Well, there you are, my lady," said Fanny, "all ready to go to the ball."

The house seemed to have come alive. Everywhere were the sounds of voices; the musicians had arrived and those guests who were staying in the house were already with my father in the ballroom. Aunt Clarissa was not here on this occasion—it was too far from London—and my father was going to receive the guests alone.

I sat on the window seat in my bedroom with Fanny while we watched the carriages arrive.

It was a fascinating sight to see the guests, in their costumes and masks, alight and step across the path to the porch. The Leverets' arrival caused some excitement because they had come in their horseless carriage. They were the only family in the neighbourhood who possessed one and when they drove out in it people would run out of their cottages to see it go by; and when it broke down and horses had to pull it along there was a lot of talk about the folly of modern inventions. But during the last year in London the contraption had been treated with more respect since the law enforcing a man to walk before it with a red flag had been abolished and the speed limit raised to fourteen miles an hour. Here in remote Cornwall, however, the horseless carriage was still regarded with contemptuous suspicion and I had to agree that to see the Leverets in fancy dress riding in the thing was incongruous.

I laughed and Fanny said: "Well, if this ain't a regular circus!"

"I was thinking it was like being in the past . . . until that came."

"You're getting too excited, miss."

"Am I?"

"Why, yes. I've never seen you like this before. Don't forget you're only going to look on from the gallery."

"I wish Gwennan were here."

"Miss Mischief will be here soon, don't you fret."

She was right. The carriage from Menfreya arrived soon after she had spoken. The first to alight was the eighteenth-century gentleman, who was Bevil; he helped his mother and Gwennan out and then came Sir Endelion. I did not notice what Sir Endelion and Lady Menfrey were wearing, for I had eyes only for Bevil.

Gwennan in her everyday cloak over a simple party dress looked quite insignificant among those brilliant costumes and I could imagine how impatient she was to get into her blue velvet gown.

One of the servants brought Gwennan to my room. I hid myself so that I should not be seen in my topaz, and Fanny spoke to the servant while Gwennan came into the room. When the servants had gone Fanny said, "You can come out now, miss." Then she helped Gwennan into her gown and left us together.

"Yours is not brown," said Gwennan. "It's a sort of gold." She smoothed down the folds of her blue velvet complacently. Then she frowned. "Yours is more unusual," she went on. "Really, Harriet, I've never seen you look like that. I know what it is. You're not thinking people are hating you, that's what. But why are we waiting? I want to go to the ball, if you don't."

I had been told where I was to take her. It was to the gallery—the imitation minstrels' gallery—which looked down on the ballroom. We had decided that we would wait there until the ballroom was crowded before we slipped on our masks and went down. "Then," Gwennan had said, "we shall not be noticed."

We reached the gallery. Heavy purple velvet curtains were fixed across it and drawn back by gold bands to give us a peephole, and two chairs had been set some way back from the rails, so that although we need not be completely invisible, we should certainly not be obtrusive.

Gwennan immediately went to the balustrade and looked down. I stood a little way back; but what a magnificent sight it was! We were almost level with the gas-candled chandeliers and the scene below was made fantastic by the colour of the costumes and the different centuries represented.

We had been watching for five or six minutes when we heard voices at the gallery door, one of which was Fanny's.

"Well, sir," she was saying, "I don't rightly think I should, but if you insist . . ."

"Of course I insist. Now, be a sport."

Gwennan looked at me. "It's Harry," she said. "Harry Leveret."

The door opened and Fanny, flushed and anxious, said: "I don't rightly know . . ."

"What is it?" I asked.

"The gentleman said . . ."

And there was Harry. He was dressed as Drake and his false beard did not match the reddish hair that showed beneath his feathered cap. He brushed Fanny aside and she disappeared; then he came into the gallery.

"Harry, what are you doing?" asked Gwennan, her voice rising on a high-pitched note of excitement.

"You didn't expect me to stay down there when you were up here, did you?"

He didn't seem at all surprised to see us in our costumes so I guessed she must have told him that we had found them. His eyes shone as he looked at her.

" We have masks, too, haven't we, Harriet?" said Gwennan. " Come on. Put them on and we'll go down."

I could see that Harry wasn't very pleased at the prospect of having me with them.

" Don't worry," I said. " I shan't be a nuisance."

" You'll find a partner," Gwennan said with that conviction she always gave to things she wanted to believe.

" Of course," I replied proudly, although I didn't believe it for a moment and now that the time had come to join the dancers I was alarmed. What would happen if my father discovered me! I had allowed Gwennan to pull me into this adventure without giving full consideration to the consequences. *She* would be all right; she would have Harry Leveret to look after her; besides, her family were not like my father.

" Of course she will," agreed Harry.

We left the gallery and went down to the ballroom. I promised myself that I could always hurry back to the gallery if I felt too lonely among all those people, and the thought gave me courage. And what comfort it was to cower behind the mask. I caught a glimpse of myself as we passed a mirror. I didn't recognise myself. Then if I didn't, why should anyone else? And suddenly I was excited—by the colour, the music, the brilliance of everything and the strange feeling that with the dress I had put on a different personality.

Harry could scarcely wait to get Gwennan to himself, and as we entered the ballroom he put his arm about her and they went into the waltz. I stood watching. The Beautiful Blue Danube! How dreamy, how romantic! How I should love to be one of those dancers.

I hid myself behind the potted ferns, watching, caught up by the music, imagining myself dancing there . . . with Bevil, of course.

And then I saw him. He was dancing with a beautiful girl dressed as Cleopatra—laughing, looking down at her, saying amusing things . . . affectionately, I was sure. I thought of the way he had talked to me when he had brought me back from the island; he had kissed me then. It had been a joke, of course.

He was dancing past my alcove again and as he did so he

looked straight at me, I was sure, although it was not easy to see because of his mask. He had come very close to the ferns; it was almost as though he had wanted to take a closer look at the figure cowering there. Then he was gone, and I told myself I had imagined it. I knew him because I had seen him arrive with his family; but then I should have known him anywhere. He wouldn't know me in the same way—besides, the dress, the snood and mask made an entirely different person of me.

The waltz was over, and there followed an interval when the dangers of exposure were trebled. Suppose I were seen hiding myself in the alcove? What should a young woman be doing at a ball without a watchful mamma or a chaperon of some sort to look after her?

The music started again. Now was the time to escape to the gallery; to sit there watching the dancers as I had been told to do. But the temptation to stay was too strong. I could not bear not to be here. Gwennan would despise me for running away, I told myself. But it was more than that. I was different in this dress. I could not forget that in the room—that strange circular opening in the buttress—I had danced.

" All alone?"

My heart began to beat uncomfortably. I stammered: "Not at this moment."

Bevil laughed. I was dreaming it all. It couldn't be Bevil.

"I noticed you," he said. "I came back scarcely hoping that I should find you here. You must have just arrived or I should have seen you before."

"Among so many?"

"I should have been aware of *you*."

This was the way he talked to women. This was flirtation, and with Bevil I found it extremely enjoyable.

The orchestra started to play. "A cotillion," he said, and grimaced. "Let us stay here and talk—unless you would prefer to dance."

"I should prefer not to dance."

He sat down next to me and kept his eyes on my face. "We've met before," he said.

"Do you think so?" I replied trying to disguise my voice. He laid his hand over mine. "I am certain of it."

I withdrew my hand and let it fall on to the folds of topaz velvet.

"I wonder where?" I said.

" We can easily discover."

" I think we're supposed to keep our identities secret. Isn't it more fun that way?"

" As long as we know curiosity will eventually be satisfied, perhaps. But I am very impatient." He had leaned towards me and touched my mask.

I drew back indignantly.

" I am sorry," he said. " But I was so certain that I knew you and it seems incredible that I shouldn't be sure who you are."

" Then I am a mysterious woman."

" But I'm sure *you* know me."

" Yes . . . I do know you."

He sat back in his chair. " You give up?" I asked.

" You can't know me very well or you'd know I never give up. But in any case, I have the whole evening before me. First let me tell you that you are enchanting. Your dress is wonderful."

" You like it?" I smiled, thinking of the shaking and hanging out in the sunshine to take off the smell of damp; and the lavender sachets which Gwennan had produced to put in the folds.

" I've seen it before."

" Where?" I asked.

" I'm trying to remember."

I was entranced. I heard myself laughing at his conversation—light, frothy, frivolous conversation; and yet there seemed to be depth in it. He *was* interested in me; he had seen me in my alcove and as soon as possible he had left the partner with whom he had been dancing and had come to me. Who would have believed that possible?

There I sat, gay as anyone at the ball, returning his quips, finding that I too had a gift of repartee that might be mistaken for wit. He was certainly not bored; but he was puzzled. He did not guess who I was. Perhaps had he known I was to be at the ball he might have done so; but he had always thought of me as a child and still did and it would not occur to him that I could possibly be there; he had been with Gwennan in her simple party dress when they arrived and had heard that she and I were to sit in the gallery to watch; he knew nothing about the discovery of the dresses. No, it would not occur to him that it could possibly be young

Harriet with whom he was enjoying such an intriguing interlude.

The cotillion was over; they were playing a waltz.

"Shall we dance?" he said.

I was surprised at myself. If I had not been intoxicated by the evening, by the presence of Bevil, by my new personality, in spite of having danced with Gwennan I should have murmured that I couldn't dance. But I was bemused; I allowed myself to be led on to the floor; I may have limped but I was unaware of it; my voluminous skirts would perhaps hide my infirmity; at least so it seemed to me. And there I was, dancing with Bevil. I do not mean that I danced well or expertly. Bevil was no born dancer anyway, but I danced, and the floor was so crowded that one's steps did not matter—and I was so happy that I felt life was wonderful and everything had changed for me.

Before the dance was over Bevil suggested that we go to the supper-room, and there he seated me at a table while he went to forage for food. He came back with a tray and glasses of champagne. It was the first time I had drunk champagne and it made me more dizzily happy than ever. I caught a glimpse of Gwennan with Harry Leveret but they were so absorbed in each other that I don't think they saw me.

After supper we went into the garden. Bevil took my hand and we walked across the moonlit lawn to a seat under one of the trees from which we watched the dancers filtering on to the lawn; through the open french windows came the strains of music.

"I know," cried Bevil suddenly. "The dress! I know where I've seen it before."

"Please tell me."

"At Menfreya."

"Oh," I said blankly, remembering that Gwennan had said he and she had found the trunk years ago. But it was surprising that Bevil should remember a dress.

"Why," he cried, "it's exactly so. The hair filet . . . the gown. It might be you, but she is not masked, of course."

"Who?"

"It's a portrait at Menfreya. I'll show it to you . . . soon. When shall it be? You must come to Menfreya and let me show it to you. Will you?"

"Yes," I said.

"I'm relieved. I had a terrible fear that you were going to disappear after to-night and I shouldn't see you again. It's a promise, is it?"

"Yes, a promise."

"When?"

"To-morrow," I said. "To-morrow I will call on you and ask to be shown the portrait."

He pressed my hand. "I know you're the kind to keep a promise."

"Tell me about the portrait."

"It's an ancestress of mine. A long-ago Lady Menfrey. My great-great-great-grandmother—or there may be a few more greats. But your dress is an absolute replica of the one she's wearing. It's as though you've stepped down from the canvas."

"I should so enjoy seeing it."

"To-morrow," he said. "It's a promise."

I wanted to catch at time and prevent its moving, but even now people were making their way to the ballroom for the dance which would precede the unmasking at midnight. I had to get away before that. I did not want to stand beside Bevil, to take off my mask and see the surprise in his face, to hear him say "Harriet!" in shocked surprise. Moreover, what if my father saw me?

For to-night I wanted to be the attractive mystery behind the mask.

We were caught up in the crowd going into the ballroom. Lady Menfrey was near us; she spoke to Bevil and as he turned to her I seized my opportunity. I slipped into a passage knowing the house as few of the others did and, reaching the main staircase, hurried up it to the gallery. It was then twenty minutes to twelve.

Later from the gallery I saw him enter the ballroom; he was looking about him searchingly, eagerly. Looking for me!

Gwennan came running into the room at five minutes to twelve. I had thought she would be caught down there, but it was like her to leave it until the last moment.

She was flushed and radiant.

"What a wonderful, wonderful ball!" she cried. "It's the best ball I've ever attended."

I laughed at her and reminded her that it was the only one so it had to be the best.

Then we were laughing together. I was different that night. I had had my adventure and it was no less wonderful than Gwennan's.

I slept very little that night but lay awake going over everything that had happened at the ball. I got up once during the night, lighted my candle and took the dress from my cupboard; held it against me and looked at my reflection in the mirror. The dress did do something to me. Even in the middle of the night I looked different ... fey ... even attractive. Yes, I was sure of it, the sort of person people would look twice at. I wasn't beautiful; even the candlelight could not fool me as much as that, but there was a certain medieval charm about my face which needed the muted colour of my dress, the period style of it, to bring it out.

It was dawn before I slept at all and then only for an hour or so. The next morning the house was in that after-the-ball chaos which I knew so well; everyone was tired and touchy, except myself. I was exalted.

In the afternoon I walked to Menfreya, where I knew Bevil would be waiting for me—only of course he wouldn't know he was expecting me. What a shock, I thought, to find instead of the mysterious woman this little more than a schoolgirl in a grey merino dress, sedate cape, untidy hair unprotected by a glittering filet. If only I could have worn the dress, how different I should have felt.

The house was quiet but Bevil was there, and I went straight into the library unannounced.

"Why . . . it's Harriet," he said. Bevil's social manners were perfect. If he was disappointed he didn't show it.

"You were expecting someone, I see," I said. "Well, I'm sorry it's only Harriet."

"I happen to be delighted." His face creased up into a smile I knew and loved.

"But you were expecting some charming woman and wondering how she would look in modern clothes. You were picturing her perhaps in a mulberry velvet riding habit with a black riding hat, her face delicately veiled to protect her dazzling complexion."

"Who is this phantom of delight and how do you come to know so much of what I'm hoping for?"

"Because you were with her last night at the ball. Prepare

for a shock, Bevil. Your partner last night wasn't all that you thought she was. I'm going to confess right away. I was disguised last night . . . unrecognisably."

"So you say! Do you think I wouldn't recognise *you* anywhere?"

"You knew!"

He took me by the shoulders and laughed at me. Then he leaned forward and kissed me as he had in the boat.

"So you knew all the time!"

"My dear Harriet, why should you know me and I not know you? My powers of perception are as well developed as yours."

"But I saw you arrive and I . . . should know you anywhere."

"And I you. Now look, what was the game last night? Gwennan was there too. It was a plot between you two girls. Where did you find the dresses?"

"Here in Menfreya."

"I guessed it."

"Promise you won't tell. Gwennan would be furious."

"And I'm terrified of her fury, naturally."

"Well, you see, we wanted to go to the ball, and we found these dresses in a trunk and so . . ."

"Two little Cinderellas came to the ball, not forgetting to disappear before midnight leaving two desolate Prince Charmings wondering what had become of them. Well, Harriet, I must thank you for an enjoyable evening. Your secret is safe with me. I said I would show you something if you came here this afternoon, didn't I? Well, come on. Let's go."

I followed him into the great hall and we went up the staircase towards the wing protected by the buttress in which we had found the dresses.

"Not scared of ghosts, Harriet?" he asked over his shoulder. "This wing isn't used much. It's said to be the haunted one. There has to be a ghost in all houses like this. You knew that, didn't you? Well, this is it. If you're scared, give me your hand."

"I'm not," I said.

"I always knew it wouldn't be easy to scare you." He exclaimed in disgust: "It's musty in here. We've always intended to open it up but somehow we never get round to it. The servants wouldn't like it. They won't come here even in day-time."

" This is where Gwennan and I found the trunk," I said.

" Really. So you have been here before. Did she tell you the story of the ghosts? A woman with a child in her arms, Harriet, who walks these musty passages . . . and a man who walks too, but they don't walk together because they're looking for each other."

I shivered, and he noticed.

" I *am* scaring you," he said. " Don't take any notice of what I say, Harriet. It's nonsense. Just one of the old legends."

" It's the cold," I said. " I'm not scared."

He put his arm round me then and held me against him for a moment ; it was nothing ; merely the gesture he would use to comfort a child. He was different from the man he had been last night and I had a suspicion that he had *not* recognised me and that to-day I had ceased to be a glamorous masked woman and I had reverted to myself, familiar, plain Harriet.

" Gwennan told me some story," I said, quickly to hide my emotion, " about a governess who was kept in a room unknown to anyone in the house except Sir Somebody Menfrey."

" Sir Bevil, if you please. One of the many Bevils of the family."

" And she died having a child and no one knew till after she was dead."

" That's it." He opened a door whose hinges gave the same protesting whine which I had noticed before. " This part of the house will have to be gone over soon," he commented. " We're a lazy lot, we Menfreys. We're not energetic like you Delvaneys. We let things drift along. How many years do you think it is since these rooms have been lived in?" I started back, for something touched my face. It was a tangle of cobwebs, slimy and cold. I felt as though the whole place was calling to me: " Keep out." But Bevil felt none of this. There was nothing fanciful about Bevil. An unlived-in room was nothing to him but an unlived-in room. There were no such things as ghosts; there were only legends.

" Here she is," said Bevil.

And there was the picture—a woman in the dress which must surely be the one I had worn the previous night. It was beautifully painted, the folds of velvet were so real that I felt had I stroked them they would have been as soft as the actual material. Her dark hair was held back in the snood of gold-coloured net set with stones of topaz.

"It's the same!" I said. "Did I wear her dress, then?"

"It might be so."

I went near to the picture. She had a sad, almost furtive expression.

"She doesn't look very happy," I said.

"Well, she was married to this Bevil—who was involved with the governess."

"Oh," I said. "I see."

He came to stand behind me, putting his hands on my shoulders. "What, Harriet, do you see?"

"Why she looks so unhappy. But the dress is lovely. What a wonderful artist who painted it!"

"I see that you are fascinated by that dress. Where is it now?"

"In my cupboard at Chough Towers."

"You'll never be able to part with it, will you?"

"I am going to pack it up and bring it back to Gwennan."

"Don't," he said. "Keep it. You might want to disguise yourself again one of these days."

"Keep it!"

"A present from me," he said.

"Oh, Bevil!"

"Come on. It's cold in here. Let's go back to the inhabited regions."

That night at the ball changed Gwennan as well as myself. She was more restless, more dissatisfied with her life. She was in one of her restless moods when we went riding together.

"Life," she told me, as we rode into the woods ducking our heads when we passed under the trees, at this time of the year laden with heavy foliage, "is very unsatisfactory with us."

Always eager to hear of the Menfreys I asked why particularly now.

"Money! It's always money. It's fortunate that Papa is not the Member now, because being a Member is a costly business. I'm so bored with having no money that I've almost decided to remedy it."

"How?"

"By marrying Harry, of course."

"Gwennan, do you think he would?"

"Do I think he would! Are you crazy? Of course he would. He's madly in love with me. That's one of the reasons why it's so hateful to be sixteen. I'll have to wait at least a year before I marry."

We had come to a clearing and she whipped up Sugar Loaf and broke into a gallop. I went forward and rode beside her. She was laughing and I think some devilish mischief was in her that morning.

"I don't want to go back to that ridiculous school of ours," she called over her shoulder.

"Well, we aren't yet. There's another week or so."

"I mean . . . ever. Academy for Young Ladies! If there's anything I hate more than being sixteen, it's being a young lady."

"I'm not so certain of the second, although the first is indisputable."

"Harriet Delvaney, don't try to talk cleverly like some frightful . . . politician."

"Was I? I didn't know."

"Some people say that if you want something to happen or not to happen . . . tremendously . . . you know, if you concentrate, it might make it work."

"Like not going back to school? Like leaping from sixteen to eighteen in a day instead of two years?"

"You're developing that acid asperity in your nature, Harriet. You're going to be one of those blue-stocking women with the serpent's tongue if you don't look out."

"And why shouldn't I?"

"Because they're fatally unattractive to men."

"I don't have to develop any new tendencies to be that. I'm it already."

"Stop it, Harriet. It's your own fault."

"What is?"

"I haven't time to solve your problems this morning. I have too many of my own. I'm determined not to go back to school next term."

I was silent wondering what it would be like to go without her. But of course she would go back.

We rashly galloped across the moors. She was certainly in a wild mood.

"Like this," she called, "I feel free. That's what I want, Harriet, to be free. Free to do exactly what I like. Not when

I'm grown up, but now! I *am* grown up, I tell you. I'm as grown up as I'll ever be."

I galloped with her, calling out to her to have a care; there were some ugly-looking boulders on the moor and if she didn't care for herself she ought to for Sugar Loaf.

"We know where we're going," she retorted.

I was thankful when we left the moor behind us. Gwennan was the most reckless person I had ever known in my life.

We came into a village I had never visited before. It was delightful with its grey-towered church, surrounded by its graveyard and its cottages bordering the green.

"It's Grendengarth," Gwennan told me. "We're six miles from home."

It was close to the village when it happened; we had turned off the road into a clearing and there was a bank ahead of us which should not have been difficult to take; but as I said, Gwennan was in a reckless mood that morning. I don't know what happened, exactly—one never does on these occasions. She was a little ahead of me when she took the bank. I heard her cry out as she shot over Sugar Loaf's head. It seemed as though time slowed down. I seemed poised in mid-air over the bank for minutes before I was on the other side. I saw Sugar Loaf running on, bewildered, and then my attention was focused on Gwennan lying still on the grass.

"Gwennan," I cried stupidly. "Gwennan, what's happened?"

I slipped from my horse and knelt beside her. She was white and still; but she was breathing. For a few seconds I remained there; then I mounted and rode back to the village for help.

I was fortunate, for as I reached the road a boy was riding past on a pony. I stammered out that there had been an accident.

"I'll go straightways to Dr. Trelarken," he said.

I returned to Gwennan and as I knelt beside her waiting for what seemed like hours I was terrified that she might be dead; I remembered her words, a short time before, that she was determined not to go back to school, and wondered whether some terrible recording angel had noted the words and this was the punishment.

"If you die, Gwennan," I whispered, "you won't go back to school, and your wish will be granted."

I shivered. Then I noticed that her left leg was in a strange position and I realised what had happened.

Dr. Trelarken arrived on the scene with two men who carried a stretcher. The doctor set the leg before Gwennan was moved and then the men carried her back to his house in Grendengarth. The doctor walked with me and asked me questions.

He knew who we were because everyone in the district knew the Menfreys and Sir Edward Delvaney. He pointed out his house, which was a white one on the pretty green I had noticed when we rode through. My horse was taken from me by a groom and as we went into the house he called " Jess! Jessie. Where are you?"

" Coming, Father," said a voice; and a young woman appeared in the hall. This was my first glimpse of Jessica Trelarken, who has always seemed to me one of the most beautiful women I have ever known.

She was tall and slender; her hair was dark, almost black, and her eyes a startling blue accentuated by the blue gown she wore. She must have been about nineteen then.

The stretcher was carried into a bedroom on the first floor and the doctor attended to Gwennan. Jess helped him; and I was asked to remain downstairs. I was taken by a maid into a light and airy room, pleasantly furnished in a conventional way, except for the painting over the fireplace of a very pretty woman who was like Jess but did not possess the same outstanding beauty. The air was scented by the flowers in a huge earthenware pot on the polished table by the window—purple buddleia and lavender, and pink cabbage roses.

I sat down and listened to the tick-tock of the grandfather clock, wondering how long it would be before I heard how badly Gwennan was hurt and gazing distractedly at my distorted reflection in the gleaming brass oil lamp which stood on the table beside the bowl of flowers.

It was about twenty minutes before the doctor appeared. Jessica was with him.

" I expect Miss Delvaney would like some refreshment," he said.

" I am sure she would," added Jessica, giving me that serene smile which I was to come to know so well.

" Gwennan?" I asked.

" Broken leg. I don't want to move her just yet. Nothing

much. She took the bank too fast, I reckon. I've seen it happen at that spot more than once."

" I should go to Menfreya at once," I said. " Sugar Loaf will go back there. They'll be frightened."

" We've already sent to explain," said Jessica. " I shouldn't be surprised if someone comes over very soon."

" And you, young lady," went on the doctor, " have had a bit of a shock. Jess, ring for that wine and some of your wine biscuits to go with it. We'll all have something."

Jessica went to the bell-pull; she moved with the grace of a jungle creature which accorded oddly with her air of gentleness.

" And after that," said the doctor, " you'll be able have a word with Miss Menfrey, I dare say."

So I sat there in that scented room drinking wine with the Trelarkens, and all the time I was thinking: It's a judgment. She decided she wouldn't go back to school with me—and she won't.

I missed her very much, but life went more smoothly without her. I worked harder than I ever had and my teachers were pleased with me; I didn't make friends with other girls; I had never found that easy, and as I was no use at games I spent the time in study. This began to show results.

But when I received a letter from Gwennan I was conscious of a yearning to be with her. It was an exuberant letter. She was pleased with life. She was getting her own way, which was what she always must have.

> My poor Harriet, to think of you in that dreadful genteel Academy for Young Ladies! What do you think? I am engaged to Harry. Of course there's opposition. " Too young! Too young," they keep screaming at me. Mind you, the family want it—both families do—and so does Harry . . . madly. So it doesn't make much sense waiting, does it?

I smiled as I read that and thought: But if you don't want to wait, Gwennan, then there'll be no waiting. I read on:

> I did think of an elopement. That would have been fun, with Harry climbing the walls of Menfreya—the steepest part, you know where the walls and the cliff edge meet.

One slip and down to certain death! But then I thought, no. A young woman—not a young lady, mind you; I have done with those repulsive things—must have a little time to look round. Well, they came up with this suggestion: One year in a finishing school during the engagement, and then wedding bells to ring in Menfreystow. It appeals to me. I expect I shall be one of the few people who have ever gone away to school already engaged. So that is to be it. I'm off to France—somewhere in the middle. Near Tours where they speak the best French, so they tell me, because I have to come back speaking like a native. Part of the requirements of a woman of education, you understand.

My bones have set perfectly, so Dr. Trelarken says. He was very pleased with my progress, and Bevil is very pleased with Jessica, his daughter. A pity he always chooses the most unsuitable people. Dr. Trelarken doesn't seem to be one of the clever doctors who choose their patients with care. Hard work and gratitude seem to be this man's reward. Very noble, but it seems the only dowry poor Jess will bring to her husband is her beauty.

Then of course the war. Bevil was determined to go and fight the wicked Boer for Queen and Country. You see when he stands for Parliament he'd do so much better as a hero returned from the wars. Besides Menfreys always rally to the cause. He was determined to go but now I think he's not so eager. It's because of Jess. Perhaps he'll marry her before he goes off with Kitchener. There's nothing like a war for making hasty marriages.

Harry won't go. He's needed at home, he says; and so does his father. Business must go on.

What a long letter this is. And I hardly ever write letters. It's because my heart bleeds for my poor Harriet who is not engaged to be married, who is not going to a finishing school in France, who is not in dear Menfreya but sitting at her study window, I'll swear, looking out over neat lawns, her books before her, being such a good little girl now that she is not distracted by her wicked Gwennan.

As usual she had disturbed me; I could not recapture the peace I had been enjoying. I pictured it all; something exciting always seemed to be happening at Menfreya. I saw

c

Bevil riding over to the Trelarkens' and Jessica coming out to stand in the porch. She would be wearing the blue dress I had first seen her in with the white lace collar; she had been lovely then; now, being in love, she must be breathtakingly beautiful.

And Bevil was in love with her, and he would soon be leaving her to go to South Africa. Yes, he would want to marry her before he went.

I thought of Bevil and the girl he had brought to the island. There must have been others in between her and Jessica. Many others. But Jessica was different. Young and inexperienced as I was, I sensed that, and I was depressed.

There was one more letter from Gwennan before she left for the finishing school.

Harry's people are taking over Chough Towers. He knows I'd never really feel happy away from Menfreya so he says that Chough will be our home. I must say I like the idea. I am already planning balls I'll have in that perfectly magnficent ballroom. Your father's lease was running out, so Chough won't be your Cornish residence much longer—it'll be mine. Of course I shall invite you to stay. I'll give you the room you now have. It will be fun, won't it? But I'll bet you're wondering what your father is going to do. He'll have to have a place near Lansella, won't he? We're very pleased with your stern parent, Harriet. Do you know what he's done? You'll never guess. He's taken the house on No Man's Island. More than that, he's bought the island from Papa. This is a marvellous stroke of luck for us. You know what a white elephant of an island it is. It's just there and what use is it—except for runaway heiresses to hide in and dissolute young men to effect seductions! What dreadful company I keep! The point is I had to be the first to tell you. No Man's Island will soon be yours. You can imagine the improvements your father will make. It'll be a palace on an island I expect before he's done with it. Papa is absolutely delighted. He goes round rubbing his hands with glee. At last we have something to tide us over!

You see, Harriet, nothing remains the same. I am leaving at the end of the week for my finishing school. I wish you were coming. You probably will. Here's another secret. Your father is talking about it and Mamma has given him all sorts of details about the place. Well, it seems our fate is not to be parted for long. I shall hope that you too will soon be acquiring an impeccable French accent. But don't become engaged, will you? I want the distinction of being not only the first but the only engaged woman to arrive at the school.

G.

PS. Bevil is no longer with us. He's become a soldier. He won't be leaving for South Africa just yet, but when he does the war will soon be over, you can be sure. Poor Jess is sad, but they're not engaged. Great relief displayed by the parents. They've been absolutely terrified —although of course it wouldn't have been such a calamity as I am obliging with Harry. See you soon, Harriet, at *our* finishing school.

G.

Change was in the air, but when I arrived home for the holidays I was faced with the greatest of them all—so far.

It was the end of the spring term and to my disappointment I had a letter from my father telling me that instead of spending the holiday as usual at Chough Towers I was to come to London. I should be met at Paddington.

I was disappointed, although neither Gwennan nor Bevil would have been there, but even so I had been looking forward to going to Cornwall, to hear from A'Lee—that infallible source of information—what exactly was happening about Chough Towers, which my father would shortly be vacating, and what improvements had been made to the Island House. But most of all I wanted to know more about Bevil and Jessica Trelarken, for I could not believe that Jessica would allow herself to be the partner in one of Bevil's casual affairs.

I could not understand, either, why my father wanted me to be in London. Surely since he disliked seeing me so decidedly he would want my holidays to be spent where he was not.

As soon as I alighted from the train I saw Fanny, who had come to meet me. She looked just the same as usual in her plain serge cloak with the cotton dress showing beneath; her black bonnet, tied under the chin with grey ribbon, did little for her face except accentuate its pallor and hide the grey-brown hair which was always scraped back unbecomingly. Her expression was anxious. I felt emotional as I watched her. She looked so insignificant—but to me she had tried to be the mother I had never known.

Her face relaxed when she saw me.

"Miss Harriet. My! How you've grown!"

"You look the same as ever, Fanny."

"My growing days are over. This is a change . . . coming to London for this holiday." She looked at me anxiously. "What do you make of that?"

"Something's happened?" I asked.

She nodded grimly.

"Oh, Fanny . . . what?"

"Your father's married again. You could have knocked me down with a feather."

"But, Fanny, whom has he married?"

"You wait, my lady; and you'll see for yourself."

"She's there now . . . at home?"

"Oh, yes. Your father can't wait to introduce you to your stepmother. He thinks everyone must be as delighted with her as he is."

"He . . . *delighted*."

"I'd say."

"But . . . he couldn't be delighted about anything."

"Well, he is about this little bundle of nonsense, I can tell you."

"Fanny, I never thought of anything like this."

"That's what I guessed. So I'm warning you. You had to be prepared . . . to my way of thinking."

She had taken my bag and we made our way to where the carriage was waiting. When we were settled in and moving out into the streets, I said: "Fanny, when did it happen?"

"Three weeks ago."

"He didn't say anything about it."

"He wasn't in the habit of sending you long explanations of what he was doing, ducky, was he?"

"But did it happen suddenly . . . like that?"

"Well, there was a bit of courting, I believe. He changed. One of the maids heard him singing one morning. We thought she was going up the pole when she told us. But it was true. Love's a funny thing, Miss Harriet."

"It must be if it came to him."

She laid her hand over mine.

" You'll find him changed," she warned.

" It must be for the better, then," I retorted, " because it couldn't very well be for the worse, could it?"

I did find him changed. But when I met my stepmother I was so astonished that I could only gasp at the incongruity of this match.

As soon as we arrived at the house Mrs. Trant came into the hall to tell me that I was to go at once to the library, where my father and Lady Delvaney were waiting for me.

As I stood on the threshold of that room, I could sense the change creeping over the house. Nothing, I thought, is going to be the same again. We have come to the end of an epoch. Lady Delvaney was sitting in an arm-chair by the fireplace. She was a young woman, petite, with fair fluffy hair, a strikingly fresh complexion, round babyish face and pale blue eyes, so large that they looked as though she were startled. Perhaps she was, at the sight of me. She was dressed in pink and white and my first impression was that she was like a piece of confectionery the cook had made for one of Papa's parties. There was a pink ribbon in her hair and her gown was trimmed with pink and white; her face was delicately powdered; her waist was the tiniest I had ever seen, and never had the term " hourglass " been more aptly applied than to her.

But the most startling sight in that room was not this woman. It was my father. I would not have believed he could ever have looked like that. His eyes had become more blue and they were brilliant as they were when he was being witty with his political friends.

" Harriet," he said rising, and coming towards me he took my hand in one of his and laid the other on my shoulder—a gesture of affection which he had never before used towards me. " I want you to meet your . . . stepmother."

The pretty creature covered her face with her hands and murmured: " Oh, but it sounds so dreadful."

" Nonsense, my love," said Father. " Harriet and you will be friends."

She rose and lifted those big blue eyes to my face—she was considerably shorter than I. " Do you think so?" she asked tremulously.

I realised that the creature was—or pretended to be—afraid of me!

"I am sure we can," I said.

Never had I found it so easy to please my father, who was now smiling at me benignly.

"I'm so glad."

"Ha!" said my father. "I told you you need have nothing to fear, did I not?"

"You did, Teddy, you did."

Teddy! That was new to me. Teddy! How absolutely incongruous! But more so that he should actually like it! What miracle had this woman been able to work?

"And was I not right?"

"Teddy, dear, you know you are always right."

She was dimpling and he was smiling at her as though she were one of the wonders of the world. I felt I had stepped into one of my dreams; they appeared to be so content with each other that they were allowing some of that contentment to lap over on to me.

"You're looking puzzled . . . Harriet." She spoke my name shyly.

"I had no idea . . . It was a surprise."

"You didn't warn her! Oh, Teddy, how naughty of you! And I'm really a stepmother. Fancy that. Stepmothers are supposed to be such horrid creatures."

"I am sure you will be a kind stepmother," I said.

My father looked emotional. Could it be, I wondered, that I had never known him before?

"Thank you . . . Harriet." Always the little pause before she spoke my name as though she were frightened of using it.

"Stepmother indeed!" said my father. "You are not six years older than Harriet."

She gave one of her little pouts and said: "Well, I shall try to do my best to be a *good* stepmother."

"In fact," I said, "I am too old to need a stepmother, so perhaps we could be friends instead."

She clasped her hands ecstatically and my father looked pleased.

"You will have time to get to know each other during Harriet's holidays," said my father.

"That," she announced, "will be the greatest fun."

When I was in my room I shut the door and looked about it expecting it to have changed. Here were the same four walls

which had seen so much of my childhood misery; here I had
come after hearing those cruel words of Aunt Clarissa and
made my plans for escape ; here I had often cried myself to
sleep because I had believed myself to be ugly and unloved.
There was the picture of the Christian Martyr which for
some reason had always frightened me when I was young.
It portrayed a young woman waist-high in water, bound
to a stake; her hands were tied with the palms together so
that she could pray and her eyes were raised to heaven. It
used to give me nightmares until Fanny explained that she
was happy to die because she was dying for her faith and it
would soon be over when the tide rose, for then she would be
completely submerged. There was the little bookcase with
my old books which had delighted my childhood. There was
the money-box from which I had extracted the shillings and
sixpences to pay my fare to Cornwall. The same room where
I had been kept on a diet of bread and water as a punishment for some misdemeanour, where I had struggled to learn
the collect of the day or lines from Shakespeare as penance.

The same room—but the house was different. My father's
resentment, the unhappiness of years, had dropped from him
—or rather it had been removed like a cloak by the delicate
fingers of this frivolous-looking piece of confectionery who
was my stepmother.

I studied my reflection in the dressing-table looking-glass.
Yes, I had changed. That little kindness my father had shown
me had lifted the scowl from my brow. I promised myself
that I was growing better looking. Gwennan was right when
she said I reminded people that I was unattractive because
of my own attitude.

I was excited because getting to know oneself was exciting.
I was beginning to believe that I had the power to influence
my own personality. I saw how happiness with his Jenny
was changing him. It was a wonderful discovery.

My astonishment grew as the days passed. My father did
not exactly allow me to penetrate their magic circle, but at
the same time he did not want me shut out entirely. It seemed
that my acceptance of Jenny and hers of me was needed to
make his happiness complete. I suppose the child I had
been—bitter, resentful—would have refused to give him
what he wanted now. But I had changed when I had put on
the topaz-coloured dress, when Bevil had shown clearly that
he had been attracted by me. I had softened in some way ;

and the new Harriet had lost her vindictiveness—she wanted to please.

So I became Jenny's friend.

Meals were different now, with William Lister and myself, Papa and his new wife. Conversation flowed more easily; neither William nor I now had to worry about making aimless remarks. Jenny did that to perfection, and all her inanities were greeted by smiles from her husband.

They often went to the theatre—which was something new to my father, who had never had time for it before; but the theatre had been Jenny's life and she loved it. Jenny would prattle through dinner about the show they had seen or were going to see and the stage personalities whom she obviously admired. Papa listened and quickly learned what she had to tell him about the different actors and actresses so that he could aspire to her kind of conversation.

One day my father said: "I want a word with you, Harriet. Pray come into the library."

I followed him there. He sat down and signed to me to be seated, looking at me with the cold distaste which had wounded me so deeply before Jenny's coming. So it was only when he was with her that he felt more kindly towards me! The assurance which had grown up about me like a shell was only a brittle covering and ready to crack at the least ill-usage, and the sullen expression, I knew, was creeping over my face; I felt ugly, for I was sure that he was comparing me with his exquisite little Jenny.

"I have been thinking of your education," he said.

I nodded and he looked at me with exasperation. "For heaven's sake, show some enthusiasm."

"I'm . . . interested," I said.

"I should hope so. I have been thinking that it is time you left that school. You certainly need some grooming to fit you for society. Your Aunt Clarissa will see you launched eventually, but you are by no means ready for that. How old are you now?"

So he didn't remember. He remembered that Jenny liked her bon-bons tied with pink ribbon but he couldn't remember his daughter's age. But perhaps he was pretending to forget, for surely he must remember the day which had been the most tragic in his life until he had met his Jenny who had made a new man of him.

"Sixteen and a half."

"It is a little early. I had thought you should wait until
you were at least seventeen, and then have a year or two
abroad. But I see no reason why you should not go now.
Your reports from school are not bad. They could of course
be better, but they are adequate. The place to which Gwennan
Menfrey has been sent seems to satisfy her parents. I do
not see why it should not be equally good for you. So you
will not be returning to Cheltenham."

I was excited. Soon to be with Gwennan again! It was
the next best thing to being at Menfrey.

"The school is near Tours," he said. As if I didn't know!
"We will see what it has done for you in say . . . six months,
and if it gives satisfaction you will stay for a year, perhaps
two."

"Yes, Papa," I said.

He nodded a sign of dismissal and I went to the door very
conscious of my limp.

On such occasions I could see how we needed Jenny. If
she went away the old relationship between my father and
myself would soon return. That realisation made me very
sad, but I was excited at the prospect of joining Gwennan.

They were going to the theatre that night. William Lister told
me that he had had difficulty in procuring the tickets, but he
had to get them somehow because Lady Delvaney was so
eager to go. It was a new departure from his duties of the
past—this securing of theatre tickets.

At dinner that evening, which was served half an hour
earlier on account of the theatre jaunt, Jenny looked prettier
than ever. She was in mauve chiffon over a green satin and
I had to admit to myself that the effect was enchanting; she
wore her fair hair piled high on her head, which had the
effect of making her seem more childish than ever. My
father I thought was drinking more than usual, and Jenny was
affecting a pretty concern.

"But, Teddy, I am really serious. If your poor head is not
better I shall insist that we do not go."

"It is nothing, my love, nothing at all," he assured her.

She turned to me. "But Harriet, his poor head was so
bad this afternoon. I made him rest and I put some of my
eau-de-Cologne on his forehead. It is wonderful. It always
makes me feel better when I'm fatigued. If you ever need
it, Harriet . . ."

"I don't have headaches, thank you."

"Oh, no, you are so young . . . But Teddy, you must take greater care. And if your head is not completely cured it shall be no play for you."

My father smiled at her fondly and declared that she had charmed away his headache.

I glanced at William, wondering what he thought of all this lovers' talk, and I saw that he was embarrassed, as I was.

Just before midnight I went to my window and saw my top-hatted, black-coated father and my glittering stepmother returning from the theatre. She was chattering. I could hear her high-pitched excited voice as they came up to their room. I sat for some time at the window wondering whether it had been like that with my mother and whether they had been delighted when they knew they were going to be parents. I tried to assure myself that he had been as excited then at the prospect of becoming a father as he was now to be the husband of a pretty young girl.

Perhaps under Jenny's influence he would grow more and more mellow and tell me.

I undressed, went to bed, and was soon asleep, to be startled by the sound of knocking on my door, which was flung open even as I opened my eyes.

My stepmother in a negligee all frills of lace and satin, her fair hair in confusion about her shoulders, her blue eyes wider than I had ever seen them, and fear written all over her pale face, was shouting incoherently at me.

"Harriet . . . for God's sake . . . come. Your father . . . Teddy . . . something's happened. Oh, Harriet. Come quickly."

My father died early next morning. Never had I felt so blank, such a sense of unreality. I could only think: Now I shall never be able to win his approval . . . never . . . never . . . never!

The strange night was over. The doctor had told us that my father had had a stroke and that there was just a possibility that he might recover; but before morning that possibility vanished. Jenny could only tremble and murmur: "It can't be true. It can't be true." The doctor talked to me instead of her.

"Had he recovered," he said, "he would have been an

invalid. I do not think he would have enjoyed living in such a condition."

We were all grateful to William Lister, who took charge of the household in his calm efficient way.

The doctor gave Jenny and me mild sedatives because he said we needed to sleep. She kept close to my side. "Can I be with you, Harriet? I can't go back to *our* room."

I felt fond of her in that moment. "Of course," I said.

So she slept in my bed until the morning.

I awoke with a feeling that I had had a nightmare. Nothing would ever be the same again. My father, of whom I had seen very little, had in spite of that been at the very centre of my existence. A burden had been lifted, but something vital to me had been taken away. I could not explain my feelings.

Jenny's were less complicated. She had lost the great provider—the fairy godfather who had found her in rags and taken her to the ball. She was frankly distressed, and although anxiety for her future may have been at the root of this, she had, I believe, been fond of him.

In due course Aunt Clarissa arrived and immediately manifested her dislike of Jenny. I found myself hoping that Jenny did not notice.

She came to my room and looked at me with a criticism which even at such a time made me wonder whether she was picturing the difficulty of finding a husband for me.

"Such a shocking thing!" She shut the door. "I never did approve of this marriage. I have never known Edward to act foolishly before. But that . . . creature! Most unsuitable! Whatever possessed him?"

"Love," I answered.

"Harriet, are you trying to be clever? It's not very becoming—and at such a time."

"It is not in the least clever to see the obvious. Papa was very much in love with her, so he married her and gave her all the things which she had never had before."

"Hm. And she took them with the utmost eagerness."

"Her eagerness to take could not compare with his to give."

"What nonsense is this? I am deeply shocked and filled with grief, but that will not prevent my making sure that we really get to the bottom of this mystery."

"Mystery? Papa died of a stroke. The doctor said so."

" Well, we shall see at the autopsy, shall we not?"

" An autopsy!"

" My dear child, there is always an autopsy after sudden death, and your father's was very sudden."

" Aunt Clarissa, what are you suggesting?"

" Merely that an ageing man, a very rich man, decides to marry a young adventuress. He does so and very shortly he dies."

" But what has she to gain?"

" Doubtless we shall hear when the will is read after the funeral. But the autopsy, I am thankful to say, comes first."

" I am sure you are quite wrong."

" And you, Harriet, are far too self-opinionated. I can see your manners are as atrocious as ever." She turned, and was about to leave me but at the door she paused. " Not a word of this," she said, " to her. If she thinks she has deceived us all, let her go on thinking it for a little while."

She left me alone and thoughtful.

Poor Jenny, I thought. She is going to miss my father's care and protection.

Later when I went down to the servants' quarters I could not help overhearing their comments.

" That's what comes of an old man trying to be a young one."

" You don't think that *she* . . ."

" Get away with you! But . . . I don't know. I reckon he's left her pretty comfortable. Well, if she wanted to be rid of him . . . and go off with some young man . . ."

I didn't want to hear any more. It was so unkind, so unfair. My father had had a stroke, doubtless because he was trying to keep pace with Jenny's youth, but that was his fault, not hers.

Suspicion crept into the house like a November fog.

The next day I saw the papers. " Sir Edward Delvaney dies through heart attack. Two months after his marriage to a chorus girl, Miss Jenny Jay, Sir Edward Delvaney collapsed in his London residence. This will mean a by-election in the Lansella district of Cornwall for which Sir Edward has been Member for the last ten years."

Bevil, who had not yet left for South Africa, came to London for the funeral—to represent his family, he said. When Mrs. Trant told me that Mr. Menfrey had asked to see me, I ran eagerly to the library. His face lit up when he saw me. I stood before him and he laid his hands on my shoulders and looked at me sadly.

"Poor Harriet," he said. "It was so sudden."

He was looking searchingly into my face; he knew, of course, what the relationship had been between my father and myself.

"It's . . . bewildering," I told him.

"Of course. We were horrified when we heard, and they all send their love to you. They want you to go to Menfreya if you would care to."

I smiled rather wanly. "It's good of them," I replied.

"Gwennan is away at her French school, of course."

"Only the other day . . . he was saying I should join her there."

"It's a good idea. A complete break. Then come back and start afresh. That's the best possible plan."

The door opened and Jenny came into the room. She was startled to see that I was not alone.

"Oh, Harriet . . ." she began; then she stood still, looking at Bevil.

"My . . . stepmother," I said.

Bevil came forward and took her hands. "I am sorry we must meet for the first time in such sad circumstances."

His eyes were shining. I had seen that look before, and I was filled with dismay.

The funeral was almost a public occasion. My father had been a well-known politician and recently had been in the news when he had married a girl young enough to be his daughter and a chorus girl at that; now he had died suddenly a few weeks after that marriage.

Whenever I smell lilies I remember that day. The odour of the oak coffin, the scent of the flowers and an air of foreboding filled the house. Every room was dark because the blinds were all drawn and everyone went about speaking in whispers and looking solemn, and when my father's name was mentioned they spoke of him as though he were a saint.

I remember the slow and solemn cortège of which I was a part and the faces of curious people peering in at us—particularly at Jenny—"That's the one . . . Some people know a good thing when they see it. Back row of the chorus and then my lady . . . and still my lady and a fortune I reckon without encumbrances. Oh, yes, *some* people are lucky."

Poor Jenny! She seemed oblivious of the whispers. I wished I could have been. Aunt Clarissa sat up straight and prim, looking hideous, I thought, in her black bonnet on which the beads glistened and the jet drops dangled. She was disappointed that the autopsy had proved my father had died solely from a heart attack.

The church seemed stifling hot; I was glad of Bevil, who stood between Jenny and me as though he was determined to protect us.

The sun was warm as we stood round the grave; I kept seeing scenes from the past between my father and myself and in vain I sought for one which had been happy. It was only when Jenny was present that he had shown any friendliness towards me; and as I listened to the sound of earth falling on the coffin I felt a great desolation in my heart because I should never see him again. I saw the tears on Jenny's face and took her hand; she clung to mine gratefully.

Back at the house we drank wine and ate the food which had been prepared for us, and Mr. Greville of Greville, Baker and Greville came to read the will.

In the library where this was to take place there was an atmosphere of tension. Mr. Greville sat at the table, his spectacles on his nose, his air solemn and unhurried as though he was going to tease those anxious people by making them wait as long as possible.

I felt wearied by the legal jargon; there was one thing which interested me more than anything else and that was Bevil's awareness of the young widow, and I was not yet sure whether hers for him was not growing.

I gathered that there were legacies for the servants who were in my father's employ when he died, that William Lister had received a small one, and that Aunt Clarissa had been remembered. I could not understand what had been arranged for myself but I believed that I should be adequately provided for and it seemed to me that Jenny had inherited the bulk of my father's considerable fortune.

I looked at her face, but she did not seem to be taking it in; she was tying her handkerchief in knots very studiously, then untying them. She was crying quietly.

Poor little Jenny. I refused to believe she was a fortune-hunter.

A great many plans were made and unmade; but it was decided that as it was my father's wish, I should be sent off to the finishing school as soon as possible.

This was perhaps the best thing that could happen as far as I was concerned; I ceased to brood on my father's death and instead wondered what the future would hold for me.

Bevil was leaving almost immediately for South Africa.

One day I went riding with him in the Row, and that was a happy occasion. Jenny could not ride so she did not accompany us, and I was glad of this, for when Bevil called at the house either she or Aunt Clarissa were present and I never had an opportunity of being with him alone.

As we walked our horses through the park, he said: "You'll feel better when you're with Gwennan. She's delighted you're joining her. Harriet, this has been a shock to you. You always hoped to make him fatherly towards you, didn't you?"

"How did you know?"

"I know a great deal about you, Harriet." He laughed. "You look alarmed. Are you afraid that I'm in possession of your darkest secrets?"

"I have no dark ones."

"I should hope not, at your age. Harriet, I'm very probably going to take over your father's constituency."

"I'm glad. It's what you wanted."

"Odd. This happens, and then . . ."

"You get what you've always wanted."

"I have to be elected first, you know."

"If you are, you'll need a secretary."

"Well?"

"William Lister is a very good one."

"And you would recommend him?"

"Anyone who could give my father satisfaction must be good."

"I'll remember that."

He smiled at me and we touched our horses lightly and broke into a canter.

Shortly afterwards I joined Gwennan in France.

THREE

Life at our finishing school was pleasant, lacking all the discipline of Cheltenham. Being Gwennan's friend immediately gave me some standing and I made a few friends, but none of course were as close as Gwennan. She was delighted to see me. I shared a room with her, which was comfortable, because as we had to speak French all day it seemed a great privilege to be able to chat away in English in our room.

Gwennan had grown taller and more voluptuous; she was a beauty. I was tall too, but thin, and in any case there was the accursed limp. However, the mistresses were pleased with me, for they were certain I should be easier to handle than the gay and attractive girls who were in their charge.

Very soon after Bevil reached South Africa he was wounded; not, however, before he had distinguished himself for bravery; and he came home in time to take part in the General Election of that September, when he was returned for Lansella with a big majority, and since his party had retained power the future looked bright for him.

Gwennan boasted of him frequently, and my opinion was demanded to endorse her claims for him. I gave this readily.

Gwennan was the most flamboyant pupil in the school and I was never more certain of the Menfrey charm. Previously I might have imagined that I had believed in it because I was a child who had lived in a particularly cold household. But now I saw Gwennan with girls from families similar to her own and she stood out as distinctly as a flame in a dark place.

I played a vicarious part in her adventures and was called on to help her out of many a difficult situation. She had admirers in the neighbourhood and often slipped out when the school had retired to bed. This nocturnal adventuring was the spice of life, she told me. And I was the one who must see that the french windows which led to our balcony were open ready for her return. I was the one who must watch and warn her when it was safe to clamber up the creeper and swing herself on to the balcony. I was the one who had to do the work which was set for her so that she

could be off somewhere else. I loved Gwennan as I loved
everything connected with Menfreya, and she was fond of
me too. I knew that if I were in a difficulty I could rely on
her.

She gave parties at midnight in our room which was of
course forbidden, but a practice which was often carried out,
and I believe the authorities knew of this and turned a blind
eye. As long as there were no guests from outside, these
parties among ourselves were considered a tradition of our
life—a semi-secret one.

I enjoyed them. I liked to lie stretched out on my bed and
watch Gwennan talk endlessly of herself or Menfreya, of her
engagement to Harry Leveret and life in Cornwall. Once
she told how I had run away and come to the island and
stayed there until I was discovered. That focused the interest
temporarily on me and I was called in by Gwennan to give
my account of that affair. I did it in my dry way which they
called cynical and I was delighted to have them all sitting
on the beds and the floor listening to me, as I related the
story in French, for there were only a few English girls in
the party.

They were happy days and I think that I was determined
to enjoy them as they passed, without thought of the future
or the past. There would never be another time like this in
my life.

Occasionally I would be uneasy, wondering what was happening not only at Menfreya but in London. Jenny wrote,
but she was no writer and her letters were brief. She was
staying on in the house for she didn't quite know what to
do and she hoped that when I came home I would be there.

There were several of these letters to me; she was such an
unsubtle person that she could never cloak her feelings and I
soon began to discover a new note in her letters. I told
myself she was getting over her loss and I had an uneasy
feeling that it might be something to do with Bevil.

I mentioned this to Gwennan. I remember she was lying
stretched out on her bed as she liked to do because from that
angle she could see herself reflected in the wardrobe mirror.

"Bevil?" said Gwennan raising her eyes and still watching
her image. "I should hardly think so. Well, not more than
a passing fancy on his part. It's Jess Trelarken for him."

I turned my face a little that she might not see the down-
ward tilt of my mouth; I need not have worried; she was

intent on Gwennan Menfrey's vivacious face in the looking-glass.

"Oh yes, Bevil has had countless love affairs. He always will, I suppose. He's like Papa. But there's always one they go back and back to, and for him it's Jess."

"And what about Jess herself? Is she going to be waiting patiently for him to come back?"

"Of course. You've seen Bevil, haven't you? He has the Menfrey fascination."

I laughed. "But not the Menfrey conceit, I hope."

"Conceit! My dear Harriet, is it conceit to face the truth? Would you have me pretend that I was plain and insignificant? What good would that do?"

"None at all, for you could never be able to convince people that you thought so. Your arrogance is the most convincing thing about you."

"Pah!" she said. "And I'll tell you something I've told you before, Harriet Delvaney: if you were less anxious to make it clear to people that you are unattractive they might possibly remain unaware of it."

"At least," I said, "I do not put myself in the indelicate position of being engaged to one man and dallying with others."

"My dear Harriet, I shall shortly settle down at a very early age. Don't you think I'm entitled to sow a few wild oats?"

"When one sows one often is obliged to reap."

"Oh, very clever and also very trite. I seem to have heard those sentiments expressed about three thousand times during a lifetime which you must admit could scarcely be called a long one."

"Gwennan, are you in love with Harry Leveret?"

"Don't be ridiculous," she said and changed the conversation.

Gwennan finished her year abroad before I finished mine. When she went home I missed her very much. And three months later I myself returned.

My stepmother was pleased to see me. She told me that she felt lonely in the house without my father. "Perhaps," she said wistfully, "I'm not the right mistress for a house like this. I've often thought I'd like a little place in the country."

"Why don't you give it up, then?" I asked. "Why not find a little place in the country?"

She looked at me incredulously. "You wouldn't mind, Harriet?"

I laughed at her. She was really rather engaging.

I went through the house. It seemed different now that my father was no longer there. I stood before his portrait in the library contemplating it. It was lifelike, but it was not the father whom I had known. The eyes were almost benign. They had never looked like that for me. The smile was amused, the eyes alert. A man who had charm for all except his daughter.

Upstairs I went; I leaned over the banisters sniffing the smell of beeswax and turpentine and remembering what I had heard that night when I ran away. I had come a long way from that little girl who had believed herself to be ugly and unwanted because someone had carelessly said she was. Gwennan told me that I was always on the defensive and she was right. Bevil only had to show me some attention and I bloomed into new personality; I only had to wear a dress which had belonged to a Menfrey woman and I became attractive.

The Menfreys were changing me, Gwennan with her often brutal frankness, Bevil with his admiration. I often wondered, though, whether Bevil's tenderness to me was the kind he gave to every woman. He was very attractive to women; he showed how much he admired women, how important they were to him; and while he was in love with beautiful Jessica Trelarken he could find time to be kind to plain Harriet Delvaney.

Once it had been thought that I should marry Bevil—but would that be changed now? For it seemed that my father had left his money to Jenny and that I, although well provided for, was not the heiress it had once been thought I should be.

I received a letter from Gwennan.

My dear Harriet, the wedding day is fixed. I've told them that I will have no one but you for my bridesmaid —at least one of them; and you are to be the chief. Maid of honour, I believe, is the correct term. You are

to come down here—at once—or as soon as you can
arrange it. Don't delay. There's so much to do and
I've such lots to tell you. Mamma wanted to bring me
to London for an orgy of spending but that is quite out
of the question. Money, my dear! It's a sad convention
that the bride's family have to undertake all the expenses
of the marriage. I'm not a rich man's wife yet. After
the honeymoon—it's to be Italy, my love, and then
Greece—you shall be our first guest at Chough Towers.
I've told Harry and he is ready to give way to me in all
things. I intend that it shall remain so all our lives.
Come as soon as you can for there is the matter of
your wedding garments, my dear. They will have to
be made in Plymouth—but I am sure we can concoct
something together quite spectacular.

Menfreystow is in a whirl of excitement about it and
believe me the main topic of conversation is The
Wedding. It's seven weeks away, but there is a great
deal to do and if you don't come soon we shall never
get you fitted for that magnificent wedding garment.
Bevil is most enthusiastic about the wedding. He's
fearsomely busy these days now that he has become
the Member for Lansella. I think he's secretly pleased
because when I marry my dear rich Harry there'll be
less obligation for him to make an m.o.c. (marriage of
convenience). I know him well. If Jess were only as
rich as my Harry there would be a double wedding at
Menfreya.

Now I am being indiscreet. But when was I not?
You must burn this letter as soon as you have read it,
just in case it should fall into the hands of (a) Bevil,
(b) Jess Trelarken, (c) just anybody but yourself.
Come soon. I miss you. *Gwennan*

I wanted to be there. I wanted to feel the sea breezes on
my face; I wanted to sleep in Menfreya and wake up in
the morning to look out over the sea to the island house
which was ours—or rather Jenny's, for everything seemed
to be hers now.

I was seated at my window looking over the square when I
saw the carriage arrive and Jenny alight, looking disturbed.

She was coming up the stairs to my room. "Harriet," she called. "Are you there, Harriet?"

"Come in," I replied and went forward to greet her. She looked bewildered, rather like a child who has been expecting a gift that has been snatched away.

"The country house . . ." she said.

"Yes?" I knew she had been excitedly looking for one for the last weeks.

"I can't have it."

"Why?"

"The money isn't mine after all."

"Do explain."

"You were there when they read the will. You couldn't have understood it either."

"I wasn't listening, I suppose. I was thinking about my father and the past and his marrying you and all that."

"I wasn't listening either. I don't understand it now although he went over and over . . . explaining and I said I did. He kept saying 'It's in trust for Miss Delvaney.' That's you, dear. It's in trust for you, which seems to mean that I'm having the interest or something while I live but when I die it will be yours. No one else is to have it but us, you see. You have your income now and the money set aside for your education and marriage portion and the rest is mine, but only for the income and I'm not allowed to touch the capital. I can't buy a house because the money is all for you. In a way I've been lent it till I die—to have the income from it; and after that it'll be for you and no one else."

"I begin to understand."

So he *had* remembered me then; he had cared for my future more than I had believed, and doubtless it had occurred to him that my flighty little stepmother would be an easy prey for fortune-hunters; and any who did not take the trouble to find out the terms of the will before marrying her would have a somewhat unpleasant shock when they did discover.

I was still a considerable heiress—or at least I should be if Jenny died.

My father was the sort of man to tie up everything very securely.

"I'm sorry about the house, Jenny."

She smiled. " Can't be helped, can it? I don't mind so much now you're home."

I was planning to go to Menfreya for Gwennan's wedding, but a few days before I was due to leave for Cornwall I received a letter from Aunt Clarissa, who asked me to call at her house in St. John's Wood.

Fanny accompanied me because when visiting Aunt Clarissa one must observe all the conventions and she would consider it unseemly for me to travel alone. My stepmother should have accompanied me but she had not been invited and in fact told me that Aunt Clarissa had, since the marriage, made it quite clear that she had no intention of calling on her or inviting her to call.

Fanny would take tea with my cousins' maid while I was with my aunt and cousins.

I was ushered into the drawing-room, where my aunt was seated with two of my cousins—Sylvia and Phyllis. Clarissa, the youngest girl, was still in the schoolroom. Phyllis was about my age and Sylvia two years older.

As we went in I was conscious of my limp and my hair which would not curl.

" Ah, Harriet." My aunt languidly held up her face that I might kiss her cheek. She did not rise and the greeting was cold—no true kiss, the touching of our skins, that was all.

" Pray sit down. On the sofa there with Sylvia. Phyllis, my dear, you may ring for tea."

Phyllis tossed back her yellow curls and went to the bell rope. I was aware of three pairs of eyes on me—supercilious, critical, *complacent* eyes. " Thank heaven, my girls are not like this one," said Aunt Clarissa's eyes.

" And how are you getting on . . . in that house?"

" Very well, thank you, Aunt."

" I expect *she* has wondered why I don't call."

" *She* has not mentioned that she missed your company."

Aunt Clarissa flushed and said hastily: " I do not think you should go back to your finishing school. Your father asked me, before he died so suddenly, to launch you with my own daughters, and that I promised to do. It is for this reason that I asked you to come here this afternoon."

" It makes me feel like a battleship," I said. " Is it necessary to launch me?"

" My dear girl, you could not be received in the right

places if you had not had a proper introduction to society. It is my duty, now that you have no father and your stepmother is . . ."—she shivered—". . . . quite unsuitable . . . it is my duty to take you under my wing. I propose to look after you at the same time as my own two girls. It will be much cheaper."

"Three for the price of one," I said.

"My dear, you have developed a habit of making extraordinary and unbecoming comments. I am planning parties and balls for your cousins, and you shall join us."

"I have no great desire for a London season."

"It is not a matter of your desire, Harriet, but what is a necessity for a girl of your class and position."

"I always think the Season is rather like a marriage market. The prize cattle are paraded and inspected."

"*Oh!*" said Aunt Clarissa, and my cousins looked horrified. "I do not know," went on my aunt, "where you learned such strange ideas. Not at your school, I hope. It must be that stepmother of yours."

Her butler arrived and ushered in the parlourmaid, who set up the tea things on the table near my aunt. While the servants were present, conversation was of the weather.

"Shall you pour, madam?"

"Yes," she answered and there was dismissal in her tone.

We ate cucumber sandwiches and toast and Sylvia carried the cups to us. I told her that I was shortly leaving for Menfreya to be bridesmaid at Gwennan Menfrey's wedding.

"Gwennan to be married! Why, she is only just out of the schoolroom."

"*She* did not need a season," I said, looking maliciously at my cousins. "And she is marrying Harry Leveret, who is, I believe, almost a millionaire."

"There is no background," declared my aunt triumphantly, but she grudgingly added: "Although the fortune is considerable. And married . . . right out of the schoolroom."

"Quite an achievement," I murmured, smiling at my cousins, "with which we could not hope to compete."

"How old is she?"

"She must be two years younger than you, Cousin Sylvia."

Sylvia flushed. "I suppose they were friends from childhood," she muttered.

They thought me malicious. My cousins would tell each other later that as I knew I should have difficulty in finding a husband myself, I hoped they would not find it easy either.

"When you return I shall take charge," said my aunt. "Lady Masterson, who is bringing her girl out, has given me a list of very charming young men whom she is inviting to her parties, so we shall not be short of them."

I felt heartily sick of the prospect and I wondered if it would be possible for me to evade it. I did not want to be paraded like some heifer. "She limps a little but there's a fortune there . . . a small one now, but if her stepmother dies, a big one. Anyone ready to take a chance?"

"You will have to develop a little charm, my dear Harriet," my aunt was saying. "You cannot hope to achieve anything without charm."

"I am not over-anxious about my state, for all I should be expected to achieve is a husband, which I may well be fitted to do without. Have you forgotten, Aunt, that my father has left me well provided for?"

There was a deep silence and then my aunt said firmly: "I am afraid, Harriet, that you have developed some very mercenary ideas. And let me tell you—your habit of expressing them in that most unsuitable way is not going to . . ."

"Buy me a husband?" I added.

"Really, Harriet. I wonder why I give myself the thankless task of bringing you out with my girls. It is a duty I anticipate with considerable misgivings."

When tea was over Aunt Clarissa told my cousins to take me to their schoolroom and show me some of the dresses they would wear for their coming out.

Young Clarissa joined us. She was very like her sisters, pretty in a superficial way, and empty-headed, which was what one would expect of girls whose upbringing had been supervised by Aunt Clarissa. They were trained to believe that the ultimate goal was the successful marriage. I wondered as I listened to their chatter how they would fare even if they achieved that goal. It would be impossible to make them understand now that what happened in the years after the ceremony was more important than what took place during the few months before.

I was a stranger among them, a cuckoo in the nest. They were afraid of my tongue but not of my face and figure. There they had the advantage and they were determined to exploit it.

I was glad when it was time to leave and riding home in the carriage I could express my irritation to Fanny.

" I wish I need never go there again. My aunt is proposing to do her utmost to find a husband for me! She is going to parade me at her wretched balls, which I shall hate in any case. It will be almost like having a placard round my neck. Excellent bargain. Slightly damaged but considerable compensations. Please apply Mrs. Clarissa Carew, Aunt of the object, for details '."

" Oh, Miss Harriet, you are a one. I don't know how you think of such things. I don't think you're the sort to be married against your will, anyway. Not if I know you."

" You're right, Fanny. But how I hate this marketing."

I was thankful that before this unwelcome season began I should be at Menfreya.

FOUR

When Fanny and I arrived at Liskeard I was surprised to find A'Lee waiting for me. I had known that I was to be met but I was expecting the Menfreya carriage.

" Miss Gwennan's orders," said A'Lee, greeting me as though I had never been away.

" But isn't this the Leverets' carriage?"

" She be almost a Leveret, Miss Harriet. She be giving her orders already."

His lower jaw shook with suppressed laughter; I was certain that Gwennan was giving the neighbourhood something to talk about.

On the way to Menfreya he told me that Gwennan herself had planned to meet me but had gone into Plymouth to see about some arrangement for the wedding.

" With most young ladies it's their mammas that makes the arrangements. Not so with Miss Gwennan. Lady Menfrey learned to do as she was told long ago, I reckon."

" And you're looking forward to the day when she's mistress of Chough Towers, I can see," I said.

" There'll be plenty and enough going on then, I reckon, Miss Harriet."

"It's good to be back," I told him. "I feel as though I haven't been away. Yet it's quite a long time, A'Lee."

"Aye, you'm right there. Quite a little maid you were when we last see 'ee. Now you'm a young woman. It'll be your turn next, I reckon."

"'Well, nobody's asked me, sir, she said,' so far."

His jaw wagged. "You were always a caution of a maid, you were, Miss Harriet. I reckon the one that has the sense to ask 'ee will be doing well for himself."

"Let's hope that I have the sense to accept him when he does. It's just struck me that this is a subject which occurs rather frequently in my life. Is it usual or is it because I have reached that tiresome stage which is known as marriageable?"

"Oh, you be a regular caution, Miss Harriet."

"Tell me, are there any changes here?"

"Doctor died some six months back."

"Dr. Trelarken?"

"Yes. He took in a partner, Dr. Syms. He be there alone now."

"And Miss Trelarken?"

"Oh, Miss Jessie, her went away . . . to London, I think. Her was staying with an aunt of hers up there and there was talk of her being a governess or companion. There wasn't no money, you know, and her'd have to earn her living like, poor young lady."

"I should think she would be . . . capable."

"Oh, yes, very capable. 'Twouldn't surprise me if her didn't marry before long. She were a lovely-looking maiden."

"Very beautiful."

"Oh, yes. I always said to Mrs. A'Lee that it done you good to look at her. There was a time when we used to think . . ."

"Yes, what did you think?"

"Well, Mr. Bevil, he were sweet on her. Mind you, he's been fond of a good many maidens in his time, I'd say; but with Jessie Trelarken it did look . . . Oh, well, it seems it came to naught. He be a big politician now, as you do know. Got in with a big majority I can tell 'ee. People here is close, you do know. They stick to their own. Reckon they sees it as right and proper to be represented by a Menfrey again."

"Oh, yes, my father was a bit of an outsider, wasn't he?"

"Well, 'tis like this here. He didn't never belong, did he?

Now you, miss, you have an air of belonging. I reckon it was because you come down here when you was a little 'un. And us don't forget that you run away from London to come to we."

"Oh . . . that was long ago."

"Us don't forget. It makes us think that you could belong with us more than most foreigners. You was a little 'un when you come here and us do know that this is where you like best to be. 'Twas always so."

"You're right. I do feel happy here."

"Then, Miss Harriet, it's where you belong to be."

"Look," I cried, "I can see Menfreya Manor."

"Aye, we'll be there in a little while now."

"It's always exciting to get the first glimpse after I've been away."

"I can see you've a love for the old place. They say Mr. Harry have promised to do all sorts of things for the house after the marriage and you can bet your dear life Miss Gwennan will keep him up to that."

"You mean repairs?"

A'Lee pointed with his whip. "Place like that do need constant repairs, Miss Harriet. Why, what it do rightly need is men working on it all the time, for being big like that . . . and having stood up these many hundred years to our gales and our seas, well, stands to reason, it wants building up like."

"And Harry Leveret is going to help. I'm so glad."

"That's why they'm so pleased with the marriage. I reckon they wouldn't be so content to welcome in Mr. Harry but for his money. If you was to ask me I reckon the lucky one in this little old wedding is Miss Gwennan. Menfreys! Why be so proud just because you can trace your ancestry back a few hundred years? Reckon we've all got ancestors, eh?"

"I reckon so," I said.

"Well, if all the tales I've heard of Menfrey doings be true, 'twouldn't be all that to be proud about."

"You're right," I answered. "Still if the Leverets are pleased and the Menfreys too, that's a fortunate state of affairs. Oh . . . look . . . there's the island."

"My word, yes. I'd been forgetting. It do belong to you now."

"Not exactly to me. My father married and I have a stepmother."

" Oh, to her, then?"

" Not exactly to her either. I'm not at all sure. In any case, it's in my family now."

" Us don't like it much . . . the old Duchy passing into the hands of foreigners, but as I said: It'll rightly be the little maid's, Miss Harriet's, now, and that don't seem so bad like."

" That's kind of you."

" 'Tisn't kind. 'Tis true."

" I shall look forward to going over to the island."

" You don't be planning to go spending no more nights there, I reckon."

" I suppose everyone here will remember that for ever."

" Oh, 'twas a right good story. It were in the papers. Daughter of the Member and all . . . and all London looking for her when she were hiding here in the Duchy . . . right here, you might say, in our very midst."

" It was a silly thing to do. But remember I was very young."

" Us didn't think it were all that silly."

His jaw began to wag again, and I was silent, for now we had reached the gates of Menfreya which faced the road and were turning in through the archway on which was fixed the ancient clock which was never allowed to stop.

I looked up. It was keeping perfect time as usual and I remarked on this.

" 'Course it be in good order," said A'Lee. " Reckon it mustn't never be aught else. 'Tis Thomas Dawney's task to see it do keep in good order and 'tis what the Dawneys have been fed and clothed and roofed for, this last hundred years—ever since the clock did stop and Sir Redvers Menfrey were thrown from his horse, they Menfreys has made sure as nothing do happen to the clock."

Through the gateway we went under the clock, past the lodge and those quarters which had been the home of Dawneys for a hundred years and there were the lawns with the hydrangeas and azaleas all in bloom and the lovely cotoneaster which was covered in scarlet berries all through the winter.

In the great hall with its pictures on the walls, its vaulted ceiling and its staircase on either side of which were suits of armour worn during the Civil War by the Menfreys of the day, I remembered that night when I was brought in from the island by Bevil, and how Gwennan had stood on the staircase reproaching me.

Now A'Lee pulled the bell rope and Pengelly, the Menfreys' butler, came into the hall and conducted me into the red drawing-room where Lady Menfrey was waiting to receive me.

It was wonderful to be with Gwennan again. She was like a flame; she seemed to have been born with a radiance which was dazzling. I felt alive merely to look at her.

She came in while I was having tea with Lady Menfrey, swooped on me in her exuberant way and carried me off to her room. She had changed, of course. She was indeed a woman—voluptuous and beautiful, eager and excited.

This, I thought, is Gwennan in love.

She talked about the plans for the wedding. "The whole neighbourhood expects a grand affair. It'll be rather like a medieval pageant, I imagine. My wedding dress is going to be a copy of one worn by my great-great-great-grandmother. I have to keep going for fittings. Such a bore, because I have to take Dinah with me. Chaperon! Unmarried young ladies are not allowed to go into the big city alone. One of the best things about being married is freedom, I do assure you, Harriet. You will be in chains still, while I shall be free."

"Some husbands I have heard can be jailers."

"Not my husband. Do you imagine I'd go from one prison to another?"

"Actually I think your family is more lenient than most."

"What are we talking about when there's so much to say? Now, you are maid of honour. Makes me sound like a queen, doesn't it? And you are going to be dressed in lilac chiffon and you'll look . . ."

"Hideous," I added.

"That's the idea. A contrast to the beautiful bride."

We were laughing together. It was good to be with Gwennan. The thought struck her, for she said so.

"I'm so glad you've come, Harriet. When I'm married you must be our first guest at Chough."

"It's odd to think of you there."

"Yes, isn't it? Mind you, we're making tremendous alterations. Harry is making it like a palace to fit his queen."

"I believe you're madly in love with him."

"Shouldn't I be? Only I'm supposed to hide it until the wedding day. He has to go on his knees to me before the day; then he forces me to mine, when I have to honour and obey."

"He wouldn't dare!"

"I should hope not. He adores me. Now listen. To-morrow, we are going into Plymouth. It's rather amusing. Dinah has a sister there and I send her off to see her. That leaves us free."

"Free for what?"

"You'll see. But first we have to go to the dressmaker's to see about that lilac gown of yours."

She was smiling, looking I thought into the future; and I realised how very fond I was of her because I sensed a new softness in her and I guessed that was being in love. Gwennan would love more fiercely than most people because everything she did was done with such verve. If Harry Leveret loved her and she loved him, they should be very happy.

Then she said a strange thing: "Harriet, I sometimes think I should have done well on the stage."

I raised my eyebrows and waited for her to enlarge on this subject, but she said nothing and went on smiling into the future.

The next day we were driven to the station and there took the train for Plymouth. Dinah, Gwennan's personal maid, accompanied us and deposited us at the dressmaker's, arranging to pick us up late in the afternoon.

I said, "We are spending a long time at the dressmaker's." But Gwennan only smiled and retorted that I must leave everything to her.

I was measured; I saw the lilac material, and Gwennan said that we should come back in three days for my first fitting. We were in the shop for only half an hour.

"I have a treat in store for you, Harriet. We are going to the theatre. You'll like it. It's rather wonderful. *Romeo and Juliet*. You remember how well you could read poetry, but you were no good in the plays, were you? You could never forget yourself. That's your trouble."

"Why didn't you say we were going to the theatre?"

"Why should I?"

"As a matter of interest."

She was silent and the smile still played about her lips.

"I might even take you back-stage after the show."

"You mean . . . you have a friend in the production?"

"You always said I surprised you and you never knew what I was going to do next. Are you surprised now?"

I agreed that I was.

"You're going to enjoy this, Harriet."

She bought our tickets and we went into the theatre. I saw from the programme that it was a repertory company who were spending a short season in Plymouth and were doing Henry Arthur Jones and Pinero besides the occasional Shakespearean production.

But I was more interested in Gwennan's attitude than anything I should see on the stage. Some adventure was in progress. I knew the signs and I began to have misgivings. Why should she be so interested in the theatre on the eve of her wedding?

She pointed to a name on the list of players. "Eve Ellington," I read. "What of it?" I asked.

"You can't guess who that is?"

I shook my head.

"Remember Jane Ellington?"

I did. I could see Jane in the centre of our room in France, reciting scenes from *Hamlet*.

"Good heavens," I said. "No!"

"Yes," she answered. "She wrote to me that she would be here and I came along to see her. Then I went back-stage as she invited me and I met some members of the company. I've been several times since."

"That's why you thought you'd like to be on the stage! Rather late to think about that when you're shortly to become Mrs. Leveret, isn't it?"

"Yes," she said, "it's very late. What you would call the eleventh hour."

"No," I said, "it's on the stroke of midnight."

"That won't be until the actual ceremony," she answered firmly.

"You wouldn't be any good. You'd never learn a part."

The curtain rose and the play began. It was cheap and tawdry, I thought, and the acting indifferent; oddly enough Gwennan seemed entranced. Romeo was handsome enough and I looked for his name in the programme: Benedict Bellairs; and I noticed that Eve Ellington played Lady Capulet. I recognised her immediately and settled down to watch her. Poor Jane, who had had such grand ideas!

When the curtain fell on the first act I said as much to Gwennan. "What rubbish," she said. "She has to start, hasn't she? I think it's quite an . . . achievement."

"You think she will be another Ellen Terry, and I suppose Romeo is Irving in embryo."

"Why not?"

"I should imagine that even in the beginning of their careers they played rather differently."

"You're too cynical, Harriet. You always are. Just because you don't attempt anything there's no need to sneer at people who do."

"Why . . . you're starry-eyed!"

"I appreciate effort, that's all."

I was silent. I was beginning to feel really disturbed.

I thought the play was never coming to an end. I kept glancing at Gwennan; she was unaware of me; her eyes were intent on the stage. This was quite unexpected; but then it was the unexpected that one must expect with Gwennan.

Eagerly she took me back-stage after the performance. I had never been behind the scenes of a theatre before and I found it exciting, though somewhat squalid. It was pleasant to see Jane again; and she welcomed me warmly. We sat on a packing box and talked. She loved the life, she told me; she wouldn't exchange it for the richest husband in the world. I guessed she was referring to Gwennan's coming marriage. Her people had been averse to her going on the stage, so she had simply run away. She reckoned she was very possibly cut out of her father's will. Who cared? The smell of greasepaint was worth all the fortunes in the world when you were eighteen and in love with your chosen profession.

Gwennan was talking to Romeo. He was still in costume and his face was shining with greasepaint; but I could see that he was very good-looking.

"I want to introduce you to Benedict Bellairs," she told me.

He took my hand and bowed over it.

"Welcome back-stage," he said.

I felt a shiver of apprehension in my spine. I did not like him.

Gwennan was secretive, which was strange, for she rarely kept anything to herself and had always said the first thing

that came into her head without consideration. That was
why the change was alarming.

I could not talk to her on the journey back because of the
presence of Dinah; but I gathered that the visits to Plymouth, which had been very frequent, invariably included
a visit to the theatre.

Why had she suddenly become so interested?

After we had retired for the night I went to her room
determined to find out how seriously she was involved. As
I knocked I heard her speaking, but she called Come in, and
I found her standing in the centre of the room, in her
dressing-gown; she had obviously been declaiming in front
of the mirror. I saw a book open on a table and I knew it
for the Shakespeare we had used at school.

"Juliet, I presume," I said.

"What do you mean?"

I glanced at the open book. "The balcony scene. Let me
hear you. 'Romeo, Romeo! Wherefore art thou, Romeo
. . . ?' Start from there. I'll be Mr. Benedict Bellairs."

She had flushed. "Trust you!" she said angrily, and
slammed the book shut.

"You certainly look stage-struck. Gwennan, what are you
planning?"

"Nothing."

"I always knew when you were scheming. Remember how
I used to guess."

"I was inspired by the performance this afternoon, that's
all."

"It's more than I was."

"Could you ever be inspired by anything?"

"Perhaps not. Unless it's your performance. Do let me
see your Juliet."

"Stop it."

"I will when you tell me how far this has gone."

"And stop that. You sound like the mistress of the house
who finds the master kissing the parlourmaid."

"Well, have you been kissing anyone?"

"Really, Harriet."

"What about this Benedict person? You aren't what you
used to describe as sowing your wild oats with him, are
you?"

"I find him interesting, that's all."

"And does Harry know how interesting you find him?"

D

"Stop it! I wish you hadn't come."

"Perhaps I'd better go back."

"Don't be a fool. How could you now?"

"But Gwennan, I am seriously concerned. You're not a schoolgirl now; you're a young woman on the verge of marriage. Have you thought of Harry?"

"I shall be thinking of Harry for the rest of my life. I want a chance to think of someone else . . . for the last time."

"Spoken like a bride!" I said. "Gwennan, it's time you grew up."

"You tell me that. You . . . *baby*! What do you know of life? Only what you read."

"It's possible that one might discover more of life through books than back-stage with a third-rate theatrical company."

"Stop it."

"You're becoming repetitive."

"And you're insolent."

I rose to go but she caught my hand. "Listen, Harriet. The company is going away the week before the wedding. Then that will be the end."

"I don't like it."

"You wouldn't, Madam Purity."

"I only hope . . ."

"Liar. Your only hope is that Bevil falls in love with you and marries you."

I turned away, but she would not let me go. "We know too much about each other, Harriet. And there's something else we know. We'd always stand together—no matter what sort of trouble one of us was in."

It was true.

The next day Gwennan and I rowed over to the island. There was the house with its four walls each looking out on the sea. It had been freshened up a little and I guessed that my father had had that done before he died, but old Menfreya furniture was still in the place.

"What does this remind you of?" asked Gwennan.

There was no need to ask. I should never see the island after a length of time without recalling the night I had spent there, and most of all that moment of fear when I had heard Bevil's voice below and he had come in with the girl from the village. I had been too innocent then to realise for what purpose he had brought her there; but of course I knew now that that would have been one incident in a long chain of similar ones in Bevil's life.

I felt vaguely depressed, thinking of Harry who loved Gwennan, and Gwennan who on the eve of marriage to him was letting her fancy stray to Benedict Bellairs; and Bevil, who like his father and most of the male Menfreys, seemed to believe it was the natural order of things to fly from female to female like a bee whose duty in life was pollination.

The boat had run aground and we scrambled out.

"Fancy," she said. "It's yours now. This little bit of land is lost to the Menfreys for ever. It's like the sea slowly encroaching on the land. And here it is rising from the ocean. A reproach to us every time we look out to sea. In years to come future Menfreys will shake their heads and say: 'Sir Endelion lost the island. That was a dark hour for Menfreya.' Unless, of course, it comes back to the family through marriage."

"Perhaps," I suggested, "the marriage of a daughter to a rich man might make it possible to buy back the island."

"It's not easy to wrest Menfrey soil from those who acquire it. Money is not always enough."

"Let's have a look at the house."

I unlocked the door.

"Typical," said Gwennan. "In our day the doors were never locked. Change and decay in all around I see . . ."

"It looks less decayed than when it was yours."

"It looks almost prim. I wonder what the ghosts think now."

"Are there more than one?"

"I think so. This is a much-haunted house. But perhaps the ghosts won't appear for foreigners. They're very particular, Cornish ghosts are."

She was unnaturally flippant. I wondered whether she was a little ashamed.

We went through the house, passing among the dust-shrouded furniture. I broke away from her and went alone to the bedroom where Bevil had discovered me. I could picture him now pulling off the dust sheet and myself looking up at him. Bevil, for whom I felt a special need . . . now!

"I should never want to live here," I said. "The best thing about it is the view."

"Just sea right away to the horizon."

"No, I mean on the other side. The coast and Menfreya."

Gwennan smiled at me fondly. " I believe you love the old place as much as we do."

We did not stay long on the island and went back to Menfreya; as we climbed the cliff garden, went through the porch which faced the sea and passed the stables and outhouses, one of the grooms came out.

" Mr. Bevil has just come home," he said.

" So he has arrived, has he," smiled Gwennan; and she looked at me slyly.

I tried to make my face expressionless, but I don't think I was very successful.

There followed some of the happiest days I had ever known. Bevil brought an atmosphere of gaiety into Menfreya— perhaps this was enhanced because I ceased to think about Gwennan. Bevil was constantly in our company; Harry Leveret rode over from Chough Towers every day and the four of us took a morning ride. Lady Menfrey, who was in perpetual fear that her headstrong family would do something outrageous, consoled herself that we chaperoned each other.

I became almost gay; on horseback I was happier than on my feet; there I felt an equal and, probably because of this, I was a good horsewoman. Everything seemed to be in my favour. Jessica Trelarken was miles away; I didn't know where and I didn't ask. Harry was completely wrapped up in Gwennan, and she in her own complicated affairs. That left Bevil and myself.

We would ride ahead of the others; sometimes we lost them.

" I don't think they'll miss us," said Bevil.

I shall never forget walking our horses through the woods with dappled shadows cast by the foliage; the feel of a horse beneath me always brings back the wild exhilaration. I discovered then that for me there would never be any other in my life to compare with Bevil. He seemed all that I had dreamed he was in my childhood when I had made of him a knight . . . my knight. The birdsong; the soft breeze coming off the sea—that gentle south-west Cornish wind that is like a caress, soft and damp, and beautifying because it makes your skin glow; the sudden glimpse of the sea, midnight blue, azure blue, peacock blue . . . pale almost to greenish blue, aquamarine—all the blues in the celestial artist's palette—and greys and greens and mother-of-pearl. But never, as I said to Bevil, so beautiful as when touched by the rosy glow of sunrise."

" Don't tell me you wake early to see it?"

" I do. But the best view is from the island house; then you can look back at the land, at Menfreya . . . Menfreya in the morning is the loveliest sight in the world. I saw it once . . ."

He laughed and his tawny eyes were on me—on my throat and my body and then they were looking into mine.

" I remember the occasion well. I found you cowering under a dust sheet and thought you were a tramp."

" I had thought you were a ghost until I heard voices. You were not alone, remember."

" Of course not. I didn't go to see the view. But one day I will. You will have to invite me, for the place is no longer ours; and I promise you I'll arrive early and we'll look at Menfreya in the morning . . . together."

" I should like that."

He looked over his shoulder.

" It seems we have lost them again," he said with a grin.

" I think Harry has taken some pains to get lost."

" And I confess I made no effort to prevent him."

" You think it wise?"

" When you know me better, Harriet, which I hope you will, you will discover that I am not often wise."

" You're all very happy about Gwennan's marriage, I believe?"

" It's ideal. Harry's a fine fellow; and they'll live at Chough Towers. It couldn't be better."

" And he's very rich."

" There's money in the Duchy if you know where to find it. Tin, china clay, the stone we built our houses with, and our seas chock-full of fish. There are fortunes waiting for the energetic."

" And the Menfreys are not energetic?"

" We never had to be, but believe me, being the Member for Lansella is no sinecure. You know that from your father's day."

" Do you enjoy the life?"

He turned to me. " I always wanted it. It seemed wrong that Lansella should not be represented by a Menfrey. It always has been and I believed when I was quite young that

I'd go into politics. I had all sort of plans for reforms. I was young and an idealist. I could have told you all the important events as far back as Peel's ministry, Russell's, Derby's, Aberdeen's and Palmerston's. I've followed Disraeli's career and Gladstone's . . . and of course Rosebery's and Salisbury's."

"Yes, I have, too."

"You. But why you, Harriet?"

"Because I used to feel sometimes that if I could talk to my father about politics he might become interested in me. I really believed that it was possible at one time."

He was looking at me intently. "Tell me, Harriet, don't you think the world of politics is a fascinating one?"

"The people are fascinating. I should love to have met Mr. Disraeli. His marriage must have been quite perfect. He with his curls, flamboyance and brilliant wit; she in her feathers and diamonds. I have always heard that they were devoted to each other; and I think that is wonderful."

"How romantic you are. I had no idea."

"It was natural that she should be devoted to him because he was Prime Minister, favourite of the Queen, and everyone waited for what he would say next; but she was, so I heard, a rather ridiculous woman, years older than he was and not very intellectual. And he married her for her money. Fancy! Yet he said later, or perhaps someone else said it, that although he married her for her money, after years together he would have married her for love."

"Marriages of convenience often turn out the best in the end. Theirs was a shining example. They have everything on their side."

"Except love?" I suggested.

"Love is something that takes time to grow, perhaps."

"What of love at first sight?"

"That's passion, my dear Harriet, a less hardy plant."

"Do you really believe that?"

"I believe only what is proved. I am a man of little faith, as you see."

"Well, let us hope that one day you will be able to prove your theories."

"I shall, Harriet, I've no doubt. It's interesting, you know, your being the daughter of the late Member."

"You find it so?"

He studied me, his eyes screwed up against the sunlight.
"You'll have to help me during the next election."

"I should enjoy it."

"A woman can be a great help—particularly the daughter
of the late Member."

"But you don't need help down here. They're only too
eager that you should represent them."

He leaned towards me and gripped my wrist. "I shall
need your help," he said; and I flushed with pleasure.

I was so happy; I had to keep reminding myself that this
was how he was with women. He knew exactly what to say
to please them best.

He was smiling at me. "I'm glad," he went on, "that you
are growing up now, Harriet. We must meet more frequently.
My chambers are not far from you. You must ask your
stepmother to invite me."

"I will."

We lightly touched our horses' flanks and cantered across
the open stretch of country which lay before us.

We reached the moor and we tethered our horses for a
while and sat on a stone wall. It was a glorious morning, with
the sun shining on the long grass picking out the globules of
moisture clinging to the blades—for there was a little mist
up there—and making them glitter like crystals. The soft
wind touched my skin and I was happy.

Then he returned to Jenny.

"You enjoy being part of that ménage, Harriet?"

"It's my home, I suppose."

"I wonder she cares to stay on in that house."

"She was planning to buy a house in the country but she
can't touch the capital my father left her. Presumably she
holds it in trust for me."

"So that's the way it is."

"I don't understand fully. All I know is that Greville,
Baker and Greville told her that she could not have the
money for the house."

"Then you, my dear Harriet, will be a considerable heiress,
in certain circumstances."

"I hope I shall never inherit, for that means she would
have to die first. I should hate that. Do you know, I've
grown quite fond of her."

"Those sentiments do you credit, Harriet."

"They do credit to my good sense. If I had inherited all my father's fortune I should be a prey to those gentlemen who are looking for a marriage of convenience. I prefer my own modest fortune and comparative safety from attack."

"Dear Harriet, your fortune, modest or otherwise, is not your only asset."

"You surprise me."

"Do I? Then it is tit-for-tat. You surprise me with your conversation."

"I suppose you previously thought I had none?"

"It is only recently that you have given me the opportunity to enjoy it."

"It is only recently that you have sought that opportunity."

He laughed and taking my hand pressed it. "Harriet," he said, "promise that you will give me many more such opportunities here and in London."

He leaned towards me and kissed my cheek. Not passionately as I imagined he kissed others, but gently, wonderingly. I thought: He is regarding me in a different light. He is getting to know me, to like me. Or was he getting to know about my fortune and liking that?

But it was no great fortune, because Jenny was only a few years older than I, and I should not be likely to inherit for years, if ever.

The thought made me happy. It was not the fortune. It was myself.

Such happiness for one unaccustomed to it was almost too intoxicating.

When we mounted our horses he said: "So your stepmother didn't know how she stood?"

"She heard the will read; she saw the solicitor but didn't take in the legal facts."

"I should have thought something so vital to herself would have made some impression."

"I was present when the will was read but I didn't grasp it. Actually my mind was wandering and I was thinking . . ."

"What?"

"Oh, what a waste it was that my father and I had never been friends and then never could be."

"One of these days, Harriet, someone ought to make up to you for all you've missed."

"That would be justice but life isn't always just, is it?"

"Perhaps we should see that it works out that way."

What did he mean? Was it tantamount to a proposal?

"I tell you what," he said, after we had left the moors, "you are rather vague about your inheritance, aren't you? You could find out, you know."

"I could go to Greville, Baker and Greville."

"You needn't do that. You could see a copy of the will in Somerset House. Would you like me to look into it for you when I'm in town?"

I felt a sudden quiver of alarm, but I said: "Yes, please, Bevil, do."

"I will," he said. "You leave it to me. Quite a cool wind blowing up."

Was it that cool wind, I thought, which was making me feel a little cold?

Looking back after a tragedy the preceding days seem to have taken on an unreality. One has been living with the obvious and yet failed to see what is under one's nose.

Those were days of sunshine and preparation, and the wedding was coming nearer. Nine days . . . eight days . . . When I had been in Plymouth a few days before, Gwennan and I had gone to the theatre and I had seen the company's bills posted outside the building with "Last Week" stamped across them.

Thank goodness, I thought. When they've gone Gwennan will settle down and forget all about them. In a short time when she had returned from her honeymoon and asked me down to stay with her as she had promised, we would laugh and christen it the Grease Paint period.

She surprised me on the last day of the company's stay in Plymouth by not going to say good-bye to them. I thought with relief: She has finished with them already.

My dress was ready and hanging in my wardrobe. It was very pretty—in clinging lilac chiffon—and I was to wear a head-dress of green leaves. The bridesmaids were to be in green with touches of mauve. The colour was certainly going to be effective.

"Green's unlucky, though," said Fanny grimly. "I'm surprised at Miss Gwennan choosing green."

"I'm not," I said.

That day was like many another. I rode with Bevil, Harry and Gwennan in the morning. Gwennan was a little absent-minded and I guessed her thoughts were with the departing company. I had no chance of being alone with Bevil, for the four of us were together all the morning.

During the rest of the day Gwennan seemed to avoid me and I guessed she wanted to be alone to think seriously of her future.

There was a card party at the Leverets' that evening. We played whist rather solemnly and left at ten o'clock. I thought Gwennan looked remote; I spoke to her once or twice and she did not answer me. I guessed she was picturing the company packing their belongings and moving on to the next town. Another little episode over. Thank goodness, I thought, that there is no time for any more before the wedding.

I slept well and in the morning Fanny came in as usual to draw my curtains and bring my hot water.

"Another lovely day," she said, "a bit misty though. Pengelly says it's a heat haze. It was really thick first thing this morning!"

I went to the window and looked out at the sea.

Another week or so and I should be back in London and Aunt Clarissa would descend upon me for the purpose of bringing me out.

I did not want the time to pass. I wanted to catch each moment and imprison it.

We would ride that morning—Bevil, Gwennan and I—leaving the stables together and riding over to Chough Towers where Harry would be waiting impatiently for us.

I went down to breakfast. Sir Endelion and Lady Menfrey were at the table and greeted me affectionately.

Lady Menfrey said that Bevil had already breakfasted but Gwennan had not been down yet. We talked about the weather and the wedding and afterwards I strolled out to the stables.

It was an hour or so later when I saw Bevil.

He said, "Are we riding this morning?"

"I hope so."

"Well, where's Gwennan?"

"I haven't seen her."

"I don't think she's up yet. Go up to her room and tell her to hurry."

I went into the house and seeing Dinah said: "Miss Gwennan is late this morning."

"She said she would ring when she wanted me."

"When did she say that?"

"Last night."

"So you haven't been up yet?" My voice had risen to a high pitch as it did when I was apprehensive.

"No, miss, seeing as she told me not."

As I took the stairs two at a time, I kept seeing her face as it had been yesterday . . . resigned. She had run away. I knew it before I opened the door and saw the unslept-in bed, the envelopes propped on the dressing-table. Trust Gwennan to do it in the melodramatic way.

I went to the dressing-table. There were three letters. One for her parents, one for Harry, and one for me.

My fingers were shaking as I slit the envelope addressed to me.

Dear Harriet, *I read.*

I've done it. It was the only way. I just could not stay. I've gone with Benedict. We're going to be married and I might go on the stage with him. Do try to make them understand. Particularly Harry. I couldn't help it. It was one of those things that had to be. This is different from anything else that ever happened to me. Harriet, we shall always be friends, no matter what happens. Don't forget, and try to make them understand.
                                                  Gwennan

I felt too numb to move. I heard the sound of laughter from the kitchen. I heard Bevil shouting to one of the grooms. All around me for a few minutes more life was going on as usual, but soon that would be changed.

I picked up the other two letters and ran from the room.

"Bevil," I called, as I ran out of the house into the sunshine. "Quickly. Come here."

He came running. "What on earth . . ."

I held up the letters. "She's gone, Bevil. There's one for me. She's run away with Benedict Bellairs."

"What? Who?"

I had forgotten, of course. There was no one in this house but myself—and possibly Dinah—who knew of the existence of this man.

"Gwennan has run away with an actor."

He snatched my letter from me and read it.

"She's going to marry . . . But what of Harry? What does it mean?"

I just stared at him and I saw the realisation spread across his face and amazement fade to anger. "You knew of this," he accused me.

I nodded.

"Then why didn't you say? You've let her do this. We'll have to get her back."

He strode into the house, and as, hurt and guilty, I followed him, I heard him shouting to his father.

Sir Endelion followed by Lady Menfrey appeared at the foot of the stairs.

"Gwennan's run away with an actor," cried Bevil.

"What!"

Bevil turned to me. "Harriet will tell you. She knows all about it."

"Harriet." It was a piteous cry from Lady Menfrey.

"I didn't know she was going to run away," I said.

"But the wedding . . ." began Lady Menfrey piteously.

"I'll bring her back," declared Bevil. "I'd better get going right away. What is the name of this man? Here . . . open you letter."

"Letter?" said Sir Endelion.

"Oh yes," said Bevil furiously. "She did it in style . . . leaving envelopes for the family . . . and Harriet."

I was stung because he was turning the anger he felt against Gwennan on me.

Sir Endelion said in a shaking voice, and I realised how upset and bewildered he was: "I'm afraid I haven't got my spectacles."

Bevil took the envelope from him and read the note aloud. The contents were much the same as in mine. She loved Benedict Bellairs; she was running away with him because she could not go on with her marriage with Harry. She hoped they would forgive her and understand.

"Understand!" cried Bevil. "Yes, we understand that she is a selfish little fool. Forgive her. Wait till we get her back."

I said: "It is of course a terrible thing to marry for love rather than for mercenary reasons."

Bevil stared at me almost contemptuously, while Lady Menfrey moaned: "This is terrible . . . terrible . . ."

"Listen," cut in Bevil curtly. "I'm going to Plymouth alone. Until I return, keep this dark. I'll bring her back and the affair need go no further. Keep it from the servants."

"You won't find the company at Plymouth," I told him. "They left yesterday."

"What is the name of the company?"

I told him.

"I'll find where they've gone and I'll bring her back with me," he said grimly.

"She won't come."

"We shall see about that."

He left for Plymouth and I went with Sir Endelion and Lady Menfrey to the library. They kept asking me questions. What did I know? What was this man like? They were reproachful. I had aided Gwennan in this deceit.

I felt wretched because of their disappointment in me but most of all because of Bevil's contempt. I had never seen him angry before but I realised that he could be very angry indeed.

I told them about her visits to the theatre; there was no point in holding anything back now.

"So you went with her when you were supposed to be visiting the dressmaker?"

I demanded angrily how they could have thought we need spend so much time with the dressmaker.

"Dinah should have warned us," said Lady Menfrey.

"You know Gwennan. She forbade Dinah to."

"Yes," sighed Lady Menfrey. "We know Gwennan."

Sir Endelion was surprisingly subdued and I guessed he was thinking of the scandal in which he had been involved and which had resulted in his having to give up his seat in Parliament.

"And you, Harriet?"

"How could I tell tales about Gwennan?" I protested.

"But you see what has happened. When Bevil brings her back . . ."

"She won't come."

"He'll make her. Bevil will get his way."

"So will Gwennan."

Lady Menfrey sighed and I guessed that many times in her life she had been confronted by the wild intractable natures of her family.

Harry Leveret came over because he wondered why

Gwennan, Bevil and I had not ridden over to the Towers.

He had to be given the letter which Gwennan had written to him; even now I don't like to think of his face as he read her words.

He was stricken. Poor Harry! He had loved Gwennan dearly.

That day was like a bad dream. Bevil came home alone, pale and angry. He had discovered that the company had moved to Paignton, whither he had been and when he had unearthed them he had learned that Benedict Bellairs had left the company, his destination unknown.

There was nothing else to be done . . . just yet.

The Leverets had come over and Mrs. Leveret sat crying. I couldn't bear to look at Harry and every now and then one of them would fire questions at me. I couldn't tell them any more than that I had been to the theatre and that Gwennan had been friendly with an actor named Benedict Bellairs. I had to repeat it over and over again until I wanted to scream at them to let me go.

FIVE

I felt wretched back in the London house. I had lost Gwennan, Bevil was furious with me, and before me stretched the dreary season through which Aunt Clarissa would guide me.

She sat in the drawing-room facing Jenny, dressed in black, which was a reproach to Jenny that his sister had not yet cast off her mourning for her brother although his wife had seen fit to do so. She looked like a crow intimidating a little budgerigar.

Her voice was high and shrill. " Of course this house would have been ideal. I remember the entertainments my brother used to give. I have seen these rooms decorated with *exquisite* flowers and even a fish-pond in the library."

My stepmother fluttered her hands, but these helpless gestures which had so enchanted my father left Aunt Clarissa unmoved.

" Of course I wouldn't dream of using this house now . . . a house which not so long ago suffered a bereavement!"

" All houses must have had their bereavement at times," I put in because I had to come to Jenny's aid. " If no parties were ever given in houses where people had died there would be few parties."

" I was addressing your stepmother, Harriet."

" Oh really, Aunt, I'm not a child to speak only when spoken to."

" Until you are officially out I look upon you as a child."

" Then I shall be very pleased to have crossed the magical barrier."

" There is one thing I must talk to you about, Harriet. Your tongue is too tart."

" I should only succeed in artificially sweetening it."

" This is absurd digression. I was saying that it is not possible to use this house, and I suggest that Harriet makes her home with me until the season is over."

Jenny looked helplessly at me. I realised that it would have to be as Aunt Clarissa suggested.

Aunt Clarissa's house was set back from the road; there were two gates at each end in a semicircular path which led to the front door. It was larger than our house in the London square but much less elegant. Aunt Clarissa's husband had not been as rich as my father—a fact which she had always resented and, I believe, continually pointed out to my poor uncle. He had died some five years ago, after a long illness, and I had heard his death called " a happy release." I could well believe it had been.

Sylvia and Phyllis welcomed me into their home with contemptuous indulgence. I was no rival, in fact I would be a foil which would enhance their pink and white pretti- ness.

There was a whirl of activity in the house. Poor little Miss Glenister, the seamstress, was working in one of the attics which was called the sewing-room from early morning until late at night. I was sorry for her; she was harassed not only by my aunt but by my cousins; and it could be a major disaster if Miss Sylvia did not like the set of her sleeves, and Miss Phyllis, after deciding that she *adored* the coffee-coloured lace on her blue velvet, suddenly decided that she hated it after all. Miss Glenister was the scapegoat, the whipping boy. Everything was blamed on her. Some- times I wondered that she did not throw her pins and cottons at them and walk out of the house. But where to? To be employed by some other family who would exact the same duties and shower on her similar blame?

When she made something for me I always declared myself delighted with it, which wasn't true; but I couldn't bear to add to her troubles.

My cousins would put their hands to their lips to hide their smiles.

"Well, *I* shouldn't care for it, cousin. But I suppose *you* feel it is not very important."

Miss Glenister would makes excuses for them. She said to me: "Well, miss, they're so pretty. It's understandable *they* would want the best."

The dresses were filling our wardrobes. Ball dresses—several of them for, as Aunt Clarissa said, it would be *disastrous* to wear a dress so many times that it was *recognised*.

"Does that mean we shall wear them only once?" I asked.

"What ridiculous extravagance!" retorted Aunt Clarissa.

"But would it be safe to wear them twice? There may be some people who will be alert enough to recognise them even after one airing. The dress detectives!"

"I beg of you, Harriet, don't imagine you are being clever. In fact you are being very stupid."

But I had shaken her and this gave me malicious delight. I took every opportunity in undermining her confidence in her daughters and their success in what I called the marriage market. I was ashamed of myself; I told myself that I despised the entire business but secretly in my heart I knew that had I been beautiful, charming and attractive I should probably have been as interested in the dresses as my cousins were, and as eager for success. The confidence which I had acquired dropped from me and I was nearer the sullen child I had been when my father was alive than I had been for a long time. I had two personalities—the one which could be gay, hopeful, amusing and even attractive, and the sullen, caustic one which was continually on the defensive, expecting attack. I was reminded of the wooden figures in the little house in my cousins' nursery: the gaily dressed woman with the parasol to indicate sunshine, the sombrely dressed man when it was dull or stormy. Sunshine brought one *me* out (that was Bevil and Menfreya) and gloom the other (that was my aunt and cousins).

The more I disliked myself the more wretched I grew. The difference now was that this mood did not manifest itself in sullen silence; I merely made use of my barbed tongue to wound them and spoil their pleasure.

I think I was most hurt by the poor little seamstress to whom my cousins behaved so badly and to whom I tried to be kind, because in spite of this she preferred making dresses for them; and although they made her shed many a tear into her seams and gathers, she admired and respected them.

What am I doing here? I used to ask myself during those days.

We were duly presented and the round of activities began.

I had to escape from the silly chatter, the poring over lists of names.

"We must try for him. *He* would *make* any party."

"He" was the most eligible bachelor in town, possessed of a barony and a fortune.

"Even better than the Earl because, my dear, *he* is hard put to it to keep up those *vast* estates and you can be sure he will be looking for a fortune. Something beyond our dowries. If your father had only . . . But we have to make the best of what we have. Lord Bars is a charming man . . . and rich . . . *rich!* Of course I know George Crellan is the son of an Earl . . . but the fourth son, my dears! If he were the second, there might be a chance . . . but the fourth! The Honourable Mrs. Crellan! . . . Yes, very nice. But I would prefer a more *solid* title . . . something that is hereditary . . . Honourables are so doubtful, I always think. There are times when it isn't good taste to use them. So we must try for Lord Bars . . ."

She saw my lips curling with contempt.

"If you think that you might have a chance with the Earl you're mistaken. *If* your father had not been such a fool as to marry that woman . . . and leave his money in trust . . . Oh, dear. What a tangle! I thought when I launched you I should at least have your fortune. And now unless she were to die . . . and she's so young . . ."

I laughed aloud.

"Harriet."

"All this is full of sound and fury and certainly signifies nothing," I said. "I don't want the Earl nor Lord Bars nor the Honourable George Crellan, I do most sincerely assure you."

"Don't worry," retorted my aunt angrily, "*you* will never have the opportunity."

"And if the gentlemen have any sense nor will my cousins," I retorted.

There was nothing to do then but leave them; and because I wanted to escape from the triviality of it all I paid a visit to my stepmother.

Jenny was pleased to see me and I thought she was looking prettier and more animated than usual.

"Bevil Menfrey called yesterday," she told me. "What a *charming* young man. He was very amusing."

I pictured the scene, Bevil's being very charming as he always would be to a pretty woman.

"He asked after you, of course."

"I don't think he's very pleased with me," I replied. "He thinks I am partly to blame about Gwennan."

"Oh, I'm sure he wouldn't think that. It would be quite unfair and he'd never be that."

"He was unfair. He blamed me. It was quite clear."

"That was in the heat of the moment. He was upset then. Naturally he didn't expect you to tell tales. I asked him if he had heard anything of Gwennan and he said no. He had made inquiries and they came to nothing and he expected she was married by now and there was no point in trying to bring her back if she was."

"And he . . . mentioned me."

"Yes. He said, 'Harriet was in the plot . . . sworn to secrecy. If only she had given us a hint . . . but naturally she wouldn't do that!'"

"So you think he really understood?"

"Of course. He would have done the same. He said he was coming to some of your parties. Your aunt had sent him invitations."

I knew I was looking radiant; but an uneasiness crept into my mind as I looked at my pretty stepmother, her eyes shining with pleasure as she recalled Bevil's visit, her skin glowing with that fresh yet transparent clarity which was so unusual and attractive.

A few days later we went to the ball Lady Mellingfort was giving for her daughter Grace. Preparations for it had gone on all day, and I was bitterly disappointed because Bevil had not called on my aunt as I had expected him to.

In the privacy of my room I practised dancing. I could dance. I had proved that in the haunted room at Menfreya and at the ball at Chough Towers, but I imagined I lacked grace.

There was only one reason why I should want to go to a ball and that would be if Bevil was there.

I was dressed in green, which my cousins had informed me was unlucky. I felt a few qualms as I put it on, for I had chosen it more out of bravado than anything else. Green silk made into a ball dress by Miss Glenister's pricked fingers and her worn-out eyes! I thought I looked plain; and I could see from the pleased expressions in my cousins' faces that they thought so too.

Sylvia was in pink and silver and Phyllis in blue and silver. The same silver ribbon for both of them; it was cheaper to buy a quantity. I had to admit that they looked very pretty in their way, which I deluded myself into thinking was an insipid one. Their maid, whom we all shared, had dressed their hair very charmingly and each wore a curl over her shoulder. No one would have guessed that the curl had been produced by being put into rags the previous night; rather uncomfortable and grotesque but Aunt Clarissa was against the curling tongs. I had brushed my own straight hair and rolled it into a chignon which I wore high on my head.

" Ageing!" commented Phyllis happily.

" At least," I said, " there shouldn't be three fairy dolls from the top of the Christmas tree."

" Jealousy!" whispered Sylvia.

" No," I retorted. " Fair comment."

I certainly did not look my best. I scorned the rouge with which my cousins had touched their cheeks. I would go to the ball plain and ungilded just to show that I didn't care.

" She looks like someone's governess," said Sylvia to Phyllis.

" Except of course that governesses don't go to balls."

" Phyllis! Sylvia!" I said sharply. " Your manners are not half as pretty as your dresses."

" What do you mean?"

" I'm acting like a governess since I look so like one."

They would have been surprised if they could have known

that there was a tight feeling in my throat and a burning sensation in my eyes. I could have thrown myself on the bed and wept. I felt so wretched, and my wretchedness was like an echo from the past when my father had shown so clearly that he did not care about me, and Aunt Clarissa had wondered how she was going to find me a husband.

The carriage was at the door and we set out. I watched Aunt Clarissa—her complacent eyes resting on her daughters. She thought they looked enchanting.

Near Lady Mellingfort's house in Park Lane we were held up in the stream of carriages which were taking guests to her ball. This was one of the most grand balls of the season and Aunt Clarissa's emotions were divided; she was delighted to be a guest and at the same time wondering how she was going to vie with such splendour when her turn came to be the hostess.

People looked in at us—some ragged with gaunt faces. I shivered. I always disliked contrasts. I wondered whether they hated us sitting there not only well fed but in our glittering garments—the cost of our gowns would have fed a family for a week.

I was glad when we moved on and arrived at the house.

I had a vision of red carpet, powdered footmen and palms in white pots, the hum of excited voices, the anxious eyes of aspiring mammas.

Then we were mounting the wide staircases to be received by Lady Mellingfort, who in white satin, diamonds and feathers was waiting for us.

It was the nightmare I had imagined it to be. Mothers greeting each other, complimenting each other on their charming daughters, lynx-eyed for a sign of superior beauty and to catch the eye of the most enticing prey.

I caused no qualms; I could read their thoughts as I was introduced.

" Sir Edward Delvaney's daughter! Not exactly a beauty! And since her father married a young woman . . . no fortune. A real outsider."

I didn't belong here. How I longed for the time when we should be saying our farewells and grateful thanks to our hostess. How much more enticing did my own room seem.

It was as I feared. I was introduced to one or two men— the more ageing and unattractive—who eyed me speculatively. I presumed my diminished fortune was of some interest to them. I danced awkwardly and chatted for a while and as I made no effort at trivial conversation they drifted away.

I saw Phyllis and Sylvia dancing; and I was sorry that they saw me too. They threw me pitying smiles which didn't quite hide their complacence.

I don't care what they say, I promised myself, I shall never come to another of their silly balls.

Then he was coming towards me. I knew that several of the rapacious mammas were watching him, but he was unaware of it. If not the most handsome he was surely the most distinguished man in the ballroom.

"Harriet!" he said in a voice which was heard by those near by and made heads turn and eyebrows raise themselves. "I've been hunting for you for the last half-hour!"

"Bevil!" I cried, and all my joy and pleasure was in my voice for the watchers to detect.

He sat down beside me. "I should have been here earlier but I was detained in the House."

"I had no idea that you were coming."

"I wasn't sure whether I should manage it. But I heard from Tony Mellingfort that your aunt and her protégées were invited so I was determined to get here some time. Are you pleased to see me? What a noise!"

I was too happy to speak in those first moments. Then I said rather quietly: "I suppose it's what we must expect . . . the music and the chatter."

"Actually I avoid such affairs whenever possible."

"I shall too, but it'll be easier for you than for me. Is there any news of Gwennan?"

"None," he said. "I have to apologise, don't I? I was angry and I thought it might have been avoided if you had told us about the affair, but of course I understand that she took you into her confidence and you're the last one who would betray that."

"I'm glad you understand."

"You met this fellow, didn't you? Oh God, what a noise! Shall we try and find a quieter spot?"

He took my hand and pulled my arm through his; several eyes followed as we found our way to an alcove slightly secluded by palms.

" That's better."

" 'Far from the madding crowd '," I murmured, my spirits beginning to rise.

" But not far enough. This actor, what was he like?"

" I only saw him on the stage and quite briefly behind the scenes."

" But how did he strike you, Harriet?"

" It's hard to say. He was so much an actor that he always seemed to be playing a part—off stage as well as on."

" I don't know what will become of her."

" She's very resourceful."

" She hasn't written to you and asked you not to tell us?" He smiled. " But then if she had you wouldn't tell, would you?"

" No. But I can tell you this: she hasn't written to me."

" I wonder whether that's a good or bad sign."

" It could be either."

" You don't deceive me, Harriet. If Gwennan had anything to boast about she would have written to you. Didn't she always?"

" Yes. But she might be afraid you would get on to her trail and try to bring her back."

" We couldn't . . . if she were married. If you do hear, will you tell me . . . providing of course you aren't bound to secrecy?"

" Of course I will, Bevil."

" Well, that's that. Now tell me about yourself. You're staying at your aunt's I gathered when I called on your stepmother the other day."

" Yes, and I shall be glad when all this is over! I hate these affairs."

" So do I."

" *You* were under no compulsion to come."

" Wrong again, Harriet. I was under the great compulsion of wanting to see you. You know that you are the most intelligent and amusing young lady of my acquaintance, don't you?"

" I know that you have the art of paying compliments!"

He leaned towards me and kissed my nose. I thought: There was never happiness such as this. Why could I have thought I didn't want to come to Lady Mellingfort's ball?

We talked of Menfreya and as I sat with Bevil in that alcove I could hear the swish of the waves and see the machicolated walls and the old clock in the tower; I could see myself riding with Bevil through the woods and lanes. I felt intoxicated by happiness.

Later, when we went into supper together, to my dismay we were joined by my Aunt Clarissa and Sylvia who I was malicious enough to note was without an escort.

"Mr. Menfrey! How delighted I am. My daughter, Sylvia."

I felt a twinge of fear as he looked at her in that warm caressing way he and his father looked at all women.

Sylvia said: "I'm delighted too, Mr. Menfrey. I've heard so much about you."

"Then there is delight all round. Harriet could talk of nothing else but her charming cousins all the evening!"

I caught my breath but he was smiling at me. He had summed up the situation.

Lady Mellingfort had thought it would be amusing for her guests to help themselves at the buffet supper; and Bevil suggested that he should bring our supper to the table.

"Take Sylvia along with you. She will help you. Go along, Sylvia, my dear."

I watched them go off together and I hated my aunt. She was hating me too.

"Really," she said under her breath. "People are *talking*!"

"You'd hardly expect otherwise. This is not a monastic order where silence is expected."

"Harriet! Listen to me."

"I am listening, Aunt."

"Your conduct has been *disgraceful*."

"In what way?"

"Secreting yourself away with that man."

"Secreting ourselves? Oh, Aunt, there was nothing secretive. We could be seen quite distinctly through the palms . . . and we were."

"That's what I mean. It simply is not done. You are under my care and I am most displeased. You monopolised Mr. Menfrey. Did it occur to you that other people might have wanted to speak to him?"

"He has a very small fortune, Aunt. Of course there's the title which he'll have one day, I suppose . . . but a country estate . . . and a comparatively small one. Not to be compared with Earls and Barons or even the Honourable Mr. Crellan."

"Will you be silent! Well, at least he and Sylvia seem to be getting along well together."

They did. My brooding eyes had watched them laughing as they selected from the delicacies at the buffet table assisted by Lady Mellingfort's powdered flunkeys.

"Oh, here they come. Mr. Menfrey, what delicious things you have brought us! Pray sit here. And Sylvia, my dear, you sit there."

Bevil had drawn his chair a little closer to mine.

"I trust," he said, smiling at me, "this will be to your taste."

He was charming to my aunt, and towards Sylvia he displayed that mildly flirtatious attitude which he seemed unable to avoid. The evening was not exactly spoilt, but I had descended a long way from the Elysian heights.

Nor did I have a chance of regaining them, and all too soon we had said our farewells, Bevil had accepted an invitation to call at my aunt's house, and our carriage was taking us along Park Lane.

We were all silent.

In my bedroom I threw my gown over a chair and got into bed where, between waking and sleeping, I imagined I was at Menfreya looking out to sea and then rowing over to the island where Bevil was waiting for me, or riding through the woods, laughing, talking; then galloping to escape from Aunt Clarissa and Sylvia who were in pursuit. It was pleasant dreaming with only the faintest shadow of doubt and distrust—a true reflection of what had happened to me at Lady Mellingfort's ball.

The next day my aunt suggested that it would be seemly for me to visit my stepmother and I quite willingly obeyed. I was surprised at this little gesture of thoughtfulness until I learned that Bevil had called while I was out—as presumably had been arranged without my knowledge—and had taken wine and biscuits in the drawing-room.

When I returned and discovered what had happened I felt murderous.

"He paid such attention to Sylvia!" cried Phyllis.

"I thought *you* were trying to flirt with him," put in Sylvia.

"Well, he is rather amusing, and in any case he *would* keep talking to me."

I could not bear to listen to their conversation; but the triumph was mine when the next day—just before we were leaving for another of the season's parties—one of the maids brought in the flowers.

They were in a charming box—two orchids—most tastefully displayed.

"Give it to me," squealed Phyllis. "Oh, I do wonder who sent it."

My aunt came bustling in. "Flowers! Not at all unusual. Don't get so excited. You'll find this is quite a practice when a man wants to show he is interested."

Sylvia was scowling at her sister and trying to take the box from her. "How do you know they're for you?"

"Mr. Sorrell was so attentive at Lady Mellingfort's and he hinted that he hoped we'd meet again so I'm not surprised . . ."

"Oh, so they're not for you?"

Sylvia was laughing at the card which she had snatched out of the box.

"For you?" asked her mother.

But Phyllis tried to take the card from Sylvia and it dropped to the floor close to me andy looking down at it I saw the writing on it. "I'll be looking for you to-night, Harriet. B.M."

"It can't be true," said my aunt.

I picked up the box. My name was written on it very clearly. I took out the orchids and held them against my dress.

My aunt had snatched the card and was reading it.

"B.M.!" she cried.

"Specimens from the British Museum, you're thinking? But I'm sure they were sent to me by Bevil Menfrey."

I took the orchids to my room. I would take pains over my toilette and choose the dress which best matched the orchids.

This was a pale green, and as I tried the orchids against it I knew it looked charming.

It was not easy to hide my elation, and my cousins and aunt were well aware of it.

"It doesn't do, Harriet," said my aunt gently, "to attach too much importance to a gift of flowers."

"I am sure it does not, Aunt," I answered demurely.

"That friend of yours, Gwennan, she was a wild creature.

It was quite shocking the way she ran away on the eve of her wedding. They must have been ashamed of her."

"Perhaps they all make a habit of running away after promising marriage," suggested Sylvia.

"They're a wild family I have always heard and their prospects are not dazzling. I heard on a very good authority that there are *debts*. They've got some crumbling old estate in the wilds of Cornwall and I doubt we should know them but for the fact that your father, Harriet, was the Member there. And he took the seat because the previous Member had resigned on account of a scandal. That was your friend's father. I think one would have to be very careful with a family like that."

"Oh, you should be," I said mischievously. "You shouldn't ask any member of it to call for morning wine and biscuits when I'm out."

The exotic scent of the orchids was in my nostrils, intoxicating me. I did not care what they said, what they thought.

I believed the night was going to be wonderful because I should see Bevil.

I was right. It was. He spent the evening with me as he had before. We danced scarcely at all. Knowing how conscious I was of my infirmity he suggested we talk instead. This we did, though not seriously, but I felt myself sparkling, or I imagined I was. Perhaps happiness like potent wine makes you believe that of yourself. But Bevil laughed a great deal and at least gave the impression of enjoying my company, for he did not stray from my side the whole of the evening and he told me he was delighted to see me wearing the orchids.

Best of all I knew that we were being watched; that speculations were being made about us.

Can it be possible that right at the beginning of the season Harriet Delvaney who has nothing, but nothing at all, to recommend her since her father married that actress, is going to be the first of the fillies to reach a winning post?

It was a triumph.

We were conspicuous, Bevil and I; for we were always together, and it was only natural that the society papers should notice us.

Aunt Clarissa pointed it out to me; she was half impressed,

half envious. It seemed to her incredible that I, with no better fortune than her girls nowadays, and not a quarter of their beauty, should be the first to be mentioned.

I had come down to breakfast to find my aunt and cousins already at the table.

"Look at that," said Aunt Clarissa.

"Oh, an account of Tuesday's ball."

"Read what it says."

"Mr. Bevil Menfrey, Member of Parliament for a division of Cornwall, is seen to be constantly in the company of Miss Harriet Delvaney. Miss Delvaney is the daughter of the late Sir Edward Delvaney who was Member for the division which Mr. Menfrey now represents. It will be remembered that Sir Edward died some eighteen months ago shortly after his marriage. Is the enjoyment these two charming young people find in each other's company due to politics . . . or . . . ?"

I laughed aloud.

"So we have been noticed."

"I only hope," said Sylvia, "that he is not amusing himself."

"I am sure he is. He's not the man to endure boredom."

"You pretend to be so naïve."

"I, my dear coz?"

"Really, Harriet, you are very flippant," chided my aunt. "This could be a very serious matter."

I did not answer. It was a serious matter. The most serious in the world.

A few days later Bevil called at my aunt's house.

By good fortune or by design he chose a time when my aunt and cousins were paying calls. I was in my room and was startled and delighted when the maid appeared, to tell me that he was in the drawing-room.

"Asking for you, Miss Harriet," she said, with a little grimace. The manners of my aunt and cousins did not endear them to those who worked for them; and consequently the servants here were delighted with my social success in putting *their* noses out of joint—of which of course they had heard, since I had no doubt this was freely discussed below stairs.

I wished that I was not in my plain lavender gingham and wondered whether I had time to change; I looked into my mirror and saw that my hair was untidy as usual. I looked very different from the young lady who had taken such pains to appear at her best at social entertainments.

I said: "Tell Mr. Menfrey that I will be with him in a few minutes."

As soon as the door closed, I threw off my gingham and put on the grey faille dress with a separate bodice and skirt. While I struggled with the hooks I was conscious of the seconds ticking away, but when I had fastened the last one I noticed again the untidiness of my hair and paused to comb it. It had taken a little more than five minutes, to make the transformation. I often thought of those five minutes as some of the most significant of my life.

I hurried down to the library to find Bevil standing with his back to the fireplace. He took both my hands in his and for a few seconds stood there smiling at me.

"What great good fortune to find you in . . . alone."

"My aunt and cousins should not be long," I answered demurely. "Unless they should be unduly delayed."

"Ladies," he said, "have a habit of being unduly delayed." His eyes were laughing at me, and I was aware that he knew I had stopped to change my dress.

"It's very becoming," he went on, "but with such intricate hooking four hands are better than two. Allow me."

He turned round and I felt his fingers as he hooked the dress and then his lips on my neck.

"Bevil!" I cried.

"My reward," he said. "You must always expect to pay for services rendered."

I did not turn round to face him because I knew that my face would betray my delight.

He said rather abruptly: "I'm glad I found you alone. There's something I want to tell you."

"Yes, Bevil?"

"Come and sit down."

He took my arm and we sat on the sofa side by side.

"I'm leaving for Cornwall to-day," he said.

I did not speak; my heart was beating too fast and my throat felt constricted. I should be denied the pleasure of his company at the next functions but he had something to say to me and he had come to say it. I believed I knew what it was and if I were right I would be completely happy. I wanted him to take me away to Cornwall, away from the

London house to which I should surely have to return very soon.

"I've got to be at a meeting there," went on Bevil. "It's absolutely essential; otherwise I shouldn't go."

"Of course."

"The politician's daughter would understand. And Harriet . . ."

The carriage had drawn up outside the door and my aunt and cousins were alighting. I heard my aunt's shrill voice: "Come along, Sylvia."

Bevil looked at me and grimaced. My aunt was in the hall. I heard her penetrating voice. "In the library." Then she was at the door, and sweeping into the room.

"My dear Mr. Menfrey, how perfectly charming of you to call."

I felt deflated. The moment had been at hand and had passed.

Bevil looked rueful too, I imagined.

And as Sylvia and Phyllis appeared and our little tête-à-tête was ruined I assured myself that if he had been on the point of asking me to marry him, it would merely be a postponement, and I should not be too despondent.

It was only later that I realised the important part chance plays in our lives and that stopping to change from gingham to faille had put an alarming question mark in my life which would haunt me for some time to come.

I felt desolate after Bevil had left. I called to see Jenny, and while I was in the house I went up to my old room to find Fanny there.

She was looking unhappy so I asked her if anything was wrong.

"I've been hearing about you in the papers," she said. "They're hinting at a wedding. I didn't much like it."

"What didn't you like?"

"You're growing up now and I reckon you think I shouldn't be talking to you like I used. But I'm taking the liberty because to me you'll always be my girl . . . well, I had you since you were a baby."

"Yes, Fanny, I know, but I'm not a baby any more, you see; and suppose I were to marry. I'm eighteen, you know."

"It ain't that, Miss Harriet, it's . . . it's the way they're coupling your name with . . . Well, I like to think of you settling down and having me with you and then the little 'uns that come along would be mine too."

"There's no reason why that shouldn't happen, Fanny."

She looked fierce. "No, there's no reason and that's how it would be. But I'd like to see you happy and . . . married to the right man."

"You surely wouldn't want to choose him for me?"

"I wouldn't think to go as far as that. But there's some you know that's wrong 'uns."

"I don't know what you're hinting."

"There's gossip and rumours going the rounds and they don't always come to the ears of them they could be most useful to. But I'm not going to mince my words no more, Miss Harriet. I'm talking about that Mr. Bevil Menfrey, that's who. Now it's no use you looking at me all cold and haughty like. I know you don't want to hear a word against him. No more do I want to say it to wound you. But a slap in the face now, is better than a lifetime of misery. Now look here, miss, don't you get into a paddy. I'm worried. I am, and it's all along of what you could so easily fall into."

"What do you know about Mr. Menfrey?"

"That he's one of them Menfreys, that's all. They're bad. It's in 'em, and there's no bones about it. Oh, I know they're nice enough to look at; they know how to lay on the charm. But underneath they're bad. Look at that Miss Gwennan—letting down poor Mr. Harry at the last minute for her own whims. . . . She's one of them Menfreys. They're not to be trusted."

"Do you know something about Mr. Menfrey?"

Fanny pursed her lips and lowered her eyes.

"Fanny!" I took her by the shoulders and shook her. "Tell me. I insist."

"You won't like it, miss."

"I'll like it still less if you attempt to keep anything from me."

"Women. That's what it is. I've heard that he keeps a mistress in a little house at St. John's Wood. And you remember Miss Jessie, the doctor's daughter? Well, she's a governess to a family in Park Lane and I hear that Mr. Menfrey's a frequent visitor—above and below stairs."

"It's all tittle-tattle," I cried.

"Perhaps it is, miss, but when I see you concerned in it then I prick up my ears . . . sharp."

"Why are you telling me all this, Fanny?"

"I'll answer that by telling you something, Miss Harriet. I've never talked to you, have I, about my little 'un . . . my little girl. Somehow I couldn't bring myself to. I could talk to you about the orphanage and all that misery . . . but I couldn't bring myself to talk about my little one. I had a baby girl. See, when I left the orphanage I went into service and the housemaid there had a brother. Billy . . . Billy Carter. He was a sailor and we got married. We hadn't been married a year when the sea took him. Going down to that place in Cornwall brought it all back. I'd lie awake at night and listen to the sea, all noisy and wild, and I'd say, 'That's the sea that took my Billy.' The baby was well on the way and I used to tell myself of nights that it 'ud be better when the baby was born. They said it was all I'd gone through . . . the shock and that. She only lived a day . . . my little baby. I thought I'd die. Then I come to you. There was a little girl baby, the same age as mine and she'd lost her mother. You see, there was a baby without a mother and a mother without a baby. It stood to reason. I was the wet nurse and so in a way I got my baby."

"Oh, Fanny," I said, and threw myself into her arms.

"My baby!" she crooned stroking my hair. "You see . . . my little one wouldn't have had a father and it was like as if you didn't have one either. But then it was different. I didn't cry myself to sleep. I had my baby to think of. It was like Providence. I'd got a baby after all. And that's why I reckon I've got a right to warn you, love. We're close, dearie, you and me . . . and if I had to look on and see you not happy, I reckon it would just about break my heart."

"Dear Fanny," I said, "don't think I don't understand. . . . Don't think I don't appreciate. We'll always be together . . . and my children will be yours as well. But you're wrong about Bevil and the Menfreys."

She shook her head sadly. "And you, my love, you're bewitched by 'em. Do you think I don't know you? Do you think I ain't seen this coming? You know I'm right, don't you? You believe what I've told you?"

I felt as though I wanted to burst into tears. It was unfair of her to thrust her sentimentality at me and then talk scandalously of the man I loved.

I turned away from her. "I don't like gossip, Fanny," I said. "Oh, don't think I don't know that your concern is all for me. I've always known I could trust you, and you know you can me. But I know the Menfreys better than you ever can."

" I'm worried," she insisted.

I put my arms about her. "Fanny, haven't you learned yet that I can take care of myself?"

But she only shook her head.

When Fanny had left me I sat on the edge of my bed. I was miserable because although I pretended not to believe Fanny's accusations against Bevil my common sense told me that there was a very good chance of their being true. It was the Menfrey way of life. Infidelity was as natural to them as breathing. I was foolishly romantic if I thought that Bevil would change the habits of a lifetime merely because he had met me. Had I not always known this? Yes. But I had had a foolish idea that once he was my husband he would miraculously become all that I desired him to be. And what I asked of Bevil was that he should be exactly as he was and had always been except in one respect—he should be faithful to one woman, and I was that woman.

Even now I was deceiving myself. I could not trust Bevil, if while he was paying court to me—and surely he was doing so—he had a mistress in St. John's Wood and at the same time was in love with Jessica Trelarken. Only a man with an elastic morality could behave so—but was that the Menfrey morality?

Could anyone who was capable of such deceit be the rock on which one longed to build one's future life? How could I trust such a man; how could I feel secure?

That was what I needed, what I had always missed. Security. The desperate desire of the young and vulnerable. My father had withheld it and I had found it in Fanny; and now Fanny was warning me, trying to protect me from straying into the morass of marriage with what she considered an undesirable husband in the same way as she had snatched me up once, I remember, as I was about to run into a bed of nettles.

I went thoughtfully back to my aunt's house.

We were in the sewing-room with Miss Glenister and there were yards of white satin decorated with tiny gold flowers spread out on the table.

Aunt Clarissa had bought the material cheaply and was crowing over her bargain. Miss Glenister was nervously measuring it and calculating what sort of a gown it would make, while Sylvia and Phyllis were quarrelling as to which of them it would most become.

I listened as I was listening during these days, with amusement and interest. I wanted to think of such trivial matters; it was one way of stopping my thoughts running in uncomfortable directions.

" Bishops' sleeves," cooed Sylvia.

" They don't become you. You are too plump," retorted Phyllis.

" Perhaps, miss, you would like a flounced skirt . . . in which, I can tell you, you look very stubby."

" Now," cried Aunt Clarissa, " if you are going to be naughty, I shall wish I had not found this bargain. Miss Glenister will say what can be done and then we shall decide for whom the dress shall be made."

" It must be in time for Lady Carront's ball," said Sylvia.

" And that is in two days' time," I pointed out.

" Oh, I'd sit up all night if need be to finish the gown," declared Miss Glenister meekly.

I fingered the material and holding it up to my face glanced at myself in the mirror.

Sylvia laughed. " Mamma did buy it for one of us, cousin," she reminded me.

" I know that, but I thought there would be no objection to my examining it."

" It is too delicate for you."

" Perhaps for us all," I said. " It is quite elegant."

" And why should we not be elegant?"

" We should if we could, of course."

" Clever, as usual. Well, your cleverness didn't stop a certain person from putting to flight, did it?"

" Who has put to flight?"

" You know full well. After making you rather conspicuous he took fright, I suppose, in case you had ideas."

I was hot with anger and turned furiously on my cousin, but just at that moment there was a knock on the door and one of the maids entered.

" It's one of the maids from Westminster Square, madam. She's asking for Miss Harriet."

I ran out of the room down to the hall where Fanny was

E

waiting. I knew at once that something was wrong . . .
terribly wrong. For a few seconds she looked as though she
were vainly searching for the right words to convey the
enormity of this calamity.

" Miss Harriet . . . it's your stepmother."

" She's ill?"

Fanny shook her head.

" She's dead," she said.

SIX

The days had become unreal. I could not believe this was
actually happening. Scenes kept coming into my mind like
hideous pictures painted by a madman. I saw the faces of
Polden, Mrs. Trant and the servants—scared yet excited,
horrified yet delighted. This was a tragedy such as they read
of, and they at the centre of it!

They were saying that my stepmother had been poisoned.
There was going to be an inquest and then they would know
for sure and they would find out why she had died, who had
been responsible for her death.

Aunt Clarissa summoned me to the library. She looked five
years older than she had that morning when she had been
discussing the gold-embroidered satin.

" Harriet, this is shocking."

" Yes, Aunt."

" Some overdose of drug, they're saying. It's terrible.
There'll be a scandal. *And* in the middle of the season. This
could be disastrous . . . quite disastrous."

" Oh!" I said, and I heard my voice breaking into a laugh
which alarmed me. " The season!"

" It's no laughing matter, I can tell you." Poor Aunt
Clarissa, she had no sensitivity of her own and failed to
recognise it in others. " Who do you think would want to
link themselves with a family in which such scandals occur?
This will be fatal to all our hopes. It couldn't have happened
at a worse time."

" It couldn't have been worse whenever it happened," I said.
" Aunt Clarissa, she's dead . . . *dead*!"

" Don't shriek. The servants will hear. They're no doubt
discussing this now. I really think, Harriet, that you shouldn't

stay here. After all if *you* aren't here, it won't be so blatantly connected with *us*, will it? Of course it will come out that she was Edward's wife. Oh, how could he have been so blind? He was always so wise . . . except in this one thing. Infatuated by this dreadful woman . . . and although she is dead I still say it . . . infatuated by a woman who as soon as he is dead kills herself . . . or worse still allows someone to kill her."

Listening to Aunt Clarissa I felt the hysteria rising in me. I said: " Are you turning me out, then, Aunt?"

She did not answer so I went on: " I'll leave the first thing in the morning."

I was exhausted that night but I scarcely slept and when I did I kept starting up in horror. Nightmares tormented me and I was glad to see the dawn.

The maid who brought in my hot water looked at me curiously. I was connected with a tragedy—sudden death, suicide . . . or murder.

I bathed and dressed very slowly, delaying the time when I must leave. How strange that I should want to linger in my aunt's house! I had always thought that I should have longed to leave it, and that this should be so, filled me with an even greater desolation. Never in my life had I felt so lonely, so insecure, so uncertain of the future.

There was a knock on my door and one of the maids entered.

" You're wanted, miss. In the library."

I nodded and pretended to look at my reflection in the mirror and to pat my hair, lest she should see the misery on my face.

I could no longer delay. I had packed my bag. I was ready to leave. I expected to find Aunt Clarissa in the library where she would tell me that in all our interests it was best for me to go and that she had ordered the carriage to come in ten minutes' time.

Slowly I went down to the library. Aunt Clarissa was there, but she was not alone.

Lady Menfrey came forward and took my hand in hers. She kissed me.

" My dear Harriet," she murmured. " My poor, dear Harriet."

And then I saw Bevil rising from the arm-chair. He took me in his arms and held me against him. I felt weak. The transition was so sudden. From despair, from the sorrow of aloneness to the comfort of the one person in the world with whom I wanted to be more than any other. I could not speak; I was afraid that if I attempted to I should burst into tears.

"My dearest Harriet," he said in a voice so wonderfully tender that it made me want to weep, "this has been quite terrible for you. You mustn't worry any more. We're here . . . we're here to look after you."

Still I could not speak.

"Harriet!" It was Aunt Clarissa. "Mr. Menfrey and his mother have travelled up from Cornwall for the purpose of looking after you until this wretched affair is over. Lady Menfrey has suggested to me that she takes you to Mr. Menfrey's house where you should remain with her until some plans can be made. I think it is an excellent idea."

I felt relief breaking over my face.

I heard myself cry, "Oh, yes, oh, yes . . . *please*."

I was driven to Bevil's small town house in a quiet little cul-de-sac on the north side of the Park. Here Lady Menfrey remained with me. There were only two servants—a maid and a housekeeper who cooked the little which Bevil had needed in the past. The place was merely the *pied-à terre* he had acquired since he became a Member of Parliament.

Lady Menfrey insisted on my going straight to bed, for she declared I was exhausted even if I didn't realise it. I was submissive; I found it the utmost luxury to put myself into the hands of this kind and gentle woman, particularly as Bevil was making every effort to show me how anxious he was on my behalf.

We talked little of the tragedy, but of Menfreya; and Lady Menfrey said that it was Bevil's wish—and hers—that as soon as the inquest was over I should return with them to Menfreya to recover from this terrible shock.

Fervently I told them that there was nothing I should like better, nothing I needed more. So it was arranged.

Thus I lived through those days that followed the tragedy; they were long, dreamlike days, but because I saw Bevil frequently and was constantly in the company of Lady Menfrey, whose main idea seemed to make me feel as though she was concerned for me as she would have been for a daughter,

I felt I had something to cling to, and she was the best companion I could have had. She was still serene, she, the heiress who had been kidnapped by Endelion and who had fallen in love so romantically and then been forced to adjust her romantic ideas and learn to live with a man who could never be faithful and whose irresistible passion had been not for her but for her fortune! But here she was, beautiful still, with a different beauty from that of the Menfreys— calm, classical features, gentle, kindly and, could I say, resigned. The result doubtless of a life of compromise and adjustment to the wild ways of the Menfreys who, although they were worldly and perhaps selfish and mercenary—for Menfreya—were the most charming people in the world.

And there was Bevil, so anxious for me, so eager that everything should be done for my comfort, tender, in a manner which conveyed to me a suppressed passion. His hands lingered on my arm; his eyes were caressing; and about him there was an air of waiting which seemed to me significant. It was as though I were already engaged to marry him. I was certain that I should soon be. Lady Menfrey conveyed it in her manner, and when she spoke of Menfreya she spoke of it as my home.

That was how I lived through those days of tension when the Menfreys sought to impose on an image of tragedy one of living happily ever after.

They succeeded and I loved them for it—Lady Menfrey as the mother I had never had and Bevil more than I had ever believed it was possible to love anyone.

There was no need, Bevil said, for me to go to the inquest. It might be unpleasant and I had not been in the house when the tragedy had occurred.

I was anxious that he should make any arrangements he considered suitable.

" And as soon as it is over," he said, " you should go to Menfreya. You can travel with Mother and I'll join you in a few days' time."

I replied that I did not know how to thank them, and that I could not imagine how I could have gone back to that house . . . and lived there through these days.

Bevil took my hand and pressed it reassuringly.

" Well, you know now that you can safely put yourself in the hands of the Menfreys," he said. I thought he was about to make some declaration of his feelings for me, but he didn't—not in words, although his looks were full of tenderness and, I believed, a desire to protect me for ever.

On the day of the inquest even Bevil and Lady Menfrey were apprehensive although they tried to hide this from me.

Lady Menfrey was in her room most of the morning, preparing to leave for Cornwall, she said, which she thought we might do the next day.

"I shall need some of my things," I said. "I shall have to go . . ."

She shook her head. "There's no need. Write from Cornwall and send for that maid of yours. She will bring what you need."

"I'll do that," I said. "But the house—what of it now? I feel that I never want to go into it again. I should never be able to forget . . ."

"There's no need to concern yourself with that as yet. Leave it as it is. There will be the servants to consider. You need help in these matters. My husband and Bevil will give you that help. Let everything stay as it is at the moment. The thing for you to do is to get away . . . as soon as this unfortunate business is over."

"Sometimes I think it will never be over."

"My dear child, what do you mean?"

"I suppose that I shall never forget . . . that it will always be in my mind. . . ."

"Oh, but tragedies seem so when they are immediately beside us."

"I find it a great relief to let you make my decisions."

"I hope you will always agree to let us help you in this way."

I was certain then that soon I should be Bevil's wife.

It was the day of the inquest, which Bevil had attended. I was in the small guest-room overlooking the tiny walled garden when he came in. Lady Menfrey was in the drawing-room and I did not go down, because I felt the need to calm myself.

I had felt restless all that day. I had pictured the courtroom so vividly that I felt I was there. So much depended on the coroner's verdict.

Eventually Lady Menfrey came up to my room and told

me that Bevil was back; he wanted to see me. The verdict was death by misadventure.

"But how?" I breathed.

"Come and see Bevil. He'll talk to you. Then we're going to get right away to-morrow."

As I entered the drawing-room Bevil came to me and took me into his arms.

"It's over," he said. "God, was I relieved! I don't know what I expected. This is the end of it. Come and sit down."

We sat on the sofa and he kissed me.

"But, Bevil," I said, "what happened? How could it be?"

"It came out that she had been taking arsenic . . . for her complexion. Apparently it's not unusual. Women take it to make themselves beautiful and unfortunately the stuff does have that effect . . . for a time anyway."

"Arsenic!" I cried. "For her complexion! Of course there *was* something about her complexion! It was quite lovely but . . ."

"Evidently the effects of the drug. The coroner went on about it. Some people use it in a lotion but others are foolhardy enough to take it internally. Where she got it, they couldn't find out. Naturally her supplier would lie low. One of her theatrical friends, I suspect. But your Fanny had seen her taking it in beverages . . . lemonade and such things."

"But the idea of taking arsenic! How dreadful!"

"Apparently it's used a great deal by doctors in making up medicines, but they, of course, know what they're doing. The coroner referred to the Maybrick case. There was quite a stir about this practice years ago during the Maybrick trial. The husband died of arsenical poisoning and the wife was accused of murdering him. She was condemned to death but reprieved at the last moment—I think because there was a doubt, and he could have taken the stuff much the same as Jenny did. You see, it's not really so unusual, but highly dangerous as in the cases of James Maybrick and your stepmother. They found a quantity of it in her room. The coroner delivered a sermon on the folly of ignorant people using drugs the power of which they don't understand—and the verdict of death by misadventure was brought in."

I couldn't shut out the vision of bright pretty little Jenny . . . dead. Bevil knew this and tried to comfort me.

"It's over now," he said. "To-morrow you'll be leaving

with my mother. I shall be with you in a few days. Will you begin making arrangements at once, because we don't want any delay."

" Arrangements . . . ?".

He laughed. How confident he was, rightly so, for I could never have resisted him even if I had tried.

" For the wedding, of course. It'll be rather unconventional, but then we are. Married from the bridegroom's house. *That* will cause a flutter."

" There is the house on the island," I suggested.

" Picture it," he said. " The bride stepping into the boat in her wedding finery. The south-west wind—if in evidence, and you could be almost certain that it would be—carrying off the veil and orange blossom . . ."

" And the boat overturning and the bride being washed ashore by the gigantic waves, late for her wedding. . . ."

" I've just remembered," said Bevil. " You haven't said you will yet."

" Will . . . what?"

He looked at me disbelievingly; he went on to his knees and taking my hand said: " Madam, if you'll marry me I will give you the keys of heaven. . . ."

" The keys of Menfreya will do for a start," I answered solemnly.

He was beside me, laughing, embracing me. " Harriet, do you know why I love you? You amuse me. That's why. And I love to be amused more—or almost more—than anything else. I want you to say now that you love me, that you adore me in fact, and that you want to be my wife as much—or almost, for I don't think anyone else could feel quite so madly eager as I do—as I want to be your husband."

" You make a wonderful proposal, Bevil," I said, " although a slightly flippant one."

" My darling, it is because my emotions are so deeply touched that I am flippant. I really should be on my knees telling you how much I want this . . . how I always have . . . and there has never been anyone else I could love as I love you. Dearest Harriet, you belong to us . . . to Menfreya. It was always meant that we should be together, there. You do agree, don't you?"

" I love you, Bevil. I couldn't deny that if I wanted to because I've made it plain in the past and I've made it plain now. But you . . ."

"Yes, what of me? Aren't I making it plain now?"

"You are telling me you love me, but you didn't always, of course. How could you love a plain child with a limp and a rather brusque and generally unfortunate manner?"

He put his lips on mine. He had all the most charming and irresistible gestures that a girl deeply in love looks for and refuses to tell herself that they may have been acquired through long practice.

"An interesting child, an amusing child, who had some crazy notion that she wasn't as pretty as some children merely because she didn't have the look of a brainless doll. I don't like dolls, Harriet, but I adore one living vital young woman whom I am going to marry whether she accepts me or not."

"You mean you would kidnap me?"

"Certainly. It's a tradition in the family."

"And therefore a good foundation on which to build a marriage."

"You have an example before you."

Had I? Lady Menfrey was serenely happy, yes. But how had she lived through the years of humiliation when Sir Endelion's affairs with other women had been the talk of the neighbourhood? Was that Bevil's idea of a good marriage? An unfaithful husband was perhaps one order of life; wifely complaisance another.

No, I thought, it should not be so with me. I was not another Lady Menfrey. But I was too content with the immediate prospect to concern myself with the future.

"The kidnapping will not be necessary," I said. "So you need not go ahead with your plans for that. Instead tell me more reasons why you want to marry me."

He put his head on one side and regarded me with mock seriousness. I thought: We shall always be able to laugh together. That had been the essence of my relationship with Gwennan—our minds were in tune. Fleetingly I thought of Gwennan who had run away on the eve of her marriage. I heard Fanny's voice of grim prophecy. "You can't trust those Menfreys."

"As the daughter of an M.P. you'll make a good M.P.'s wife."

"A very practical consideration."

"Why not be practical? Choosing a wife is a matter worthy of the utmost consideration. Far more than selecting a Member, you know. They can be out after five years. A wife must last for a lifetime. So, an M.P.'s daughter is the perfect wife for a rising M.P., particularly when it was for the same constituency."

"So you will expect me to help you in elections, and the necessary nursing process in between."

"Certainly, I shall. You'll be excellent."

I felt the tears in my eyes then and I could not stop them. I was so ashamed for he had never seen me cry before. In fact I couldn't remember when I had.

He drew away from me and I have never seen tenderness such as his as he took a handkerchief and wiped away my tears.

"At such a time," he scolded. "Tears . . . and Harriet!"

"They don't go together, do they? Don't imagine I'm going to be a weeping wife. It's because I'm happy."

He too was moved and he sought to hide it.

"You don't know anything yet," he said. "This is only the beginning. We're going to be known throughout the Duchy as the happy Menfreys."

Before I left for Cornwall I went to see Mr. Greville of Greville, Baker and Greville that he might explain my financial position to me. He told me that the death of my stepmother had made me the heiress to a considerable fortune. Everything would now be mine when I reached the age of twenty-one or on the occasion of my marriage, which must have the approval of himself and the other executor of the will.

"I have already heard from Mr. Menfrey that you have promised to marry him and I can set your mind at rest without delay. There will be no objection and your fortune will pass into your hands almost immediately after the marriage has taken place."

"What of the second executor?"

"Sir Endelion Menfrey." Mr. Greville's rugged features were as near a smile as they could come. "I think your father would be very pleased by your engagement. It was a match which was talked over by him and Sir Endelion when you were a child."

"Then," I said blankly, "we are doing what was expected of us."

The plump white hands were spread out on the desk and

their owner surveyed them with satisfaction. "I am sure," he said, in his precise dry manner, "that this is a highly desirable union and I can tell you, Miss Delvaney, that it simplifies matters greatly." He picked up some papers on his desk as though weighing them, and looked at me over his gold-rimmed pince-nez. "Now, your allowance will go on as usual until we have the formalities settled. I hear that you will shortly be travelling down to Cornwall in the company of Lady Menfrey. Excellent! Excellent! And the marriage will take place there. Congratulations. I do not think there could have been a more satisfactory finale to these unfortunate happenings."

I felt as though I were being neatly filed away in a cabinet labelled " Heiress safely disposed of as prearranged. Unfortunate matters satisfactorily settled."

And as I went out to the carriage I wished that my father and the Menfreys had not discussed my future so thoroughly. I wished that Bevil and I had met a few months before and been swept off our feet by an irresistible passion.

I was beginning to suspect that for all my display of cynicism I was at heart a romantic.

"There is no reason for postponing our departure for Cornwall," said Lady Menfrey. "There you will be able to plan what you intend to do about the house . . . about everything. Bevil will naturally see that what you want is carried out, when you have made your decision."

I thought of the house where life would be going on as it had before the accident. It would be a silent house. I imagined the servants speaking in whispers, tiptoeing past the room where Jenny's body had been found. They would be wondering what the future held for them and it was unfair to keep them in suspense.

Fanny would, of course, come with me, but the others would have to find fresh places and were no doubt anxious about their future. I discussed this with Bevil and as a result I again went along to see Greville, Baker and Greville, and it was decided that annuities should be arranged for Mrs. Trant, Polden and the elderly servants and gratuities for the younger and that although they should remain in their posts for the next two or three months they should begin making other arrangements and if any succeeded in finding new places they would be released.

I felt relieved having settled this and went along to the house the day before I was due to leave for Cornwall.

I asked Mrs. Trant to summon all the servants to the library and there I told them of my situation and what had been arranged. I felt deeply moved to see their relief, and on behalf of them all Polden expressed gratitude and their wishes for my happiness.

" You'll be selling the house I reckon, Miss Harriet," said Mrs. Trant.

" Certainly."

" Well, miss if ever you and Mr. Menfrey should be needing the services of any of us . . . you would only have to say so and speaking on behalf of us all we should be glad to leave what posts we had and return to you."

I thanked them all and then went up to my old room with Fanny to discuss what I wanted her to bring to me in Cornwall when she came down a few days after me.

I tried to be practical when we reached my room.

" I shall discard most of these things," I said. " We shall pass through Paris on our honeymoon and I intend to buy some clothes there. So just a few things will be needed, Fanny."

" There'll be your books and some of the little things you cherished."

I thought of them. My postcard album; letters which I had always kept; little things which had pleased me; a box covered in shells in which I kept buttons and needles; a musical box which played Widdicombe Fair and which William Lister had bought for me when he had taken a brief holiday in the Devon village; a row of pearls which my father had given to me; his Christmas present—he preferred to forget my birthdays—over the years; one pearl added each year. I had never liked it although now, looking at the perfectly shaped beads of that deep creamy colour, at the flashing diamonds in the clasp, I realised that it was a beautiful ornament and probably worth a great deal. But to me it had been symbolic of his lack of interest. Custom demanded that he give me something, so there was the pearl, costing so much more than the baubles Fanny had given me, yet far less precious.

I thought again of how much I owed Fanny, who had understood how a child would have felt on waking on Christmas morning and looking in vain for the bulging stocking. She it was who had told me the Christmas legend; she who had bought those oranges, nuts, bags of fondants, those fascinating cut-out cardboard marvels, penny plain and tuppence coloured, those sixpenny dolls. Fanny had put the happiness into my Christmases when she roamed the market stalls looking for gaudy glittering objects which would delight a child, not my father in the thickly carpeted jeweller's salon selecting the pearl to add to my necklace which would prove an investment.

I put a few things on my bed—the music box from William Lister, my books—yes, they must come, all of them, because they had provided the escape from fact. *Elsie Dinsmore*, *Misunderstood*, *The Wide Wide World*, *Peep Behind the Scenes*, *A Basket of Flowers* . . . stories of children whose lot had been as unhappy as my own; *Little Women* (how I had thrown myself into that delightful family, taking on the parts of Meg, Jo, Beth and Amy in turns); *Jane Eyre* and *Wuthering Heights*. Stories of endurance and triumph. I could never part with them. Fanny watched me. "You don't want *that*," she said.

It was the cut-out cardboard stage—tuppence coloured.

"Fanny," I said, "I remember the first time I saw it. It was . . . wonderful. Six o'clock on Christmas morning."

"You would wake early. I used to lie there listening for you. I was awake at five on those mornings. You used to get out of bed in the dark."

"Yes, and feel the stocking; and then take it back to bed and hold it . . . guessing. I had a pact with myself that I mustn't open it till the first streak of light was in the sky; because if I did it would disappear and all be a dream."

"You and your fancies!"

"If it hadn't been for you, Fanny, there wouldn't have been a stocking."

"Oh, some of the others would have seen to it."

"I don't think so. They were the best mornings of the year. I remember waking up a week later and the terrible disappointment because it wasn't Christmas, and that I should have to wait fifty-one weeks for the next."

"Children!" said Fanny, smiling tenderly.

I stood up suddenly and threw myself into her arms.

"Oh, Fanny, dear Fanny, we'll always be together."

She was militant in her fierceness. "You bet we will, miss. I'd like to see the one as could part me from you."

I released her and sat down on the bed.

"I shall be glad to be finished with this house. I don't remember ever being really happy here except on those Christmas mornings and times with you. Do you remember how we used to go out into the markets—how we used to toss with the pieman and buy hot chestnuts?"

"You always loved the markets, miss."

"They seemed so exciting and colourful and those people who were so anxious to sell their goods . . . they were poor and I was rich . . . but I used to envy them, Fanny."

"You didn't know what their lives were, miss. You just thought selling there in the market was a nice sort of game, and never having felt chilblains driving you mad with the itch and soreness, and the rheumatics bending you double, you just thought what a good time they had. You can't always know what's going on out of sight, can you?"

"I was too sorry for myself in those days, Fanny. Now all that is over. I shall expect you in Cornwall by the end of the week."

"You can depend upon it, miss, that as soon as I've cleared up here I'll be on that train. And what about all the furniture and everything?"

"I suppose the good pieces will come down to Menfreya; the rest we'll sell. Mr. Bevil will make the arrangements."

"I reckon he'll be making all the arrangements in the future, miss."

I smiled, and I suppose my happiness shone through the smile, because she was silent for a moment; then I noticed her own expression harden and I understood, because Fanny was not usually one to hide her true feelings, that she disapproved of my engagement.

"I hope so, Fanny. As my husband it is natural that he should!"

"Oh, yes, he'll make them all right."

"Fanny, for heaven's sake stop it. This is a time for congratulations—not doleful prophecy."

"The time for prophecy is when it comes naturally to make it."

"What on earth do you mean by that?"

"I'm not at ease in my mind, miss. Couldn't you wait a while?"

"Wait, Fanny? What for?"

"You've been rushed into this."

"Rushed. I've been waiting for Bevil to ask me to marry him for years."

"I'm afraid. . . ."

"Don't be. Now I'm not going to discuss this with you any more. Everything will be all right."

"There's one thing I'd like to know."

"All right. What is it?"

"Did he ask you *before* your stepmother died . . . or after?"

"What does that mean?"

"It means a lot to me, miss. Before you had only your income, didn't you? I don't understand these things much but I reckon when your stepmother died, all that money was yours . . . without strings like . . . as there was with her. Well, you see if he waited till after she died . . ."

I could have struck her because I was so angry, and I knew myself well enough to understand that I was whipping up anger to hide fear. Why had she put that vague uneasy thought of mine into words so that now I could no longer ignore it? I had to bring it out and examine it in the light of day.

"What nonsense," I said. "He was going to ask me before she died . . . only we were interrupted."

If only Aunt Clarissa had not come in at that moment when he had called on me! I was certain then that he was about to ask me to marry him. But was he? If he had meant to ask me wouldn't he have made the opportunity?

Fanny was looking at me steadily, her eyes dark with fear and suspicion. She was firmly convinced that Bevil was marrying me for my money; more than that, she had watered those seeds of doubt in my own mind so that they were already springing into life.

She twisted her hands awkwardly. "You see, Miss Harriet, I want you to be happy. I just want everything of the best for you. And when things start to go wrong they have a habit of going on that way."

"What on earth do you mean?"

"I can't help thinking of that poor lady. She's on my mind. I see her looking at her lovely skin in the glass and then putting that stuff in her drink . . . and then going like that."

"It's horrifying. I'm trying not to think of it, Fanny, but I can't get her out of my mind. Dying like that . . . without being prepared."

"Without being prepared," whispered Fanny. "Yes, that was how it was. She didn't have a warning. She was there one day and gone the next. I expect my Billy had a warning. He'd hear the storm rising, wouldn't he? They'd be fighting the storm and they'd know there was danger all around . . . but she, poor lady, she didn't know. . . ."

"We've got to stop thinking of it, Fanny."

"Thinking can't do no good," she agreed.

"Now stop worrying about me. Everything will be all right."

Her mouth was set; her eyes hard; she looked like a general going into battle.

And although she had made those doubts spring up in my mind I knew that as long as Fanny lived I should always have someone to love me.

Lady Menfrey and I were met at Liskeard and I shall never forget driving to Menfreya. The lanes made narrower by the summer foliage on the banks had never seemed so green and colourful; I sniffed the warm breeze as we came near to the sea and when I saw the towers of Menfreya I could have wept with emotion. Now it was more than a house which had caught my fancy, more than an ancient fascinating house: it was my home.

There was the house on the island; and there was the cliff with the walls of Menfreya rising stark above it on the coast side, as though it were part of the cliff face itself.

Through the porch under the clock tower with the ancient clock which was never allowed to stop, into the courtyard, where we alighted. Sir Endelion was standing in the great porch waiting to receive us.

"Welcome, welcome, my dearest child."

I was taken into his embrace; I was kissed.

Never had a bride been more warmly welcomed by her new family.

Those days at Menfreya stand out in my memory. I wanted, I told them, to explore the house—every room and passage, every alcove, every nook.

"I think it's the most wonderful house in the world," I told Sir Endelion and Lady Menfrey on that first day.

"That's fortunate since it's to be your home, my dear," replied Sir Endelion.

"I want to see everything. . . ."

"You'll find that the east wing is in need of repair."

I smiled, remembering the table with the rubies which were no longer there. Menfreya needed money to be lavished on it by those who were fortunate enough to be taken under its roof. But I should never grudge spending my money on the preservation of the house.

The day after my arrival Sir Endelion himself took me on a tour of inspection. He was delighted to show me everything, and told me as we studied the shield over the fireplace in the great hall that nothing in the world could have made him happier than this engagement.

"It was what your father wished and it is what I have always wanted. The union of our two families. Your name, my dear, will be inscribed on the shield, for there are the names of all the families who have been linked in marriage with the Menfreys."

I studied those names and I wondered what the owners of them had felt when they had come to this great house as brides. Very soon Delvaney would be added to them and I thought of the names going on when my sons brought home their wives.

It was a happy sense of belonging, and that was what I had always wanted.

There was so much to see and admire, so much which I had never seen before and which now had a special interest because it was to be my home. There was the wonderful mosaic floor in the great hall; the staircase and the suits of armour, the inevitable portraits in the gallery. There were so many in whom I discovered the Menfrey look. They could have been Bevil or Sir Endelion dressed in the costume of another period.

I went into the chapel which was never used but on whose altar fresh candles were kept; I was shown the secret room in the buttress, and Sir Endelion told me the story of the Menfrey who had kept the woman he loved there, unknown to his family.

"The story is that the clock in the tower stopped and no

one could make it go. Then the master of the house came home and went to the secret room and found his mistress and her child dead. But don't you believe all you hear about the Menfreys, my dear. There are enough stories about our evil doings to make a One Hundred and One Nights Entertainment. I don't think you'll find us as black as we're painted. Tell me, Harriet, you don't think we're half bad, do you?"

"I have known you too long to be afraid of what I may discover."

"And soon you'll be one of us. Bevil's a lucky fellow. I've told him so, and I don't think you're going to be so hard done by either."

I loved seeing the place and hearing the stories.

But Lady Menfrey was eager that preparations for the wedding should be put in hand without delay, so we went to Plymouth and chose the material for my wedding gown, and there we passed the theatre in which Gwennan had met Benedict Bellairs and I was sad thinking of Gwennan and wondering why she had never written to let us know what was happening to her. What fun it would have been if she had been with me now! Sisters in truth! If only she had married Harry Leveret and was now settled happily at Chough Towers with him, how pleasant it would have been!

We chose the white satin for my wedding gown and I was to wear the veil which Lady Menfrey herself had worn and which had been worn by her predecessor.

She did not mention Gwennan and I was surprised, for I had thought that coming into Plymouth must remind her.

Bevil came down to Cornwall and the banns were put up. When I went driving with him through the countryside, we called on several of the neighbouring squires and were greeted with a great show of friendliness.

"I knew your father. Such a charming man. How happy he would be if he could see this day."

"So appropriate. I am sure you will be a great help in the constituency."

"Such a suitable match. We are all quite delighted."

Bevil would give imitations of our hosts as we drove along. It was a little malicious but very funny and I found that I was constantly laughing in his company. It was the laughter of happiness, but then that is the best laughter of all.

I was learning about Bevil. He had a quick wit; he was hot-tempered; he was kind, but when he was in a rage he seemed capable of injustice; repentance quickly followed, and although inherent pride made it difficult for him to admit he was wrong, his sense of justice was even greater than his pride. I was never quite sure whether he was as much in love with me as he implied. He was fond of me—he always had been—but was he more in love with the suitability of the match than with my person? I felt fearful and wondered whether he could have been equally fond of any girl who obviously cared for him and had enough money to make her good for Menfreya. Sometimes in my room I looked at myself critically. My appearance had improved since my engagement, for happiness can give some beauty to any face, but I could not help being conscious of the manner in which his eyes would light up at the sight of a pretty girl; he had a special smile for them all, even a milkmaid whom we passed in the lanes.

When we called on Dr. Syms I wondered what Bevil was thinking. Here it was that Gwennan had been brought when she had had her accident and he had first seen Jessica, but if he was remembering those days he gave no sign.

" Dr. Syms," he said jovially, " you'll come to the wedding?"

" I'll be there, duty permitting." Dr. Syms, chubby-faced, middle-aged and energetic, was beaming his congratulations. " But if somebody's baby chooses to make an appearance at that time . . . well, I shall hear all about it, for there seems to be nothing else people can talk of but the Menfreya wedding."

Mrs. Syms took us into her drawing-room and we drank wine while we talked of the wedding and the constituency and what was likely to happen at the next election. She was, I discovered, an ardent worker for the party.

" I'm sure you'll be such an *asset*," she told me. " An M.P. needs a wife; and your being the daughter of the previous Member is going to appeal. I hear your father was such a fine Member; and now that he is gone and we're back in the old tradition of a Menfrey for Lansella, it's so charming that our present Member should be the husband of the daughter of the old one. It'll be as though the seat never really went out of the family. That will mean a great deal here."

I began to get a glimpse of what my future life would be. I should work for the party; I should have to open bazaars and perhaps speak from platforms. It was exciting though a little alarming, but Bevil would be there. I pictured myself making witty speeches—Mrs. Menfrey, the wife of the M.P.—and a pleasant picture of the future began to grow.

"I'm so glad we came here," Mrs. Syms told me. "It's more interesting than being in the town. Yes, we were in Plymouth, but there seems to be so much more social life in a place like this. Mind you, it's strenuous. Poor Dr. Trelarken killed himself with the work. Such a charming man . . . his daughter, too. You knew her, of course."

"Very slightly."

"Rather sad. The poor girl was left almost penniless. I hear she went to London or somewhere to be a governess. It's no life for a girl—and one so beautiful. She was a real beauty. She might marry—but it's difficult for a girl in her position. Life can be very difficult in those circumstances . . . very difficult indeed."

When we drove away, I said, "She's a talkative woman."

"She talked enough for a politician. Actually she ought to be in Parliament herself. A pity they don't let women in. Perhaps they will one day."

"They're very different from the Trelarkens." I heard the high-pitched note in my voice and I wondered whether Bevil recognised it. It was a sign of emotion.

He was silent and I glanced sideways at him to see that he was smiling.

"Poor Jessica," I went on.

"Bad luck for her," he agreed.

"I always remember my own governess, Miss James. She was a timid woman who seemed to be in fear of losing her post—timid, that is, except with me, whom she was inclined to bully."

"It's no life for a woman in the wrong family."

"I wonder how Jessica likes it?"

He did not answer, and I was afraid that if I pursued the subject further I would be unable to control my feelings and let loose my suspicions and jealousies.

There was no time for brooding. Only three weeks to the

wedding! Lady Menfrey had decided to fill the house with guests who would be mainly friends from London—parliamentary friends who Bevil hoped would be my friends, since I was going to be of use to him in his work. There would be local friends too.

William Lister, my father's old secretary, who now worked in the same capacity for Bevil, was making most of the arrangements. It was pleasant to see him again and I was delighted to guess that he was happier working with Bevil than he had been with my father.

Fanny had arrived to look after me. She irritated me by her obviously resigned attitude; it was as though she was facing some unavoidable disaster and she was determined to put on as good a face as possible. But this was just a small irritation in a wonderful existence. I was happy. Bevil was constantly in my company. He had even wanted to come to the dressmaker's to see me fitted into my dress, until his mother indignantly forbade it as unlucky. We discussed our future life, which seemed to be suffused by a rosy light like the dawn, and I was reminded of that time when I had run away and awakened after a fearful night to see Menfreya in the morning.

I was fanciful. I was happy. I was going to surprise him by the manner in which I would help him. I read politics and Bevil was first amused then impressed when I could discuss Free Trade and Protection with him.

I was glad enough to leave to him the disposal of the London house. He said that William Lister would deal with all that while we were away on our honeymoon. My father had collected some valuable pieces of furniture, and Lister, who was an expert on such things, would see that anything of value was brought down to Menfreya, where there was plenty of room to house it. The rest could be sold.

We were going to the South of France—to a little town in the mountains from which we should be able to look down on the Riviera. He had been there before and it was ideal for a honeymoon. Moreover the weather at this time of the year would be perfect.

The wedding was almost on us and when I could rid myself of a slight uneasiness I was completely happy. I kept thinking of Gwennan who had run away and I was terrified that something would happen to prevent my marriage. Then I thought of all the women whom Bevil had loved and I wondered how different his feeling for me was from what he had felt for others. He assured me that it was, and with such sincerity that I believed him; but I was beginning to know Bevil very well indeèd. When he desired something he did so with such enthusiasm that he believed he desired it more than anything else in the world. But one desire passed, and there was another to replace it. Deep down in my heart I knew that happiness was not a prize on the mountain top which, when you had reached it, was yours for ever. Happiness was a prize, but it was only yours for a brief moment and guarding it was as difficult as attaining it in the first place. Happiness came in moments. Elusive. Unpredictable. It came when Bevil's eyes opened wide in appreciation of some bright remark, when he turned to me in a sudden realisation of the bond between us, when he said from the heart, " I love you, Harriet Delvaney. There's no one quite like you." He used my surname often in moments of emotion; I suspected, because he did not want to betray the depths of his feelings. He, who was accustomed to quick desires, violent and irresistible while they lasted, was a little surprised that love could walk side by side with passion. At least that was what I liked to believe.

Our wedding day arrived. It was the beginning of September. I awoke early and looked across the sea to the house on the island. The sea was tinged with pink as it had been on that other morning and the rosy glow was on the house.

Since Sir Endelion was a sort of guardian as my father had made him an executor of his will, he would give me away. The bride given away by the bridegroom's father! That had surely happened rarely, and the best man was Harry Leveret who was to have married Gwennan. An odd choice, but Harry himself had suggested it. It might be that he wanted the world to know that he no longer cared for the girl who had treated him so badly.

There was I in white satin and the flowing Menfreya veil and my orange blossom. They all declared that I looked lovely, and for once I almost believed I did.

I looked at my reflection in the glass. " Don't worry, Fanny. I'm going to be lucky. I've made up my mind about that."

" You're tempting Providence."

" Don't be such an old ghoul, Fanny. You didn't want

me to become a Menfrey, did you? Well, I'm going to be one, and there's nothing you can do about it."

" No," she said, " there's nothing I see to do."

" Now I know what they mean by a skeleton at the feast."

Lady Menfrey was coming into the room. " How are you getting on, dear? Oh, but you look lovely! Doesn't she, Fanny?" Her eyes filled with tears. She was thinking of the abduction, the seduction and the hasty wedding. Like me she had been an heiress. If she had not been, there would have been no abduction, no seduction—but perhaps there would. The only certainty was that there would have been no marriage.

" Dear, I think we should be getting along now."

To the village church with Sir Endelion. " You look lovely, my dear. I'm proud to give you away. . . . This is a happy day for us all."

Bevil was already there and his eyes were on me. There were special glances for me alone. A pity we have to go through all this fuss, he meant. A simple ceremony would have been so much better . . . and then away to that little town overlooking the coast where we can be alone and I can show you that I love you as I never loved anyone before and that if your stepmother had not died and so released your father's fortune I would have married you, Harriet Delvaney . . . no, Harriet Menfrey now.

So we walked down the aisle to Mendelssohn's Wedding March. I saw the faces in the pews that watched us . . . blurred and intent. No relations of mine were present. Aunt Clarissa had pleaded her inability to leave home at such a time, but I knew the truth was that she could not have borne to see me married when Sylvia and Phyllis had failed to secure husbands.

Out to the carriage and back to Menfreya, Bevil beside me, holding my hand tightly, laughing now and then—a new Bevil, I thought, serious, contemplating the future. I was so happy I felt that if I could have had a wish it would have been to prolong that drive for the rest of my life, to sit there in the carriage with Bevil beside me, serious and tender, telling himself—as I was sure he was—that this was the beginning of a new life for him. He was going to love and cherish me, for better for worse, as he had vowed to do ; it was going to be an end of the life of light adventure. He was going to be the reformed rake who made the best of husbands.

Under the clock which only stopped when a Menfrey was going to die a violent death, into the courtyard where the stones were worn with the wheels of carriages and the hoofs of horses over the centuries.

I had come home—a Menfrey.

Bevil must have been thinking the same for he said:

"Well, Harriet Menfrey, we're home."

Happy women, like happy countries, they say, have no histories; so there is little to report of the first weeks of my honeymoon.

We went first to Paris, where I bought the clothes I had promised myself. An exhausting business, standing before mirrors, listening to cooing compliments in French-English. But I did acquire some charming clothes; and Paris when one loves and is loved is one of the most wonderful cities in the world.

The Eiffel Tower, the Bois de Boulogne, the Sacré Cœur and the Quartier Latin—they are all sanctified memories to me still. Bevil beside me, laughing, making me do the talking because I had a better command of the language than he had, for he refused to attempt to discard his English accent. I remember the soft lights of restaurants and the looks of those who served us who, with true Gallic intuition in such matters, knew that we were lovers. We betrayed it—both of us. That was the joy of it—he as much as I.

But our ultimate destination was that little town in the mountains, so we left Paris and made our way south.

The Provençal flower season was over but how I loved the country with its magnificent mountain scenery and its glorious coast. I was immediately enchanted by our hotel, and when I stood on the balcony and looked away to the sea I thought I had never seen anything so beautiful.

They were happy days.

Madame the proprietress knew Bevil. He had been there before.

"And this time he comes with Madame Menfrey. That is very beautiful."

Her dark eyes were speculative, though, and I wondered with whom Bevil had stayed in this hotel before. Perhaps alone, but it might have been that he had made friends in the town. During the ten days we had spent in Paris I had had no such thoughts; I had begun to believe I had conquered them; but here they were, at the first sign of suspicion.

But I forgot it when we went down to the dining-room which opened on to the terrace with its views over the mountains. There we dined by candlelight and all my happiness returned.

"We should stay here for four or five weeks," Bevil said, for he wanted me to love Provence as he did. Here life was lived simply, and that was how to get the best out of a honeymoon. "No distractions," he said. "Not that anything could distract me from Harriet Menfrey—but it's the simple life for me."

I was content enough. In the mornings we explored the old town with its winding streets and worn steps and alleyways. The dark-eyed children watched us almost furtively. We were so obviously foreigners; and the stall-holders were delighted when we paused to buy fruit and flowers in the market square. We sat outside cafés and watched life go by. During the afternoons we would sit under the palm trees in the garden and lean on the stone balustrade looking over the mountains away to the sea. We hired horses and rode into the mountains, through lonely villages, along dangerously narrow paths. Bevil insisted on leading my horse along such places and although I was a good horsewoman and capable of managing my mount, I enjoyed the protection. Sometimes we stopped at inns for *déjeuner*; we tried all the native dishes and the wine of the country and we would sit sleepily content half through the afternoon before we rode on.

We rarely made plans. We let each golden day take care of itself. How I loved the warm sunny days and the evenings when the sun disappeared taking the heat with it. Then I put on a warm wrap and we went out sometimes to walk in the cool mountain air.

One late afternoon we rode into the mountains. We were going into one of the villages for dinner, where Madame had told us we could see some Provençal dancing.

We set off promising ourselves a ride home by moonlight. We were very gay and happy as we rode along and we sang together a song which Monsieur, Madame's husband, had taught us. The words were set to the Maid of Arles music and was about three wise men coming to Bethlehem. Whenever I hear that tune I am back on that rough mountain path singing, with Bevil beside me . . . a happy moment which was, in a way, a finale to the complete contentment. But, perhaps fortunately, I did not know this then.

> *Trois grands rois,*
> *Modestes tous les trois,*
> *Brillaient chacun comme un soleil splendide;*
> *Trois grands rois,*
> *Modestes tous les trois,*
> *Etincelaient sur leurs blancs palefrois.*
> *Le plus savant*
> *Chevauchait devant,*
> *Mais, chaque nuit, une étoile d'or les guide;*
> *Le plus savant*
> *Chevauchait devant,*
> *J'ai vu flotter sa longue barbe au vent.*

Bevil, singing out of tune in his atrocious British accent, made me laugh immoderately, and he cried: "Well, you do better, Harriet Menfrey."

"That won't be difficult," I retorted. "There's so little competition."

And as I sang he told me: "Your voice isn't half bad, sweetheart. And you speak the language like a native."

So we went on singing until we came to a little village, where we were warmly welcomed by Madame and Monsieur. We had been expected, they told us. They would have been disappointed if the English milord and his bride did not come to visit them. Madame from our hotel mothered us, but she gossiped about us, evidently. In any case in that small dining-room we were given the place of honour near the violins which would provide the music for the dancers.

Food was served with the ceremony to which we had become accustomed; the wine was brought and poured as though it were nectar of the gods and Madame and her waiter watched us as though they were admitting us to Paradise while we tasted the highly-spiced food and declared it to be delicious.

It promised to become one of many happy evenings until the English couple came into the room. Immediately I noticed Bevil's astonishment; and as the woman's eyes fell on him she stopped short—as surprised as he was. She was delighted, too.

As she approached our table, I noticed her bright honey-coloured hair and long grey eyes, that her lips were smiling, her body voluptuous and that in spite of this she walked with a jungle grace which was made more obvious because her companion moved clumsily beside her and was inclined to be chubby.

Bevil had risen.

"Am I dreaming?" she asked. "Pinch me, Bobby . . . then I shall wake up."

"I hope it's not a nightmare," said Bevil.

"It's the nicest sort of dream. What are you doing here, Bevil?"

Bevil was smiling at me. "This is an old friend," he began.

She grimaced. "Did you hear that, Bobby. An *old* friend. I don't like the description. It could be ambiguous."

"Only to the blind," replied Bevil.

"You should introduce us, my dear," said Bobby.

"Of course," put in Bevil. "This is my wife."

The woman's grey eyes swept over me and I fancied they missed little.

"This is my husband."

Then she laughed as though it were a great joke that Bevil should have a wife and she a husband.

"Don't tell me," she went on, "that *you're* having a honeymoon, too."

"It calls for some sort of celebration, I'm sure," said Bevil. He turned to me. "Lisa and I knew each other . . . a long time ago."

Madame was at our table. "You are friends? You would like to dine together?"

"What fun!" cried Lisa. "Now, Bevil, you can tell me *all*."

Madame signed to the waiter to bring chairs, and soon we were all seated round the table and the fuss of serving began. She was Lisa Dunfrey, Bevil told me. Not now, she reminded him. There was Bobby. Lisa Manton. "You know," she said, "Manton Biscuits. Bobby makes them, don't you, darling? Not personally, of course. Merely profitably. But, Bevil, this is so amusing. Both honeymooning at the same place!"

I wished that Bobby and I could have found it so amusing.

He hated it as much as I did, for she turned her attention to Bevil and left him to me.

The weather was glorious, said Bobby. What did I think of the mountain scenery? How did I like French food?

He was no more interested in my answers than I was in his questions; we were both listening to the conversation of his wife and my husband; and none of us paid any real attention to the Provençal dancers who performed so charmingly for our pleasure.

I knew the look which came into Bevil's eyes when he was attracted by a woman; I had seen that look for me; now it was there because of Lisa. If Bobby and I had not been there would they have resumed a relationship which they both seemed to look back on with nostalgia, I wondered.

At one point she turned to me and said: "So you're Sir Edward Delvaney's daughter. I saw the announcement in the papers, and I remember thinking that it would be a very *suitable* match for Bevil."

"Thank you," I replied. "I hope yours is as suitable."

She laughed and looked into her glass. "Oh yes. Isn't that satisfactory? All so suitably married—all at the honeymoon stage together. And Bevil has his politics. . . ."

"And you your biscuits," I replied.

She surveyed me coolly and turned back to Bevil. I gazed at the dancers not seeing them—instead seeing Bevil and this woman together making love. Was this a foretaste of the future? Would I now and then meet friends of Bevil's and suffer the acute jealousy which was tormenting me now?

I thought the evening would never end; but at last there was no longer any excuse for staying and we left them there to return to our hotel. I was relieved to feel the night air but I had lost my peace of mind.

"How well did you know her?" I asked.

"Know whom?" he queried unnecessarily.

"The beautiful Lisa."

"Oh, I just knew her."

It told me nothing and yet I imagined it told me so much.

When we reached the hotel Madame wanted to know if we had enjoyed the dancing. Bevil was unusually quiet but I managed to reply brightly that it had been a most illuminating evening.

Bevil made love to me fiercely that night and I asked myself as we lay in the darkness: Is it Lisa to whom he is making love? Am I the substitute?

We didn't meet them again and in a few days Bevil had recaptured his high spirits and I was able to hide my misgivings. The honeymoon continued, but nothing was quite the same.

SEVEN

We had been in Provence six weeks. It was a long honeymoon. November was with us and the rainy weather had set in. It fell in torrents bouncing up and down on the balcony and flooding the bedroom; the clouds completely blotted out the mountains and the sea, and without the sun there was a decided chill in the air.

It was time to leave for home.

It was good to be back in Menfreya. My spirits were lifted by my first glimpse of the house, and as we drove under the old clock tower I told myself that I was going to be happy in my new home. I was determined to be all that Bevil wanted in a wife.

It soon became clear that a ministerial crisis was brewing. Balfour had replaced Salisbury as Prime Minister not long after the new King's coronation, and Chamberlain, with his following, was threatening to resign over Protectionists' proposals. I must understand these problems thoroughly, if I was going to be of any real help. The duty of a politician was to make laws which would improve the well-being of the country; it seemed to me that that was a noble ambition. I was fired with enthusiasm. When I told him this he kissed me and said I was going to be the ideal politician's wife. He would grow enthusiastic over some wrong which in his view was a particular evil. He would discuss the problems with me and I found myself caught up in his zeal.

He took his duties so seriously. In the town of Lansella he had chambers, and there, when he was in Cornwall, he spent two mornings a week so that those whom he represented in Parliament might come to see him with any problems they wished to discuss. I sometimes went there with him and to my delight found that I could be of use and that he realised it. Then I forgot that honeymoon incident which had so disturbed me; I was even able to tell myself I had imagined the whole thing.

Bevil's career began to obsess me as it did him. I was delighted to find that although he was ambitious—he dreamed of Cabinet office and the ultimate prize of the premiership—he really had the good of his constituents at heart, and was determined to make himself as accessible as possible. This meant a great deal of hard work; there was a constant stream of people to see, a tremendous amount of correspondence; and although William Lister was very efficient there were many ways in which I could make myself useful.

I was happier than I had ever been.

It has always astonished me how changes come into one's life. The gradual change becomes acceptable but sudden shock, presenting itself without warning to shatter the existence so completely that nothing will ever be the same again, makes one uneasily aware of the perpetual uncertainties of life.

That is what happened to me on the April morning. There were wild violets under the hedges and cowslips in the meadows and I was waking every morning to find my room full of sunshine and the sound of the waves as they slowly advanced and retreated in a steady soothing rhythm.

It was Bevil's day for receiving people in his Lansella chambers and I was alone that morning as he had work to do with William Lister there. I went down to devilled kidneys and bacon which were in a chafing dish on the sideboard. Breakfast was from seven-thirty till nine at Menfreya, and this morning, as neither of my parents-in-law was down and Bevil had already left, I was alone. I was studying the papers carefully when one of the servants brought in the letters and laid them on the table.

I glanced at them and the handwriting on one of them made me catch my breath.

" Gwennan's ! "

I slit open the envelope. There was a Plymouth address at the top of the letter. I read:

Dear Harriet. This is like old times, isn't it? I expect you've been wondering what has been happening to me all this time. I am about to satisfy your curiosity, if you still have it and want it satisfied. This is between us two. I want to see you first and in secret. Will you come to this address either to-day or to-morrow. I shall be here. There is a condition. You must come alone and tell no one. I hope you will. I rely on you.

Gwennan

PS. It's easy to find. When you come out of the station turn right, then turn left as far as you can go. Turn right again and you'll see it. No. 20. I shall be waiting.

She knew then that I was at Menfreya; she knew that I was married to Bevil, for the letter was addressed to Mrs. Menfrey. I was thankful that I had been alone when I received it.

As I walked through those streets which grew more and more squalid with every step, I was being prepared for what I should find. Number 20 was a three-storeyed house in the final stages of decay. The front door was open and as I stepped into a hall an old woman called out to me. She was sitting in a rocking chair in a room on the right, the door of which was wide open. I saw a line of washing in the room and several children in ragged garments.

"I want Mrs. Bellairs," I told her.

"Right at the top," she said.

I felt sickened as I mounted those rackety stairs; it wasn't the smell; it wasn't the obvious dirt and poverty; it was the fear of what I should find when I opened that door beyond which Gwennan was waiting for me.

I knocked. I heard her voice with the lilt in it which was so like Bevil's.

"Harriet. So you came . . . you angel!"

"Gwennan." I stood there staring at her. Where was my beautiful Gwennan with the scornful flashing eyes, the springing tawny hair, the Menfrey look? In her place was an emaciated woman, so gaunt that it took me some seconds to assure myself that it was Gwennan. Her body was wrapped in a dressing-gown that might once have been gay. I noticed it was torn in places.

I could have wept at the change in her since I had last seen her. I wanted to hide from her the horror in my face so I drew her to me and held her fast.

"Oh, Harriet . . . you sentimental creature! You always were, I knew it."

"You had better tell me everything," I said. "Where is Benedict Bellairs?"

"I don't know."

"So you've left him?"

She nodded. "It was the biggest mistake I ever made, Harriet, when I ran away with him."

"So it went wrong?"

"Almost from the start. He thought that I had money of my own. He'd heard of the Menfreys . . . old family . . . traditions, and the rest. And then . . . I brought nothing."

"So you found your marriage was a mistake and . . ."

"It wasn't exactly a marriage. I thought it was, but he was married already. I was a simpleton, Harriet. It didn't take much subtlety to deceive me. I went through a form of marriage . . . but he didn't even commit bigamy for my sake. It was a friend of his who played the parson. Another actor, so he did it rather well."

"Gwennan!"

"You look shocked. I read about you in the papers. 'Daughter of Lansella's late M.P. marries the present Member. Miss Harriet Delvaney, daughter of the late Sir Edward, was married to Mr. Bevil Menfrey, M.P. for Lansella and district.' So, Harriet, you got your wish then. You always wanted Bevil, didn't you?"

I nodded.

She smiled rather sadly. "Tell me what happened when I left."

The same Gwennan. Her own affairs were always more interesting than those of others and she made no attempt to hide this.

"Consternation."

"I'll bet there was. And Harry?"

"He was heartbroken."

"Poor Harry! He would have been a good husband to me."

"What happened after this . . . mock marriage?"

"I became with child, as they say."

"You have a child?"

"It's for that reason that I've asked you here, really. I'm sinking my pride for him."

" Where is he?"

She went to a door and opened it. In a small room was an old wicker basket, and in this a child lay asleep. He was pale-faced and not very clean, but he had the Menfrey tawny hair and I recognised him as one of them.

" Benedict," she said gently.

" Benedict Bellairs," I added.

" Benedict Menfrey," she corrected me.

" Of course."

" It's a difficult situation, Harriet."

I agreed. " Why did you ask me? Tell me everything, Gwennan."

" I asked you because you're one of the family now and I expect more help from you than the others. I want to come back to Menfreya, Harriet. I can't stand this life any longer. And I want him brought up at Menfreya."

" Well, of course you'll come back."

" And how explain . . . ?"

" It could be done. You've lost your husband, so you've come home. It's a delicate situation but could be arranged."

" I wouldn't come unless they wanted me."

" But, Gwennan, of course, they'll want you. You belong to them."

" Dear old Harriet. You've got *such* nice thoughts. Harriet, we real Menfreys—not those by marriage—may not be so kind. I want to come back. I want my baby to come back. But I don't want any recriminations. I don't want any grudging admittance."

" You want them to kill the fatted calf for the prodigal daughter?"

" No. I want to come back . . . and I want you to arrange it. And I want Benedict to be known as Menfrey. I want to forget there was ever such a person as Benedict Bellairs."

" But the boy is named after him!"

" Well, we were together when he was born. It was only afterwards . . . when I didn't get well again . . . that things really went wrong between us."

" When you didn't get well again? You're ill, Gwennan. You don't look . . ."

" I'm no beauty now, you mean. I've been through hard times, Harriet."

" I can see it. Tell me what's wrong, Gwennan."

F

"Oh . . . nothing that the sea breezes can't cure."

"What are you doing now? How are you living?"

She shrugged her shoulders.

"Oh, Gwennan, you must come back with me," I cried in horror.

"We'd look well walking together, wouldn't we? The M.P.'s wife, the lady of elegance, and what I've become."

"I can't leave you here."

"I want you to go back and tell them that you've seen me. I want to be invited back to Menfreya. I hoped I would never have to do this, but I am doing it now."

"I'll go back at once. But you should come with me, Gwennan. I hate leaving you here."

She shook her head.

"You're coming back with me," I insisted.

"When Bevil or my father comes to fetch me, Harriet."

"I shall go straight back and they'll be here to-day."

"Will they, do you think?"

"Of course they will. I shall insist."

"*You*, Harriet?" She laughed.

I emptied my purse, leaving myself just a few shillings I might need on the return journey and I was angry with myself because I had not brought more with me.

I kissed her and left her.

"I'll see you soon," I said.

I ran to the station, and while I waited for the train I sat thinking of her in a hundred different scenes. Gwennan on horseback riding through the lanes about Menfreya; at the Chough Towers ball; going into Plymouth to be fitted for her wedding dress. I could not bear to remember her as she had been and think of her as she now was.

How long that journey seemed, and when I arrived at Liskeard, as I had not known what time I should return, I had to take the local train to Menfreystow and then walk back to Menfreya.

As I was about to run into the house Bevil came riding into the courtyard.

"Bevil," I cried. "I must speak to you at once."

"I've something to tell *you*."

He was excited, but my thoughts were so full of Gwennan that I could think of nothing else. He called to one of the grooms to take his horse and he followed me into the house.

"Bevil . . . come up to our room. I want to talk to you."

He took my arm. "You'll never guess. It's incredible. What do you think, Harriet?"

"Bevil, I must tell you. I've been to Plymouth . . ."

"Harry Leveret. He's standing against me. What do you think of it? Have you ever heard anything like it?"

"Bevil, I've . . ."

"Of course, I don't think he's got much chance. But it's going to be more of a fight than I anticipated. A local man like this . . . !"

He did not notice how overwrought I was. He could think of nothing but the new situation created by Harry Leveret's standing against him.

We reached our room. I shut the door and blurted out: "I've seen Gwennan."

That shook him. He stared at me blankly for a few seconds then he said sharply: "Where?"

"In a squalid room in Plymouth."

"Good God!"

"She's got a child."

"And this . . . actor?"

"She's left him. She was never really married to him."

He was bewildered. I could see him trying to imagine this terrible thing which had happened to proud Gwennan; and at the same time one thought would keep intruding into his concern for his sister. He was picturing her coming back to Menfreya with her child. There would be scandalised comments; his father's indiscretions would be recalled. "These wild Menfreys," they would say. "Are they the people we want to represent us in London?" And there was Harry Leveret, waiting, ready to slip into Bevil's place.

"She's ill. She wants the boy to be brought up here . . . as a Menfrey."

"It can't be, Harriet!" he said, and his voice was almost a whisper.

"When you've seen her, Bevil, you'll realise it must be."

"There must be some way out of this. We'll take care of her, but if she comes here . . . with a child and no husband . . and a possible election in view . . ."

"I know it will be difficult," I said. "But this is Gwennan."

"You must leave this to me," he replied firmly.

I looked at him intently, wondering how well I knew my husband. I was disappointed. I had thought he would feel as I did, and that was that we must tell the family at once of Gwennan's plight, and we must bring her back to Menfreya without delay.

"I will go and see her to-morrow," he said. "In the meantime, say nothing to the others."

I had to be satisfied with that. I was certain that when he saw Gwennan he would be as horrified and moved as I was, and I was sure that Gwennan would soon be home.

It was late the next day when Bevil returned from Plymouth. I was alarmed when he came alone.

I was waiting for him as he entered the house.

"Gwennan . . ." I began.

"She's all right," he said. "You needn't worry."

"All right, but . . ."

"She decided that she wouldn't come back after all."

"Wouldn't come back! But . . ."

"She saw what it would mean if she did. She didn't want to make trouble. She says that she's caused enough already. She'll be well looked after."

I was suddenly angry. He had been there, talking to her, making her see how her presence might influence his career. He had made it impossible for her to come back.

"I'm going to see her," I said. "I'm going to talk to her."

He shrugged his shoulders. "Don't you believe me, Harriet?" he asked coldly. He was tired, I could see— physically and emotionally so. I understood that Gwennan's return would not send up the family's credit in the neighbourhood, but it seemed to me that the only thing that mattered was that we should look after her.

"I don't know what to believe," I said.

"In that case, rest assured that I have done all I could for her."

"All you could?" I demanded. "For whom? For Gwennan or the good name of the family, which is so important now with an election pending?"

"For heaven's sake, Harriet, don't be a fool. It hasn't been very pleasant, I can tell you. Gwennan won't come home. But she will be all right. She'll have an allowance and the child will be cared for. You didn't mention this to my mother? She'd be most upset."

I shook my head.

I went up to our bedroom and sat at the window over-looking the sea. I thought: He was determined not to have her back. He thinks it's enough to see that she has money. But it isn't enough. She's crying out for Menfreya. I thought of her mother—kindly, ineffectual. She had accepted the rule of the Menfrey men, as I would never do. I was one of them now, but I was always determined to be myself.

That was my house on the island there. If Gwennan couldn't come to Menfreya she could come to the island house. From there she would see Menfreya and she would be happier for it.

I had made up my mind. To-morrow I was going to Plymouth to see Gwennan.

In the morning Bevil was like his old self. It seemed to me that in his mind the affair of Gwennan was neatly marked off as finished. He would probably see his solicitor and arrange for an allowance to be paid to her and later he would look after the boy's education. He might even visit her at regular intervals. But in my opinion that wasn't the sort of attention Gwennan needed.

I said nothing of the affair and this must have deceived him. He talked as usual while we breakfasted together.

"There's going to be some pretty hard campaigning, and I want you to appear with me. We ought to make a tour of the villages and outlying districts. I think you might develop a flair for that sort of thing, Harriet."

I was pleased to be included. To be with him, sharing his life, was what I wanted more than anything. I was interested in the lives of the people whom we represented. I loved the work I did when I went to Lansella. Very often we were able to help some of the old farm workers who were afraid of being turned out of their cottages. Bevil had very strong feelings about looking after the elderly. He said it was inherent in the old landowning classes and had been bred over the generations. He wanted to modernise some of the fishermen's cottages along the coast which had been standing for several hundred years and although highly picturesque were scarcely sanitary. There were all these matters to be dealt with; and Bevil was working indefatigably for the people. He would work for those people, I told myself, yet I suspected he would not allow his own sister to come back to her home, and all because he feared a scandal. I under-stood his fears to a certain extent. The battle for his seat was going to be a fierce one and danger had loomed up from an unexpected quarter. I knew very well what would be said by our opponents. The father involved in a scandal and as a result there was not a Menfrey in Parliament for several years. Now there's Gwennan Menfrey who went off to Plymouth and comes back with a baby and no father for it! These are the Menfreys for you. Are they the sort of people you want to represent you in Parliament?

Radical strength was growing in the country. The influence of William Ewart Gladstone, though he had been dead for some years, was becoming a legend even in constituencies which had been notoriously Tory for generations.

Harry Leveret had a score to settle with the Menfreys and he had the resources of a millionaire to put behind his campaign.

"We've got a fight on our hands, Harriet," said Bevil, "and you're going to help me win it. This afternoon I'm going to take you into Lansella to meet agents and some of the workers. I've told them my wife wants a part in the campaign."

I was scarcely listening. I thought: I'll go to Plymouth as soon as he has left and I'll be back in time to go to Lansella with him. But I must see Gwennan. I must under-stand why she has changed her mind.

I loved Bevil but I must retain my own personality. I should never become the kind of woman Lady Menfrey was —without a will of her own, a slave of her menfolk. If Bevil and I were going to build up a worthwhile relationship he must understand that I was no shadow of another person —not even him. I must be myself.

As soon as Bevil had left I sent for the carriage and drove to Liskeard where I caught the train to Plymouth. I would return by the midday train and the carriage was to meet me.

For the second time I walked down the narrow street and opened the door into the squalid house which was let off in rooms.

I went up the stairs to Gwennan's room and knocked. There was no answer. I opened the door.

"Gwennan," I called. "It's Harriet."

She was not there. No one was there. I went down the stairs. The door which had been open on my previous visit was still open. The woman was still on her rocking chair. I think she was the landlady—a sort of concierge.

"I've come to see Mrs. Bellairs," I said.

"She's left. Went away with a gentleman who came for her."

"Where's she gone?"

"She didn't leave an address."

"She left with the baby?"

"With the baby and the gentleman. She owed me three weeks. He paid me right up to the end of the week . . . and only right, I say, after being kept waiting like that."

"But she must have left an address."

"She did not. Hustled out quick she were. She just went off with him."

So that was why Bevil was complacent. He had taken Gwennan to some place and was not going to let anyone at Menfreya know where.

I was shocked and very wretched. I went to the Hoe and sat there for a long time thinking about Gwennan and Bevil and was very unhappy.

I did not realise how long I remained there until I looked at my watch and saw that I had missed the train.

I did not reach Menfreya until late afternoon.

When Bevil came home that night I was in our room.

He was angry—reasonably so, I told myself.

"You made me look rather foolish," he burst out.

"I'm sorry."

"So you went to Plymouth. You didn't believe what I'd told you. You went to see for yourself. On a fool's errand."

"It was meant to be an errand of mercy."

"I had to make excuses for you at Lansella. I said you were not well. I've made arrangements for you to say a few words at a meeting next week."

"What am I expected to say? What a kind husband I have and I am sure they can put their trust in him because his conduct towards his sister . . ."

Bevil was really angry; I could see by the glint in his eyes.

"I told you that Gwennan would not come back and that I was arranging that she would be looked after. You're telling me that you didn't believe me. You wanted to see for yourself. That's it, isn't it?"

"How can you behave like this to your sister?"

"It was her wish."

"It was your wish, Bevil. Do you think I understand nothing?"

He took my arm and shook me. "I'm tired of this, and I don't like being made to look foolish."

"I'm sure you prefer to look cruel in your wife's eyes rather than foolish in your friends'."

His grip on my arm was painful and when I winced he said, "I must live up to your opinion of me."

"I think we should have an understanding," I said, wrenching myself free. He was beside me.

"An understanding, certainly."

"Because I married you it doesn't mean I share your views. I won't be brutal because you are. Gwennan wants to come back to Menfreya."

"She does not."

"She did until you saw her."

"I have told you that she prefers things to be as they are now. Can't you believe me?"

I did not answer, but turned away from him.

"Where are you going?" he asked.

"I think one of us should use the dressing-room."

"But I do not."

"You don't wish to use it . . . then I shall."

"I don't wish either of us to."

Of course he was stronger than I. I had never thought that I should fight physically to resist him. But I did; and the more I struggled the more determined he became to subdue me.

He was cruel; he was brutal.

I said breathlessly: "Are you mad? I am not a village girl to be raped when the fancy takes you."

I was useless against him. I was in his power. It was the most shattering experience of my life.

Fanny brought the breakfast tray to my bedside.

"You look tired," she said.

"I didn't have such a good night."

"Mr. Menfrey was off early. Here, let me put something round your shoulders." She picked up a bed-jacket and as I put my arm into it the sleeve of my nightdress was pulled above the elbow. On my forearm was a long bruise.

"My patience me!" cried Fanny. "Where did you get that?"

I stared at it in dismay.

"I . . . I don't know."

"I've got some lotion that's good for bruises. It takes them out in no time."

It was when she was putting on the lotion that she discovered the bruise across my shoulders.

"You don't remember how you got that either, I suppose," she said.

Angry lights shot into her eyes. I knew what she was thinking. She had never liked Bevil and I recalled how she had warned me against him.

Now she would dislike him more than ever. She had made up her mind that he ill-treated me physically.

I sat on the platform beside Bevil and looked down at the sea of faces. He appeared to be relaxed; he had just made an excellent speech and he had been most attentive to me; but he was afraid.

The relationship between us had undergone a change. We were polite to each other; I guessed he was a little ashamed of the force he had used but he had not referred to it and I knew it was meant to be symbolic of our relationship. He was the master, he was telling me. He expected obedience from me, and as long as I gave it I should be treated with respect; but if I had to be taught a lesson, he was ready to do the teaching however unpleasant.

My love for him was unchanged. It had been with me ever since I was a child, and I did not believe it could ever fade. Whatever he was, I wanted him. I knew that the only thing I should not be able to endure would be his indifference. He knew this for although I had deeply resented the affront to my dignity by his display of force, my passionate need of him had betrayed me.

What did I want? I asked myself. Did I want a hero who did not exist? Bevil was the man for me—the wild Menfrey who knew what he wanted and how to take it.

But I hated what I was sure he had done to Gwennan, and if I could I would have brought her back to Menfreya. I would have done so to satisfy myself, however much Bevil had hated me for it.

He had won this battle because he had been cleverer than I. Then he had behaved like the conqueror to the vanquished. Now he was showing me that he was prepared to forget my folly and take me back. So here I was sitting on the platform with him and at any moment now I would be called upon to say those few words which would show the audience that I adored my husband, that I supported him in everything he did, that we were devoted to one another and that there would never be a scandal surrounding us like that which had forced his father to retire from politics.

And Bevil was uncertain. I could sense it. He knew that I had a will of my own and that Gwennan was between us. The moment came and I rose. I was aware of the bird in the hat of a woman in the front row; all the curious eyes on me; the rows of faces. In my hand was the short speech which the agent had prepared for me and which I had memorised.

It was typical of a thousand such speeches.

I started to speak and what I said was not what was written on the paper. I saw Bevil sit forward. He was alarmed. Then . . . he was smiling. I saw the faces changing; they became alert and interested.

I can't remember what I said but I was being natural; I was telling them why they must support my husband.

It was over in three minutes, but there was loud applause and I sat down, trembling slightly. I had been a success.

That was a wonderful evening. Bevil said: "You're a find, Harriet Menfrey." And he was tender and loving and I was almost happy going home with him. I should have been completely so if I could have forgotten Gwennan.

I did not mention her, and Bevil was not a man to sense the moods of others. To him everything was as it should be. He had married a woman who would be a good politician's wife; she had brought money to bolster up the family fortune; she had too much spirit at times to be comfortable, but he knew how to subdue that, for he was the all-powerful male and she was, in spite of her sharp tongue, only a woman. Not a beautiful woman, either, and therefore not spoilt.

Bevil was very satisfied with his marriage on that night.

During the weeks which followed I was constantly with Bevil: He took me everywhere with him and gradually our relationship slipped back to what it had been in the days of our honeymoon. How glad I was that I had over some time steeped myself in politics so that I could talk intelligently of events. I was never happier than when I saw Bevil sit back, his arms folded, a look of gravity on his face, eyes lowered to hide the satisfaction in them, when I made some well-thought-out comment, or my occasional platform speech.

For the first time in my life I was completely unconscious of my limp; I knew that no physically perfect woman could have delighted Bevil more than I did . . . at that time.

But life does not remain static.

It was about two months after I received that letter from Gwennan that the next arrived. This was short.

Dear Harriet. This is very urgent. I must see you. Please come to me here as soon as you receive this letter. Don't let anything delay you. Please, Harriet.

Gwennan

On the top of the letter was a Plymouth address.

Bevil was in the dressing-room when I opened the letter. I dared not show it to him, for I believed he would put everything possible in the way of my going and I was determined not to fail Gwennan this time.

I had hidden the letter when he came out and sat on the bed chatting about the day's programme. I was to be with him all the morning in the Lansella chambers because one of the tasks I had been able to do particularly well was to listen to the women's problems, record them and advise on them.

I could not say I was going to Plymouth. I pictured him struggling with me, finding the letter and perhaps going in my place.

We would return to luncheon at Menfreya, and in the afternoon I should be free because he had an engagement which did not include me.

Never had a morning seemed so long; I was terrified that something would happen to prevent my leaving, but at last I was free.

It was about four o'clock when I arrived at the station and took a cab to the address Gwennan had given me.

We drew up before a small but respectable hotel, where I guessed Bevil had installed her.

When I asked for Mrs. Bellairs the receptionist opened her eyes wide and told me to wait a minute please. She went away and in a few minutes the proprietress of the hotel came hurrying out.

"I'm so relieved," she said. "Please come in here."

She took me into a pleasant but modest reception room.

"You're related?" she asked.

"I'm her sister-in-law."

Her relief was obvious.

"She died early this morning."

"Dead . . ." I repeated stupidly.

"It was inevitable. She was so weak and had evidently neglected her health for a long time. It was too late when she came here and we knew the end couldn't be far off. I've notified her brother."

"When?"

"The letter was posted this morning."

"And the child?"

"He is being looked after by one of my maids. I am grateful that you came. We naturally want instructions. You will be Mrs. Harriet Menfrey, perhaps?"

"I am."

"I have a letter for you. She asked that it should be delivered into your hands personally if that were possible. I will bring it to you."

For a few seconds I could only stare at the familiar handwriting and think of Gwennan . . . dead.

My dear Harriet,

I am writing to you in case there is no time for speaking. I'm dying. I've known it for months. I went through a terrible time after Benedict had gone. I was worried and there was no money. At one time I wanted to come back to Menfreya to die but I saw that that wasn't possible. When Bevil came to see me I realised it. It wasn't anything he said; in fact he said I must come back to be looked after, but I could see that it wouldn't be any good. You can't go back and make things as they were. The moving finger writes and all that. I knew that I couldn't face the explanations, having the child, the mess I'd made of everything. It would have been too humiliating and I'm too proud. So in spite of Bevil's persuasion I didn't come. I'd made up my mind; he saw that, because we do understand each other.

Well, now there's Benny, and I'm writing this to you, Harriet, because you're the one I want to look after him. I want him to go back to Menfreya but I want you to be a mother to him. He'll be at a disadvantage as you were when you were little and you will understand that more than anyone else.

I may be dead when you read this. I'm dying now, Harriet. It was such a different sort of life after Menfreya. Late nights, crowded rooms, cheap theatrical lodgings—and then of course the wretched poverty. I suppose I couldn't stand it. Bevil has been good to me. He brought me here and since then I've been able to see that Benny was fed and clothed. I longed to come back but I couldn't face it, Harriet. But when I'm not here Benny must go to Menfreya.

Now, Harriet, this is my dying wish . . . as they say. Take my boy and bring him up as yours. Don't let anyone else have him, and think of me when he needs you. Remember it's Gwennan who needs you, Harriet . . . then as now. He is Benedict Menfrey. Remember that. Let him be known by his true name; and if you and Bevil should fail to have a child, then Menfreya will be his by right.

I had hoped to see you before I died, but then I cannot be sure when my time will come. It might be suddenly and, like the foolish virgin (for the adjective certainly applies to me if not the noun), I should be caught without oil in my lamp, so that I should leave my boy stumbling on alone in the darkness.

Harriet, we were very close, weren't we? I know you were always a better friend to me than I to you. That is why I am asking you to do this for me now. And I am happy to go now that I have written this letter for I trust you.

My love to you, my dearest friend.

Gwennan

For a few moments I couldn't speak. The proprietress of the hotel tiptoed out and left me alone. Gwennan was dead. I was terribly unhappy yet angry. It need not have happened, I kept telling myself. If she had married Harry she would be alive now. It was not as though there had been a grand passion between her and Benedict Bellairs. She had acted once too often in her wild irresponsible way and now this lovely vital girl was dead.

And Bevil? I had misjudged Bevil, and felt sick with shame. How stupid I had been! Impetuous, foolish, suspicious. How he must have despised me for that ! And yet I was glad because he had not been unkind. He had tried to bring her back and it was she who had refused to come.

I folded the letter, put it into the pocket of my coat and went out into the hall. The proprietress, who had been waiting outside, brightened when she saw that I had pulled myself together.

" And the child," I said, " where is he?"

" I'll take you to him."

I nodded.

" First," she said, " would you like to see her?"

I hesitated. How would she look, in death, my proud and lovely Gwennan? I thought of the shock I had received the last time I had seen her. I did not want to remember her like that.

" She looks at peace," she murmured.

So I followed her up to the room in which Gwennan had lived since Bevil had taken her from her poor lodging. It was small, rather dark, but neat and clean. She lay on the bed, looking different, but her tawny hair was brilliant against the pallor of her skin. But what struck me so much was the serene expression on her face. I had never seen her look like that before. My eyes went to the blotter on the little table. The lid of the ink pot in the stand was open ; the pen was lying across the blotter and I pictured her sitting there writing the letter to me.

Gwennan, I thought, you can rely on me no matter what happens.

I turned and went out of the room.

" I had her laid out," said the proprietress. " I suppose her family will see that everything is taken care of."

" Yes," I said. " Her brother—my husband—will come as soon as he receives the letter. I came in response to a letter from her. He does not know yet, but as soon as I return he will . . . Besides, he will soon have your letter."

She nodded. " This sort of thing is so upsetting to the rest of the residents. I know you will understand."

" I do."

"And the child?" she asked anxiously.

"I will take him back with me."

"I am sure that will be the best possible arrangement. I'll take you to him now."

He was sitting on a red hearthrug thoughtfully examining the toes of his little boots when I opened the door. A young girl was sitting in a chair watching him.

She smiled at me. "He's been as good as gold," she said.

I went over and knelt down on the hearthrug. There was no question about this one's being a Menfrey. He had the same tawny hair and eyes; and the sparkle was there in his eyes.

"Hallo, Benny," I said.

"Hallo."

"I'm Aunt Harriet."

He nodded. "Aunt Harriet." He had no difficulty with the name, which told me that he had heard it before.

He gripped my arm to help himself up; then he came close to me and studied me intently. I looked at the smooth skin, the short nose, a replica of Gwennan's with its flaring nostrils. I would never forget Gwennan while there was her son to remind me.

"Are you coming with me?" I asked.

He nodded, his eyes immediately asparkle with the spirit of adventure which had been the characteristic and perhaps the ruin of his mother.

"We're going to Menfreya," I said.

His lips formed the name with ease and I knew he had heard that before too.

"It's time we were going," I told him.

My return could not have been more dramatic. I had managed to get a fly at Menfreystow station but it was almost eight o'clock when I reached Menfreya and there was beginning to be great concern about my absence. I might have gone out during the afternoon without saying where, but I should most certainly be back in time for dinner.

Bevil had invited guests and dinner was about to be served —Lady Menfrey was fortunately there to play hostess, but of course they were expecting to see me.

I could sense the tension as I stumbled into the house carrying the sleeping child in my arms.

I heard Pengelly's startled exclamation; and suddenly it seemed Bevil, my parents-in-law and their guests had all appeared on the staircase.

Often I recall that scene with a smile. It must have seemed like a nightmare. The truant returned—not alone, but carrying a child in her arms.

I heard Bevil's voice. "Harriet! What in God's name . . ."

I said: "Gwennan is dead. I've brought her baby home."

Lady Menfrey came running down the stairs. "Harriet . . . Harriet . . . what do you mean?"

Bevil was beside me; I was aware of strange faces; but I was so exhausted by the journey, by my emotions, by my fears for the child's reception, that I felt I could endure little more.

"You'll be hearing to-morrow," I said to Bevil. "There's a letter from the hotel where she is. She died this morning. He's to be called Benedict Menfrey. That is her wish."

Lady Menfrey took the child from my arms; the tears were running down her cheeks but I could see that she would love the child—already she had someone to fill Gwennan's place in her heart. It must have been what Gwennan had hoped for.

"You're exhausted," said Bevil sharply.

"It's been an exhausting day. . . ."

"We have guests," he said, not sharply but in a bewildered way.

"I'm sorry," I replied.

A woman whom I knew as the wife of one of the party workers took my hand and squeezed it. "Don't you worry about us, Mrs. Menfrey. You need to rest . . . now."

I smiled at her gratefully and Bevil said: "You should go straight to bed, Harriet." He turned to the guests. "Please excuse me for a moment."

He followed me to our room. He shut the door and I waited for the storm to burst. What had I done? I had jeopardised his chances. The scandal Gwennan had brought on the family would now be publicly known—and it was all my fault.

I felt the stubborn lines forming about my mouth. I held my head high and limped painfully to the bed. I sat there looking at him.

"There was nothing else to be done," I said in a cold

angry voice. "I should never think of doing anything else."

And then I thought of Gwennan lying on that bed white and calm in death as she had never been in life and I covered my face with my hands.

I felt him take them very gently in his. "Harriet," he said; and his voice was tender.

"Dead!" I said. "Gwennan! She was always so full of life."

He did not speak but looked at me sorrowfully.

"The child is going to stay here," I went on, forcing anger into my voice to hide my grief. "I shall look after him. And if you won't have him here, then . . . I shall take him away."

"Harriet, what *are* you saying?"

I tried to draw my hands away from his grasp, for I was afraid of my emotions. It was too much to endure. Gwennan dead . . . never to see her again . . . and Bevil hating me because I had gone against his wishes and brought the child to Menfreya.

He put his arm about me and held me against him. "Of course the child will stay here. And so will you. Listen to me, Harriet Menfrey, you think you've married a brute. . . . Perhaps you have. And I'll tell you this. There is one thing he won't endure. That is life without you . . . so get that into your head."

"Oh, Bevil, Bevil," I said weakly.

He just held me and I felt comforted.

He was practical suddenly.

"I'm going to send Fanny to you," he said. "My mother is looking after the boy. There's nothing to worry about." He kissed me. "You must know that."

He left me and went back to our guests, who I was sure would be agog with curiosity. I wondered what story he was telling them, but I was too tired to care.

Fanny came to me and I let her help me to bed; and when I was there I lay back on my pillows quietly, and although I was relieved because I had brought the child to Menfreya, thinking of Gwennan brought a sadness which was like a physical pain.

Benedict's presence was easily explained at Menfreya. Gwennan had eloped with an actor, whom she had married against the family's wishes; she had died and now her son was at Menfreya, which was a perfectly natural state of affairs. The boy was known as Benedict Menfrey, which was just like the Menfreys. It wasn't the first time the family name had been retained. There had been a daughter who had inherited the estate and when she married, her husband had to change his name.

It was a house of mourning, and when I humbly told Bevil how sorry I was for misjudging him he said: "You were right in a way, Harriet. I should have insisted she came home."

William Lister, that silent-footed and efficient young man, who had the great quality of seeming to remain unnoticed except when he was wanted, went to Plymouth with Bevil and between them they made arrangements for the funeral; and Gwennan was buried in the Menfrey vault in the churchyard on the hill just outside Menfreystow.

The child made a difference to the household, and he was soon a great favourite with his grandparents and most of the servants. Lady Menfrey was happier than I had seen her for a long time and I realised how deeply she had felt the loss of her daughter.

Benny asked now and then for his mother, but we told him she had gone away and that was why he was staying with us. Sometimes he cried for her; then we would think up little treats to comfort him and gradually we began to divert his thoughts from the past. Menfreya was full of delights such as he had never known before. The house was a continual source of wonder; the suits of armour, the old pictures and tapestries. Benny had never seen anything like it. He seemed to be everyone's pet. He struck up an immediate friendship with his grandfather and Bevil; he was so obviously one of them.

There was great excitement when Lord Salisbury died and a crisis arose over the Protectionist proposals. Bevil came home demanding to know where I was.

I was actually dressing for dinner and he came bursting into the bedroom.

He told me what had happened.

"It may mean an election in the near future. Then we should have to go into battle in earnest."

"We shall win, of course."

He sat down on the bed and taking my hands pulled me down beside him.

"You like a fight, don't you?" he said.

"No, I don't think so."

"Ah, but when a fight has to be fought you go into it in full cry."

"Shouldn't one?"

"Of course. You fight the good fight with all your might. Twice armed is he who has his quarrel just. Is that right? You should know. Harriet, are you looking forward to our fight?"

"I'm determined to see you victorious."

He laughed. "Spoken like a good and virtuous wife. You know, Harriet, my darling, a good wife is more valuable than rubies. It says so in the Bible."

"The Menfreys had an opportunity to put that to the test."

"What do you mean?"

"I'm thinking of the table with the rubies missing from the top. I was told they were used one by one and when they had disappeared, the Menfreys were obliged to seek rich wives."

"Who told you that story?"

"Gwennan, I think."

"Poor Gwennan! Still, the boy's here."

"I'm so ashamed when I think of the conclusions I jumped to."

He laughed at me. "Well, I didn't behave very well either. And I'll tell you something that came out of that, Harriet. Beast that I was, and even more loathsome beast that you believed me to be, you still love me."

"Well, idiot that I was . . ."

"You're right," he said. "I still love you."

He kissed me hard on the lips and I said: "Please, not bruises. Fanny noticed."

He frowned. "That woman doesn't like me, Harriet."

"Oh, she's only mildly disapproving. I'm her child, remember. She doesn't think anyone's good enough for me."

"She may be right. And as long as I have your approval, what do others matter? I need it, darling. Now we have to fight an election together. My formidable Harriet. You're going to be very busy in the next few months, years perhaps.

Too busy to spend your days entirely looking after young Benny."

"His grandmother will be ready to step into the breach."

"She's not always well, and I was saying to her that I thought it was time we had a nursery governess."

"She agreed with you, of course."

He grinned at me. "It's obvious, you know. I need you more than Benny does."

I was so happy to be wanted that I couldn't hide the fact.

After that there was talk about the governess we would get. Both Sir Endelion and Lady Menfrey thought it was an excellent idea. They doted on the boy and were very anxious to have the best for him, but nothing was done about it and I fancied Lady Menfrey was not very eager that we should get someone quite so soon.

"He's young yet," she said, for she enjoyed looking after him herself.

Sir Endelion went to London for a visit to friends and it must have been two or three weeks after his return when we received a letter. He did not say anything about it immediately but it was clear that something had happened which amused him. He kept chuckling to himself, and one evening at dinner he made an announcement.

"While you've been talking about what you'll do I have gone into action," he said. "I've found you your nursery governess."

We all looked at him but he was intent on watching Pengelly pour the claret into his glass.

Bevil was smiling. I guessed he was pleased because it had been his idea in the first place that Benedict should have a governess and leave me free to help him.

Sir Endelion waved a hand. "You'll be surprised," he said.

"You mean, Endelion, that *you* have engaged a governess?"

"That's what I said, my dear."

"But how could you know what qualifications and er . . ."

"I've no doubt that this one is going to give great satisfaction."

"But really . . ."

"You wait. She's coming at the end of the week."

"But I don't understand."

"You will, my dear."

Lady Menfrey looked uneasy. Bevil met my eye and grinned. "It's what we want," he said.

"But such an odd way . . ." began Lady Menfrey.

"She wanted the job; we had it. Simple as that," said Sir Endelion.

He kept laughing to himself.

"You wait and see," he said.

Bevil and I rode over to Lansella; it was one way of exercising the horses, enjoying a ride and combining this with business.

It had been a busy morning and as we rode home we discussed the queries which always seemed so amusing in retrospect.

Lady Menfrey called to us as we came into the house.

"She's come. She's here now. You'll never guess. I was never more surprised."

"A guest for luncheon?" I asked.

"Oh . . . no. The nursery governess."

We hurried in and as we were about to mount the staircase she appeared at the top of it. She was standing there above us, her beautiful oval face composed, dressed in dove grey; plain almost to severity, it only served to show her perfections. Her features were perfectly modelled, Grecian and classical; her dark hair waved loosely about her well-shaped head; her blue eyes were long, deep-lidded and black-lashed. She smiled and it was her smile which alarmed me. It was so gentle and yet so full of wisdom . . . which later I thought of as cunning.

She said: "You look surprised. Sir Endelion came to the house where I was working and I had an opportunity of speaking to him. I had heard about the little boy. One does hear these things. And when I knew you were looking for a nursery governess I told him I should like the post."

I felt numb with apprehension, and as Jessica Trelarken slowly descended the stairs I felt my contentment fading away. I dared not look at Bevil for fear I should understand too much. I remembered how he had in the first place suggested we look for a nursery governess. Had he planned then to bring Jessica into the house? I remembered his attitude when Sir Endelion had made his announcement. Had he known then? Had he asked his father to invite Jessica to the house?

The future seemed very uneasy. I knew that life at Menfreya would change for me when Jessica Trelarken came into it.

EIGHT

The first indication of the effect Jessica would have came almost immediately on her arrival. It was dinner time on her first evening. I had dressed in a gown of dark green velvet which I had always thought rather becoming and I wore the garnet ear-rings, brooch and bracelet which Lady Menfrey had given me. They had been hers, she told me, and the previous Lady Menfrey's before her, so she was keeping them in the family.

While I looked at myself in the mirror—feeling pleased with the effect—Bevil came in and taking my shoulders stood behind me looking at our reflection.

" Very effective," he commented. " You look as if you've stepped out of one of the canvases in the gallery. But then you often do."

I waited for him to say something about the new governess, but he didn't, and that, even at this stage, seemed suspicious. Surely it would have been the most natural thing in the world to talk about the new arrival, paricularly as we had known her in the past.

So we went down to dinner. It was Sir Endelion—in his new puckish mood—who called attention to the fact that no extra place had been laid.

Lady Menfrey said: " But we are expecting nobody."

" What of Miss Trelarken?".

Lady Menfrey looked uneasy. " But Endelion, she's the governess now."

" Now! But her father used to come here to dine. You can't banish people below stairs when in the past they've dined at your table."

" She isn't banished below stairs," pointed out Lady Menfrey. " She has a tray in her room. That has always been the custom with governesses. They always had trays in their rooms because naturally they would not expect to eat in the servants' hall."

Bevil said nothing, but I could see that the bronze colour of his skin had deepened. He was concerned about the outcome of this; and I felt certain that if I had not been there he would have joined in to support his father. The advent of Jessica had already changed him; he had become less frank, as though he were a man with something to hide.

" My dear, you can't put Jessica Trelarken in the servants' hall. She's a lady."

"She's a governess now, Endelion. Alas, so many ladies have to become governesses . . . or companions. It's the only course open to them when they're left penniless as poor Jessica was."

I was watching Bevil. I thought: She will be here every evening. It's impossible. She must stay in her room . . . at least that.

I said: " My governesses never dined with my father. They always seemed to prefer a tray in their rooms."

"My dear Harriet," laughed Sir Endelion. " This isn't your governess. It's Jessica Trelarken. An old friend of the family. That's so, eh, Bevil?"

Bevil hesitated for a second. Then he said: "The Trelarkens used to dine here now and then. I suppose we ought to show Jessica that we don't regard her as a servant."

" Governesses are not servants," I said. " They take some meals with their charges."

" She can't dine with hers at this hour," retorted Bevil. " Unless she takes it at his bedside while he sleeps."

Pengelly was hovering. My newly sharpened wits, which were already beginning to frighten me, assured me that in the servants' hall they would be talking. Of course *she* didn't want her. Nor did my lady. It was the men who were determined to have her. Titters! The suspicion running through the house penetrating every corner.

" Has Miss Trelarken's tray already gone up?" asked Lady Menfrey.

" No, my lady. That'll be after the family has finished," said Pengelly gravely.

" Then," put in Sir Endelion, " lay another place. Then go to her and tell her we expect her to dine here with us."

Pengelly inclined his head, signed to one of the girls to lay another place, and disappeared.

In five minutes Jessica came in. She was wearing a plain black silk dress which she must hurriedly have slipped on when she received the summons, but there was no sign of hurry about her.

She hesitated at the door but I believed that to be studied hesitation.

Sir Endelion said: " Sit down, my dear. Of course you're to dine with us. Trays in rooms! Who ever heard such nonsense. Many's the time your father has sat at this table."

" Thank you," said Jessica calmly. Pengelly held the chair while she sat.

She smiled, demure, serene, but unsurprised. It was clear that she did not think it strange that the governess should dine with the family. It could not have happened in other places where she had worked. But this was different. This was Menfreya.

Oddly enough the change affected everybody. Jessica Trelarken seemed to illuminate the house in an oddly sinister way, making me see everything and everyone differently, so that I felt unsure of myself and wondered whether after all, I was naïve and without knowledge of the world.

She was so serene, but I was soon asking myself whether it was not a deadly serenity. Everything about her was quiet. She moved noiselessly; I often found that she had come into a room without a sound; one was unaware that she was there until one looked up and caught the blaze of her beauty.

Her beauty! No one could be unconscious of it. It was rare beauty and none could deny it. It was perfection of feature; there was not a flaw in that perfect face. Her skin was smooth and seemed to glow. I had seen such a complexion only once or twice before; her hair was smooth yet vital. She had everything, this woman—except fortune.

And it was inevitable that the presence of such a person in the house should have its effect upon us all. She seemed to bring out characteristics which had lain hidden within us. My father-in-law had always been charming to me; I had not seen a great deal of him, but when we had met, our encounters were pleasant. I believed that he welcomed me into the family because I was an heiress, perhaps, but nevertheless he had been very friendly—fatherly, one might say. Now I was aware of a puckish streak in his character. He had known

that Bevil had at one time been attracted to Jessica Trelarken; then why had he brought her into the house? There
were times when I believed that he was mischievous—like
a boy who puts two spiders into a basin and takes pleasure
in watching them fight. Perhaps, I thought, he never forgets
that he once lost the seat for the Menfreys and it was only
recently that it had been regained.

Whenever such thoughts occurred to me I dismissed them
as hastily as I could. I was sure that but for Jessica Trelarken they would never have come into my mind.

Then there was Lady Menfrey. I had never thought her a
very strong character; I knew she had given way to her
family continually; but now she seemed cowed; and I
noticed that she meekly accepted Jessica's authority.

Fanny? She had become wary—furtive, almost. In the past
she had always been frank with me; now I had the feeling
that she was holding something back.

Bevil? Naturally he who had always admired attractive
women could not but be affected by her presence; in particular he had admired Jessica and it was clear to me that he
still did.

And myself most of all. I seemed to lose that attractiveness
which being Bevil's wife had given me. I had tried to follow
—and with some success—that rather strange look of another
century which the topaz gown and snood had brought out in
me. People said of me : " She's not conventionally good-
looking, but that strange other-worldliness about her is
attractive." I knew it made me stand out, even among prettier
women; and I wanted to stand out—for Bevil.

With the coming of Jessica it seemed to drop from me. I
felt plain as I had been in my childhood, and the feeling had
its effect on my looks. My limp seemed more obvious; but
perhaps that was because when I was happy I could forget
it; and I was certainly not happy now.

Worst of all I was becoming suspicious. Distrust had
crept into my mind and it would not be dismissed. I was
becoming watchful and alert; and each day these feelings grew
stronger.

I tried to throw off my jealous fears, but they persisted.

Ever since Benedict had come to Menfreya I had been his
special friend, for he had seemed to put me in the place of

the mother he had missed; I had always spent some of the day with him and he looked forward to my visits. Sometimes I took him out for a walk or now and then I rowed him over to the island house, which he loved. He was always clamouring to be taken and the row across delighted him.

One morning about a week after Jessica's arrival, as Bevil had gone to Lansella alone, I went to the nursery to see Benedict.

Jessica gave me her cool smile, which I had begun to compare with that of the Gioconda. She looked neat and of course beautiful in a lilac-coloured gown with trim lace collar and cuffs. She had few clothes but what she had were in perfect taste. That was something she possessed—a sense of how to make the most of her clothes; but it may have been that beauty such as hers would make any dress look wonderful. I immediately felt awkward in her presence and I wondered then whether she deliberately made me feel so with those cool glances of hers. She moved with a grace which I could never imitate and there was a natural charm in all her gestures.

"I came to see Benedict," I said.

"He's playing with his bricks."

"I thought I'd take him out. Perhaps over to the island as the wind's dropped. He loves that."

"He's already been out this morning. I'm afraid he'd be over-tired and that'll make him cross. Then of course he won't want to eat his dinner. You know what children are."

She was smiling so disarmingly.

"Oh, but . . ." I began.

"Had I known you were coming I should have made him wait for his walk. But I do think regularity is important."

"I see."

I walked to the door of his playroom; she was beside me.

"Please don't tell him you were going to take him to the island."

"You're afraid he would want to come?"

Again that smile. "He'd want to go, of course. It's just that I know he would be over-tired."

I went into the room. "Hallo, Benny."

"Hallo!" He didn't look up. But that was nothing. He was absorbed in building a brick house.

"Your auntie is here," reproved Jessica.

"I know." Still he did not look up.

She smiled at me.

I knelt down and looked at the brick house. "It's going to fall soon," I told him.

He nodded, still not looking at me and that moment the bricks clattered to the floor. Benedict let out a shout of delight.

Then he picked one of them up and his pleasure faded as he noticed that the coloured picture was slightly torn. He said mournfully: "Wants Jessie."

I took it and said: "Oh, that can easily be stuck on."

He took it solemnly from me and handed it to Jessica. "Poor brick wants Jessie," he said.

She took it. "I've stuck some of the others," she explained. "I'll see to it, Benny."

She raised her eyebrows as though to say, You know what children are.

But that too seemed to me like a sign.

Jessica now joined us every evening for dinner. She had three dinner dresses—one black, one grey and one of blue velvet. They were all simple and by no means costly but she managed to look magnificent in them; and in mine—some of which I had bought in Paris on my honeymoon—I felt gauche and often overdressed. That was the effect she had on me; and moreover I had an odd feeling that that was what she meant to do.

There was nothing of which one could complain. An onlooker would have said that merely by being present Jessica put others into the shade. But I felt she was aware of this and that she was nursing a secret triumph.

She was like a magnet at the table, drawing to her the attention of all the men. Sir Endelion was gallant; Bevil was always conscious of my being there, always eager to draw me into the conversation, but I sensed it was a studied eagerness, calculated to hide his true feelings; even William Lister, who also took meals with us, would turn to her with frank admiration.

If she had been a pretty, frivolous little fool like poor Jenny, it would have been bearable, but she wasn't. She was clever and well educated; and what was most disconcerting was my discovery that she was determined to show her knowledge of politics, for this subject was naturally one most frequently discussed at the dinner table.

Her voice was soft and gentle but because she spoke slowly and her enunciation was perfect, clearly audible.

I listened to her and was aware of the men all watching her. Lady Menfrey at the head of the table was trying to look alert as she did when the conversation was political, but I knew that she was really wondering whether she should send for more blue wool for her tapestry or whether Benedict was going to have a cold since he had sneezed twice during the day.

"I've had many a discussion with my father on that point," Jessica was saying. "He had very firm views. Of course we didn't always agree."

"The doctor was a man who had very strong views on Tariff Reform, I remember well," put in Sir Endelion.

"My mother used to say that once my father made up his mind on a subject he made it up at the same time not to change it."

They all laughed.

"Many's the time he's come here and we've argued almost to blows," said Sir Endelion. "A good fellow, the doctor. I don't care half so much for this new fellow."

"His wife is a strong supporter of the party," I put in.

"That's true." Bevil smiled at me; it might have been my imagination but I was certain that he forced himself to turn from Jessica to me.

I was beginning to dread these meals, yet previously I had so enjoyed them. I liked the political talk; William Lister was always deferential to me, and both Bevil and Sir Endelion paid me the compliment of listening gravely to me. Now it seemed that Jessica was usurping my place even here.

Then she said: "I met Harry Leveret yesterday afternoon. I was riding not far from Chough Towers. He's in residence there now."

That was another thing; Jessica had always been fond of riding and Sir Endelion had suggested that if she liked to give one of the horses a little exercise she should do so. Jessica had responded with enthusiasm.

They were all alert now. Lady Menfrey looked frightened, and started to play nervously with her cutlery. I could see the pain in her face. She was thinking of that dreadful day when it had been discovered that Gwennan had run away.

Jessica gave her gentle smile which I always felt was like a mask spreading across her face.

"He was very friendly," she went on.

"Why not?" I retorted, and my voice sounded harsh. "He has no quarrel with you."

"He knows I'm here, of course. He talked . . . about the future." She paused and looked from Sir Endelion to Bevil, including Wiliam Lister in her gaze. "He said that he's now accepted as candidate for his party."

"So it's settled," said Bevil.

"Yes. There was something else he said. Perhaps it's impertinent of me but . . . I let him sound me as to your feelings. He thinks you're probably piqued because he's going to stand against you."

"I must say it was a surprise," said Bevil. "Why didn't he come out into the open with it? It all seemed somewhat secretive to me."

"That's what he thought, but he said that the Leverets and Menfreys had always been friends and he doesn't see any reason why you shouldn't continue to be. He asked me whether I thought that if he asked you to dine at Chough Towers you would refuse."

Sir Endelion burst out: "I don't like his politics. I'm surprised at him! Thought he was a business man. What's he doing suddenly going into politics like this?"

"If he asks you and you refuse," said Jessica hesitantly, "he might make things awkward. What I mean is, he might let it be known. . . . Do you see what I mean?"

"Exactly," replied Bevil, leaning forward and looking at her with approval.

"He could say that he had been badly treated by the Menfreys once. . . ." She smiled deprecatingly and I thought of how deeply Harry had been wounded at the time of Gwennan's disappearance. "And that now . . . just because he doesn't agree in his political opinions his friendship has been rejected. I may be wrong but I don't think it would be looked on very favourably."

She paused again. Then the conversation broke out; and the outcome was that it was decided that when Harry Leveret invited us to Chough Towers we would accept the invitation.

Bevil and I dined at Chough Towers. It seemed strange to

be in the house again, particularly as it was furnished almost as it had been when my father had rented it. There were some additions, of course, and it was clear that Harry was going to do a good deal of entertaining.

He was different from the young man who had come to the gallery to look for Gwennan, and I guessed that the loss of Gwennan had had a great effect on his life. It had made him grow up suddenly and he had ceased to be a light-hearted boy. I was certain that he had loved Gwennan dearly, and had wanted alliance with the old family of Menfrey. Although he seemed insignificant I sensed in him a driving desire to succeed, which he must have inherited from his father, who from humble beginnings had built up the fortune which had made him a millionaire.

We invited him back to Menfreya and the relationship between the two families was re-established. Jessica appeared to have been right, for the move was approved of. When the election did come—although it seemed as though it would not be just yet—it was going to be a clean fight in the constituency and most people—except Harry and some of his supporters—believed that Bevil would certainly hold the seat.

A few days after Harry's visit to Menfreya I went into the library and saw Fanny standing at the window very still, crouched behind the curtains, so that she would not be seen.

"What are you looking at, Fanny?" I demanded and I went swiftly to the window.

"Nothing . . . oh, nothing," she replied, hastily turning away.

But I had seen them—Bevil and Jessica. Benedict was playing a little distance away, but it was on Jessica and my husband that Fanny's attention was focused.

"Is anything wrong?" I asked.

"I hope not, Miss Harriet," she answered tartly.

I knew exactly what was in her mind and she knew what was in mine. I wanted to rebuke her, to tell her she was being foolish; but when I looked into her loving face I knew that if I suffered she would suffer with me.

I shrugged my shoulders and turned away.

A week or so later, going down to the dining-room, I found to my dismay that both Bevil and Jessica were missing.

We had taken our places at the table—Sir Endelion and Lady Menfrey, William Lister and myself, expecting at any moment that the missing pair would arrive. The fact that they were both absent, immediately aroused my uneasiness.

"What is keeping them?" murmured Lady Menfrey. "Mr. Lister, have you any idea?"

"None at all," replied William. "I haven't seen Mr. Menfrey since four o'clock."

"I hope Benedict is not unwell and Jessica feels she should be with him."

"I'll go up to the nursery," I said, and immediately slipped away.

I ran all the way, and when I opened the door of Benedict's room I saw that he was in bed, fast asleep.

I went into the schoolroom and through to Jessica's room and knocked on the door. There was no answer, so I went in. The room was as neat as it always was. A sudden fear made me open the drawers in the chest of drawers. With great relief I saw that her things lay neatly there. I opened the cupboard door. There hung her dresses.

I faced the fact then that I had actually believed that she and Bevil might have gone away together.

I went back to the dining-room. "Benedict is asleep but Jessica is not in the nursery or in her room."

We dined at eight and it was now ten minutes past the hour. Pengelly, hovering with his maids, wanted to know if he should serve.

Lady Menfrey often looked at Sir Endelion before giving an order. It was a habit which mildly irritated me because I believed that she could have at least been mistress in the house if she had asserted herself.

I said rather sharply: "They know dinner is at eight. They won't expect us to wait. Let us begin."

I sounded as though I cared more for my food than anything, when in fact I was wondering how I was going to make a show of eating.

Pengelly said: "Thank you, madam." And the soup was brought in.

"It's so unlike Jessica," murmured Lady Menfrey. "She's usually such a punctual person. Her father always was, I remember."

"And Bevil?" said Sir Endelion. There was speculation in his eyes and he looked more puckish than ever. "Have *you* any idea, Harriet, my dear, where he might be?"

"None," I replied. "Unless he was suddenly called to

Lansella, but in that case he would surely have left word."

"Into Lansella with Jessica Trelarken? Now that's hardly likely, I should think. Why if he'd taken anyone into Lansella it would have been you, my dear."

"I should have thought so."

"It's Jessica I'm wondering about," said Lady Menfrey. "I do hope there hasn't been an accident. Oh, Pengelly, send to the stables and see if any horses are missing. I remember poor Gwennan's accident . . . and how Dr. Trelarken's houseboy came over to tell us. Yes, go at once, Pengelly. I am most anxious."

We were through the soup course before Pengelly came back.

"None of the horses is missing, my lady."

Sir Endelion sat back in his chair looking at me.

"It's strange," he said. "*Both* of them."

The meal seemed interminable. I played with the fish on my plate, anxious that none of them should know how worried I was. I caught William Lister's eyes on me. He knew; and he was kind and sympathetic. I believed he was as worried as I was.

"Miss Trelarken knows many people in the neighbourhood," he suggested. "It may be that she has gone visiting and forgotten the time."

"That's what it is!" cried Lady Menfrey triumphantly and she began to eat steadily. She had something to cling to now. Jessica was visiting friends and had forgotten the time; Bevil was in Lansella on Parliamentary business; they would soon return and it would all be explained. She wanted peace in the household so desperately that she would pretend it existed when it didn't.

William Lister seeing that he had soothed her went on: "I'm sure something must have turned up at the Lansella chambers demanding his immediate attendance."

"Wouldn't he have told somebody that he was going?"

"There may not have been time," he said lamely.

"Of course," cried Lady Menfrey. "That's it. There wasn't time."

Her husband was smiling at her sardonically. I guessed he believed that they were together. And if they were, I asked myself, if they had disappeared so blatantly, what could it mean?

But Bevil would never leave Menfreya. How could he give up everything? He was not a romantic boy to elope on impulse, leaving his wife and his career. There was some other explanation. But I was becoming more and more certain that they were together somewhere.

The meal had come to a dismal end.

"I'm afraid," said William Lister looking at me almost pityingly, "there may have been an accident."

"Oh no, no!" insisted Lady Menfrey. "Jessica has forgotten the time and Bevil has been called to Lansella."

William and I exchanged glances. We didn't believe it.

We went to the drawing-room where coffee was served. We were all tense and nervous. We talked desultorily but all the time we were straining our ears for the sounds of arrival and none of us was really paying attention to what was said.

It was impossible to keep the disappearance secret. I was aware that the news was spreading with the speed and efficiency of jungle drums. The servants would be discussing the possibilities of what had happened to keep Bevil and Jessica away at precisely the same time and the story would be carried round . . . to Menfreystow and on to Lansella, which would surely not be good for Bevil's reputation. That was what I could not understand; how had he, who cared so much for his career, allowed himself to be caught in such a situation? Could it be that he was caught up against his will? Or had he forgotten the passing of time?

In any case, if they did not return soon we should have to do something about it.

That was a very uneasy evening; and it suddenly occurred to me how lonely I was. I could not quite trust Sir Endelion, for since he had brought Jessica into the house, I was learning something of his character. He had been wild in his youth and I could imagine his going through life tempting fate. He wanted something to happen . . . and was ready to risk disaster rather than suffer boredom. I understood this feeling but I knew I could not rely on him. And Lady Menfrey? I thought of her kindness to me at the time of Jenny's death. But then she had been acting in accordance with her family's approval. She was too much a seeker after peace to be a rock in the case of trouble.

William Lister was beside me; his face was puckered with anxiety.

"I know how you're feeling," he whispered.

"There must have been an accident," I said. "We'll have to do something."

"Yes," he agreed. "And soon."

"What?" I asked.

"I'll go into Lansella to see if he's there. He may well be delayed on business and a message to us could have gone astray."

"The two of them must be together," I pointed out.

He nodded wretchedly.

"An accident involving them both," I went on. "It could be so if they had gone riding together . . . but all the horses are in the stables. What can it be!"

"It would be better to take some action. The reason I wanted to wait was . . ."

"I know. You were hoping they would turn up and you didn't want a thing like this talked about."

"I'm sure it was what Mr. Menfrey would wish. But I think the time has now come for action. I'll go over to Lansella immediately. I think it'll be quicker and there'll be less noise about it if I ride over. I can find out if he's been to the chambers and see if the agent knows anything. If I can't get any satisfaction there we shall then have to let the police know."

I had begun to tremble; he leaned towards me and lightly, shyly touched my hand. "You know I'll do everything possible . . . for you."

"Thank you, William," I said; and I believed there was someone whom I could trust.

So William rode over to Lansella and I waited, tense and anxious, for what would happen next.

We sat in the red drawing-room—a disconsolate party, and it was about an hour after William had left when we heard Bevil's voice. We all hurried to the window but could see little, for there was no moon, although the sky was clear and full of stars.

"He's back!" I cried; and I ran out of the room, along the corridor to the top of the staircase. I saw him standing in the hall, Jessica beside him.

"Bevil!" I cried. I discovered I was so pleased to see him that I could not keep the joy out of my voice.

"Harriet!" he answered me. "The most maddening thing happened."

As I went down the stairs I was limping badly. Jessica was watching me; she was pale and her hair was loose and untidy; it was slightly damp, too, but this did not detract from her beauty. Her eyes seemed larger and more luminous; it occurred to me that she at least had enjoyed the adventure.

"What happened?" I demanded.

Jessica held up something. I didn't recognise what it was. She explained: "We went to get this and then . . . found we were caught there."

"Caught?"

"It's all quite simple," said Bevil. "Oh, hallo, Mother. Hallo, Father." Sir Endelion and Lady Menfrey had appeared on the staircase. "We went to retrieve that thing and then the wretched boat slipped away somehow."

"Slipped away!" I was repeating the significant words interrogatively—always an irritating habit, I have thought, in other people. I couldn't help myself. I was frightened.

"Perfectly simple," said Bevil. "Benedict and Jessica were over on the island this morning and he left his teddy bear there. He wouldn't go to sleep until Jessica promised to bring it back to him. She asked me to row her over."

I wanted to know: Why did she ask you? Why could she not have gone alone? But I didn't. I couldn't betray my feelings before them all.

"So," went on Jessica, "he kindly did so and when we had found the bear and came down to the shore the boat was gone."

"Where to?" asked Sir Endelion, a lilt in his voice as though he was enjoying the adventure vicariously.

"That's what I'd like to know," put in Bevil with an attempt at anger.

"You couldn't have tied it very securely," mocked Sir Endelion.

"I'm sure I did."

"So the boat's lost, eh?"

"No. A'Lee brought it in. He saw it drifting out to sea," he said, "and he was bringing it in to Menfreya beach when he passed the island and we hailed him. He's just brought us back."

"Oh dear," sighed Lady Menfrey. "You missed dinner and

must be hungry. I'll tell them to get something for you at once."

She sensed the disbelief, the growing storm, and she wanted to be away.

Sir Endelion said: "Well, you're not the first one to be marooned on an island. It was always a favourite place of yours."

I remembered then, myself cowering beneath a dust sheet and Bevil's coming here with one of the girls from the village. This time I had not been there to prevent the culmination of the adventure.

What, I asked myself, had happened this time in the house on the island?

Bevil was looking at me and I was determined not to betray myself.

"Well," I said coolly, "you've returned."

I caught a glimpse of Jessica's face as I walked back to the stairs. She smiled faintly. Apologetically? Defiantly? I couldn't say.

It was half past eleven when Bevil came up; he had been closeted with William, who had returned from Lansella and I was sure was deeply regretting that he had gone there, for his journey had only spread the story.

He looked at me coolly, and I knew well that it was a habit of his when disturbed to feign nonchalance.

"Still up?" he said unnecessarily.

"But ready to retire," I retaliated. "Wrapped in dressing-gown and thought."

"What's wrong?"

I felt that sharpness of tongue which I had developed as a weapon in my early days beginning to take command. "I'm not sure."

"What do you mean?"

"That's what I want you to tell *me*. What exactly happened?"

He looked impatient. Another sign of guilt? I asked myself.

"You heard what happened. We went to look for the toy and the boat slipped away."

"You tied it badly then."

"I suppose so."

"Deliberately?"

" Now look here, Harriet . . ."

" I think I have a right to know the truth."

" You know the truth."

" Are you sure?"

" I am not on trial. If you decide not to believe me there's nothing I can do about it."

" We'll have to do something about it. There'll be gossip. Perhaps there already has been."

" Gossip. I should have thought you'd have known better than concern yourself with that."

" Then it shows how little we know each other, for *I* should have thought *you* would have known better than to become the subject of it."

" I couldn't help what happened to-night."

" Bevil, that's what I want to be sure of."

" Of course you can be sure of it. Good God, what are you suggesting?"

" She's a very beautiful woman."

" And you're an extremely jealous one."

" And there are going to be a lot of curious ones when this is discussed throughout the constituency."

" I wish you wouldn't try to be clever, Harriet."

" I'm not trying."

" Well, let's accept the fact that you are, without effort. What a stupid thing for Lister to do."

" We had to do something. I agreed with him that he must go to Lansella. It was my fault. We had no idea what could have become of you, Bevil." My voice had become earnest, almost pleading. I was fully aware while I quarrelled with him how very much I loved him, how I needed him; and I was afraid, because I believed I needed him far more than he needed me. " You'll have to be very careful about your relationship with Jessica."

" *My* relationship? What do you mean? She's Benedict's governess."

" Nursery governesses have figured so frequently as the heroines of romance that they are becoming so in ordinary life, and when they are, besides being nursery governesses, very beautiful, and the master of the house cannot hide his interest . . . when he disappears for hours with her—however innocently—and a hue and cry is sent out, there you have an explosive situation. If the master of the house is a landowner, a king in his own kingdom, he can go his own wilful way, but should he be a Member of Parliament, guardian of public morals, a figure of righteousness, he's sitting on a powder keg."

" Quite a speech!" he said and began to laugh. " You're good at them, Harriet. But I sometimes fancy you let your love of words run away with your common sense. Shall we let that be a peroration?"

" If you wish it."

" One thing more. What I have told you about to-night's affair is true. Do you believe me?"

I looked into his eyes. " I do now, Bevil."

He drew me to him and kissed me, but without the passion for which I longed. It was like a kiss to seal a bargain rather than one displaying affection.

I wanted to say: When I'm with you I believe you. Perhaps I'm like your mother. I believe what I want to believe. But when jealousy should rise up again it will bring the doubts back.

I slept late next morning and when I awoke Bevil had gone. Fanny brought in my breakfast on a tray. She set it down and stood at the end of the bed looking at me. She would, of course, have heard all about last night's adventure.

" You look worn out," she said as though she were angry with me, as she used to be when I caught a cold as a child. " I suppose you've been worried about the absentees last night."

" It's all over now, Fanny."

She sniffed disbelievingly.

" Here!" She had brought a bed-jacket and put it about my shoulders. I saw her sharp eyes examining me for bruises. Fanny would never forget anything she did not want to forget.

She poured out the coffee and said " There!" as she used to when I was a child.

I drank the coffee but could not eat with any relish. I kept going over that moment when I had stood on the stairs and seen Bevil and Jessica together, and the words Bevil and I had flung at each other later in this room still rang in my ears.

Fanny clucked her tongue and said: " I don't know, I'm sure. All I can say is, you can't trust 'em. We're better off without them."

"Who, Fanny?"

"Men."

"You don't mean that."

"Oh yes I do."

"If Billy had lived . . ." It wasn't often that I talked of Billy; I usually waited for her to broach the subject.

"Billy," she said. "He was like the rest, I reckon. Billy wasn't as much for me as I was for him."

"But he loved you, Fanny. You always told me so."

"He had a mistress, you know. He went from me to her. That's how it is with men. They don't love like we do."

"Fanny!"

"I never told you that, did I? No, I wasn't the only true love for Billy. He had this other love . . . and you might say he deserted me for her."

I was startled. I had never heard her talk like that before. Her eyes were wild and she seemed to be peering beyond this room into the past.

She was talking to herself. "There was the little one . . . and he gave me that . . . but I lost my baby . . . that baby . . and then I found my other baby."

I put out my hand and she took it. The touch seemed to bring her out of her trance.

"Don't you fret," she said. "I wouldn't let nothing bad happen to you. I'm never going to leave you, miss. So don't think it."

I smiled at her. "I didn't think it, Fanny," I said.

"All right then. Eat up that egg and don't let's have any nonsense."

I obeyed, smiling to myself. I had thought I stood alone—but there was always Fanny.

I was very anxious to hide my fears, so I asked Jessica to ride with me the next day, and we went into Lansella together. People threw us some curious glances but I was sure that to be seen together was the best way of allaying suspicion. Jessica behaved as though nothing had happened, but I was very unsure of her. There were moments when I thought she was secretly amused at my anxiety to make people believe we were the best of friends.

I promised I would go and have nursery tea with her and Benedict next day and when I arrived I found Benedict alone in the nursery standing on a chair.

"I'm a monkey," he told me. "Monkeys climb; did you know?"

I told him I did know.

"I'll be an elephant if you like. They have trunks and walk like this." He climbed down, got on all fours and lumbered about. "Would you like me to be a lion now?" he asked.

I said I would rather he were himself for a while, which amused him.

Jessica came out and I was at once aware of his affection for her, and was ashamed of the surging jealousy within me. I should have been pleased that we had a good nursery governess for him; Jessica had certainly shown herself skilful in the nursery and to have won his affection did her credit. I thought: But she is usurping my place . . . everywhere . . . throughout the house.

Then I felt ashamed and said quickly how well Benedict was looking and how grateful we all were to her for her care of him.

"It's my job," she replied. "But I never thought I'd be a governess to Gwennan's child that day when they carried her into the house."

"Poor Gwennan. Benedict is so like her. I see her in him every time I look at him."

I had sat down and Benedict came to put his hands on my knees and look up into my face.

"Who's he like?" he asked.

"He was like an elephant just now and now he's like himself."

That made him laugh.

Jessica brewed tea in the brown earthenware nursery teapot. "It always tastes so much better in these old brown pots," she said lightly as she poured. "Is it because we always remember them from our childhood?"

She talked about nursery days in her home, when her mother was alive. She was the only child and must have been beautiful from the day she was born; they had doted on her. How different her childhood had been from mine!

"I used to sit on a high stool in the dispensary," she told me, "watching Father make up the medicines and he used to say 'This for the Influenza.' Or 'The Ulcer came in to see me to-day.' He thought of all his patients as the disease they had. Mother used to say it was bad for me to hear so much of illnesses but Father said it was right for a doctor's daughter."

She was being affable. Perhaps, I thought, she was as anxious to reassure me as I was to reassure the community.

"You take sugar?" she asked.

I nodded. "Yes, please. I have rather a sweet tooth."

Benedict was staring at me. "Show me!" he cried. "Show me the sweet tooth."

I told him that it meant I liked rather a lot of sugar in my tea, and he was thoughtful.

"If it had been possible," Jessica was saying, "I should have liked to be a doctor."

"A noble profession," I agreed.

"To have the power . . . to a certain extent . . . over life and death . . ." Her eyes glowed. I was struck by the way she put it. Power?

My thoughts were diverted immediately because Benedict had taken a spoon and before we had noticed what he was doing had put a spoonful of sugar in my tea.

"That's for your sweet tooth," he shouted.

We were all laughing. It was quite a pleasant tea-time.

We were at dinner discussing the ball we were giving at Menfreya. A fancy-dress ball, we had told Harry Leveret when he had called with his mother for a game of whist the previous evening. The Leverets came frequently since the reconciliation; and with William and Jessica we were able to make up two tables.

"I always remember," Harry had said, "the fancy-dress ball your father gave at Chough Towers."

I remembered it in every detail. I had worn the dress which had somehow been important in my life because it had marked a turning point. That night I had realised that I could be attractive, because the dress had brought out my rather medieval looks and I had been accentuating them ever since.

The dress still hung in my room. I looked at it often and longed for an opportunity to wear it, though I had worn the snood now and then.

I was delighted therefore at the prospect of an opportunity to wear it again, but I knew I should not do so without arousing poignant memories of Gwennan in the gallery with me, of our creeping down, two young girls on the brink of adventure. I wondered whether Harry remembered too.

"I remember my father's parties." I smiled, thinking of the London house and the elaborate displays. I saw a child leaning over the banisters, listening and hearing no good of herself.

"Memories?" said Bevil tenderly. He had been at great pains since the island adventure to show me he cherished me; and I had been feeling happier. If only Jessica were not here, I thought, I believe I could be completely happy.

But there she sat, smiling serenely, listening intently; and the free and easy way in which conversation was carried on showed clearly that she was accepted as a member of the family.

"Costume always provides a problem on these occasions," said William. "But I do know an excellent firm who supply them." He smiled at me. "I used them in your father's time."

"I have my costume," I replied promptly. "I wore it at one of my father's affairs."

Jessica had leaned slightly forward. "Do tell me about it. What does it represent?"

"It's just a period dress. Actually it must have belonged to one of the Menfreys because there's a portrait of her wearing . . . well, if not the identical dress, one so like it that I can't tell the difference."

"How exciting! I hope you'll show me."

"Certainly."

"I suppose," went on William, "I had better see about hiring some costumes. You must tell me what you would like to be."

"I think I shall try to make my own," said Jessica. Then she looked a little startled, but even at that moment I felt she was not truly so, and entirely sure of herself. "That is . . . if I am invited."

"But naturally," cried Sir Endelion.

She smiled deprecatingly. "After all I am only the nursery governess."

"Oh, come, come, my dear." Sir Endelion was giving her his goatish look. "You mustn't think of yourself as anything but a friend of the family."

"Well, then," said Jessica, "as Mrs. Menfrey is providing her costume, I shall do the same."

I took out the dress and held it against me. I was certain my eyes seemed brighter and that my skin took on a new bloom. I let the dress fall to the floor while I put on the jewelled snood. Then I held up the dress again.

Even as I smiled at myself I felt the pain of memory. I could never forget Gwennan.

"Gwennan," I whispered to my reflection, "if only you hadn't run away, if you'd lived and married Harry and gone to Chough Towers and had your children there, it would have been wonderful. You would have been my sister and Jessica Trelarken would not be here looking after your son."

But life had to be accepted for what it was.

I felt a desire then to look again at the circular room which was said to be haunted by the sad governess, and to see once more the woman who had worn a dress so similar to mine that it could have been the same one.

I had been meaning to talk to Bevil about the house, for it seemed wrong to have so much of it that was never used. We ought to go through those old rooms and have them renovated so that we could give house-parties, fill the place with gaiety as Harry was doing at Chough Towers.

A few days later I found time to go and look at the portrait of the woman in my dress. As I made my way to the deserted wing I assured myself that I was not a nervous type and I was even inclined to be sceptical of the supernatural, but when I pushed open the door and stepped into the wing, I was not so sure. Perhaps it was the protesting whine made by the door which set my nerves on edge. I had forgotten it and it startled me as it broke the silence. I laughed at myself and went along the corridor where Gwennan had once led me. It was gloomy for there was only one window high in the wall, and that was in need of cleaning. It was ridiculous. This part of the house should be attended to. I could imagine Sir Endelion shrugging his shoulders and not wishing to go to the expense of opening up the wing and Lady Menfrey, of course, agreeing with him.

I started back. It was as though a clammy hand had touched my face. I cried out involuntarily and my own voice echoed back to me. In those seconds I felt an icy shiver run through my body.

Then I put my hand to my face and realised I had, as on another occasion, walked into a cobweb.

I wiped it off as best I could and tried to laugh at my folly, but I knew my nerves were taut and I could not prevent myself peering over my shoulder.

I wanted to turn back, but I knew if I did I should despise myself so I went forward and came to the door which had replaced the sliding panel. Again that protesting whine as I stepped into the circular cavity of the buttress.

A faint shaft of light came through the slit in those massive walls. There was the long mottled mirror, the trunk—and that was all.

I caught my breath in a little sob, for the door had moved on its hinges and I heard again that noise which sounded like a groan.

Could it be true, I asked myself, that a woman had lived here, and the rest of the household were unaware of it? I pictured her lover looking like Sir Endelion. No, he would have been young and would have looked more like Bevil. I imagined him, silently coming here to see her.

I touched the walls; they were very cold. She had had little comfort here. But what would have happened to her if she had been driven from the house by the mistress—the woman in my dress—and had nowhere to go? Any shelter was better than none—besides, she had the support of her lover.

I walked round the circular room through the narrow opening, up the twisting narrow flight of stairs to the parapet round the buttress tower. The air seemed so strong after the confinement of the circular room that I felt intoxicated. I stood there breathing deeply. Far, far below me the sea was whirling playfully about the rocks sending up little spurts of white spray. I could just see the tips of the treacherous Lurkers and . . . the island.

Then I was alert. It was the sound of a step on the stone stairs. I was mistaken. Naturally one became a little fanciful in a place which had such a legend. No. There it was again. Is it true then, I asked myself, that the governess who died here could not rest and returned to the scenes of her last days on earth?

I tried to laugh at myself, but I felt trapped—shut in by the stone staircase leading to the haunted chamber on one side, and on the other was the sheer drop to the sea.

Seconds seemed like minutes; I had turned and, gripping the parapet, kept my eyes on the narrow opening. I heard the sound of deep breathing and there was a shadow in the opening . . . and the governess was looking at me. For a moment I believed I was seeing a ghost, and then I caught my breath, for it was not the governess of long ago who had come to haunt me, but the governess of to-day who had followed me here.

" Jessica! " I cried.

She laughed. " I believe I startled you. I'm so sorry. Actually I saw the door to the wing open and I couldn't resist exploring. I've never been to this part of the house before."

Had I left the door open? I didn't believe I had.

" It needs repairs and a lot of attention," I said, trying to make my voice sound matter-of-fact.

She came and stood beside me on the parapet, her eyes level with mine.

" Is it true," she said, " that this part of the house is haunted?"

" You wouldn't believe that sort of nonsense, I'm sure."

" I'm Cornish, and you know what we Cornish are. It's all very well for you prosaic English. . . ."

" Yes," I said coolly, " I know that you're a superstitious race, but I should have thought *you* had too much common sense to believe these stories."

" During the daylight I'm sceptical, but not always when darkness comes . . . or when I'm in a place like this. This story was about a governess, wasn't it?"

" So the tale goes."

She laughed. " I'm naturally interested in a Menfreya governess. Do tell me the rest."

" She became pregnant, hid herself up here, gave birth to a child and died. No one knew she was here except her lover, and he was away. When he came back he found her and the child dead."

" Quite a feat, keeping someone hidden away in the house where his family were living."

" The room was supposed to be sealed off then."

" It almost is . . . now."

We were silent; I was aware of our isolation. I could well imagine the long-ago governess's loneliness and terror when she knew her child was about to be born. I shivered.

"I wonder what really happened," said Jessica quietly. "Do you think the wife murdered her?"

"Murdered her! That's not the story."

"It wouldn't be. But do you think she didn't *know*? She must have seen how things were between her husband and the governess. I mean . . . wouldn't a wife know?"

I repeated blankly: "That's not in the story."

She gave a little laugh. A gull suddenly swooped to the sea and his melancholy cry was like jeering laughter.

Jessica laid her hand on my arm. "I think the wife knew. I think she came up here and murdered her after the child was born. Murdered them both. It couldn't have been difficult in those days to make it seem as though she died in childbirth. Imagine the wife's feelings! Her husband is in love with another woman! She'd feel murderous, wouldn't she?"

Was it my imagination, or was she closer to me than was necessary? Was that a grim purpose I saw in those beautiful unfathomable eyes?

As she gripped me more firmly and swayed towards me, a frantic fear possessed me, and I wrenched myself free so violently that she fell against the wall of the tower. I saw her trying to steady herself, her face drained of all its colour. I caught her as she slid to the floor, breaking her fall.

"Jessica!" I said. "What's wrong?"

Her eyes were closed, her dark lashes long and black against her pale skin. She had fainted.

I propped her against the wall and forced her head down. I was wondering whether to leave her and run for help, when she opened her eyes.

She looked bewildered.

"You fainted," I said.

"Fainted?" she repeated. "Oh . . . I . . . I'm all right now. It's passing."

I knelt beside her. "What happened?" I asked.

"It was nothing . . . just a faint. It's the height . . . I could never endure heights. It upset me suddenly."

"Shall I call someone?"

"Oh, please, no. I'm all right. Getting better every minute. It was nothing. Just a momentary thing. Really, I've almost recovered."

"Do you often faint?"

"Oh . . . people do now and then. I'm sorry it happened."

"Let me take you back to your room."

"Thank you."

She stood a little unsteadily but she looked more like herself now. She turned to smile at me. "Please don't make a fuss. It was nothing. Just a little dizziness. Will you forget it happened and not mention it?"

"If you wish."

"Thank you."

We returned to the circular room and as we left it she said: "I'd like to see the portrait of that Lady Menfrey you mentioned."

"Now? Wouldn't you rather go to your room and rest?"

"The dizziness has passed. It was really the picture I wanted to see."

"It's along here."

I took her to the room where the portrait hung. She looked at it and then at me. "The features are not really like yours," she said, "but I can imagine in a dress like that, you could belong to her period."

"Wouldn't we all in the clothes of the period?"

"That's what we'll no doubt find out at the ball when we see the guests in their costumes. So she was Lady Menfrey at the time the governess died. I still suggest she murdered her."

"You think she looks like a murderess?"

"Do murderesses look the part? I don't think so. The most unexpected people commit murder. That's why murders are committed. If people looked the part the victims would be on their guard and the murder would be prevented. No. She knew that the governess was going to have her husband's child. Imagine her feelings. How would you feel? They must have hated each other—that wife and governess. It's reasonable to suppose that one might attempt to murder the other."

"I don't believe it," I said.

She smiled—completely serene once more, as though that incident on the tower had never taken place.

"It makes a better story," she murmured.

The hall at Menfreya is the most magnificent part of the house. The vaulted ceiling with the carved wooden beams; the fine old staircase with the armour said to have been worn by a Menfrey who crossed to France with Henry VIII; the gallery with the pictures; the arms on the wall; the dais on which the musicians now sat. It was a beautiful sight, particularly as the greenhouses had been denuded to provide pots of the most exotic blooms, while our native hydrangeas —pink, blue, mauve, white, multi-coloured—in enormous tubs draped in purple velvet had been placed at intervals about the room. Leaves decorated the staircases and I was reminded of the entertainments my father used to give.

Fanny helped me to dress. She was silent and I wondered whether she knew something which she was withholding from me for fear of hurting me.

Yet as I looked at my reflection in the mirror, the topaz colour of the dress bringing out something in my eyes, the jewelled snood doing the same for my hair, I felt invulnerable.

"I'll brush your hair to make it shine," said Fanny. "We've plenty of time." So she took off the snood, laid it on the dressing-table, and putting a white cloth about my shoulders brushed my hair.

"You're happy to-night," she said. Her eyes met mine in the mirror. She looked like a prophet standing there, the brush raised in her hand, her eyes intense. "I pray you stay that way," she added.

"Don't be long, Fanny," I said. "Don't forget I'm the hostess to-night. I must see that everything is in order."

Guests would not be announced as at an ordinary ball. They would be ushered in by Pengelly and others of the menservants, all splendidly dressed in blue satin coats, frogged with silver cord, white knee breeches and powdered wigs; and then in their masks they would mingle and assemble for supper, and afterwards unmask. We had decided on a masked ball because they were always so much more exciting, we thought. The air of mystery they gave to the proceedings added to the gaiety and we believed that people enjoyed hiding behind anonymity and it gave an added zest to attempt to guess who one's partner was.

The Menfreys would move among the crowd so that none would know that we were not guests ourselves until the unmasking when we should receive their thanks and congratulations.

I should be watchful of a man in a Roman toga. But then I should know Bevil anywhere. Two Roman togas had been delivered, William had told me in dismay and wondered whether to send one of them back. He had ordered a Persian costume for himself, a Roman one for Bevil.

"There simply isn't time to do anything about it," I told him. "There will just have to be two Romans from Menfreya. You can be sure there'll be others."

He agreed.

Sir Endelion was a Cardinal—Wolsey, Mazarin or Richelieu, I was not sure, but he could have passed as any of them. Lady Menfrey was ironically Katharine of Aragon.

I thought of the change in Sir Endelion. But was it change? Hadn't the mischief always been there, waiting to be brought out? Perhaps I had much to learn of those about me.

I shivered.

"Someone's walking over your grave?"

"It's more likely to be a draught from that window."

Fanny went over and shut it. "Your hair's shining. I used to like to see it look like that. Now where's that thing?"

"Thing seems disrespectful, Fanny. It's a snood or a filet."

"Well, bless me, it's a pretty thing, anyway. I don't know. It does suit you. You seem different somehow . . . when I put it on."

"How . . . different, Fanny?"

"I don't know . . . as though you don't belong here . . . but somewhere else."

"What do you mean?"

"Don't ask me. It just came into my head." Her face puckered suddenly and I thought she was going to cry.

"Fanny," I cried. "What's wrong?"

She threw her apron over her head suddenly and sat down. I went to her and put my arm about her shoulders.

"I'm a silly thing, I am. It's just that I wanted to see you happy. . . ."

"I am, Fanny. I am, I tell you."

She looked at me sadly and I remembered how she used to look at me in the past and mutter: "You can't fool Fanny."

I recognised Jessica at once. She was the only one in that assembly who was simply dressed; and how clever of her, for she was the one who consequently attracted all the attention. She had made the dress herself. Almost Puritan in its simplicity, it was made of lavender-coloured silk; the skirt cascaded to her feet; the bodice was meant to convey primness but on her it had the opposite effect, by accentuating her perfect figure. Her dark hair was smoothed down on either side of her face to a simple knot in the nape of her neck. She had come as a governess of another age. I caught my breath when I saw her.

"I see you recognised me in spite of my mask," she said. "What do you think of my costume?"

"It's so . . ."

"Plain? It's supposed to be a governess's, you know."

"It's charming. What made you decide on that?"

"You're going as a long-ago lady of the house, which is what you are. Why shouldn't I come as what I am? It was easy to make and I thought no one else would come like this. The idea came to me when we were talking in that eerie part of the house the other day."

"I see."

"Do you think *that* governess looked like this?" she asked. "I think she might have. I looked up the costumes. And this is about the same period as yours. I wonder if anyone will notice it."

"I should hardly think so."

"Rather amusing if they do."

I turned away from her and as I made my way across the hall I was joined by a Roman toga and for a moment I thought it was Bevil. "You are looking striking in your costume." The voice was William Lister's.

"Thank you. I've already seen two other togas. I told you there would be plenty. We might have strayed into the Appian Way."

"Practically every country and period is represented."

"I'm going to the supper-room to make sure everything is in order there."

"I'll come with you."

"No, do please go and look after Mary Queen of Scots. She looks as if she's in Fotheringhay rather than Menfreya."

I saw a Cardinal's costume pass by with Marie Antoinette. My gallant father-in-law was regaining his youth.

We had decided on music from all countries and the "Blue Danube" Waltz was being played as I made my way to the supper-rooms. There were three of them all beautifully decorated with flowers and leaves, and small tables with dazzling napery had been set up in each. I spoke to Pengelly, who assured me that everything was in order, so I returned to the ballroom.

"Will you join me in the dance?"

Another Roman. For a moment my heart leaped. I thought it was Bevil putting on a disguised voice to amuse me; but that illusion quickly passed.

The floor was too crowded to dance very successfully but that did not worry my partner, who was obviously not a good dancer and wanted to talk.

"I must confess I know who you are," he told me.

"Is it so obvious?"

"Not at all. But I've seen you in that dress before."

I had caught the voice now. I knew that mouth. It had grown tight-lipped when Gwennan had gone away.

"So it's you, Harry."

"I'm betrayed."

"You gave it away by mentioning the dress."

"That seems years ago."

"Harry . . ."

"Yes, go on. You're wondering whether I mind talking about it. Well, it's in the past and she's dead now."

"Oh, Harry," I said, "it was so silly of her. It wasn't as though . . ."

"As though she really cared for him? No, perhaps not. But she didn't care for me, either. I don't think she cared for anyone but herself. She was a Menfrey."

I heard the bitter note in his voice and I felt a great pity for him. He hadn't forgotten; perhaps he hadn't forgiven.

"She suffered terribly, Harry."

He was silent and I saw his lips harden, almost as though he were glad that she had. Poor Harry, he had loved her; there seemed to be some power the Menfreys had of binding people to them. I thought of my own feelings for Bevil; nothing he did to me could alter it. And so it might be with Harry, who continued to brood over Gwennan.

I wondered then whether he had decided to go into politics to turn his thoughts from that tragedy, and whether he wanted to stand against Bevil as a sort of revenge.

"You're sorry for me, Harriet," he said suddenly, reading my thoughts. "You're thinking that Gwennan jilted me and now I'm going to be humiliated once more when the people here show me they don't want me to represent them in Parliament."

" Why here, Harry?" I asked. " Why not somewhere else?"

" You don't like the idea of my standing against your husband?"

" No. After all you're an old friend of the family. I know we pretend that isn't important, but it is . . . in a way. I'd like to see you putting up somewhere else."

" You don't think I have a chance here?"

" The Menfreys *have* held the seat for a long time."

" There was a period when your father represented Lansella. That could happen again."

" But . . . he was of the same party."

" The allegiance to a certain party doesn't have to go on for ever."

I could see the grim set of his lips and I believed that he had an idea that if he won the seat from a Menfrey, life would have, in measure, made up for the humiliation he had suffered through Gwennan.

It seemed a crazy notion and I didn't like it.

" You're going to be disappointed, Harry," I said.

" Spoken like the wife of the reigning M.P. I wouldn't expect anything but that from you, Harriet."

" Why don't you think about trying to get a chance somewhere else?"

" This is my place," he said, " as much as the Menfreys'. Should I be driven out by them? It's going to be a fight."

We sat down for a while and he brought the conversation back to Gwennan. I could see that he was dwelling on the past, that he couldn't get her out of his mind. It was natural, I thought, for this ball must have recalled that other when they had been together, she so gay in her home-made blue velvet, enjoying the adventure of the ball she was not supposed to attend. Harry would be carried away by all that charm, exhilarated as never before. No wonder he was full of regrets.

I excused myself to make sure all was well, for after all I was hostess, even though disguised.

I was relieved to get away from him, for he depressed me. I danced now and then ; I sat out and talked ; it was clear that several people knew who I was. Perhaps my slight limp betrayed me. I talked a good deal of politics ; I mingled with the guests; I danced with my father-in-law and with Bevil, who was gay and very affectionate.

"You're an asset to the party, Harriet Menfrey," he told me with a laugh. "How Harry Leveret thinks he's going to beat us when you're around, I can't imagine."

I told him I had danced with Harry, who seemed to be brooding about Gwennan. Bevil wasn't interested in Harry; he told me I looked wonderful, a most exciting ghost from the past. "We ought to bring that picture out and have it cleaned. It should hang in the gallery. Perhaps we'll have you painted in that dress to hang beside it. That would be amusing."

It was wonderful to be with Bevil; I could understand Harry's bitterness.

But of course Bevil and I could not be together all the evening. It was our duty, he said, to attend to the wilting wallflowers. He went off to a talk to plump Helen of Troy and I to an ageing Sir Galahad.

Now and then I caught sight of the eighteenth-century governess. I knew that she was never without partners; her beauty shone through any disguise, and how clever she had been to come so simply clad! It struck me that she would always be clever.

It was after I had left the supper-rooms that I caught sight of her dancing with Bevil. I turned away. I did not want to see them.

All the time I was dancing I was wondering what they were saying to each other. How were they together? The ball had turned sour for me and I wished it was over. Harry Leveret had disturbed me, and I felt then that once having loved a Menfrey there was no escape. That was how it would be with me. I was afraid of Jessica Trelarken, and I was afraid of Bevil. I did not understand her and I understood him too well. Why had she come here as a governess? Was she trying to draw some parallel? Was she saying it is happening now as it happened then?

I suddenly saw it with clarity, how it must have been all those years ago. The governess who lived in those rooms, had she some irresistible attraction like Jessica's? I could imagine the husband who could not let her go, who kept her there, close to him . . .

It was silly. I was not being reasonable. The past could not intrude like that on the present. I had a husband who was fond of female company; there were men who could not be content with one woman, and by a fortuitous chain of events we had a governess who happened to be possessed of rare beauty.

I imagined the rest.

I felt a desire to get out of the ballroom, and slipped into the grounds. The wind caught playfully at my hair but it was safely held in the filet. A strange urge came to me and I took the path which led to the cliff-side garden and then went into the garden itself. I paused to glance back at the house. It was beautiful in moonlight; the lighted windows, the sound of music before me, and behind me the sound of the waves on the sand and rock.

It was high tide and the island seemed farther away than usual; the tips of my slippers were wet, as a wave, wilder than the rest, splashed me with its spray. I looked across at the island and saw the light in the window. I caught my breath and stood still, watching.

I did not know how long I stood there, for as I did so I was back in the past when I had lain beneath a dust sheet and Bevil had towered over me, the girl from the village standing by.

Who was there now? " Bevil always uses the house for his seductions," I could hear Gwennan's voice laughing in my ears; and it seemed that the night was full of ghosts—not of a governess who might have died in childbirth, not of a woman who might have murdered her, not so far back as that . . . Gwennan . . . mocking me, yet my friend. I felt Gwennan was warning me on that night.

And as I stood there I saw a figure emerge from the house. It was not easy to see who, from this distance, but a white toga is easily distinguishable. He was joined by a woman, and because she was in a simpler fancy dress than those of everyone else it was easy to recognise her.

They were together on the island. They came down to the shore; the man in the toga was doing something to the boat. They were going to row back.

Anger constricted in my throat. I would wait for them. I would be there when the boat touched the sand.

But no . . . they were not coming back. They had been making sure that the boat was securely tied. Once before they had not tied it securely enough.

I thought: I will go over. I will confront them. This time he'll not find me cowering under a dust sheet.

I was untying the boat when I heard a cry from behind me.

"Stop, miss."

Fanny was running down the cliff path and came panting to stand beside me.

"What are you doing here? You were going to get into that boat!"

"I had a fancy to go out to the island."

"Are you mad? On a night like this with the sea choppy? If that boat overturned you'd be dragged down in those skirts before you could say Jack Robinson."

She was right.

"Oh, I know," she went on grimly. "I saw. But it's not for you to go over there. Now you'd better get back to that ball and forget about it."

"Not just yet, Fanny. I want to stay out here for a while."

"It's too chilly. Come on."

We climbed up to one of the arbours and there we sat together for a while.

Fanny looked fierce. I wanted to talk to her but I dared not. I was trying to pretend that I had imagined I had seen them on the island.

At length we returned. I didn't see Bevil and Jessica again until the unmasking. Then they were not together.

It was the early hours of the morning before the last guests had gone and I was alone with Bevil. I kept on my dress to give me confidence. I was going to speak to him because I couldn't remain in suspense.

I gripped my hands behind my back to give me courage. He was humming one of the waltz tunes, and coming to me, put his arms about me and tried to dance round the room with me.

"I think our ball was a success," he said. "We must do more entertaining."

"There's something I have to say to you, Bevil."

He stopped and looked at me intently, noticing the gravity of my voice.

"I left the ballroom at one time," I said. "I went down to the beach and saw two people on the island."

He raised his eyebrows. "You mean—our guests?"

"One of them was Jessica Trelarken. The other was in a Roman toga."

"The Romans were ubiquitous to-night." He spoke lightly.

"Bevil," I said, "was it you?"

He looked startled, he hesitated and my heart leaped with fear.

"On the island? Certainly not!"

I thought: Would it be part of his code to lie, to defend his mistress in any way necessary?

"I thought . . ."

"I know what you thought. Because of that unfortunate affair of the teddy bear. . . ."

"You weren't really there, Bevil?"

"I really wasn't there," he replied mimicking my earnest tone.

Then he took the snood from my hair and threw it on to the dressing-table. His hands were on my dress.

"How does this thing unfasten?" he asked.

I turned my back to show him. I believed him—because I wanted to so much.

A few weeks later Bevil had to go to London and I went with him. Although I loved Menfreya so much I was delighted to get away from Jessica.

I was very happy in Bevil's little town house; I met many of his political friends and because I was able to talk to them about politics and the party I was a great success and Bevil was proud of me.

"Of course," they said, "as Sir Edward's daughter you knew all about it before you married." They thought Bevil had made a very wise marriage; they envied him, they said; and he liked to be envied.

I enjoyed calling on Aunt Clarissa. Phyllis was engaged but the match was not up to their expectations. I was sorry for Sylvia, who was still unattached. But I couldn't help being amused at the different treatment accorded my new status. Aunt Clarissa rather implied that I owed my good fortune to her endeavours. Bevil and I laughed a great deal about this when we were alone.

Yes, they were happy days.

It was while we were in London that I had the idea of turning the island house into a holiday home for poor children who had no opportunity of having a few weeks by the sea in summer. This notion had come to me when I had made a sentimental journey to the markets I had long ago visited with Fanny. I saw them through different eyes now, and longed to give those little coster children a taste of sea air.

I was excited by the project and delighted when Bevil agreed with me that it would be a fine way of using the house which had been so useless. I decided that as soon as I returned I would make preparations and it might be that we could start our holiday scheme at the beginning of the following summer.

By the time we returned to Menfreya the autumn was well advanced. Benedict was pleased to see us and found primroses in the lane which he brought to me. They were a rarity at this time of the year, but I have seen them occasionally in November, as though the balminess of the weather had deluded them into thinking that the spring had come.

"For you," he told me; and I was delighted, until I realised that Jessica had prompted him to make the offering. I sometimes had the notion that she was trying to placate me.

It was soon after our return that the rumour about the island became the prevailing topic for several days.

Two of the local girls, out after dusk, hurrying along the cliff path, were sure they saw a ghost on the island. According to their account, they had both seen the apparition, had looked at each other and then started to run home as fast as they could.

They were questioned by their parents. "A ghost? What did it look like?"

"Like a man."

"Then perhaps it was a man."

"'Twas no man, we know."

"Then how did 'ee know 'twas a ghost?"

"We did know, didn't us, Jen?"

"Yes, we did know."

"But *how*?"

"'Twere the way he stood there."

"How do ghosts stand?"

"I dunno. But 'taint like ordinary folk. Looking to Menfreya he was. . . ."

"How?"

"How ghosts do."

"How's that?"

"I dunno. You just know it's how they be when you do see un, don't 'ee, Jen?"

"Aye, you do just know."

"I wouldn't live in that house for a farm."

So the story went round. A man had appeared on the island and although it wasn't possible to see him clearly they knew he wasn't any man of the neighbourhood. He wasn't anyone they had seen before.

Bevil laughed at the story. "It means they're running short of scandal. They must have something to talk about."

But I thought of the night when I had hidden under the dust sheets; I thought of the night of the ball. I had seen two of our guests there then. Could it be that they had found the island house a pleasant meeting-place? Could it be that the man who had been there that night was the "ghost" seen by the two girls?

I wondered.

The Cornish people love a ghost. There are more ghosts in Cornwall than in all the rest of England; they can be piskies, knackers, little people, spriggans—but they are ghosts all the same; and when the Cornish discover one, they don't let him go lightly.

The cliff path was often deserted after dark, but several people claimed to have seen the spirit of the island. He varied from a knacker to a man in a sugar-loaf hat, small but lit by a phosphorescent light so that he could be clearly seen; he was tall beyond ordinary men, some said, and they saw horns sticking out of his head. To others he was an ordinary man in a sou'wester—a man who had been "returned by the sea."

I used to sit at my window looking out to the island and I could understand how these fantasies were created. The shifting light could play tricks, and with the help of the imagination and absolute belief almost any image that was desired could be created.

One old man, Jemmie Tomrit, who lived in a two-roomed cottage in Menfreystow, was deeply affected by the story. He was a fisherman of ninety—a man respected for his longevity; he was the pride of his family, who were determined to keep him alive till he was at least a hundred. He was a mascot, a talisman. There was a saying in the town: "As long-lived as the Trekellers." And old Jim Trekeller had lived to ninety-two, his brother to eighty-nine. So the Tomrits were hoping to have the name Trekeller changed to Tomrit if they could manage it.

Therefore the old man was never allowed out in a cold wind; he was cosseted and cared for and when he was missing from home there was a general outcry.

He was found sitting on the cliff close to Menfreya " looking for the ghostie," he said.

And the Tomrits were angry with Jen and Mabel who had come home with tales of ghosts on the island, because the old man was always trying to get out to the cliffs to stare at the island. He muttered to himself and hadn't been the same since ; and when he had tried to get out of bed at night and had fallen and bruised himself the Tomrits had called in Dr. Syms, who had said it was a lucky escape, for it might have been a broken thigh, which could have been dangerous at his age. And if he was getting an obsession about the island, well they must remember that he was a very old man and old men must be expected to ramble on a bit—it was called senility.

"Grandfer senile!" cried the Tomrits. " 'Tis they silly girls that be responsible for this. 'Tis a lot of silly nonsense. There be no ghost on No Man's Island."

Then the most important topic in Menfreystow was, would the Tomrits be able to snatch the title from the Trekellers after all ; and the island ghost slipped into second place, and after a while was only mentioned now and then, although it was remembered at dusk when people found themselves on the lonely cliff path.

I caught a bad cold during November and Fanny insisted that I spend a few days in bed. She made me her special brew of lemon and barley water which stood by my bed in a glass jug over which she put a piece of muslin, weighted with beads at the four corners to keep out the dust.

I had to admit it was soothing.

Bevil had to go back to London and I was sorry I couldn't accompany him. So, he said, was he ; but he thought he would not be away for more than a week or so.

The weather turned stormy and my cold had left me with a cough over which Fanny shook her head and scolded me.

"It's wise to stay in, dear," said Lady Menfrey, "until the gales die down. Going out in this weather's no good for anybody."

So I stayed in my room, reading, going through letters which had come to the Lansella chambers and answering some of them. William told me that he was carrying on at the chambers in Lansella while Bevil was away and it came out that Jessica was helping him.

I was astonished.

"But what of Benedict?"

"His grandmother takes charge of him while she's away. She's glad to, and I need help at the chambers. Miss Trelarken has an aptitude for the work and the people seem to like her."

Occasionally during those days, a feeling of dread would come over me. I felt threatened but I could not be sure from which direction.

Fanny was aware of it. Sometimes I would see her sitting at the window staring broodingly across at the island as though she hoped to find the answer there. I wanted to talk to Fanny, but I dared not. Already she hated Bevil; I could not tell her of my vague fears; but her attitude did not help me.

I woke up one night with the sweat on my face, startled out of my sleep. I heard myself calling out, though I did not know to whom.

Something was wrong . . . terribly wrong. Then I knew. I was in pain and I felt sick.

"Bevil," I called, and then I remembered that he was in London.

I got up and staggered through to Fanny's room, which was just across the corridor.

"Fanny!" I cried. "Fanny!"

She started up from her bed. "Why, lord save us, what's the matter?"

"I feel ill," I told her.

"Here!" She was at my side. She was wrapping something round my shivering body. She got me into bed and sat by me.

After a while I felt better. I stayed in Fanny's room and although next morning I no longer felt ill I was weak and exhausted.

Fanny wanted to send for the doctor but I said no. I was all right now.

It was just weakness after the cold, Fanny said; but if I felt like that again she was going to have no more nonsense.

It was only a few days later when that incident, coupled with what happened to Fanny, took on an alarming significance.

It was Fanny's custom to awaken me in the morning by drawing my curtains and bringing me my hot water. Therefore I was surprised on waking and looking at the clock to see that it was half an hour later than my usual time for rising.

A terrible fear came to me then. There was only one thing which would stop Fanny coming and that was that she was ill. Putting my feet into slippers and wrapping a dressing-gown about me I hurried across the corridor to her room.

The sight of her horrified me. She was lying in bed, her hair in two thin little plaits jutting out at the side of her head, her face a greyish colour.

"Fanny!" I cried.

"I'm all right now," she assured me. "I thought I was going to die."

"What?"

She nodded. "The same," she said. "I feel that weak I couldn't get up to save my life."

"You mustn't, Fanny," I said. "I'm going to send for the doctor."

She gripped my wrist.

"Lovey," she said earnestly, reverting to a pet name of my childhood. "I'm frightened."

"Why, Fanny?"

"It was the lemon barley," she said. "You haven't been taking it lately."

"No. I didn't fancy it after that night I wasn't well."

"I saw it standing there. It had been there all day. I didn't think I ought to waste it and I drank the lot."

"Fanny, what are you saying?"

"It was in the lemon barley. I was with your stepmother when she had a bad turn once. She said to me: 'It's all right, Fanny. I've taken an over-dose of my medicine.' You know what that medicine was. They told us at the inquest. It killed her in the end."

"Fanny!"

"It was meant for you. There's something going on in this house."

"You mean somebody's trying to poison us?"

"They didn't know *I* was going to drink it. It wasn't meant for me."

"Oh . . . Fanny!"

"Yes," she said. "I'm frightened, I am."

I was silent. Thoughts were crowding into my mind too jumbled, too horrifying to express. I kept seeing Jessica's face with the unfathomable smile. And I thought: No. It's impossible.

"Fanny," I said, "what are we going to do?"

"We've got to catch them, that's all. We've got to watch."

"We must call in the doctor."

Fanny shook her head. "No," she advised. "Then they'd know we were on their track. They'd try something else, and we wouldn't be prepared for it. They mustn't. They'll think you didn't drink and it was thrown away. Let them think that."

Fanny's eyes were wide and staring. I didn't like the look of her at all and was in two minds about calling the doctor.

I told her so and she shook her head. "You must never take anything in your room. That's the only way you'll be safe."

I said: "You could make more lemon barley. We could have it analysed. That's what we ought to do."

"No," she said. "They're cunning. While we're doing that they'll try something else."

"Fanny, this is madness."

"Who came into the room to-day, do you remember?"

"Everybody. William with some papers from the chambers. Lady Menfrey brought in the flowers. Sir Endelion came to see how I was. Miss Trelarken came in and brought Benny to see me. Then there are the maids."

"You see, it's awkward and we don't know, and they might not try it again. I feel better now although I believed I was near death in the night. Oh, my little miss, I don't know what this means, but I don't like it. I never have liked it. I feel as though something's calling me to get away . . . that's how I feel."

"I'm sure we should do something, Fanny."

"We must give ourselves a little while, though . . . a little while to think."

She was so distraught that I promised her to do nothing . . . yet.

After the first shock I found myself disbelieving Fanny's theory that the barley water had been poisoned. I had had a cold; perhaps it was a gastric chill. It had made me feel sick; Fanny had caught it; she certainly seemed ill after that bout in the night. I said to myself: We're hatching this between us. It's suspicion and jealousy that haven't any foundation in fact. Bevil said he wasn't on the island; and even if he were unfaithful, he would never allow anyone to harm me.

Poison! It was impossible.

Fanny had changed; she had grown even thinner and her eyes seemed sunken; there was a wild expression in them which alarmed me; she was more possessive than ever and would scarcely let me out of her sight.

About a week after Fanny's sickness I went down to the Lansella chambers and there received another shock when I realised how insidiously Jessica was undermining my position.

One of the callers, when received by me, said as she sat down: "Last time I saw Mrs. Menfrey. Such a lovely lady! So kind and gentle. I'm not surprised our Member is proud of her—as I've heard he is."

"I'm Mrs. Menfrey, the Member's wife," I said.

"Oh!" she cried, turning faintly pink. "Well, I must say I'm sorry. . . . I thought, you see, from the way she was . . . er . . . she didn't say she wasn't when I called her Mrs. Menfrey . . . which I'm sure I did."

When I next saw Jessica I said to her, "I hear you were mistaken for me at the chambers."

She raised those perfectly-shaped eyebrows to signify surprise.

"Yes," I went on, "one of the callers said she had seen the Member's wife last time she had come. It was you."

Jessica shrugged her shoulders. "They form their conclusions."

"She was so certain because she'd addressed you as Mrs. Menfrey and you hadn't corrected her."

"Oh, they imagine these things."

I looked into her face and noticed the calm smiling mouth, the beautiful eyes which betrayed nothing, the perfection of her smooth, fresh-coloured skin. In that moment I thought: If she wanted my place she'd be ruthless enough to do anything to get it.

NINE

Bevil had returned and Christmas was upon us. I awoke early to the sounds of bustle, for the servants were all up at dawn to prepare pies, game and poultry. They were so excited that they couldn't keep quiet and on Christmas Day no one expected them to.

Bevil gave me a diamond bracelet; and Benedict came racing into our bedroom to show us what he had discovered in the stocking which Jessica had given him to hang on his bedpost.

" Look, Uncle Bevil. Look, Aunty Harriet."

We looked and admired, and I thought then how pleased Gwennan would have been if she could have seen him; she would smile ruefully, though, because by doing what she had wished for her son I had brought Jessica into the house.

When I heard Jessica calling him I took him by the hand and led him away; she was in the corridor, wearing a blue twill dressing-gown, only elegant because she was wearing it; and her hair hung in a thick plait down her back. She looked more beautiful every day.

Later in the morning Bevil and Sir Endelion went hunting; the sound of the horns echoed through the house and when they returned, according to custom, the log fires were blazing —elm and oak between which the very sweet-smelling bog turf had been spread.

The carol singers visited us, their voices untrained but enthusiastic.

> " As I sat on a sunny bank
> A sunny bank, a sunny bank
> As I sat on a sunny bank
> A Christmas Day in the morning."

The sunlight filled the house, and through the open window

came the soft south-west wind. There would be rain very likely before evening. It was a typical Cornish Christmas weather—no snow for us. We might see a few snowflakes during the New Year but there was rarely enough to settle. Our Christmases were warm and damp.

We all gathered in the hall—decorated with holly and ivy—for the wassailing when the bowl of spiced ale was set on the table and Sir Endelion drank from it the health of all who lived in the house, and then passed it round so that we might all drink too.

Bevil held the bowl out to me and his eyes were wide with affection.

"Happy Christmas, Harriet," he whispered; and I wondered whether I had been passing through a phase of madness to doubt him.

I wore my topaz gown that evening; and since it was Christmas Day we dined in the great hall as had been done every Christmas since Sir Endelion and Bevil could remember. When the guise dancers arrived we danced with them; then we sat and watched while the villagers crowded into the hall to see the guisards perform their play. We of the house handed round the spiced ale and punch, the saffron cake, potato cake, pasties and gingerbread as Menfreys had been doing for generations.

That was a happy day.

There was consternation at Menfreya a few days later.

Fanny told me when she brought up my breakfast tray. Her face was working oddly, so I knew she was upset.

"What is it, Fanny?" I asked.

"That clock's stopped," she said tersely. "That tower clock."

"It's impossible."

"No. It's happened. Stopped at twenty minutes to three. There's a regular row going on downstairs I can tell you. Dawney's just come up to the house to see Sir Endelion and *him*. They're in a nice rage, I can tell you. It's never happened in a hundred years or more . . . so they say."

"A great deal of fuss about a clock!" I replied.

She gave me an odd glance and set the tray down on the bed. I looked at it with distaste. A boiled egg, thin bread and butter, coffee and marmalade. It was what I usually had since after my cold I took it in bed, but I had little appetite for it this morning.

She stood at the bottom of my bed. "You know what they're saying. It means a death in the family."

"Old wives' tale," I said.

"Still," she added, "they're in a state."

When she left me I tried to eat a little because I did not want anyone to know how upset I was. How had the clock stopped? It was Dawney's first duty to see that it never did. It was oiled at the right time, watched over, tended with care, just to make sure it continued to work.

It may have seemed foolish to pander to the superstition; but this was Cornwall and the Menfreys were a Cornish family.

I guessed that the news was already over the neighbourhood. The clock has stopped! It means one of the Menfreys is threatened.

They would watch us now; they would see death shadowing us. It was obvious that some portentous event was about to take place. We had had the ghost on the island; and now the clock was stopped. In these they would see omens.

It was unnerving to know that people were watching you expectantly. When Bevil or I came riding into the courtyards the grooms would come out to see if we were actually home. I was sure they expected us to be brought home on a stretcher. I had a strange feeling that they had selected me for the victim. Then the uneasy feeling came to me that they knew something which I merely suspected. Did they know more of the relationship between Bevil and Jessica? Was it true that when a man preferred another woman to his wife everyone knew of this before the wife?

It was all very well to laugh at superstitions, but at heart most of us are susceptible to them. I was becoming nervous. I remembered the two incidents of the barley water, known only to Fanny and myself. But perhaps to others. Those who had tried to poison us? But that was absurd. No one had. It was Fanny's ridiculous suspicions. Which I shared. Or did I? I was not sure.

Fanny didn't help. She watched over me with persistence, and if I were later home than she expected me to be I would find her in a state of terrible anxiety. Once I heard her praying . . . to Billy. In moments of crisis nowadays she always turned to Billy.

Sometimes I wanted to get away from the house and I liked to wander away from Menfreya along the cliff path to Menfreystow. There I would sit, overlooking the sea, and think about the past—my past with Bevil, being discovered by him on the island when I had run away, the joy of meeting him at Lady Mellingfort's ball. But chiefly I thought of that occasion when he had come to my Aunt Clarissa's house to see me and I had stopped to change my dress. That was before Jenny's death, before I had inherited so much money. If only he had asked me to marry him then! I wanted so much to believe that was what he intended to say to me.

Suspicions coloured all my thoughts, all my memories of the past.

And while I was sitting on the wooden bench which had been set on the cliffs for the use of weary walkers, old A'Lee came along the path and saw me.

He greeted me and I saw his chin wagging involuntarily, which was a sign that he was amused.

"Why, if it's not Mrs. Menfrey."

"How are you?" I asked.

"Oh, we're fighting fit up at Chough Towers, Mrs. Menfrey."

Fighting fit! He was reminding me of the rivalry between us and on whose side he was.

"Mind if I take a rest awhile, Mrs. Menfrey?" he asked. "It's long since you and me had a little chat like. Regular friends we was, once upon a time."

"Why not now?" I asked.

His chin started to wag. "You being one of them, and me being on the other side, like . . ."

"Mr. Harry and my husband are good friends," I said.

That made the chin wag more furiously than ever. He changed the subject and nodded to where the island jutted out of the sea.

"They say it be haunted by the spirits of men as died violent deaths there."

"Several men?"

"I did hear it were a regular practice for men to go on to that island and never be heard of no more—but maybe they was, when their bodies were washed up on the shore."

"How could that have been?"

"The house was said to be used as a dumping ground for smugglers, and that it was the excisemen who went searching for contraband in Little Menfreya who never came back again alive."

"One of your Cornish legends?"

"Like as not. There's plenty on 'em. And now this clock have stopped. I don't like the sound of that, Mrs. Menfrey."

"Well, you see we're all still here."

"Don't 'ee laugh at it. 'Taint lucky to laugh. That clock ain't stopped for years and years. Menfreys wouldn't let it, so 'twas said."

"So it hasn't stopped before in living memory!"

"There's stories enough. Don't 'ee go out when the weather be rough, Miss Harriet." He had slipped into the use of my old name and I fancied his attitude changed towards me when he did. I had become the child for whom he had been sorry, and was no longer one of the enemy. "I remember a story my grandfather told me about one of the Menfreys. There was an accident. A gentleman who was staying there was took out in a boat by Sir Bevil and this fine gentleman couldn't swim. Sir Bevil he were a fine swimmer like all the Menfreys. I used to watch young Mr. Bevil . . . our one, you know, m'dear . . . darting in and out of the sea. Like a fish he were."

"Yes, and what happened to this other Bevil?"

"He took the fine gentleman out for a row and the boat capsized. The fine gentleman were drowned and Sir Bevil swam ashore."

"He didn't attempt to save his friend?"

"The sea were high and 'tweren't possible . . . so he said. Though he said he'd tried. But 'twasn't so. Years passed and he took to religion. It would have made you split your sides with laughing. He'd have all the girls and boys taken in fornication, as he'd call it, and punished. The boys would be whipped and the girls shamed in the church. That were how religion took him although some of the girls and boys might have been his own flesh and blood for he had the Menfrey taste for love-making—in his sinful days. Well, it so happened that he came near to death and knew it and he was afraid that all his latter-day goodness wouldn't make up for this big sin of his and on his death-bed he confessed.

He'd gambled with the fine gentleman, who had won his estates from him, and that included Menfreya itself. He wanted the fine gentleman's wife. So there was only one thing he thought he could do and that was remove the fine gentleman. So he bored a hole in the boat and filled it with something . . . he didn't tell what . . . he couldn't go into details for his breathing was getting shorter and there wasn't much time left . . . and he took the gentleman out and soon the boat started to fill with water. The fine gent panicked and the boat overturned. All Sir Bevil had to do was swim for the land and hope fine gent wouldn't be rescued. And if he was, it was an accident . . . that was all."

"Is it possible to bore a hole in a boat and make it sea-worthy for a time?"

"Certain sure it is. If the hole were filled, well 'twould be like the bung hole in a barrel, wouldn't it?"

"Yes, but it would be obvious if a hole was bored. . . ."

He lifted his shoulders. "Sir Bevil, so 'twas said, filled up the hole with some'at as would slowly melt."

"Is there such a thing?"

"Salt packed tight, maybe. Sugar. That would be better. Tight packed sugar would take a little time to melt in cold sea water."

"What an idea!"

"Yes, b'aint it."

"Well," I said, "that happened long ago. Or perhaps it didn't happen at all."

"I allus had to make up stories for 'ee, Miss Harriet, didn't I now? When you was a little 'un and come to the Towers . . . a sad little 'un on account of your papa never having the time to be nice to 'ee . . . I used to say to myself, 'Now how can I amuse Miss Harriet?'"

"You were good to me, A'Lee."

"Aye. I were."

"And it was a good story. Did it really happen?"

"Which one, Miss Harriet? The ghosts on the island or Sir Bevil and the boat?"

"Both."

"Well, that be a queer thing about us Cornish, m'dear. We do love a tale and the more ghostly it be the better we do like it. I often think on them days when we used to be friends like. 'Tis a pity . . ."

"We're still friends, A'Lee."

"Yes," he said. "Nought on 'em can alter that." There was some truth in it, for he was worried, and I knew he was thinking about the clock's stopping.

There was a knock on my door. It was eleven in the morning. Bevil had gone off to Plymouth for the day on special business.

"Come in," I said, and Jessica entered, looking coolly beautiful in a gown of lavender cotton and white lace collar and cuffs. I could never see her without imagining her and Bevil together as lovers and it was difficult to compose myself in these circumstances.

"There is someone asking for Mr. Menfrey." I saw now that she was paler than usual and that she was greatly disturbed. "It's most extraordinary."

She held out a card to me and I read,

J. HAMFORTH AND SONS, UNDERTAKERS
Fore Street,
Lansella

"I don't understand it at all," she went on. "I thought perhaps you . . ."

I said: "I will go down to see what he wants."

He was waiting in the library, black-coated and solemn, and when I entered he started and turned pale. We knew each other slightly, for his premises were in Fore Street close to Bevil's chambers and naturally Bevil and I were well known in the district.

"Mr. Hamforth . . . what is it?"

"Excuse me, ma'am . . . I . . . This was a shock and I couldn't believe it when I received the letter."

"Letter," I said. "What letter?"

"The letter telling me to call to . . . er . . . to see about the . . . arrangements."

"What arrangements?"

He bit his lip; he lowered his eyes because he simply could not look at me. I had a feeling that when I had entered the room he looked as though he were seeing a ghost.

A ghost! There was something very strange going on here.

"You came to make arrangements about a funeral?" I said sharply.

" Er . . . yes, ma'am, Mrs. Menfrey."

" Whose . . . funeral?"

He did not answer, but I knew.

" You thought it was to be mine?"

" Well, ma'am, that was what . . ."

" What you were told?"

" That I was to come at once to Menfreya, that I was to make the arrangements."

" For *me*?"

He was embarrassed, poor man. He had never before had to face the task of preparing a woman for burial before she was dead.

" I was upset," he said. " So were my wife and my clerks. They'd been to some of the meetings and they'd seen you there."

So they all knew. In Lansella they would be talking about my " death." It would be all over the town. News like that travelled quickly. I was certain that Mr. Hamforth's trap would have been seen coming to Menfreya. Death at Menfreya! The clock which had not stopped for a hundred years had stopped recently. And now the undertaker was up at Menfreya.

" This is the most extraordinary affair," I said.

" I've never known anything like it before in all my experience, ma'am."

" No, I don't suppose you have. But I want to know how it happened."

" There was a letter came this morning. It was a queer sort of letter. But I didn't think of that then."

" A queer sort of letter? Where is it?"

" I brought it with me and showed it to the young lady."

" To Miss Trelarken?"

" Yes. She was puzzled and asked to see it. You see I told her that I had come to make arrangements and she couldn't make out what, so I showed her the letter and she said she would take me to you as Mr. Menfrey was not at home."

I was relieved. There was a letter. This was some sort of practical joke and we could get to the bottom of it if there was a piece of tangible evidence like a letter.

" Give me the letter, please, Mr. Hamforth."

He took out his pocket book and fumbled through it. He looked puzzled; then that expression lifted and he said: " Of course, the young lady took it and didn't give it back."

I went to the bell rope and when a maid appeared said: "Tell Miss Trelarken to come here without delay."

She could not have been far away, for she came almost immediately.

I said: "We want the letter."

"The letter?" she repeated.

"The one Mr. Hamforth gave you. The one which was sent asking him to call here."

"Oh, yes. But . . . I gave it back to you, Mr. Hamforth."

"No, miss, you didn't."

"But surely . . ."

They looked at each other in amazement and I felt a sick fear rising within me.

"It must be somewhere," I said sharply to Jessica. "Look in your pocket."

She tried the two pockets of her gown and shook her head. She appeared to be very distressed—or was she putting on a good act? That was the thought that occurred to me then: she was acting.

What did this mean? Had she and Bevil arranged this? Were they together in some diabolical plot against me? If I were no longer here there would be no obstacle in her way . . . and perhaps his.

"It must be somewhere about," I said. "I am very anxious to see that letter and to know who wrote to Mr. Hamforth telling him to come and bury me."

We searched the library and then Jessica said: "But it was in the hall. I was about to go out into the garden when you came, Mr. Hamforth, and we stood in the hall for a while. It was after you had given me the letter that we came into the library."

I led the way to the hall and we searched everywhere, but we could not find the letter.

"It's very strange," I said, and the terror was growing in me. "At least, you both *saw* the letter. How was it worded?"

They looked at each other.

"It was written in a hand I did not recognise," said Jessica. "It asked Mr. Hamforth to come and make arrangements for the funeral of Mrs. Menfrey."

"There must have been a signature," I insisted.

"It was, I thought, written by Mr. Menfrey's secretary," said Mr. Hamforth.

"By Mr. Lister?"

"It was not written by Mr. Lister," put in Jessica. "I know his handwriting well. It was signed for B. Menfrey and there was an initial which I couldn't read."

I looked from Mr. Hamforth to Jessica.

Who had done it and why? Could it be that someone had chosen this macabre way of warning me?

Bevil came back from London that night. I was in bed but not asleep. I had been lying awake going over the events of the day. I kept seeing Mr. Hamforth's horrified and bewildered face, and Jessica's, not smiling now, but as unfathomable as ever.

Bevil came into the bedroom.

"Wake up, Harriet. I've some exciting news. Balfour has invited me to a week-end party. There'll be several others there."

"That's wonderful. But . . . have you heard about Hamforth?"

"Hamforth? What's Hamforth got to do with the Prime Minister's invitation?"

"Nothing. He came to-day to measure me for my coffin."

"What!"

I explained.

"Good God! Who would do such a thing?"

"I should like to know that. There was a letter but Jessica Trelarken put it down somewhere . . . and it was lost."

"But what was the idea?"

"First the clock stopped . . . and now this. It's evident that I'm the victim."

"Harriet, for God's sake, don't even think such a thing."

"It seems as though someone's warning me."

"We'll get to the bottom of this nonsense. I'll go and see Hamforth to-morrow."

"He can tell you no more. If we could find the letter . . . But you see, Jessica had it . . . and lost it. It seems so odd."

"She must have been as unnerved as you."

"At least they hadn't come to measure *her* for her coffin."

"What a macabre notion of a joke. My poor Harriet." He had his arms round me soothingly. I wanted to lie against him, to sob out my fears.

He put out the light and came to bed and we talked for a long time about the Hamforth affair and of what the Prime Minister's invitation could mean.

Bevil went to Lansella the next day. I didn't go. I couldn't bear to face everyone who I knew would be talking about my "death." I would wait a while, I promised myself, until the talk had died down.

Fanny came in with my breakfast tray. She said I shouldn't hurry to get up.

She looked extraordinarily drawn. I was sure that the Hamforth shock had frightened her as much as it had me.

"Fanny," I said, "you mustn't worry."

"Worry!" she said. "I'm well-nigh out of my mind for wondering what's the right thing to do."

"Do you think we ought to tell about the lemon barley? Everything seems different now."

"You needn't worry about that," said Fanny nodding at the tray. "I went down to the kitchen and cooked it myself."

"Oh, Fanny, I'm safe while you're here."

"I wouldn't let no harm come to you."

"You see, Fanny. I'm being warned. Who would warn me?"

Her face screwed as though she were going to cry.

"Did someone stop the clock to warn me? Did they send that letter to Hamforth's to warn me? Then it looks as if whoever did these things wants me to be prepared. It wouldn't be the same one who wanted me dead, would it?"

She spread out her hands and stared down at them, shaking her head.

Suddenly she stopped and looked at me sharply. "There's something I've got to tell you. It's that Miss Trelarken. You can always tell. I can see it in her face. It does something to a woman. I know, I tell you."

"Know what?"

"I went into her room this morning. The little boy came down to the kitchen before she was up. I took him back and she was there without her dress. In her petticoat she was. She always wears those full skirts, but in her petticoat you could see."

I stared at Fanny.

"I swear it's true," she said, "that Miss Trelarken is going to have a child."

"Fanny, it's not possible."

"I'd say it was."

"No," I said. "No." I felt sick with the horror of it. I couldn't bear to read the suspicions and conclusions in Fanny's eyes.

It was growing so like that other story that it was becoming like a nightmare. The pregnant governess. The wife in the way. What had she said: "They would hate each other. They would want to *murder* each other."

It couldn't be so. I had become obsessed by the governess story. And then suddenly I remembered how she had stood close to me on the parapet before she had fainted.

It was true, of course. Jessica Trelarken, like the governess in the story, was going to have a child.

Evil thoughts crowded into my mind. Was the ghost on the island, seen by the girls, Bevil keeping a secret tryst with his mistress? Hadn't he always used the island for his youthful adventures? I imagined the desperation of lovers, the whispered conversations, the hopes, the fears. And then . . . the poisoned lemon barley. Jenny had died through taking arsenic which she had presumably procured through her theatrical friends. And Jessica? I knew now that her complexion, so perfectly smooth, so fresh yet somehow translucent, was as Jenny's had been. Did Jessica have arsenic in her possession as Jenny had had? How could she get it? Easily. Her father would use it in making up his medicines and a quantity of it could have been in his dispensary at the time of his death. Jessica would have known what it was. She would have read of Jenny's experiments and might well have tried some herself. What was more natural than that a woman who saw the effect of her beauty on all around her should attempt to enhance it?

If Jessica had arsenic in her possession, it was reasonable to suppose that some belonging to her had found its way into my lemon barley.

She had hankered after my position when she came to Menfreya—and now, perhaps, if Fanny was right, she desperately needed it. And how could she attain it while I stood there to prevent her?

Was Jessica trying to kill me?

Then who had warned me? Surely someone who knew what she was trying to do. But then why not tell me simply?

Why go to such lengths as stopping the clock and sending the undertaker to measure me for my coffin?

There was only one answer. Whoever was trying to warn me did not want to disclose his—or her—identity.

A'Lee's mischievous face came into my mind. Could it be? He had always been my friend. Perhaps he had seen them on the island. Was he not the one who had brought them over on the night they had been caught there?

The thoughts whirled round and Fanny sat by my bed, frowning as she pulled at the corners of her apron.

Luncheon was a quiet meal that day. I shared it with Sir Endelion and Lady Menfrey; they were subdued as we had all been since the Hamforth affair. Jessica had lunch in the nursery with Benedict, for which I was glad; I was sure if I saw her my looks might betray the suspicions which Fanny had started in my mind. William Lister did not join us; he was busy in the study, and Bevil had not returned from Lansella. I supposed that the new development hinted at by the Prime Minister's invitation was being discussed.

I went back to my room after luncheon. Menfreya was quiet at that hour. The servants were all in their own quarters; my parents-in-law were resting. Jessica remained in the nursery with Benedict, and William was at work.

There was a knock on my door and Fanny came in.

She said: "I'm going over to the island. Would you come with me? I did want to talk to you about some of the work over there. Besides . . ."

I had talked to Fanny a great deal about my projects for the island house and she had been wholeheartedly in favour. I guessed she would be a great help to me when I started my holiday scheme. Perhaps, I thought, she wanted to discuss something with me, but it was more likely that she wanted me to be with her.

"Put on a warm coat," she said. "The wind's that chilly. Here. Wrap yourself up well. You go on ahead, I'll catch you up."

Before I had reached the shore she was with me. We pushed out the boat and rowed over.

I smiled sadly at her and said: "Fanny, the fact is you don't want me out of your sight, do you?"

"That's about it," she said. "But there's things I want you to see over there."

I tried to draw my thoughts away from fears and think of the summer when the house would be full of children. It seemed a long way in the future.

"I could put up six little beds in the big front bedroom," I said; "and then there are the other bedrooms. The island will seem a paradise to them. We shall have to make a rule that they don't attempt to row themselves to the mainland without an adult, though."

Fanny was nodding, pleased to see my thoughts moving in a new direction.

We went towards the house and she said: "When I was in the kitchen the other day I noticed this here cellar. You can lift up one of the stone flags. You'd hardly notice it was any different from the others . . . unless you knew. But that was the idea, of course. You come along and I'll show you."

Fanny stood at the door of the house overlooking the sea and Menfreya as though momentarily reluctant to tear herself away.

"It's a sight," she admitted grudgingly.

And a sight it was, even on this January day with the sea a darkish green crimped with frothy waves. I stood with her looking back to Menfreya—grey, almost menacing in the afternoon light.

Fanny's eyes were gleaming with an expression I did not understand.

"Come on in. I want you to see this cellar."

I followed her into the kitchen where with some effort she lifted the flagstone. "You've got to understand it," she said. "It's not easy to open." Having exposed a cavity in the floor, she turned to a cupboard and taking out an iron candlestick stuck in a candle and lighted it.

"There are some stone steps leading down into this cellar," she said. "I'm going to have a look."

"You must be careful, Fanny."

"I'll be careful all right. It's where they used to hide the kegs of whisky, Jem Tomrit told me."

"He told you?"

"Yes, he told me. You remember how upset he was when he thought there was a ghost on the island. He saw a man there . . . clear as he saw me, he told me. He said it was a ghost of one of them that had been drowned at sea. Here, hold this candle a minute. Give it to me when I'm down."

She descended and held out her hand for the candle. I

heard her exclamation when I handed it to her. "Oh, I say!"

"I'm coming to have a look."

"You take care. These steps are steep. Give me your hand."

I descended four or five steps and saw that Fanny was right. We were in a sort of cellar. I saw there were several more steps to be descended as I peered down.

I went down a few steps to stare into the darkness below me when suddenly there was a thud and the shaft of light which had come through the trap door from the kitchen disappeared.

I looked behind me.

"The trap door has fallen, shutting us in!" I said.

"Yes, Miss Harriet." Her voice was soothing. "Don't worry. It'll be all right."

"It's so dark."

"Your eyes will get accustomed to the gloom in a minute."

I descended a few more steps and it was as though my foot was seized in an icy grip. Water!

"Fanny," I cautioned. "Be careful. There's water down here."

"It gets flooded by the high tides."

"Well, the thing is to get that door open and let in some light. This candle's not much good."

"Look over there," said Fanny. "There's light over there."

"Why, yes. It's coming through a grating."

"That grating is in the garden. It was overgrown by brambles till I cleared them away."

"Why?"

"I thought it best."

"So you knew about this, Fanny?"

"Oh, yes, I knew. I told you I went to see Jem Tomrit. I used to sit with him and make him talk to me. He was worried. You see, he thought the ghosts had come back to the island . . . the ghosts of dead men, and he was afraid they'd come to haunt *him*."

"Why should they?"

"Because he was a murderer of men. This was where they used to bring the smuggled goods and when the excisemen was on their tracks they'd lure them here. They used to let them search the place and they'd leave the trap door not exactly open, but so as it could be seen there was a trap door there. Down they'd go . . . never to come out alive."

"It's a horrible place. I've seen enough of it."

"Well, when the tide's high the water comes in. It comes through that grating, see. . . . That's what it's put there for. This was built with an express purpose, so Jem Tomrit told me. Do you know what to-day is?"

"To-day, Fanny?"

"Well, this Jem Tomrit told me a lot, he did. There's times when the tide comes up higher than ever. It's called spring tides and there's a reason for it. The moon and the sun or something. Don't ask me. It happens at this time of the year, seemingly. Well it'll be to-night at half past eight."

I had begun to shiver—not so much with the cold dampness of this place but by the strangeness of Fanny.

"At spring tide this cellar is flooded right up to the top."

"Fanny," I said, "let's get out of this place. It's damp and cold. We'll explore it properly later."

"How are we going to get out?" she asked.

"The way we came in, of course."

"It's a snap lock. It shut itself. You can only open it from outside. The smugglers saw to that."

"That's absurd."

"I'm only saying what Jem Tomrit told me."

"Then somebody's shut us in."

"Yes," she said slowly, "someone's shut us in." She sat down on one of the steps and covered her face with the hand which was not holding the candle. "I had to be with you. I couldn't leave you alone."

"Fanny," I said, "you know something you haven't told me."

"Yes, Miss Harriet."

"You know that someone is trying to kill me?"

"Yes."

"And you're trying to stop them. But what are we doing here! Are you telling me that someone has shut us in this place?"

She rocked herself to and fro.

"You'll drop the candle," I said. I was not completely frightened yet, because Fanny was beside me. It was like waking from a strange nightmare during my childhood and screaming. Fanny had come to comfort me then; her presence meant security. She gave me that reassurance now.

"You knew about this place," I said, "because Jem Tomrit

told you. You say it's flooded at high tide and to-night there's a spring tide. That's at eight-thirty. It's not four yet. We'll get out before high tide. We shall be missed."

"Who'd think of looking here?"

"There's another thing that struck me. If the water floods this place at high tide, where does it go afterwards? A certain amount sinks into the sandy floor, I suppose, but wouldn't there be much more water than this?"

"There was a big stone over the grating. Jem Tomrit told me how they used to take it away when they'd got prisoners here. Then they'd bale out after."

"There's no big stone over the grating now," I said.

"It was hidden by brambles . . . and it's been taken away. So now it's how it used to be when this cellar was used for murder."

"Fanny," I said, "you're not being very clear. You say *you* cleared the brambles. Then who took the stone away? Who shut the trap door just then? Fanny! Somebody is in this house now. They heard us go into the kitchen. They knew we had come down here and they shut us in!"

"He was here," she said. "That was what frightened the wits out of Jem Tomrit. He saw him and he thought it was the ghost of a dead exciseman, but it weren't. It were my Billy."

"Your Billy. But Billy died years and years ago . . . before I was born."

"Billy loved me true, but there was one he loved better. It was the sea. The sea was his mistress and he'd leave me for her. You ought to have heard him talk about the sea. You knew then what he loved best. When he went away he said: 'Don't be frightened, Fanny. I'll come back for you . . . I'll come back one day. I'll take you to sea with me, one day. You wait for that, Fanny . . . and you be ready when the time comes.' Then suddenly it came to me what he meant. There'd be a sign. And now it's come."

"Fanny," I said, "what has happened to you? Let's get out of this place."

"We'll get out of it in our own good time. He'll be waiting for us. We'll be with him . . . the two of us . . . safe and sound."

"You're not being sensible, Fanny. Do you remember how you used to tell me to be sensible? I'm going to try and open that trap door."

"You'll hurt yourself, lovey. I told you it can only be opened from the outside."

"I don't think you're right, Fanny."

"I am. I made sure. I didn't want anything to go wrong."

"Fanny! Fanny! What are you saying?"

I sat down on the cold step beside her. This companion of my youth, this beloved nurse, this woman to whom I had always turned for comfort, had become a stranger.

"Fanny," I said gently, "let's try and understand what this is all about. Let's sort it out, shall we?"

"There's nothing to sort out, my pet."

I stared into the darkness and wondered how much water there was down there, how much truth was in this story of smugglers and excisemen. I thought of Menfreya—my parents-in-law resting till tea, which they would probably take in their own rooms. Bevil would return. Perhaps for dinner? Perhaps after. But surely I should be missed by dinner-time? When I didn't appear they would send a maid to my room to see if I wanted anything sent up. I should not be there; then they would grow a little anxious. Dinner at eight—high tide at eight-thirty. They would never be in time.

But I couldn't believe in death. Not death at Fanny's hands. In fact I couldn't believe this was really happening to me. It was like one of those fantastic nightmares which used to haunt my childhood.

I walked to the top of the steps and tried to push open the door. It was unyielding. Of course it hadn't been opened for years. It was bound to be difficult. I didn't believe this story of spring locks.

I could not accept Fanny as a murderess. I sat down beside her. I thought: It must be four o'clock. How soon before the water starts coming in? Slowly at first and then . . . the flood. Four hours . . . to wait for death.

I couldn't accept it.

"Fanny," I said, "I want to understand what this means. I want to talk to you."

She said: "You're frightened, are you?"

"I don't want to die, Fanny."

"Lor' bless you, there's nothing to worry about. Billy talked to me about death by drowning. He said it was the easiest way out. Billy will be there waiting for me . . . and I couldn't leave you behind, could I? I didn't want you to die like your stepmother. Drowning's better. 'It's easy,' said to myself. You see they wanted you out of the way . . the two of them. They couldn't fool me. He was never th one for you. I warned you against him. He was too fon of women . . . just as Billy was too fond of the sea. I' have liked Billy to take a nice comfortable job ashore. H wouldn't. Not him. You see, he couldn't leave it alone It's the same thing. With Billy the sea and with him . . women. And since she came . . . with her wicked ways . . I knew I couldn't leave you . . . I knew her. She was goin to get him and now she's carrying the child, she's desperate She'd got the stuff for her complexion just like your step mother . . . but that poor lady killed herself with it . . *she* was going to kill *you*."

"Oh, Fanny, do you believe that?"

"I believe what I see and I was frightened for you. I used to lie awake and my head would go funny . . . dizzy like, with the worry of it. And then Billy came for me and I said to myself I can't leave her. It would be different if *he* was different, if *she* wasn't there. I daren't go and leave her. You see, when I lost my little 'un you were my baby I couldn't leave you, could I? I'll take you to Billy with me, and we'll all be together."

"Fanny, you stopped the clock."

"I wanted you warned. You remember how upset you were when your stepmother died. You said, 'She wasn't warned.' So I warned you. I stopped the clock."

"And then you sent that note to Hamforth's."

"Yes, I did. I wanted you to be ready, you see. I didn't want you to have too big a shock."

"So *you* took the note you'd sent."

"I thought that was best. She laid it down on the table there in the hall and I found it and took it away. It was best that way."

I was silent. I thought: She is mad. My dear Fanny is mad. She is going to commit suicide and kill me because she loves me.

I felt hysterically weak. I stood up and began pounding against the trap door.

"There," she soothed. "There's nothing you can do. Can't open it from down here. They fixed that when they used to get the excisemen down here. Jem told me all about it You'll only hurt your poor hands. Don't you fret. There's

nothing to be done but wait. There's going to be a gale.
A gale and a spring tide. It'll be easier that way."

I was frightened. To be sitting here with Fanny had seemed
in a way cosy so that I could not altogether believe in her
wild plan.

She was so calm, so certain, sitting patiently waiting for
the end. I could not imagine how it would come. The water
would push in through the grating, I guessed, and then what
would happen to us? Would it come as high as the top
steps? I remembered that I had heard it said that the
gardens and kitchens were often flooded at high tide. This
was spring tide, a gale was blowing—and we were underground.

I guessed it to be about six o'clock. No one would have
missed us yet. High tide would have come and gone before
they did.

And here was I shut in a cellar with a mad woman.

I had accepted the truth. Until now she had been only
Fanny—dear, familiar, comfortable Fanny. Now she was the
woman who wanted to kill me.

"I must get out!" I cried suddenly. "I must get out!"

I stood up and pushed with all my might against the trap
door. It was useless. It did not move. Was she indeed right
with her talk of spring locks?

The grating! I thought. Was it possible to find a way
through that? I had a vision of myself climbing the cellar
walls to the grating, forcing it up in some way.

I started down the steps and plunged knee-deep in water.

Fanny was startled out of a reverie.

"What are you doing, you foolish girl! Now you're wet
through. A nice cold you'll be getting and we have to stay
here in our damp clothes."

"Fanny!" I cried hysterically. "What is that going to
matter?"

"Colds can lead to congestion of the lungs and that's no
joke."

"Let's get out of here. I need dry things . . ."

"You're shivering, dearie. Don't you fret. We'll soon be
with him and past all trouble."

"Fanny, please listen to me. We've got to get out of
here. We've got to get out . . ."

"There, ducky," she said, "don't you fret. Fanny's here."

I sat down helplessly beside her and she put an arm about me.

"Don't be frightened. It's only the wind you hear. By golly, there's going to be a storm to-night."

The candle was lost. We had dropped it into the water. I heard the plop as it fell and the feeble flame was extinguished.

I had lost all sense of time. I felt as though I had been for hours in this dark damp place.

I was gradually beginning to understand that I was in truth facing death, that the woman beside me meant to murder me; she and I would die together and the last words I should hear from her would be a heartfelt endearment.

I'm going mad, I told myself. This can't be true.

I heard the crash of the waves against the rocks. The tide was coming in . . . the spring tide.

High tide at eight-thirty! I thought. What was it now? Seven? Later?

I stood up. I would try again. I began to shout for help. I hammered on the stone which shut us down.

Fanny's voice was dreamy. "You remember how I used to read you stories to send you to sleep? You remember Aladdin and his wonderful lamp? Do you remember how the wicked magician shut him in the cave . . . ? This is like it."

"Fanny, this isn't a cave. It's a cellar below sea level and the tide is coming in."

"It all came right for Aladdin. It's all coming right for you."

"They'll miss us at the house, Fanny. They'll look for us."

"They won't look here."

I was silent. She was right. What could possibly lead them here?

"And even if they knew we were here," went on Fanny, "they'd be hard put to it to get across if the sea's anything like as wild as it sounds."

"I don't want to die. I don't *want* to die."

I began to shout for help. It was foolish. Who could hear me?

Then I heard the water spilling over on to the grating, and falling into the cellar.

The tide was almost upon us.

I had dragged Fanny to the topmost step. I had turned my back to the grating. I was standing up hammering ineffectually on the trap door.

Fanny was still. I sensed a certain ecstasy.

At any moment now, we should be swept from the steps. This was death. And only now that I stood face to face with it did I know how desperately I wanted to live. I was calling out without knowing what I called. I realised that it was " Bevil! Bevil! "

Here I was trapped with the water rising. A picture of the Christian Martyr flashed into my mind. I remembered that calm face ; the hands which were bound at the wrists palm to palm in prayer, the wooden stake to which she was bound and the water up to her waist as she awaited the rise of the tide.

With such serenity was poor simple Fanny facing death.

There was a crash as the heavy waves pounded in ; the water came tumbling through the grating. I closed my eyes and waited. I was on the top step but the water was washing about my ankles. In a few minutes the grating would be covered by the sea and then . . . the end.

I put my hands over my face.

" Soon now, my love," whispered Fanny.

" No," I cried. I hammered on the trap door. " Bevil! " I cried. " Bevil."

Then miraculously Bevil's arms *were* about me. There was a faint light above me.

I heard his ejaculation: " Good God! "

And I was not sure what happened next.

I was lying on a bed and Bevil was beside me.

" Hallo," said Bevil, smiling.

I was puzzled. One moment I had been in the horror of the flooded cellar ; the next I was in bed.

" You look as if you're . . . pleased to see me," I said.

" I am," he answered.

I was in the house on the island. Outside, the storm was raging ; the tide was receding but the kitchen was flooded. I could hear voices from below.

Bevil was still at my bedside.

I called to him and he took my hand.

"Hallo," he said. "All right now."

"What happened?"

"You were in that cellar. It must be years since it was opened. But rest now. You've had a shock."

"I want to know, Bevil. The tide was rising, wasn't it?"

"In a short time the place would have been completely flooded. Thank God we were in time—but only just."

"The spring tide . . ."

"Now you're not supposed to talk."

"I can't rest until I know. How did you get here, Bevil?"

"I came looking for you."

"But why . . . *why* . . . ?"

"Good God, you don't imagine I'd let you get lost, do you?"

"But how did you know?"

"Never mind now. I'm here. I found you. And you're safe."

"Bevil, you're *glad*?"

He lifted my hand to his lips and kissed it passionately. No words could have told me more than that quick gesture. It was enough to set me at rest. I closed my eyes.

It was some hours later when they removed Fanny's body. They had tried to save her but it was impossible.

When they had opened the trap door she had been with me. They had distinctly seen her. She had slipped, they said, and disappeared; but I knew that she had not wanted to be brought out of the cellar alive.

My poor loving Fanny! When, I wondered, had the madness started to canker her brain? Was it with those early tragedies—the loss of husband and child? Poor Fanny, the gentle murderess who had killed for love. I had heard of murder for gain, for jealousy, before, but never for love.

And how had Bevil come in time? Because he had not intended to let the matter of the letter to the undertaker pass. He was going to find out who sent it; he wanted to know why. He had questioned Hamforth and come to the conclusion that if he could find the letter he would have a piece of tangible evidence in his hands and he would not rest until he knew who had written it.

Jessica remembered seeing Fanny in the hall when she was talking to Hamforth, so Bevil sent for Fanny, who could not be found.

And where was I, Bevil wanted to know. It was soon discovered that I too was missing.

Bevil, Jessica and William Lister had sat in the library talking over the affair of the undertaker.

Why, they asked each other, had Fanny done such a thing, for they were certain it was Fanny since it seemed very possible that she had taken the letter: and why should she want to if not to prevent its being traced to her? And why should Fanny write such a letter?

Jessica supplied the information that Fanny had been visiting Jem Tomrit and that Mrs. Henniker, his daughter, was uneasy about it. The old man talked constantly of the past since he had had that scare seeing ghosts on the island, and it wasn't good for him. She had always believed that Jem could live to a hundred as far as his body was concerned; it was his conscience that was worrying her—and him—for it wouldn't let him sleep at night lately. He talked, too, wandering in his mind, and had said that he and his mates had murdered some excisemen by locking them in the underground cellar and letting them drown.

Bevil said: "We're going to see Jem Tomrit."

So they did and Bevil made him talk. Fanny had been asking questions about the house on the island; again and again he had told her the story of the murdered excisemen who had been lured into the cellar and left to drown.

"We're going to the island . . . gale or no gale," said Bevil.

He didn't know, of course, that Fanny's plan was that we should die together. Bevil merely thought that we had gone exploring and that the snap lock might have shut us in.

Back to Menfreya to find one of the boats missing. The sea by this time was high and the tide coming in fast. But they came over somehow. Bevil and William Lister and Jessica.

And they brought me out in time.

I lay in bed on the island thinking about it. They say that when you drown your life passes before your eyes in pictures. Well, I had come near to drowning and now I lay still thinking of scenes from the past.

Gwennan had gone and something of the old life disappeared with her. It would be the same with the passing of Fanny.

But Bevil was left to me. I owed my life to Bevil—to his determination, his energy, his will to save me.

Yet . . . by saving me he would lose Jessica.

That was the thought which uplifted me like a buoy in a raging sea of doubt.

If he had wanted to be rid of me, what an excellent opportunity he had had.

We had to stay the night on the island for the storm grew more fierce. Never have I heard such wind, never known such an angry sea.

Bevil came to the room to tell me that there was no hope of leaving for Menfreya till morning.

" In any case," he said, " you're not fit to go. You have to rest."

" I slept in this room once before," I said. " Years and years ago. . . . It was when I ran away from home."

He smiled at me indulgently. I could see how glad he was that I was safe. " You seem to have a talent for doing crazy things."

" And the next evening," I said, " you came over here. Do you remember? You found me under a dust sheet in this very room."

He wrinkled his eyes, trying to remember.

" You had brought a girl over. I'm afraid I interrupted that little romance."

He laughed. " What a memory you have!"

" I'm sorry."

" What?"

" For interrupting then . . . and now."

" What in God's name . . . ?" His brow was wrinkled as though he was truly mystified.

" Jessica is very beautiful and she would have made an excellent M.P.'s wife."

" Let's hope she doesn't. It's odd how people blurt out things at odd moments. While we were coming over in the boat . . . and I thought we'd never get there, and the sea was hell . . . she told me she was going to marry Leveret. That . . . the marriage was necessarily going to be somewhat soon and quiet."

"You mean . . ."

"It's true. They've been using the island as a rendezvous, and that's the reason for the mysterious lights and figures that have been seen here."

"So it was Harry!"

"Yes. And she more or less admitted that she'd been helping him for months. A sort of spy in the enemy camp. That time when the boat slipped away it was engineered at Harry's request with the help of that old rascal A'Lee . . . to make a scandal for me . . . if you please. His tactics will have to be better than that if he ever gets into politics."

"If," I said happily.

"Not in Lansella, eh, Harriet Menfrey?"

I could sense his happiness, and it was because I was safe. For a moment I forgot everything else—the terrible loss of my beloved Fanny, the nightmare hours before her death . . . so much that needed to be explained.

At length Bevil said: "Good God, I believe you thought that I actually . . ."

"You and Jessica," I said. "Well, it wasn't such a wild conclusion to arrive at, in view of . . ."

He was serious, then he said: "Poor Harriet! I'm afraid you have had a lot to put up with. The fact is, I'm a very imperfect specimen."

"I too," I said.

"I'll take you as you are. Will you, Harriet, take me?"

"It sounds like something out of the marriage service."

"It's appropriate. That's what we're talking about . . . being married."

He bent over and kissed me and it was as though we had sealed a bargain.

It was some time afterwards before events fell into place and the picture was clear. I mourned Fanny for a long time—and still do. How I wish that she had not lost her reason. I wish that she could have been the nurse to my children that I always imagined she would be. I think that I could have nursed her through that terrible time if only we could both have been rescued. It was her fear for me which sent her toppling over the edge of sanity into madness. I believe that when her body was poisoned, as it assuredly was, her mind was tampered with too. There was tangible evidence, so we thought, of the desire of someone in the house to kill me, and it was this which had decided Fanny that when Billy was calling her she must take me with her.

When I discovered the truth I was amazed that the web of suspicion in which I had become entangled was of my own weaving. The unwanted child I had been had always regarded happiness with suspicion; because my father had not cared for me, I had made myself believe that no one ever would. I did not realise until this time that my life was in my own hands. It was a marvellous revelation because never before had the future become so full of exciting possibilities. And understanding myself I became more tolerant of others. I could be tolerant of Jessica's hopes and fears. Adventuress she may have been; she may have come to Menfreya hoping for an easy life there; she might have hoped to lure Bevil from me, or perhaps to marry William Lister, until she had seen the more inviting prospects Harry Leveret had to offer. I could not be sure; but the woman I had become was less censorious than the old. Jessica had fought for her own happiness, as I had for mine; and I hoped she would find what she sought with Harry.

By chance I discovered how Fanny and I had been poisoned. It was shortly after Jessica had left when I took tea in the nursery with Benedict and he gleefully put spoonfuls of sugar in my tea.

"You've got a sweet tooth," he chuckled. Then he said: "You like this sugar better than Jessie's?"

Jessie's sugar, he told me, had been kept in a bottle in her cupboard and by standing on a chair he could reach it. He had brought it for my lemon barley when I was sick to make me get well quickly.

I went over to see Jessica at Chough Towers when her child was born. Being a mother had changed her in some way. I myself was pregnant at that time and I understood the change; it almost made us friends. She admitted that she had read about the arsenic when Jenny died and had tried it herself now and then. She was horrified when she heard how Fanny and I might have been poisoned.

Well, that was all long ago, but I often think of that night when, rescued by my husband, I lay in the bed in the island house listening to the storm, and how it wore itself out during the night, until the sound of the waves dropped to a murmur.

When it was light I got out of bed and stood at the window to watch the sunrise. Bevil was sleeping in a chair near my bed and I did not wake him.

The sea was still and only the brown edge to its skirt was an indication of how violent the storm had been.

And there was Menfreya touched with the faint rosy glow, and as I looked I remembered that morning all those years ago when I had looked and thought that the loveliest sight in the world must be Menfreya in the morning.

I thought of all that had happened there through the centuries and in my own short life and all that was yet to come.

Gwennan was gone; Fanny was gone; but I had Bevil and we should go through life together.

Bevil had come to stand beside me and we both remained at the window looking across the sea.

"Who would believe that's the same sea as the one that was raging last night?" he said. And he looked at me and I knew that he read some of the thoughts that were in my mind.

Tragedy had come close, but luck had been with us.

Bevil was still shaken when he considered how miraculously my rescue had been timed.

"It's like being given a chance," he said.

"This day is starting well," I answered. "Look at the sky. And look at Menfreya. . . . It's so beautiful in the morning."

Victoria Holt

The supreme writer of the 'gothic' romance, a compulsive storyteller whose gripping novels of the darker face of love have thrilled millions all over the world.

The Shivering Sands 30p
Her haunting novel of suspense and treachery, set on the edge of the Goodwin Sands.

King of the Castle 30p
A young woman becomes enmeshed in the secret past of an aristocratic family.

Mistress of Mellyn 30p
A lovely Victorian girl becomes a governess in a cold, brooding Cornish house.

Bride of Pendorric 30p
The phrase 'until death us do part' takes on a more ominous meaning for a young bride.

Menfreya 30p
The terrible legend of an old house comes dangerously, and murderously, to life.

Kirkland Revels 30p
An innocent, newly-married girl enters her new home and finds she has crossed a threshold of terror.

The Legend of the Seventh Virgin 30p
Old memories and mysteries are stirred to life in a quiet corner of Victorian Cornwall, bringing to light an ancient vengeance.

The Queen's Confession 40p
Her enthralling re-creation of the life of Marie Antoinette.

New in paperback July 1972

The Secret Woman 35p
Victoria Holt's bestselling new novel of danger and romance on a tropical island.

 *Fontana Books*

Victoria Holt also writes as

Jean Plaidy

'One of England's foremost historical novelists.'
Birmingham Mail

The Tudor Novels
The Spanish Bridegroom 30p
Gay Lord Robert 30p
The Thistle and the Rose 30p
Murder Most Royal 35p
St. Thomas's Eve 30p
The Sixth Wife 30p

The story of Mary Stuart
Royal Road to Fotheringay 30p
The Captive Queen of Scots 35p

Robert Carr and the Countess of Essex
The Murder in the Tower 30p

Life and loves of Charles II
The Wandering Prince 30p
A Health Unto His Majesty 30p
Here Lies Our Sovereign Lord 30p

The French Revolution series
Louis the Well-beloved 30p

The persecution of witches and puritans in the 16th & 17th
centuries
Daughter of Satan 30p

Catherine de Medici
Madame Serpent 35p
The Italian Woman 30p
Queen Jezebel 30p

All available in Pan Books

Catherine Gaskin

Fiona *30p*
Her new bestseller. A young governess on a Caribbean island
encounters mystery and danger in a land of slaves and over-
lords, hurricane winds and forbidden drums. 'Compulsive
reading.' *Sunday Mirror*

Also by Catherine Gaskin in Fontana

Sara Dane *40p*

Blake's Reach *30p*

I Know My Love *30p*

The Tilsit Inheritance *35p*

Corporation Wife *35p*

The File on Devlin *30p*

Edge of Glass *30p*

All Else is Folly *30p*

Daughter of the House *30p*

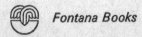

Fontana Books

D. E. Stevenson

'Miss Stevenson has made herself mistress of the light novel that is consistently charming without being foolish.' *The Times*. 'D. E. Stevenson has made peculiarly her own this province of feminine fiction—the kindly, ironical observation of ordinary life which retains a wonderful zest and freshness in its presentation.' *Glasgow Herald*

Her books include:

The Young Clementina 25p

The Musgraves 25p

Winter and Rough Weather 25p

Bel Lamington 25p

The English Air 25p

Fletcher's End 25p

The House on the Cliff 25p

Sarah's Cottage 25p

Spring Magic 25p

Music in the Hills 25p

Katherine Wentworth 25p

Charlotte Fairlie 25p

Rosabelle Shaw 25p

Smouldering Fire 25p

The Blue Sapphire 25p

Young Mrs Savage 25p

Celia's House 30p

Sarah Morris Remembers 25p

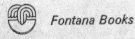 *Fontana Books*

Fontana Books

Fontana is best known as one of the leading paperback publishers of popular fiction and non-fiction. It also includes an outstanding, and expanding section of books on history, natural history, religion and social sciences.

Most of the fiction authors need no introduction. They include Agatha Christie, Hammond Innes, Alistair MacLean, Catherine Gaskin, Victoria Holt and Lucy Walker. Desmond Bagley and Maureen Peters are among the relative newcomers.

The non-fiction list features a superb collection of animal books by such favourites as Gerald Durrell and Joy Adamson.

All Fontana books are available at your bookshop or newsagent; or can be ordered direct. Just fill in the form below and list the titles you want.

— —

FONTANA BOOKS, Cash Sales Department, P.O. Box 4, Godalming, Surrey. Please send purchase price plus 5p postage per book by cheque, postal or money order. No currency.

NAME (Block letters) _____

ADDRESS _____

_____

_____